DON'T MISS THESE EXCITING
TIME PASSAGES ROMANCES,
NOW AVAILABLE FROM JOVE

This Time Together
SUSAN LESLIE LIEPITZ

An entertainment lawyer dreams of a
simpler life—and finds herself in an 1890s cabin,
with a handsome mountain man . . .

A Dance Through Time
LYNN KURLAND

A romance writer falls asleep in Gramercy Park,
and wakes up in fourteenth century Scotland—
in the arms of the man of her dreams . . .

REMEMBER LOVE

Susan Plunkett

JOVE BOOKS, NEW YORK

REMEMBER LOVE

A Jove Book / published by arrangement with
the author

PRINTING HISTORY
Jove edition / December 1996

The Putnam Berkley World Wide Web site address is
http://www.berkley.com/berkley

ISBN: 0-515-11980-6

A JOVE BOOK®
Jove Books are published by The Berkley Publishing Group,
200 Madison Avenue, New York, New York 10016.
JOVE and the "J" design are trademarks
belonging to Jove Publications, Inc.

PRINTED IN THE UNITED STATES OF AMERICA

10 9 8 7 6 5 4 3 2 1

In memory of my brother, Andrew Joseph Fassbender

March 31, 1959–January 14, 1993

With love forever

Chapter 1

THE HUM OF test equipment, computers, and a violent storm echoed off the walls of Westminster Labs. As they had thousands of times before, Dr. Winifred McCanless's pale blue eyes sought the picture on her desk. A handsome young man in cap and gown with the UCLA mantle of summa cum laude laid around his shoulders grinned back. Winifred's heart ached with the rawness of a festering wound. Her eyes closed to a vision of her brother on his graduation day. Five months ago, Joey had stood on the threshold of realizing his hopes, dreams, and aspirations. He had been alive. Over the past seventeen years, Joey had grown from being her surrogate child into her best friend. She'd love and miss him until the day she joined him.

As had happened many times since his death, Win felt Joey's palpable presence expand until it filled the white and chrome laboratory. At that moment, the perception became so strong that she almost cried out loud.

Part of her was sure if she turned around, he'd be sitting there on a stool, his straight brown hair drooping over his

1

forest green eyes, a mischievous grin crinkling the stubble and freckles on his cheeks. The sensation flooded her with heart-clenching emotion and caused a tight-chested breathing that threatened to suffocate her.

Sudden tears scalded her eyes and closed her throat. An uncontrollable spasm of grief shook her six-foot frame. Then came a stab of loss, piercing her heart with an intense brutality. After a moment it passed, leaving her invisible wounds bleeding with grief.

The digital clock flashed midnight. Chill bumps rippled across Win's arms in reaction to the sudden temperature drop in the isolated laboratory. Reflexively, she saved the computer file and peered expectantly across the stainless steel and white room.

"Joey?" Lightning flashed through the rainy night beyond the lab's only window in response.

"I know you're here, Joey." Two tears spilled over the dam of her pale lashes.

The memories persisted. In a flash of lightning, her mind's eye conjured the morgue where the chill reached beyond the warmth of living flesh and touched the soul with an icy fingertip. A man in green medical garb pulled open a square icebox door and rolled out a slab. How long had she stared at the mutilated face she had laughed with over breakfast that same morning?

Shuddering, she eschewed the memory of identifying Joey's body. She tried pulling away from the black time two weeks after his graduation. The impact of the drunk's car had fused the vehicles into an indescribable mass on the Hollywood Freeway. The paramedics had told her that Joey died instantly. Somehow, that bit of knowledge imparted little comfort. The other driver had not worn a seat belt. The collision had thrown him clear of the wreckage and oncoming traffic. He had suffered cuts, bruises, and some broken bones. In a few years, he'd be out of jail.

Joey would still be dead.

She would still be alone.

The world would still turn.

Even now, she railed against the finality of Joey's death. That mangled body in the cold, dark morgue shouldn't have been Joey. *It shouldn't have been Joey!*

But it had been. A piece of her heart had withered and died that day. In its place burned an oozing black hole no one saw.

Thunder growled, shaking the building. The computer screen blinked, commanding her attention to the urgent project displayed on the monitor's great eye. She cleared her throat and brushed away the moisture from her cheeks. Steeled to finish the task, Winifred mentally folded away the mantle of grief until the next emotional tornado swept it free again.

The lights flickered and died, plunging the sterile, climate-controlled lab into darkness, then flashed on again with unexpected brilliance. The anxious knot in Win's stomach tightened. Holding her breath, she typed furiously, hoping the separate power source for her computer held long enough to finish and send the file to the Westminster Labs' mainframe computer twenty miles away.

Outside the window beside her desk, trees snapped and swayed under gale-force winds. Talons of lightning clawed at the sky, forcing her to squint against the sudden flare. The ground trembled with the power of the thunder.

The lights blinked again.

Win closed program files in preparation for sending the file to safety.

Again the lights flickered and died. This time, the lab stayed dark. Only the ghostly glow of her computer screen and the reddish-amber exit sign over the door illuminated the room.

The floor vibrated and glass rattled in response to the tempest's fury. She had to get out of the lab. And she would, just as soon as she finished keying the backup program and sending the file.

An electric current charged the air. The tiny hairs on the

back of her neck and along her arms quivered and stood on end.

An explosion rocked the building. Sounds of shattering glass, crumbling test scaffolds, and a distant alarm assaulted her ears.

All the hair on her body raised. In a crystallized instant, time stuttered. The air around her glistened and distorted the walls.

Everything moved in slow motion except her nervous eyes and speeding heart. Her finger descended toward the send key at a snail's pace.

An eerie greenish glow lit the far side of the lab. It percolated along the undulating walls. Explosive thunder filled her head and chattered her teeth. Her body hung in a state of increasingly slower motion.

The greenish glow blossomed over the ceiling and floors. Like a cancer, it consumed everything it touched. Still, her athletic body resisted the slight effort to press the send key. The deadly glow drew closer, creeping along the wall behind her, approaching with every frenetic heartbeat.

The warm, metallic taste of doom filled her mouth.

The green glow slithered over the lab table nearest her desk. How strange. She no longer heard the glass beakers and bottles exploding, but she saw it happening.

She glanced down. Her finger had finally depressed the send key.

Win stared at the electric force looming from all sides in rapt fascination.

I'm going to die.

The calm realization emerged from the logical part of her mind as a pure thought void of emotion or the regret most twenty-nine-year-olds might experience. It was a fact. Dr. Winifred McCanless knew how to recognize and deal with facts.

"Not until you've lived, Sis," came Joey's reassuring voice through the green glowing energy charge consuming the room.

"Joey!"

Forks of powerful lightning struck the west wing of the Westminster Research Laboratory, peeling away the heavy roof and the third floor and exposing the steel shells of the containment labs. In what became a brief, devastating chain reaction, the metal attracted more lightning. Like an angry child venting frustration with boundless energy, the lightning struck the research wing repeatedly. The ensuing explosions leveled all three floors. Nothing and no one survived.

NEW ARCHANGEL (SITKA), ALASKA
1866

The final addition to Ransom Hamilton's well-planned future awaited him on the deck of the *Ompalada*. He watched the ship sail into the harbor. Tonight, he and Cassandra would consummate their proxy marriage. Within a few years, the walls of the great house he'd built would ring with the sound of children. His children.

He examined the sky. The schooner *Ompalada* had beaten the storm into port. The way the heavy, dark clouds roiled over the water promised a severe blow. Already, men secured cargoes and battened down the hatches of the dockside ships. With luck, the storm would wait until he had Cassandra and her trunks ensconced at the house. A flash of lightning and rumbling thunder dimmed his optimism.

Fresh excitement rippled the air. He hoped Cassandra was as anxious as he to consummate the marriage. Damn, but it had been a long time since he'd had a woman. Months. A married man, which he considered himself when he signed the documents, owed his wife fidelity.

Over the twelve years of his association with Cassandra's father, Archibald Forsythe, Ransom had watched Cassandra grow into a beautiful young woman. Although he had preferred being married in San Francisco with all the pomp and ceremony Cassandra deserved, he hadn't dared leave his trouble-plagued business for the journey down the coast and back. Fortunately, Cassandra's practical nature hadn't demanded a courtship and utterances of ardent devotion before or during marriage. She possessed the attributes necessary in a wife, including self-sufficiency and a rounded education. A simpering, clinging vine of a wife would merely increase his burden, not ease it. Cassandra's even temper and patience stood her in good stead as a mother, too. He had seen the way she cared for her feebleminded sister, Felicity. Cassandra possessed an infinite capacity for love and tenderness.

Nature had also blessed her with a deliciously curvy body for which he had elaborate plans this evening. Just thinking about the night ahead quickened his pace down the wharf.

Sidestepping a stack of barrels two men lashed into place against a wharf piling, Ransom hastened, as though his speed could spur the *Ompalada* on faster.

In minutes the storm descended. The temperature plummeted and the sea churned a gray froth. Whitecaps foamed into life with increasing violence. An eerie, howling wind whipped at the *Ompalada*'s dropped sails and screamed through her rigging.

Halfway down the dock, Ransom glanced up and saw Cassandra sauntering along the shattered deck. The missing rail section bespoke a tumultuous voyage.

Apprehensive, he watched her approach the edge of the ship's deck as though it were a calm, sunny day. Urgency knotted his stomach into a clenched ball.

"Cassandra! Get back!" he shouted. Desperate to warn her away from the perilously close break in the rail and the building pitch of the sea, Ransom broke into a run, dodging a coil of rope beside a dock strut. He wove across the floating dock as it shifted beneath his feet. His worried shouts and the thunder of his booted feet on the planks sent men scurrying.

Just as he reached the side of the *Ompalada*, the ship lurched. The dock tilted sharply with the roll of a great wave. Ransom went sprawling across the damp wooden planks. He scrambled to his feet, all the while eyeing the broken ship rail.

Over the keening cry of the wind and land-bound gulls came a rise of screams from the *Ompalada*'s deck. Ransom watched in horror as Cassandra tumbled into the gray water.

Instantly, he shrugged out of his coat and yanked off his heavy boots, then dove into the cold, angry sea.

Heart pounding against his rib cage, knowing he had little time, Ransom groped though the murky water. He wouldn't let her die.

After surfacing, he took his bearings and gasped several massive gulps of air, then dove again, frantic for his bride. Kicking and digging straight down in the water with strength born of desperation, he groped for her clothing. The cold pressure of the entire ocean closed against his heart, crushing the brilliance from his dreams.

Again, he surfaced, gasped fresh air, and dove, this time altering his descent toward the dock moorings. Every bone-chilling second carried Cassandra farther from his reach and out of his life.

Stretching his arms in wide arcs, he became a rash predator hunting the dark water, determined to find his prey. A feathery touch tickled the back of his hand.

When he reached out again, his fingers closed on something filmy. He kicked hard, propelling himself toward the fabric. Then there was more of the gauzy material. Much more. Yards of fabric. He hauled it in like a sail in the face of a storm until he found substance.

Cradled in the arms of the sea, the limp, unconscious form floated in angelic suspension.

Embracing his threatened future, he battled up from the murky depths and the hammering waves. He broke the surface with a lung-searing gasp.

A barrage of shouts penetrated his dim awareness. Six

feet away, a dozen men called and reached for him from the gyrating dock.

The chill of the ocean coaxed him into icy paralysis. Suddenly weary, his arms loosened around his precious burden. In that instant, fatigue stretched the distance to six miles.

Move, his mind commanded. *Move or drown*.

Clutching his dream, he kicked and caught an incoming wave. His eyes remained riveted on the dock and the line of outstretched fingers promising help and warmth.

The next wave lifted them. Seizing the momentum, he lunged toward salvation a long three feet away.

Again, he made the supreme effort, his body barely obeying his mind.

Finally, strong hands grappled at his outstretched hand and hauled him against the bobbing dock. His precious burden slipped into the safety of willing arms. Then he heaved himself out of the chilled water.

Once on the dock, someone stripped him of his vest and shirt. Warm blankets were wrapped around his head and shoulders. A blast of wind knifed the air. Ransom shivered, but he remained rooted in place, desperate to know how Cassandra fared. She *had* to live.

Two men worked on reviving her while onlookers offered conflicting instructions and advice.

Ransom drew the blankets around him as a cloak against the certainty of death. Something was wrong with his eyes. Perhaps the cold pressure of the sea had affected his vision. He blinked several times, sure his eyes deceived him. When the shimmering image solidified, his heart nearly stopped.

"Your wife . . . " the captain of the *Ompalada* started. "I am so sorry, Mr. Hamilton."

Ransom shook his head, gradually comprehending the identity of the woman. Relief flooded his senses, followed quickly by sorrow. It wasn't Cassandra.

Simpleminded Felicity Forsythe, incapable of more than rudimentary social manners, had required constant care.

Ransom groaned in anguish for the death of the sweet young woman-child.

If Felicity had accompanied Cassandra, something must be terribly amiss with Arch. He hoped not. Arch was a pillar, a man with judgment more sound than a double eagle. Arch had been Ransom's mentor and financial partner twelve years earlier when he sailed from San Francisco and launched his current fortune and future.

Crouched beside Felicity and using the throng of bystanders as a windbreak, Ransom brushed long, curling, golden-brown clusters of hair from Felicity's colorless face. She had been under the frigid water what? Five? Six minutes? Longer? He didn't know. Staring at her lifeless body, a tremendous sorrow squeezed his heart.

Even in death, the beautiful young woman who never spoke a harsh word in her life appeared innocent, almost ethereal.

"I'm sorry," Gerald Wagner said, tucking another blanket around his friend's shoulders. "It's a long story, Ransom, but Felicity was your wife." Nearly as tall as Ransom, Gerald's ten additional years of age showed in the silver that streaked his black hair and the weathered lines on his still handsome face.

"No. I married Cassandra," Ransom said absently, stroking Felicity's icy cheek with the back of his shaking, chilled hand. "Where is she?"

"Arch married you to Felicity," Gerald insisted in his gravelly voice. He drew a deep breath and exhaled audibly before continuing. "Cassandra had already married some Aussie and was on her honeymoon by the time I found out just how badly Arch deceived us. I'm sorry. Maybe I should have sent word, but I thought it best to tell you personally."

For a long moment Ransom gaped at his friend without comprehension. As the magnitude of Gerald's statement penetrated his cold-numbed brain, he stopped shivering. He closed, then opened his mouth, but no words formed. The anger mixed with sorrow twisting Gerald's lined face and burning in his ebony eyes confirmed the truth.

A crackle of lightning followed instantly by thunder shook the dock. As though caught in the eye of a hurricane, Ransom numbly watched Adele Clairmont break through the throng of spectators and throw her wailing, screaming body onto Felicity. The nurse and companion had been with the Forsythe family since before Felicity's birth. She had cared for Felicity every day of her life.

"You were ta wait for me," Adele cried. "You dinna ever disobey before. Why this time? Why now? 'Twas only a minute." Her perfectly arched eyebrows drew together in the center over her teary brown eyes. Wind tugged at the neat, brown bun pinned at the nape of her slender neck.

Gerald Wagner grasped Adele's shoulders and lifted her from the frigid, still form of her charge. She fought him briefly before accepting the comfort of his arms and turned, sobbing into his rough wool sea coat. The buffeting wind carried her grief through the silent crush of onlookers.

Staring at the serene, lifeless face, grappling with the perplexing revelations and their consequences, Ransom stood. A veil of incredulity dulled his sharp mind. Surely, he misunderstood.

Disbelieving, he found remorse in Gerald's wavering gaze. "Felicity was my wife?" Ransom asked in a grating whisper.

Both Adele and Gerald nodded, then avoided his vacant gaze.

Ransom stared at them for another minute before turning his attention on the unmoving form at his feet. His wife. His dead wife. Before questions inundated him, a profound soul-searing loss tightened his gut in an unmerciful grip and twisted hard, driving him to his knees.

He couldn't drag his gaze from the sooty line of dark lashes lying against Felicity's colorless cheeks. How could he be married to her? Would she have even understood what marriage was?

A thunderous fury for Arch's odious betrayal surged from the pit of his soul. "No-o-o-o-o!" he bellowed in denial.

How could Arch have done this? How could he have married that sweet little innocent to him? Christ! What had he done to make Arch hate him and betray their trust and friendship of more than a dozen years?

A great gust of wind rocked the dock. Lightning flashed in blinding bursts. Instant thunder rolled, rumbled, and reverberated through the electrically charged air.

As quickly as the tumult struck, it subsided, leaving the dock becalmed. In that moment, Felicity's body spasmed and jerked, rising several inches into the air, then flopped back on the stained planks. Before anyone reacted, she coughed, gasping for breath, and turned into a shivering mass of teeth-chattering life.

Chapter 2

Swirling black eddies laced with vivid colors pierced the mind-dulling pain, sparking Winifred's consciousness. A scream of protest welled up in her throat, where it died. She struggled to draw a full breath. Fiery ice ripped at her lungs with a thousand razor edges. Her airways burned as though she inhaled a caustic acid instead of sweet air. Each shallow intake birthed a fresh round of torture.

The white spots dancing behind her eyelids sparked a memory.

Lightning.

She had been struck by lightning.

The fire bolt must still be lodged in her chest and burning her alive.

Then came the cold.

Freezing cold.

Only a cryonics crypt was so cold.

In the chaos of disconnected memory, she knew that she had died and been frozen in a cryonics crypt. Her best friend, Alexis, and her lab partner, Boyd, would do that for her—and in the interest of science. Weren't they laughing about that very scenario last month in the coffee room? They would preserve her until medical technology advanced sufficiently to heal her. Visions of bilious nitrogen clouds condensing into ice crystals on her naked body flitted through her disjointed consciousness. Only coming back to life after being frozen for who knew how long could be so painful. Every nerve burned.

Paralysis gripped her limbs. Not even her eyelids budged. Despite the agony, she fought to move, to do anything to understand the source of her punishment.

Suddenly, agonizing spasms squeezed her burning lungs. A bone-jarring coughing seizure sent her whole body convulsing against something as hard as steel. Someone or something turned her onto her side and braced her. The last vestige of warmth gushed from her body into the chilled mist in the form of stinging bile. The horrific pain that followed put her on the edge of oblivion. She lay still, fighting the ebony waves of unconsciousness.

Gradually, a strange world, rife with foreign smells and peculiar noises, seeped through the agony. Every small gasp for oxygen cost dearly. Did anyone know how much it hurt to be thawed out and returned to life?

Through the cacophony of chaotic logic and sound, a gentle voice touched an aching chord. At first, the words made no sense. The reassuring tone promised warmth and tender care.

Alexis?

Alexis, stop the pain. Please, stop the hurt . . .

When the voice resumed, she realized it was not Alexis.

Again she tried forcing her eyes open, but her stubborn eyelids remained sealed. Between the colossal effort of drawing a decent breath and recovering from the bone-jarring coughing fits, the plea to stop the pain died before reaching her lips. Not that her burning throat could utter it.

It took a moment before she realized that she was moving.

She was being carried.

Despite the pain, it felt like floating. The protective tenderness created by the cradle of strong arms momentarily quelled her discomfort. A tiny whimper escaped from low in her throat.

Without warning, uncontrollable chills seized her. Then, eager fingers tore at her. At first, she thought they were skinning her, then she realized they were removing her clothing. Clothing. Why was she dressed in a cryonics crypt? Each movement charted new dimensions of misery and a fear of endless torture.

Then a soothing Scottish voice spoke and tempered her fright.

Someone propped her head against a soft, puffy pillow. Dim words of encouragement penetrated the haze. Strong hands began rubbing nerve-tingling warmth into her legs through layers of thick blankets.

Gentle, firm fingers held the back of her head as a heated glass of liquid touched her icy lips. Reflexively, she drank. The liquid created a delicious path to her stomach. She gulped the entire contents, spreading wonderful numbness over her raw nerve endings.

Using sheer determination, she forced her eyes open. A tall man with angry aquamarine eyes shimmering like iridescent opals glowered down at her. His intensity mesmerized her.

Why was he so angry? Was he angry at her? Nah, he couldn't be angry at her. She hadn't even opened her mouth yet.

Even with wet hair and wrapped in a blanket, he was easily the most fascinating man she'd ever seen. The sharp angles and planes of his face kept him from being handsome. Still . . .

Thinking him a replica of the hero in a romance novel she once read on an airplane, she closed her eyes, suddenly tired beyond belief. Etching the vision of the angry, intriguing man in her mind, she drifted into an exhausted brandy-enhanced sleep.

Gerald Wagner's claim that Felicity was his wife settled into Ransom's reality as he carried her into the bowels of the *Ompalada*. Moments later, Adele directed him to Felicity's first-class cabin. The heat of Ransom's blossoming fury warmed him with each step.

As Felicity's husband, he had been the logical person to assist Adele. Although quite familiar with the intricacies of removing the layers of clothing proper ladies wore, Ransom's cold, shaking fingers obeyed reluctantly. Getting Felicity out of the soggy yardage turned into an ordeal.

Felicity was a small woman, and Ransom could have easily lifted her with one arm under normal circumstances. The debilitating effects of the cold sea made holding her dead weight while Adele removed the seemingly endless layers of clothing a chore. The more of Felicity's shivering, blue-tinged skin Adele revealed, the warmer Ransom became. The woman might not have a brain in her head, but Lord, she had a body sculpted for a man's pleasure.

Revolted by the turn of his thoughts, he cradled Felicity in his left arm and ripped off her chemise and pantalets. Standing, he held her securely and tried not to stare at her full breasts with puckered nipples begging for the warmth of his mouth. Adele hurriedly towel-dried her, then drew back the thick quilts on the bed. All the while, Adele spoke softly to the charge fate offered her a second chance of caring for.

With a whispered oath of relief, Ransom laid Felicity in the center of the bed, then turned away as Adele covered her. His physical reaction to Felicity's voluptuous peaks and contours disgusted him. Even when he blinked, he saw her tiny waist, the marvelous flare of her creamy hips fashioned for making love and bearing children, and the tantalizing nest of dark brown curls guarding the gates of her womanhood.

He tucked the blanket tightly around his shoulders and watched Adele rub Felicity's legs through the comforter. The innocent face framed in a wild mass of golden brown curls drew his unwilling gaze. *Damn. She's too demented to dally with and too delectable to deny. How the hell could Arch do this to her? To me?*

Needing a drink to dull the growing realization of Arch Forsythe's betrayal, Ransom found a bottle of brandy and a couple of glasses. He poured a healthy measure into each glass, then warmed them on the brazier before handing one off to Adele for Felicity.

Ransom Hamilton could count on one hand the number of people he trusted without reservation. In a less than an hour, that precious number had dwindled by one. The betrayal struck at the deepest level.

"Where's Arch?" His icy fury chilled the cabin.

Adele continued holding the brandy to Felicity's blue-tinged lips. "Mr. Forsythe died shortly before we left Seattle, Mr. Hamilton. He tried very hard to stay alive until he could talk to you . . . "

"His deeds say it all, may he rot in hell!" Ransom glared at the limp yet seductive form of his unwanted wife. "The son of a bitch! Say the truth, Adele. He preferred death over facing me." He slammed the wall with his fist. "And to think I admired that old man. I revered him like he was something worth emulating." Swearing a profane oath, he subjected the wall to another burst of outrage.

Aside from the anger at Arch and the self-loathing for his unexpected physical reaction to the mindless woman-child shackled to him through the web of legalities, Ransom felt empty. His dreams were dashed. Gone with Cassandra. In their place stood a pallid specter of an almost-woman he could never in good conscience make his wife. It would be the equivalent of taking advantage of a child. Never mind her seductive body and the fact she might enjoy the multitude of delights he could teach her. The point was that Felicity was feebleminded and he needed a wife with a sharp mind, not just an alluring body. He needed Cassandra, dammit!

He waited while Adele tucked the blankets around Felicity and moved away. "Why, Adele? Why did Cassandra marry someone else?"

Adele turned on him, hands on hips, and glared up into the rage glinting in his eyes. "Perhaps if you had taken the time to write to her occasionally, Mr. Hamilton, she might not have been swept off her feet by Mr. Malcolm. But, you know Cassandra. When she dinna get more than a couple of letters the first year you were gone . . . "

"What the hell do you mean? *A couple?* I wrote every damn week! For two damn years. It was Cassandra who didn't write!" Muttering under his breath about untrustworthy, blame-shifting women, he poured more brandy.

Adele held her ground. "Ye may have written, Mr. Hamilton. I'd not be calling ya a liar. But believe me when I tell you, she barely got a handful in all that time. Surely, not more 'n half a dozen in the two years since ya last visited. She wrote you every week the first year. I posted them meself. So donna be blaming Miss Cassandra for getting on with her life. Ye may be willin' ta wait until yer thirty and two ta wed, but Miss Cassandra was not willin' ta wait until she was."

Adele sloshed a couple of fingers of brandy into the snifter she used for Felicity, then downed the fine liquor as though it was sassafras tea.

"Goddammit! I got five letters from her in all that time! Five! If she wrote so diligently, why didn't I receive them?" he shouted, stirring Felicity and not caring. The anger of Adele's lies heated him from the inside out. "Every one else got what I sent out. Contracts. Bank drafts. Letters. Why the hell wouldn't Cassandra get the letters I wrote?"

The magnitude of the destruction of his plans and dreams unraveled him. A small glimpse of what his future held, married to Felicity, knifed through his gut and sharpened the pain of betrayal. Losing the bride he'd built his future around was one thing. Betrayal and deception into marriage with a simple-minded nymph was quite another.

Gone was the hope of filling the grand house he had built for his wife and future children as long he remained married to a woman with the mind of a child.

Gone was the dream of teaching his sons to sail the seas, cut the timber, and build the next generation of ships.

Gone was the chance for ending the long, lonely winter nights and filling them with at least satiation, if not laughter and love.

Even with Cassandra, he had not expected love. Sexual gratification. Friendship. Respect. But not love. Not for years. Maybe not ever.

In the numb fog of his ravaged dreams, Ransom stared down at Felicity. He felt no relief that she would live nor any remorse for the deed that saved her. If there was truly an innocent victim in the room, it was she. Felicity had never been capable of treachery or so much as a lie. Watching the gentle rise and fall of her breasts beneath the blankets, he pondered how little her mind was capable of. Yet, her body told another story. He'd have to watch over her like a doting father once she recovered. The men of Sitka would be on her like cold on a glacier if they thought he'd cut her free.

"How long ago did Cassandra get married?" he asked tightly, denying the loss, still seeking reason and logic from the chaos of his shattered plans.

Adele pulled a chair beside Felicity's bed and sat. With her hands folded in her lap, she took a deep breath. "Cassandra met John Malcolm a year ago at a dinner party she attended with her father. Mr. Malcolm courted her relentlessly, swept her off her feet, he did." Adele drew another deep, stabilizing breath. "They were married last September and left for Europe on a long honeymoon Mr. Forsythe gave them as a wedding present."

Ransom caught the nervous glimpse she stole at him and remained silent.

"I think Mr. Forsythe hoped Cassandra would want to be

quits with Mr. Malcolm after the honeymoon, but to my knowledge, she be holding fast with her choice. We had to leave before they returned. And they should be back in San Francisco by now, or very soon."

"Why?"

"Why what?"

"Why did you have to leave before they returned? Why couldn't you have waited and brought . . . " He shook his head, then ran his fingers through his salty hair, pushing it out of his face. It made no difference. He was married to Felicity. Cassandra was married to what's-his-name Malcolm.

"Mr. Forsythe was afraid to wait any longer. He'd been ill, but he wouldna talk about it. Of course, I knew. I couldna help knowing, seeing him 'most every day for the past twenty years. He was very sick. I know he tried to live long enough to see you again, Mr. Hamilton." She lifted her chin and met his gaze without flinching. "He couldna help dyin' any more than Felicity could help being born the way she is."

A sharp knock on the door signaled a temporary halt. Both knew the conversation was unfinished.

A scowling Gerald Wagner opened the door and thrust a bundle of fresh, dry clothing and boots at Ransom. He cast a long, dark glance at Adele, who met his black eyes with unperturbed resolve.

"Think what you will, Mr. Wagner," she said firmly, then headed for the door. "I'll be outside while you change, Mr. Hamilton. Please let me know when you're finished."

Both men watched her go, each wearing an expression that would have sent most men scurrying.

Ransom dropped his boots on the floor and tossed the dry clothing onto the chair Adele had vacated, then stripped off his wet trousers.

"Just tell me how the hell this happened!" Ransom seethed between a line of clenched teeth while drying his cold, damp skin with the blanket. "How the hell did you let that old fox marry me to his simpleton daughter?"

"I'm sorry, Ransom."

"I don't give a damn how sorry you are. Just tell me what the hell happened in San Francisco."

"I made the same mistake you did, Ransom. I trusted him. As soon as he read the papers and we discussed the reasons for a proxy wedding, he was anxious to get it done. I agreed. I figured the sooner it was over, the sooner we'd get back to Sitka. He told me Cassandra was ill and Felicity could stand in for her."

Gerald Wagner glanced at sweet, sleeping Felicity. Ransom muttered something vile under his breath as a chink of Gerald's anger-tempered armor came unhinged in a visible softening of his weathered features. "Felicity thought the wedding was a game. A great dress-up, like whatever she imagines a ball must be. She wore a white wedding dress and veil. Arch walked her down the aisle."

Wagner turned away from the visage of innocence and met Ransom's black rage. "You had a church wedding. Seven people attended, including the organist. It was over in minutes. Then came the paper signing. Since I don't make it a habit of attending weddings—they make me nervous—I didn't realize the priest never mentioned any names. It wasn't until later, after I learned of Arch's deception, that I found out they make the people getting married, even by proxy, say the names."

Gerald splashed brandy into an empty snifter and sipped the golden liquid. "I'll have to admit, I was nervous the whole time I was in that church, Ransom. Gettin' married for you was too much like getting married for myself."

"You're not the one stuck with the results of this debacle. I am." Ransom punched a leg into his dry trousers. "Now, tell me how he pulled it off." The deep-seated fury prowled for an outlet. He held it back, needing to know the whole of the deception.

Gerald stared at the wall. "Old Arch was smooth. Real smooth. During the paper signing, he read everything aloud, saying 'bride' or 'groom' whenever it came time for a name.

Since you'd already signed the papers, I signed as a witness without checking the bride's name. Not that it would've mattered, then. I should've checked the papers *before* the ceremony. But, so help me God, it never occurred to me he'd do something like that.

"It's my goddamn fault you're married to her, Ransom. When ya strip it all away, that's the truth. I failed you. I didn't look out for your interests. I've been going back and forth as your emissary for years and never messed up. Until now. That's why I had to be the one to tell you." Gerald hung his head, obviously struggling to comprehend the act of duplicity responsible for ruining his friend's life.

"I trusted Arch. I would've bet my life he'd never do anything like change Cassandra's and Felicity's names. And I'd have lost," Gerald said, resigned.

"So would I, Gerald. Arch was the last man I thought would betray either one of us."

"Yeah, well, before he died, Arch asked me to give you this when I saw you." Gerald withdrew a hefty packet from inside his coat. "The old man apologized for dyin'. He said he owed you a proper vent for your anger. He knew the price you'd pay for what he did, and he didn't pretend otherwise."

Ransom hesitated, inclined to toss the packet into the brazier. True, with Arch dead, no target existed for his anger. They were all victims of the old man's manipulations. And the old man had died. Ransom cursed with vehemence, caught between grieving for his friend and mentor or spitting on his memory. With another invective, he snatched the packet from Gerald.

Tethering his anger, Ransom broke the seal on the bundle and rifled the contents. Along with a number of deeds and contracts was a will and an envelope bearing Ransom's name. Thinking the letter might contain business instructions and some attempt at an explanation, Ransom plucked it from the stack.

"I'll see to getting the cargo unloaded," Gerald said. "If

it'll make you feel any better, I'll meet you behind the stables tonight. I won't raise a fist, either."

Ransom shook his head. Much as he felt like lashing out, he loathed beating Gerald into a pulp, which was exactly what would happen if he got started and Gerald didn't defend himself.

"I'd feel better if you did." Gerald opened the cabin door.

"No you wouldn't." Ransom continued buttoning up his clean shirt. "We would both feel worse. Nothing would change for the better. You'd end up battered and bloody, and I'd feel guilty as sin for hitting a man who didn't defend himself. I haven't sunk that low, Gerald.

"Go. Take care of the cargo. Find Miss Clairmont and tell her I'll sit with Felicity while she gets something to eat. I doubt she'll leave . . . "

"I'm right here, Mr. Hamilton," Adele said from the passageway. "Thank you for your consideration. I'll prepare a tray and return shortly, and I'll answer any questions I can."

When the door closed, Ransom glanced at the silent scrap of femininity bundled in quilts, then sank into the chair near the brazier. Forearms resting on knees, he toyed with the letter from Arch. He debated tossing it into the coals, but if it contained business directions, he had best read it. Then again, if it offered excuses where none were acceptable, why waste the time? Nothing Arch could put in the letter could mitigate such cold, calculated deception. Nothing.

Even so, he opened the envelope and withdrew the heavy paper. Arch's familiar scrawl appeared shaky, like Ransom's fragile state of calm. He read the letter. Then he read it again, shaking his head in denial as his gut roiled with unwanted understanding during the second reading.

When he finished, he lifted his head and stared at Felicity. Complete anguish claimed the rest of his being in a misery-making vise. For a moment, he knew himself as the sorriest son of a bitch north of the equator. He was sorry Cassandra married the Australian; sorry Felicity nearly drowned; sorry Arch felt compelled to protect Felicity through deceit; sorry Arch died; sorry he lost the old man and the opportunity of blasting him for betraying their friendship. Most of all, right now, he was sorry he understood Arch's motives. Considering the destruction of his future, Ransom preferred embracing his wrath. But he couldn't watch gentle Felicity sleep and focus the tumult of his anger on her.

"Damn you, Arch." Ransom stared at the pages in his hand and marveled at the pressures Arch had endured before the perfect solution dropped into his lap.

Gerald Wagner's arrival with the proxy marriage papers had given Arch the golden opportunity to have Felicity taken care of by a man he trusted. Arch had grabbed it in both hands. He had never wavered.

Grudgingly, Ransom understood the desperate actions of a dying man and the reason Arch compromised the integrity he valued so highly. Old Arch loved his little daughter more than life, and he proved it by exacting an unspeakably high price for her safety.

"Why didn't you write? Why didn't you tell me you were dying, Arch? We could've worked something out."

Ransom wondered about Cassandra's husband. With Cassandra married to a man Arch did not trust, there remained no one left to care for Felicity and handle the enormous wealth Arch had bequeathed her. By marrying her to Ransom and leaving her the beneficiary of his fortune and Ransom the administrator, Arch met his end at peace. The letter was a statement of trust instead of a plea for forgiveness or understanding. Arch had held no illusions about the effect of his duplicity. He had expected neither forgiveness nor understanding. Instead, he had counted on Ransom's honor.

Ransom couldn't fault Arch's argument for marriage over guardianship. If John Malcolm was the kind of man Arch suspected, he might use Cassandra to drag the guardianship through the courts and possibly win. Arch asked only that Ransom maintain the marriage until John Malcolm revealed his true colors. He believed that after a time, Cassandra would leave her husband. Once she did, Ransom could dissolve the marriage with Felicity.

Ransom swore under his breath, reading Arch's implications between the lines.

In the end, he controlled the entire Forsythe fortune in exchange for delaying his future another year or so. Yes, he'd wait for Cassandra. Where else would he find another woman like her? The amount of money required to support Felicity in style for the rest of her life was a pittance in comparison with the totality of Arch's wealth.

Ransom dropped his head into his hand and rubbed his temples. The last paragraph of the letter haunted him. Apparently John Malcolm was unaware that Cassandra wasn't Archibald Forsythe's child and would inherit only her mother's legacy.

Ransom straightened. He summoned the emotional detachment responsible for his business successes and examined the problem of Felicity. He needed a level head for sorting out this thorny predicament.

For the moment, he did not want a level head. And he did not want to deal with Felicity. Damn, what he wanted was to walk away from this mess.

A solid rapping at the door preceded Adele's return. Ransom stiffly motioned her to the chair beside Felicity's bed, then closed the door. "How bad is she?"

Adele set the food tray on the nightstand before checking Felicity. She smoothed the curls clustered around Felicity's head away from her face. "I'll not know until she awakens . . ."

"Felicity's physical stamina is not in question. The woman is as healthy as a horse. She will live. Hell, she'll outlive all of us. I want to know what her mind is like." Ransom closed his eyes and saw Felicity wander toward the broken rail on the ship. "I already know she lacks the sense God gave a mosquito."

"Deductive reasoning is not Felicity's strong suit," Adele

agreed slowly. "She has never disobeyed before today. She has proper manners for most home occasions, but she gets easily distracted when taken into the city or among strangers.

"She has a limited vocabulary and upon occasion can put together a few intelligible sentences." Adele stole a glimpse of Ransom's dark expression and continued, undaunted, all traces of her Scottish brogue replaced by polished parlor English. "I would not expect her to engage in entertaining conversation. She enjoys hearing the written word read aloud and is capable of asking a question about the topic she's just heard."

Ransom wheeled on Adele, his black brows nearly burrowed together over his glittering, angry eyes as stormy as the Arctic Ocean in winter. "Stop with the platitudes and fancy descriptions, Adele. Does she or does she not have the mentality of a ten-year-old?"

Adele straightened in her chair. "In truth, Mr. Hamilton, I would say a well-mannered five- or six-year-old."

"Thank you for your directness, Miss Clairmont." He grabbed the packet of Arch's papers, then stomped out of the cabin.

Frustrated, Ransom considered his options. As long as he refrained from consummating the union—and could prove it—an annulment was possible. Perhaps things were not as dire as he feared initially.

An annulment would work just fine. It would take time and money, but considering the stakes, he'd make the time. Money was the one commodity of which he had plenty. The lawyers in San Francisco could quietly lay the groundwork before the summer ended.

The real question was what to do with Felicity and Adele until he made arrangements for their return to San Francisco. First, he needed to contact the Forsythe family attorney, Thomas Nolan. In the meantime, Adele had to stay with the girl at all times.

Suddenly, his stomach clenched and his steps faltered.

Then again, maybe things were worse than he thought.

One deception might be a warning of others. What if Felicity wasn't a virgin? Could he still get an annulment?

His fingers dug furrows through his thick, wavy hair as he started down the gangplank. A new thought sent him stumbling and nearly over the side.

What if Felicity was already carrying a child? Was that the unspoken root of Arch's vile deception? Had something awful happened? Had Felicity wandered off and been taken advantage of? Hell, she probably wouldn't know anything was wrong if she suffered no injury beyond the initial physical discomfort of losing her maidenhood. Even then, she might not remember what took place.

Lord knew the woman lived in a different world where broken ship rails and storm-tossed seas posed no danger. What if . . .

No. Arch's honor, blemished as it was, would never have allowed deceit that foul.

Would it?

A few hours ago, Ransom would've bet his life that Arch wouldn't have changed the names on the marriage documents.

And he would have lost.

Presently, it seemed wisest to expect the worst.

Ransom groaned, his thoughts brimming with vile possibilities.

A cold wind whipped through the *Ompalada*'s rigging. Ransom bent his head into the blast and the all-consuming black thoughts rooted in the pain of betrayal and the price of understanding.

Chapter 3

"ASPIRIN," WINIFRED PLEADED in a whisper, afraid that speaking louder would split her head in two. In truth, she needed something more effective—maybe morphine.

How much sweeter it would be to slip back into those delicious dreams filled with the aquamarine eyes of the most intriguing man she'd ever seen. An optimist at heart, she speculated that if she opened her eyes she might see him again . . . not that he'd look back with the same kind of sexual interest he created in her. However, fantasies needed fodder, too. Decisive, she opened her eyes.

It took a moment to realize she was staring at a wooden planked ceiling. She blinked hard, wishing to trade the ceiling and the numerous questions it inspired for the image of the comely stranger. Winifred shut her eyes and willed her headache away.

Years of martial arts training and the physical brutality of neighborhood basketball pickup games where she was the only female had schooled her in drugless ways of banishing pain. As the center forward for three years running on her championship team at UCLA, the technique had served her well.

"Oh, little one, are you awake?"

Winifred ignored the question. No one in her right mind called her *little one*. The only time she had felt herself on the short side of any scale was during an exhibition basketball shoot-out with the Los Angeles Lakers professional basketball team. Then, her six-foot height had seemed inadequate on the court.

"Your fever is gone. I am so pleased. Perhaps we can leave today," said the woman. This time, the voice sounded vaguely familiar.

A soft, gentle hand swept across her brow and filled Win with an aura of comfort. Calm, secure, she inched her head toward the voice and opened her eyes.

A pleasant woman of forty dressed in clothing straight from the costume department at Universal Studios smiled at her kindly. Only a few gray strands showed in the dark brown hair drawn into a bun at the nape of her neck; her brown eyes held a sadness.

"Good morning, my sweet little one." A generous smile accompanied the glide of her hand along Winifred's cheek. "Can you tell me how you feel?"

Not quite believing what she saw, Winifred shut her eyes, then pinched herself. When she opened them again, she pushed into a sitting position in disbelief. The woman perched on the edge of the sturdy chair gazed at her in a blend of amusement and concern.

The small room crammed with an antique armoire, a chair, and a washstand beside the bed perpetuated the serene atmosphere. The planked ceiling contrasted sharply with the burgundy papered walls and the fine antiques. A thick carpet reminded her of the rugs sold by the Persian carpet dealers perpetually going out of business. It covered most of the rough planked floor in a fine array of intricate patterns.

Her fingers smoothed the thick quilt covering her, appre-

ciating the handwork. "Where am I?" Winifred asked in a
raspy whisper.

"You're in your cabin, dear. Safe and warm. Here." The
woman pivoted on the edge of the chair. "Have some chocolate before it gets cold. We have some wonderful Russian
pastries, too. I'm sure you'll like them."

Dumbfounded anyone would bring her something resem-
bling breakfast in bed, Winifred gaped at the woman for a
few seconds before asking, "Who are you? My fairy godmother?"

A genteel laugh filled the small cabin. "It's just me,
Adele, sweetheart. Were I your fairy godmother, I'd wave
my magic wand and grant even your slightest wish."

Winifred relaxed against the plush feather pillows.

What happened? How on earth had she gotten into this
bed with a pseudo–fairy godmother attending her like she
was Cinderella?

Slowly, the fog cleared from her memory. She recalled
her excitement over having her cancer drug findings con-
firmed and fixing the samples and data for transit to Caulder
Labs in Boston . . . Finishing up her procedures in the lab
. . . The storm . . . Joey so close she could almost touch him
. . . Then the electrically charged air and the lightning strike.
She'd been certain she'd die.

Was she dead? Were Alexis and Boyd's efforts with cryo-
genics in vain? Was this a place where she awaited judgment
like Meryl Streep in the movie *Defending Your Life*?

A quick review of the last twenty-nine years based on the
Ten Commandments promised her a short stay—if that was
how things worked. *Hell, I didn't have time for sinning. All
I had time for was work and school and basketball so I could
keep my scholarships and a roof over our heads.*

Basketball may have paid her way through her bachelor
of science in chemistry, but brains won the scholarships and
grants that paid for her Ph.D. Both avenues placed a greater
emphasis on aptitude and consistent results than on physical

beauty. However, formal education was only part of her knowledge trove.

Raised in East L.A. and caring for her younger brother, Joey, most of his life, Winifred had acquired street savvy early. When she was twelve, her father abandoned the family and her world had started crumbling. Two years later, her mother went for cigarettes and never returned.

Uncle Hiram McCanless, a fisherman, took the youngsters in and helped Win with the social workers when he was in town, which was only about half the year. An incident on the street the first week they lived with him prompted Hiram to enroll Win in karate. A quick learner, physically strong and agile, Win excelled.

After a couple of years with Hiram and the East L.A. Karate Dojo, few people bothered ten-year-old Joey McCanless. His sixteen-year-old, six-foot-tall sister could kick the stuffing out of three or four toughs at the same time. And she had.

Even after earning her Ph.D., she lacked any serious opportunity for activity smacking of sin. Not one for self-delusion, she knew she wasn't the type of woman a man gazed upon with lust in his heart and an erection in his Dockers. Her early years left invisible scars. Too often she'd seen children brought into the world without a thought for their welfare. She wouldn't consider sex with a man unless she was assured of marriage and they used birth control.

For better or worse, the problem of "yes" didn't arise. Win never met a man who wanted to marry her. Sleep with her during her glory days at UCLA? Yes. Marry her? No.

Finally, Win met her caretaker's patient gaze.

"Are you ready for your chocolate now, dear?" Adele stirred the liquid in the big mug, all the while lifting her eyebrows and smiling encouragement.

What the heck, Win figured. Surely turning down a bedside angel bearing goodwill, hot chocolate, and pastries was sinful. Win sipped the chocolate and nibbled at the pastries. "Why are you here?" she managed between bites.

"To help you, Felicity. You've had a nasty accident. Please, dear, never disobey and scare me like that again. I believe you took ten years off my life and at least that many from poor Mr. Hamilton's, too." Adele smiled mischievously and daubed at the corners of Win's mouth with a soft linen napkin.

"Felicity? Is that what I'm called here?" Win rolled the name around on her tongue. It sounded soft, frail, and oh, so feminine, just the opposite of Winifred Beatrice McCanless.

"Well, yes, dear. That is your name." Adele poured more chocolate into Winifred's cup from a china teapot kept warm by an embroidered cozy.

"How did I get here?" Win met Adele's gaze with growing curiosity.

"We came from California on this ship, the *Ompalada*. Do you remember San Francisco, Felicity?"

"San Francisco?" She hadn't been to San Francisco for more than basketball games. She and Joey had planned an excursion to northern California for the August after his graduation. Instead, Joey went to the cemetery and she nearly went crazy with grief. Only the long hours of intense research at the lab had kept her from plunging over the edge headfirst. Had it not been for her work, she would have lain in bed until her broken heart stopped beating and her misery ended.

Suddenly tired beyond reason, Winifred settled into the pillows and listened as Adele related the glories of San Francisco, a place the older woman obviously loved. With the pleasant sound of Adele's voice in the background, Winifred drifted toward sleep.

A few hours later, Winifred woke feeling stronger. If this was her new life, she'd better explore it. As she threw the quilts back, Adele entered the cabin with a shriek of protest.

"What?" Winifred demanded. "I need a bathroom."

Adele's smooth brow drew together in a furrow. "I've ordered a bath for you, Felicity. We'll complete your toilet before we leave the ship. We must make Ransom Hamilton a bit less regretful of the situation."

While she wondered who Ransom Hamilton was and just what situation Adele referred to, she really needed a bathroom. She shoved her feet over the side of the bed, thinking it strange they didn't touch the floor.

On second thought, it was strange that she could *see* the floor without her glasses. She alternately squinted and blinked. No. No contact lenses. Perhaps being here had cured her faulty vision. "Definitely a plus," she mumbled, scooting toward the edge of the bed where Adele restrained her.

"I don't want you out of that bed."

"If you don't let me up, I'm going to wet this bed," Winifred warned.

In steely calmness, Winifred followed the direction of Adele's finger to a screen in the corner of the room. Her stride was off slightly, as was her balance. Odd, her body lacked the smooth athletic fluidity that she took for granted in L.A.

What she discovered behind the screen banished all thoughts of her physical anomalies. Instead of running water, a commode, a sink, and a toothbrush, she found a contraption straight out of a museum basement. Without the benefit of a cultural history class a decade earlier, she'd never have recognized the chamber pot chair beside a slipper tub.

Musing that there were a few things she didn't understand about this place, she availed herself of the facility.

It was the cussing, she decided. She kept meaning to watch her language, but the words slipped out when she least expected them. Maybe if she'd cussed less on the basketball courts or when alone in the lab, she'd deserve a place with a modern bathroom.

The bath and hair washing became an adventure beyond Win's wildest expectation. The air of fantasy settling over her conjured the sensation of being part of the background in a rock video. The eerie perception increased with the realization that her hair had grown two feet. If she recalled correctly, lightning fried hair, it didn't make it grow at a phenomenal rate. With hair this long, a bad hair day could be fatal.

After three swipes of the towel, she pronounced herself dry. She opened the armoire, intent on finding comfortable clothing. The swinging door on the left revealed a mass of lace, frills, and feminine fabrics.

"How about a sweat suit? Or jeans and sneakers?" she asked Adele, marveling at the tiny shoes at the bottom of the armoire. "Whose are these, anyway?"

"Why, those are your clothes, Felicity. Come, I'll help you dress and fix your hair. You know, it's the way things are done now." Adele guided her into the center of the cabin.

Not quite willing to defy this ministering angel, Win lamented the need for wearing the old-fashioned garb in the closet. Lord! Petticoats, corsets, bloomers. The gap between the limbo caretaker's taste in fashion and her own preference for a pair of jeans yawned across the centuries.

She sighed. If this was limbo, it was temporary and so were the clothes. Always a team player, she'd follow the agenda without complaint—for now.

As Adele recounted the previous day's events, Winifred forgot the atrocious clothing and the tugs and pulls on her hair.

"Back up, Adele," Win requested, tilting her head opposite the way Adele pulled. "Are you telling me I wandered off the edge of this ship? I fell into the water and drowned?"

"Oh, little one, I was so afraid you were dead. So was poor Mr. Hamilton when he pulled you out of the ocean. But then, in a few minutes, you coughed and shocked all of us. My dear, you gave us such a scare. You must do as I say, do you understand?"

"A few minutes? How long was I underwater? Didn't I swim?" Winifred felt the color drain from her face.

"No, precious baby, you have always shied away from water. That's why I wasna concerned when I went back for our cloaks." Adele framed Felicity's face with her hands. "You were in the water at least ten minutes, though it seemed an eternity when Mr. Hamilton was searching for you. Once you were on the dock, it seemed forever before you started breathing. It was probably just a few minutes."

This was not limbo. It was the *Twilight Zone*! Suddenly panicked, Winifred grabbed Adele's hands. "What's my name, Adele?"

Adele smiled with infinite patience as though her charge's forgetfulness was a common occurrence. "Felicity Forsythe Hamilton, sweetheart. Can you remember that for a few hours?"

The sincere request kept Winifred from hurling a scathing retort that would have frosted the older woman's hair. Instead, she began piecing things together. Adele didn't consider herself a limbo angel or a fairy godmother. What was going on here?

Adele opened both doors of the armoire and turned her charge toward the full-length mirror inside the right door.

Winifred's mouth fell open at the reflection. Yesterday she was Winifred Beatrice McCanless standing at ground zero in a lightning strike. This body belonged to Felicity Forsythe Hamilton, who drowned because she walked off the side of a ship.

Impossible, she decided.

Still . . .

Instead of being six feet tall with brown hair, pale blue eyes, and sporting thick glasses perched on her pug nose, she was barely five-feet-two, petite, and . . . and beautiful! The startling blue eyes staring back were a much deeper blue than hers had been, and they were framed by long, thick black lashes instead of Coke bottle bottoms in heavy frames or contact lenses so strong that she told people she had her eyelids stretched to wear them. Health pinked her smooth ivory cheeks with a glow that darkened the faint blush of

freckles running over the bridge of her delicate nose. Her
full ruby lips parted in awe. Absently, her hand touched the
mixture of chestnut-and blond-highlighted brown hair
catching the glow from the lamp and fingers of sunlight
streaming through the porthole.

All rational thought fled Winifred's mind. The vision in
the mirror gawked back in surprise at a truly beautiful
woman.

Stunned, she retreated, her gaze captivated by the reflection. The memory of an old movie flashed into her mind.
She saw Natalie Wood, clad in a blue dress and wearing
long, white gloves extending past her elbows. Natalie's hair
was also piled atop her head, though not quite as heavily as
Win's.

Win reached toward the mirror in the same astonishment
that Natalie Wood portrayed so many years earlier when she
said, "Mama! I'm beautiful."

During her twenty-nine years, Win McCanless had experienced a multitude of emotions, but she had *never* felt beautiful. Powerful, agile, brilliant, flexible, skillful, intelligent,
confident, but never beautiful—until this moment in someone else's body.

She staggered backward and bumped against the bed.
This wasn't her body.

Distantly, she heard someone beating on the door.
Shocked by the realization of occupying a dead woman's
body, she let Adele drag her away.

The next thing she knew, she was gazing up at the chiseled face of the man with the aquamarine eyes. In her
dreams he had been laughing and happy. In reality, he was a
mountain of smoldering rage. Anger radiated from him.

Words withered in her throat when Adele introduced her
to her husband.

Chapter 4

THE VISION OF loveliness Felicity presented at the cabin threshold sent unwanted desire shooting through Ransom. Her intense gaze sparkled with an unmasked blend of curiosity, innocence, and astonishment. If he hadn't known better, he'd have sworn a spark of intelligence flickered behind those expressive ocean blue eyes.

Sadly, he knew better. The birthing that killed her mother had left her damaged. Arch had consulted the greatest medical minds of the day on Felicity's behalf. Seeing her so perfect and lovely made accepting the extent of her impairment more difficult.

Felicity wore a blue poplin dress with a narrow band of pleated fabric at the end of the skirt and a similar pattern on the sleeves. Bias folds of blue satin with a darker blue silk fringe finished off the fashionable vision of innocence.

While he contemplated the tragedy of Felicity's childlike mind, his body responded to the delectable feminine morsel ripe for seduction.

He noticed the way a sprinkling of small freckles played

across her nose and that the shape of her sensuous mouth was made for kissing. Everything about her was slight and delicate from her small, straight nose to the gentle curve of her neck. The lush swell of her breasts and small span of her waist flaunted her femininity.

The memory of her naked body surfaced unbidden. He battled down the arousal tightening his pants. The last thing he needed on top of his current business trouble, the takeover of Arch's interests in Seattle, Sitka, and San Francisco, and an overdue whaling ship, was a simpleton wife so gorgeous and innocently sensuous she aroused him whenever he saw her.

No. This needed to stop right now. How? he wondered, feeling the mire of events broaden. Unreasonable anger darkened his mood.

Gripping Adele's hand as though she was the last bastion of protection, Win's heart lurched in the face of the black fury barely contained by the giant filling the doorway. Peril and menace radiated from him in waves. The highly charged reactions of fight or flight sent color into her cheeks.

Ransom Hamilton exuded a raw sensuality she recognized as a magnetism capable of drawing women of all ages. His commanding presence warned that many a watchful female eye and hopeful heart waited for the telltale nod or smile that transformed his darkly angular features into an angelic promise of sensual ecstasy. Thick, black lashes clustered in a squint around his fiery aquamarine eyes.

A tall, well-muscled man obviously conditioned by physical labor, his stern, chiseled appearance cast a formidable presence. Intimidated, she inched away when he moved into the center of the cabin. He reached back with a long arm and flipped the door shut. The man towered over her, reminding her of the startling change in her own altitude. Despite the rapid pounding of her heart, she kept her gaze fixed on him. The close fit of his black trousers left little to the imagination where his long, muscular legs were concerned. His gray jacket had a waist seam and buttons on the cuffs that matched those on the slightly darker gray brocade vest. Beneath the vest, a stark white shirt gaped at the throat. Raven hair curled around the collar of the impeccably tailored jacket hugging his broad shoulders. The only real color about the man came from his eyes. But the fine fit of his expensive attire couldn't displace the aura of untamed danger surrounding him.

"Felicity, dear, this is your husband," Adele said quietly, touching her shoulder. "This is Ransom Hamilton. Do you remember him? I know it's been a long time."

She'd never met him, so how could she remember him? But now, she'd never forget him. Ransom Hamilton. Handsome Ransom Hamilton, she decided in near hysteria, biting back a giggle tickling her throat.

She jumped when his large hands settled on her shoulders. Before she could cringe or shrink away, he guided her to the edge of the bed. A masterful pressure eased her down until she sat. Although gentle, his handprints left the impression of a branding iron. Heat coursed through her body, lodging in some of Felicity's more favorable and private places.

"Husband?" Win squeaked. For an instant, she both pitied and envied the woman who called him *husband*. Oh, Lord! If Adele's version of her identity was true, she was that woman. Good grief! Had the woman who occupied this body been this hunk's wife? At least her taste in men was better than her choice of clothing.

The researcher in her channeled the chaos. Given the change of physical identity, who was she in a legal sense? Was she, Winifred McCanless living in Felicity's body, married to Ransom Hamilton? How could she be? She'd never promised anything in front of a preacher or justice of the peace. What a mess!

Surely the legal statutes covered this kind of situation. Racking her memory, she couldn't recall a similar case, but the Supreme Court must have a ruling on the validity of such a marriage. They had a ruling for everything else.

Determined to learn what she could, she managed a tremulous smile at Ransom, noting with a quiet sigh of relief that his expression softened when she did so.

"Are you feeling well enough to leave the ship, Felicity?" Ransom asked patiently, dragging the chair in front of her.

Caught up in the strange sensations playing havoc in her body, Win nearly missed the question. By the time she found an answer, his captivating bass voice seduced her attention in another direction.

"I know you'll miss your beautiful home in San Francisco, but we will try to make your visit fun. There are activities you can do here in the summer and interesting places to visit, too. Would you like to see the Russian fort? They have real cannons. And men in colorful uniforms. When we go, you must be very good. You will have to stay very close to me. Understand?

"Do you think you can just sit there while Miss Clairmont and I prepare your things? You're going to stay at my home for a while. I think you will like it. You'll need all your pretty dresses up at the house, so we'll pack them up and take them with us."

With her jaw clamped shut, she glared at him. Keen disappointment dashed Win's hopes of having found a nearly perfect man. Forget the legal complexities of any sort of marriage! The man had the IQ of a gerbil.

Ransom glanced over his shoulder at the ever-patient Miss Clairmont. "How limited is she? Can she understand what I'm saying, Adele?"

Win's mouth sagged open. Damn. Maybe he wasn't stupid. It sounded like he thought *she* was stupid, or at least mentally deficient. Well, Mother Nature may have been in a stingy mood when it came to Win in the looks department, but her mood turned generous when she handed out the brains.

Left eyebrow raised, a frown deepening in a warning, she leaned toward him.

"Why don't you ask *me* if I comprehend the placating tone and condescending demeanor you've employed to coerce me into acceding to your wishes?" Winifred demanded, her eyes narrowing, her hands curling into fists. "I am perfectly capable of answering direct questions and can actually comply with reasonable requests when couched in the appropriate vernacular by sensibly speaking individuals."

No sooner did she finish speaking than Adele sighed and collapsed into a heap of skirts and petticoats.

Cussing under her breath, Win scrambled off the bed. She brushed past the useless man gaping at her and dropped to the floor. Cradling Adele's head in her lap, she gently rubbed the woman's pale cheeks.

"Make yourself useful, Mr. Hamilton. Get out of that chair and go find some smelling salts for me!"

Adele moaned and her eyelashes fluttered.

"Never mind. She's coming around." Smoothing a cluster of hair from Adele's forehead and cheek, she addressed the dazed woman. "Just lie still for a moment, Adele. Breathe deeply and relax. We'll get you onto the bed." She slipped her arm beneath Adele's legs in order to lift her. Ransom gently pushed her aside.

"What do you think you're doing? You can't pick her up. I'll take her." He scooped Adele up with an easy grace and laid her on the bed. "You've done enough for one day."

"What do you mean, *I've* done enough for one day? I haven't done anything." She popped to her feet and glowered at him, hands on hips. "You're the one treating me like an imbecile. I've merely set the record straight."

He wheeled on her, his expression as menacing as a district gang war in August. Her mushrooming outrage burst into broken shards of fear. "Be quiet." His voice reverberated like a softly struck bass drum. "Do not say another word unless you're spoken to. Understand?"

As quickly as it came, the fear left. In its wake, anger

lapped at the shores of her reason. The desert of her mouth found an oasis. She had stood her ground with men as big as he and lived to walk away. He was just a man. That's all. Winifred smoothed her skirts with trembling hands. "Oh, I understand perfectly, you egotistical, overbearing chauvinist. But I do not take orders from you." Who did he think he was, telling her to sit down and shut up like some twitty brat?

"Yes, you do, Felicity." He grasped her shoulders and pressed her into the chair. When she started rising, he pointed at her. "Stay!"

"I am not your dog!" No way was she going to be married to this dictator. A man could ride on his intriguing eyes, rugged looks, and nicely proportioned body only so far in life. He crossed the line when he ordered her to sit down and shut up.

"No, goddammit, you're my wife! And I said stay there!" He turned his attention on Adele, obviously expecting his wife's compliance.

"Not even in your dreams, mister," Win mumbled, then escaped the chair.

"Oh, my! What's happened, Mr. Hamilton?" asked a bewildered Adele from the center of the bed. "Where did my sweet Felicity learn to speak like that? Has she changed? Is she smart now? Is it truly the great miracle we've been praying for?"

Win pursed her lips, restraining the ire rising in her throat. Seeking something to occupy the burst of energy she'd enjoy unleashing against Ransom Hamilton, she opened the trunk and started emptying the contents of the armoire into it.

"Oh, Mr. Hamilton. Stop her! She canna do that," Adele protested, pushing up from the pillows.

Ransom scowled at Winifred struggling with the trunk at the end of the bed with both hands. "What the hell do you think you're doing?"

She ignored the heated anger and confusion emanating

from him. "What does it look like I'm doing?" Three shoes clunked individually as they hit the bottom of the trunk. "Packing. These are my clothes, aren't they?"

"Yes," he answered with a forced patience, "those are your clothes."

"You did plan on taking them with us when leaving the ship, didn't you?"

"Yes." The curt answer heightened her determination to ignore his glowering disapproval.

"Then I ought to pack them so we can leave. Right?" She didn't expect an answer and kept her head down. The intensity of his forbidding glare seared her head and shoulders.

It seemed she had two hundred pounds of clothing for a one-hundred-pound-capacity trunk. Employing the cramming techniques a proficient athlete used for packing a gym bag, Winifred literally stuffed the trunk.

The task kept her from acknowledging the two sets of eyes scrutinizing her every move. Nervousness sent her fingers fumbling over unfamiliar territory. If she had a basketball in her hands she wouldn't be nervous—she'd know exactly what to do—bounce it off Ransom's head then run like hell! Although irate, he wouldn't be standing there like the great thunder god of the north boring holes into her with that icy glare. At least he wasn't speaking in that disturbing tone rumbling from deep in his chest.

A woman who directed her own affairs and who was physically stronger than most men, Win decided it was time she left the ship. She reached for the handle on the side of the trunk. When she yanked to hoist it up, she lost her footing and nearly dislocated her shoulder. She went down hard, her legs splayed straight out with layers of petticoats billowing into her face. The bruise on her posterior was nothing compared with the one suffered by her dignity. More insulting, the trunk hadn't budged.

Stunned, she massaged her shoulder and pushed to her feet, stepping on her dress and petticoats twice in the process, then frowned at the trunk in disbelief. Adele's gasp and near swoon preceded the hot sensation of Ransom Hamilton's glower.

A day ago, hoisting the trunk onto her shoulder and carrying it out would have required very little effort. Today, she couldn't move it. Gradually, she realized her smaller size robbed her of strength as well the ability to see over a crowd.

Considering Felicity's taste in men, Win decided it was far more advantageous being an intellectual, athletic, six-foot-tall woman of the 1990s. Helplessness was more alien and frightening than her strange surroundings and the notion of having Ransom Hamilton as a husband.

But nobody had consulted her about this switch. For a moment, she thought how funny Joey would have found her predicament. His macabre sense of humor, which had always made her laugh, would have deemed this whole situation hilarious.

In the halls of memory, she heard Joey teasing that she was the only person in the universe who would complain about being placed in a gorgeous body somewhere else in time instead of dying outright.

The realization of a time change straightened her. How did she know that? Slowly, she met the two pairs of eyes tracking her from across the small cabin.

Short of a nuclear war, even primitive ships had more modern bathroom facilities than this one. No woman born after 1960 voluntarily wore torturous clothing, not after panty hose, jeans, and T-shirts. Not even Felicity Forsythe or Adele Clairmont.

Her heart lurched with anxiety and her knees took on the strength of Jell-O. She forced a couple of deep breaths and beat down the waves of excitement, terror, and the awesome truth threatening to consume her.

Why was she alive in this strange woman's body instead of dead wherever dead people go? Somehow, she'd found her way to this time and place. Was there a way back? What would happen to her work at Westminster? Was there anything left of the lab?

She gave herself a strong mental shake. Logically, things like this did not happen. Gazing around her, an aura of detachment insulated her from her surroundings. Perhaps the lightning bolt drove her into a wormhole in time and slammed her into this body. Impossible. But what other explanation was there?

Answers eluded her. All she wanted was to be off this ship, then go someplace quiet where she could think. It didn't even matter which century, just so she could sift through the sudden changes in her life. Or was it her death?

She didn't know whether to be overjoyed at the challenge ahead, relieved that she wasn't totally dead, or just plain terrified that she was losing her mind. Emotionally, she teetered on the edge of a high precipice with the feeling that someone was breathing down her neck.

"My dear Felicity, tell me what has happened," Adele pleaded as Ransom assisted her from the bed.

With new insight, Win regarded Adele as the mother lode of answers. Win relaxed slightly at the prospect of a talking database.

"I don't know, Adele. I feel like a different person since . . . since my accident the other day," Win offered. "I guess I haven't been myself." *Truer words were never spoken.*

Adele draped a loving arm around Win's shoulders. "You'll be fine after we reach your new home and you take a nap. Maybe the incident caused some positive changes. It really doesna matter, sweet. We love you just the way you are."

Other than Joey, no one had ever told Win they loved her. It made her uncomfortable, as though something might be expected that she couldn't give.

"Yes. Perhaps a nap would help," Win agreed. "I'm sorry I caused you such distress, Adele." She turned toward Ransom. "Shall we go?" Her eyes narrowed on the grim face forging a permanent scowl in her direction.

Moments later, holding her cloak securely in the front,

Win accompanied Ransom across the deck and down the *Ompalada*'s gangplank. Her body still didn't function the way it should, and her slippery, slick-soled shoes further tested her confidence.

"When I get you home, I want you to stay there. Understand? Wandering about unescorted is dangerous," Ransom said, barely affording her glance.

"Look, Mr. Hamilton, we need to talk. I'm not who you think I am. Felicity really did drown. She's quite dead, I assure you. I'm Dr. Winifred McCanless from Westminster Research Labs in Los Angeles. Westminster doesn't exist right now, at least not in your time, and I'm not sure how I got into this body but . . . ."

"We will let that be our little secret, Felicity," he hissed, tightening his grip on her arm.

"Winifred." Two could play this game, she decided, sorely tempted to give him a strategic shove off the gangplank. This wasn't going well. Either she couldn't think of anything to say or she couldn't keep her mouth closed and fed his ire with each word.

"Right, Winifred."

Gooseflesh rippled under his seething glower.

She thrust out her chin and glared at him in defiance. "Make that Dr. McCanless. I don't know you well enough for first-name familiarity." If he was going to humor her, he'd better do it right!

"We can keep that little secret between the two of us, all right . . . Dr. McCanless? Now, you'll wait right here while I fetch Miss Clairmont, then we'll be on our way home." Without waiting for an answer, he stomped up the gangplank.

Watching the stiff set of his broad shoulders, Win doubted she could convince Ransom Hamilton of the sudden and drastic change in his wife. The man's air of superiority infuriated her. If he used that condescending tone again, she'd forget he wasn't a physical threat at this point and beat the hell out of him. Considering her smaller stature, maybe she'd just hurt him.

Chapter 5

WRAPPED IN THOUGHT, Winifred glared at Ransom striding up the *Ompalada*'s gangplank. Something touched her arm, and her attention flew to the source. Surprised, her eyes widened at the very old Indian and his young companion standing before her. The wrinkle-faced man she thought might be a shaman wore a woven reed cloak decorated with patterns of animals, birds, and fish. His iron gray, shoulder-length hair hung straight. A colorful band held his mane in place and rode low over bushy gray-white eyebrows. Twinkling brown eyes returned her fascination.

The shaman spoke softly to his companion, who in turn told Win, "You are the woman who gave life to the dead. The woman who is two women, but one woman. A young spirit from far away asked the gods for this body as her spirit entered the land of death. She is now free. Raven told of your coming. He say you are White Raven's. The spirits smile on you, Two Women."

Win beamed at the shaman, then at his companion, only to return to the shaman with a wisp of a smile. "You know about me?" Disbelief mingled with relief. At least one other person was either as crazy as she or understood the impossibility of her situation. She wanted to laugh and cry simultaneously. Her considerable self-restraint contained both. The genuine warmth in the shaman's gaze soothed her anxiety. Regardless of what happened with Felicity's husband, she wasn't alone. *Thank you, God.* "What is White Raven?"

The Shaman raised a rattle and shook it twice.

"The Wolf, the Raven, and the Eagle smile on you, Two Women. You are a child of the Great Spirit. More human than any human being. You are protected by the spirits and loved by human beings. A great totem will be made telling your story. When the time is right for you, we will speak again," said the young companion. He offered the old shaman the strength of his arm.

Unwilling to relinquish such open acceptance, Win reached out. The old shaman's warm, leathery skin felt the way she thought a grandfather would feel. "Wait. Please! How will I find you? How can . . . ,"

"You have only to want to see us. We will come," the companion interpreted. "You are not alone. Watch for the spirits. They are here. When the time is right, we will speak of many things. Until then, you are safe with White Raven. It is a test of the spirit for both of you, but especially for him. The spirits watch which way you choose and what you do with this great blessing. You are here for yourself, Two Women, and for White Raven. Your destinies are one." He glanced over Felicity's shoulder, nodded, then led the shaman away.

"Please, you must tell me who or what is White . . . " She started after them, but Ransom's agitated voice brought her up short.

"Don't even think of moving from that spot without me," he commanded. "Look around, woman. You've managed to halt all the work on this dock."

In her confusion and silent joy, a response for the annoyance Ransom presented eluded her. He tucked her hand into the crook of his arm and escorted her down the dock. Maintaining her balance in the stiff, heeled shoes on the rolling planks required her full attention. She barely noticed the stares they drew from the sailors and dockworkers.

No sooner were they on the blessedly solid wharf than Ransom stopped. Win glanced around. A dapper man almost as imposing as Ransom approached. In open fascination, Win watched the stranger remove his hat and bow. He caught her hand and brought it to his firm, warm lips. Sparkling blue eyes bespoke a sense of humor and radiated personal charm. His even features and thick brown hair curling around his ears and neck would have made him ideal for a Mr. March of a male beefcake calendar, especially if he smiled as he did now and revealed the dimple in his right cheek.

She bit back the impulse to giggle, suspecting that Ransom, with his complete lack of a sense of humor, might throw her back into the cold sea if she did. Altogether, it was a pleasant experience being bowed to and having her hand kissed as though she was royalty.

"Felicity, may I present my good friend, Baron Ivan Korinkov of St. Petersburg. He is a distant relative of the czar." Ransom squeezed Felicity's elbow. She glanced up. He scowled. "My bride, Felicity. I'm afraid she's unfamiliar with protocol. My apologies. I hope you'll make allowances for her ignorance of our social customs, Ivan."

Ivan's captivating smile formed instantly. "I am sure I could forgive so beautiful a woman anything. You have done very well, my friend. "

Win stared up at the handsome Russian, captivated briefly by the warm sparkle of his blue eyes and dazzling white smile, then she stammered a greeting.

Ruminating over the shaman's reference to a White Raven, she missed Ransom's conversation with the baron. She noted her surroundings. Wherever they were, four things stood out as plentiful: mud, ocean, trees, and stench. All in all, the odors of the busy wharf were worse than her experience in New York during a garbage strike in summer. The smell of rotting timber, fish, sewage, seaweed, and some other noxious smell emanating from several buildings farther down the wharf created a foul vapor.

The melody of workers talking, laughing, cussing, and singing in a variety of languages enthralled her. The waterfront hummed with vitality. Only Ransom's hand closing firmly around her upper arm kept her from exploring the beckoning sights and sounds. Gazing across two docks at the crippled whaling ship, *Lisa,* she marveled at the history unfolding before her eyes. In a sense, it was better than the virtual reality computer program the software people next door to her lab were working on. She was actually here.

Here.

There was no *off* switch.

She was truly here. Lord, it was real.

Astonished, she glanced at Ransom, intent on asking just where and when *here* was.

"We're lucky the *Lisa*'s back remained unbroken. Once we replace the masts and check the rest of the structure, she'll be seaworthy," Ransom told Ivan. "I have another ship, an iron hull, ready to replace her in a few weeks."

"Very shrewd of you to build the shipyard here, my friend. Not only do you expand your fleet, you have made a fortune off your fellow traders by fixing their ships," Ivan said admiringly. "You've made me very glad I went in with you on the packing plant, too. My cargoes bring me top market price in Russia."

Ivan smiled at Felicity. "When you've rested from your long voyage and settled into your new home, I would be honored if you and Ransom would join me for dinner, Mrs. Hamilton."

"Thank you, Baron Korinkov. I'd like that very much," Win said, unsuccessfully dampening a small smile in response to the glint of amusement in the baron's eyes.

The baron kissed her hand before taking his leave. This time, Win bowed her head. There was much more to this regression in time thing than she would have ever imagined. When she had Adele alone, she'd conduct the most diplomatic inquisition the world had ever seen.

"I thought you said she knew rudimentary protocol and manners," Ransom murmured as he escorted them down the wharf. The grim set of his jaw, the tic in his left cheek, and the tight grip he held on Felicity betrayed his anger.

"I'm so sorry, Mr. Hamilton. She does. Or she did. I don't know what she knows anymore." Flustered, Adele wrung her hands and stole a nervous glance around Ransom at Felicity.

"Please, find out. Make sure Felicity is schooled in social protocol. Ivan is a friend and therefore, forgiving of her faux pas. I know this isn't your fault, Adele. But I am counting on your assistance in this, ah, situation."

"Thank you for understanding, sir. I'm sure Felicity and I will be in proper form in no time."

This dictatorial man was almost more than Winifred could bear. She paused before entering the carriage. "I noticed you introduced me as your bride. That leads me to assume we haven't been married very long. Could I possibly be fortunate enough for us to have not consummated this marriage?"

"We are both fortunate in that regard, madam." Ransom assisted Adele into the carriage.

"Thank heaven," Win said, sighing in relief. "I want an annulment."

"I am already considering it."

The doubt narrowing his eyes mirrored her own. Feeling she had little to lose to such an arrogant boor, she smiled pleasantly, then asked, "Do you think you could tell me where we are and what year this is?"

The tic in Ransom's cheek twitched faster. "New Archangel, or Sitka, if you prefer. It's June twenty-fifth, 1866, Felicity, so the sun will shine about eighteen hours today, unless it rains. Any other questions?"

Immediately, her scientific mind went into gear. "So, at winter solstice there's only about six hours of daylight and it's probably colder than h . . ." She sank into the carriage seat and pulled her cape around her. Preferring to watch the rear ends of the matching grays, who she mentally dubbed Seattle Slew and Northern Dancer, pulling the carriage, she tried ignoring Ransom and Adele. But her intentions proved futile when Ransom sat beside her and ordered the driver home.

Even in the roomy carriage, Ransom's long legs appeared cramped. He sat with his knees open, his left thigh pressed against Winifred's. The man was a veritable oven. The heat he generated through layers of material radiated along her body.

Asking him to move constituted an admission of his effect on Felicity's body. She preferred prolonged torture to giving him that kind of satisfaction. Earlier in life, Winifred had learned not to give anyone a weapon that might be used against her later.

Focusing on safe and logical concerns, she thought about her work. What would happen to the drug Dr. Johanson validated . . . when? Was it yesterday or someday in the distant future? What if there were no copies of her updated notes for Boyd? And there wouldn't be, unless the backup program had finished running. Try as she might, she couldn't remember if there had been enough time for the file transfer. If lightning destroyed the link before the process completed . . . If Boyd didn't remember the exact changes she'd made . . . The notes were gone now. So was Dr. Winifred Beatrice McCanless.

Oh, if only it was as easy as writing down the formula and process, putting it in a bottle and tossing it into the sea for Boyd to retrieve. But it wasn't. Time wasn't tide, though it seemed to have swallowed her as easily as the vast, cold ocean claimed the persona of Felicity Forsythe Hamilton.

Her gaze roamed to Ransom who, like Adele, stared at her. Despite his surly, angry nature, he was an interesting man in both physical size and looks. A pity he was such an uptight chauvinist.

"What?" she demanded, her eyes darting from Ransom's unwavering scrutiny to Adele's growing concern, then back. "Did I grow a wart on my nose since we left the ship?"

Color popped into Adele's cheeks and she resumed twisting her handkerchief. "I'm so sorry I'm making you uncomfortable, my dear. I just canna help looking at you. Yer so, so changed, yet ya look the same. I can hardly believe our good fortune. 'Tis a miracle, it is. A miracle on the dock. Praise the saints above for answering our prayers."

Nonplussed, Win checked Ransom's face for agreement and found a curious lack of expression. While she couldn't go along with Adele's assessment of what happened, circumstances denied any other explanation. A public admission of possession of Felicity's body could get her burned at the nearest totem pole.

"Okay." Narrowed eyes met the aquamarine lasers boring through her. "What's your excuse?"

In a voice as dark as a winter midnight and as sharp as a knife edge, Ransom answered, "I do what I wish, madam, and make excuses to no one."

Careful. He's dangerous. "Good. Then I'll expect you to start the annulment proceedings this afternoon."

"In that case, madam, you can expect disappointment."

"Then *I'll* start the proceedings," she snapped back, believing the subject closed until his laughter shook the seat. The sound lacked any semblance of mirth. Gooseflesh rose on her arms and sent a shiver down her spine. Even so, she couldn't drag her gaze from him. Yes, this man was very dangerous. Something about him drew her like a moth to a flame, and she'd seen plenty of dead moths. Recalling the image in the mirror, she wondered if perhaps she wasn't a butterfly, delicate, pretty, and colorful.

Her thoughts were interupted as the driver turned the

grays down the graveled drive of an expansive two-story mansion with a widow's walk peeking over the roofline and a round turret on the southwest corner. In any time, the house was a castle. As they drew nearer, she noted the heavy brick construction and the fluted marble pillars framing the porch running along the main entrance. Freshly painted shutters stood sentry at every window.

Ransom called her twice before she heard and allowed him to help her out of the carriage. Once on the ground, she held onto his arm until he met her gaze. "Please, we must discuss what's going to happen with our futures. Things aren't as they seem, Ransom."

"After dinner." He released her as quickly as if she was made of hot coals.

"One more question." She gestured at the center of the circled drive. "Why is there a totem pole in the middle of your yard?"

He shrugged, dismissing her question. "Doesn't everyone have one?"

"No. I didn't notice any of the other houses with totem poles."

"I'll speak with you after dinner, Felicity. I have work to do. Save your questions for when I have time to answer them." He gestured toward the house.

She might have protested if it hadn't started raining. She locked her jaw and hurried toward the house. Once across the wide porch and through the massive double doors, she forgot about the totem pole. The house was enormous. Sparsely decorated in subtle, masculine furnishings, it overwhelmed her. A curving staircase yawned from the second floor. White marble covered the expanse leading to the staircase. Thick carpets punctuated the creamy smoothness. She marveled at the rich surroundings, which were unlike anything she'd seen outside of a museum. A wave of incredulity swept over her.

The house provided a stark contrast to her meagerly furnished studio apartment. Now, standing in a foyer large enough to swallow her entire apartment, she could only gape at the opulence. As a veil of illusion skimmed her consciousness, she thought all she needed was for the ghost of Rod Serling or Vincent Price to float down the elegant curving staircase and bid her welcome.

Chapter 6

Standing in front of the cheval glass in the beautifully decorated yellow bedroom that Meggie MacGregor, the housekeeper, had assigned, Winifred's trepidation eased. Her fascination with the woman in the glass grew into an excitement almost as great as that she had felt at Coretta Swin's costume party when they were both seven. Then, Winifred still held dreams of marriage, babies, and a nice apartment. Ten years later, those dreams had faded into distant memories that emerged in the darkest hours of the night. Twenty-two years later, those dreams had yielded to reality and disappeared.

Staring at the reflection, she contemplated how much of life she had already missed. She'd never dated, never fallen in love, never even kissed a man in passion. Had she been born with this alluring body, what might she have experienced? What might she have missed? The questions without answers seemed limitless.

For a moment, the image brightened and changed. In her mind's eye, she saw Winifred McCanless, the basketball player, in an eighteenth-century costume. Her short, brown hair refused the style guaranteed by the spray gel and brute force of the curling iron she had struggled with daily. Her wide-set pale blue eyes focused on the pug nose balancing her thick glasses. Without surgery, it would never be straight again. It had been broken too many times during neighborhood pickup basketball games with the boys and on the wooden courts of some of the most prestigious universities in the country. No championship season ended without Win McCanless getting a broken nose.

Scrutinizing her appearance, she shook her head sadly. That woman no longer existed. In her place stood a petite stranger straight out of the Academy Awards edition of *People* magazine.

According to Adele, sweet, unemotional Felicity had possessed the mentality of a six-year-old. The teary-eyed nanny kept thanking God for the miracle on the dock.

Win couldn't tell her she wasn't really Felicity. This was Felicity's body, therefore, she must be Felicity. Hell, physically she was, and maybe that wasn't too bad. The only thing different about Winifred Beatrice McCanless was the packaging. Since the miracle, no one would know her true identity unless she told them. Even then, who would believe her? But she had to convince Ransom that things were not as he perceived. The validity of their marriage was in question.

She suspected that Ransom's mother might find great joy in that tidbit of knowledge. Cordelia Hamilton had greeted her and Adele at the door upon their arrival. Cordelia possessed excellent bone structure and clear moss-green eyes. She had the kind of regal beauty that aged well. Her complexion remained smooth and unlined. Only the silver threads in her raven hair betrayed her years. Her promise of warmth became flash-frozen with the revelation that Felicity was now her daughter-in-law. Cordelia had turned on her heel and summoned Meggie MacGregor to show them their rooms.

Considering Cordelia's silent hostility during dinner, at the moment, Winifred preferred to be anyone other than Felicity. "Talk about a bed of thorns," she muttered, "I could sure use a rose or two."

She checked her appearance in the mirror, again marveling that this pretty, petite person was her. If Ransom hadn't expected her in the library, she'd spend the next hour exploring in wonder the image gazing back at her.

Mustering her resources, she strode from the room, then paused. The mental map she'd created of the house plotted a course toward the stairs. As she descended, she felt small and insignificant in view of the phenomenon responsible for her presence. She gave herself a locker room pep talk as she approached the library.

Squaring her shoulders and lifting her head high, Winifred turned the large brass knob. Despite the towering bookshelves crammed with books and the massive masculine furniture dwarfing her, Ransom's presence dominated the room.

"Please, sit down, Felicity. Would you like some coffee? Sherry?" With his broad back to her, he sorted through the crystal decanters.

"I'll have whatever you're having, thank you." He glanced over his shoulder, his brow furrowed in disapproval. "Or whatever is appropriate," she hurriedly added, not wanting the evening launched on a sour note. She and Adele hadn't discussed the proper drinking protocol yet. Right now, a Miller Lite would taste great. No need for a glass, the bottle was fine, thank you.

Ransom poured a healthy splash of sherry into a glass and handed it to her. "If this is not to your liking, I'll get you something else."

"I'm sure it will be fine." She tested the liquid with her upper lip, then ran the tip of her tongue over the moisture for a taste. When she lifted her gaze, Ransom was staring at her mouth. A warm flush crept up her neck and pinked her cheeks.

Ransom scowled and abruptly turned away. "Arch was a wealthy man, Felicity. He would have given every penny he had for the way you are now. Believe me, no one wishes he'd lived that long more than I. He might not have felt it necessary to deceive me and put your name on the marriage papers."

"Deceive you?" Was that the reason for his surliness? "I take it I'm not exactly what you wanted in a wife." A dozen new questions popped into her mind.

"As you may know, I wanted your sister as my wife." He faced her from across the room.

"And I would have preferred that you be a young Larry Bird," she muttered into her glass. "It's good to want things."

"I beg your pardon?" He closed half the distance of the room.

"I said, I would have preferred you married her, too."

Ransom braced against the massive library table like a cat ready to pounce. "Regardless of our marital arrangements now and in the future, I will, of course, make sure you have every comfort and want for nothing for the rest of your life. That should be a long time, considering your remarkable recovery from near disaster."

Not quite sure she'd heard correctly, Win leaned forward. "I learned a long time ago that if something sounds too good to be true, it probably is. Did you just say you were going to take care of me in a style to which I'd like to become accustomed? What's the catch? And who is this Arch person, anyway?"

Ransom's left eyebrow twitched before knitting with the right in surprise. "Catch? There is no catch. Archibald Forsythe, *your father*, took great pains to make sure you'd enjoy the comforts and protection of his wealth after he died." Ransom snorted and shook his head in lingering disbelief. "He gave you me. In so doing, he violated damn near every principle he held dear. He doted on you from the day you were born, but I never expected him to trade his honor and my friendship for your security . . . though it shouldn't have surprised me."

He polished off his brandy and poured more. "As far as our marriage or lack thereof, I, ah, need to know, ah, if you're a virgin."

His unenthusiastic resignation to the role of her provider and protector paled against her incredulity. "A virgin?" No one had ever been concerned with her virginity.

The heavy pall her silence cast in the large room heightened Ransom's obvious unease.

"Do you understand what I'm asking?"

The ominous question quelled the mirth tickling her throat. "I know what a virgin is, Ransom. I just don't know if Felicity ever, well, had sex. I sure didn't, and I was twenty-nine when I woke up in her body." She paused, wondering how she'd find out if Felicity was a virgin.

"Which brings up another point you keep overlooking. I may be in Felicity's body, but I'm not her. I'd never wander into the ocean! In my own time, it would've taken three men your size to push me in," she said. "Of course, in my time I stood six feet tall with my toes hanging out and I was an excellent swimmer.

"So that raises another interesting glitch. Since this is Felicity's body, but she doesn't live in it anymore, are we married? Personally, I vote no. Of course, explaining this minor change of ownership might be as complicated as getting a straight answer from a politician."

When he held his silence, she settled on the couch and watched him struggle with his blatant skepticism. His lack of success sent laugher bubbling up inside of her. "It's okay, Ransom. If it hadn't happened to me, I wouldn't believe it, either. Ask me something. Anything about the future up until the mid 1990s and I'll answer, or try to."

His silence refused her challenge.

"You're thinking that I'm crazy, right?" He'd be fun to goad if the topic was less serious. "Adele filled me in on Felicity's unfortunate condition. Did you consider her crazy?"

"No," he answered warily, studying his glass.

Brimming with enthusiasm, she fetched a book from the bookcase and resumed her place on the couch. Holding the sherry in her left hand, she opened the book with her right and began reading aloud. At the end of the paragraph, she snapped the book shut and raised blue eyes ablaze with triumph. To her dismay, he betrayed no reaction.

"Was that supposed to prove something?"

Steeled with fading patience, she drew a slow breath. "Felicity couldn't read. I can."

"So? How do I know that isn't part of what Adele considers her miracle on the dock?"

The man was intentionally dense. "Sure. The miracle. That explains everything. It was a miracle, all right. You just refuse to see it for what it is, Ransom." Agitation warmed her. "Trust me, if six-year-old mentalities could become what I am, know what I know, and argue with you, the waters would be so full of them trying to drown themselves you couldn't get a ship into port! Can you honestly stand there and say you believe I can recover from irreversible brain damage by drowning?"

Statue still, he met her gaze, his mask of indifference etched into his angular features. Not so much as an eyelash flickered.

She pressed on with the biggest bomb in her arsenal of arguments. "Okay, Mr. Hamilton, fasten your seat belt and hold onto your flask and gas mask. I'm taking you on a brief tour of the future."

She settled back on the couch and tucked her feet under her skirts. "For starters, Alaska will be purchased from Russia next year for $7.2 million dollars. It'll be called Seward's Folly and eventually yield some of the largest oil fields on the continent. Alaska becomes the forty-ninth state in 1959. Juneau is the capital. Sitka keeps that honor for some time, so don't dump your real estate yet."

Captivated by the play of soft light on the sherry swirling in the glass, her defensive shields fell. Her voice became rich and animated as she spoke of the future while viewing it through the crystal glass. "Oh, Ransom, there'll be so many changes. Let's see, the Klondike gold rush takes place in the Yukon in 1896 or '97."

She studied Ransom as he listened, caught between thinking her crazy and believing she was from the future. She talked through two more glasses of sherry and as many hours.

"I don't know how, who, or what, Ransom. I just know it happened to me. Consequently, I don't have the luxury of disbelief. The truth is, in some ways, Felicity knew more about life in this time than I do. I know about surviving on the streets, about basketball, chemistry, working and studying and competing to be the best at anything I do. Beyond the day-to-day relationships with my male coworkers, I know nothing good about male-female relationships, except what I saw at the movies or on TV."

Unexpectedly, Ransom asked her to explain TV. Jumping at the chance to encourage the interest she deemed a hopeful sign, she snatched a piece of paper from the table and sketched out the circuitry for a television set complete with cable system and satellite relays. When she finished, she saw a tight, polite smile and glazed eyes.

Blushing at her own overzealous explanation, she bowed her head. "I'm sorry. I guess starting with the first atom is a carryover from my days as a teacher."

"In this other place, you were a teacher?" he asked, his left eyebrow raised in skepticism.

"Yes, during my doctorate years I taught organic chemistry. It was really bonehead stuff, nothing exciting like molecular or nuclear chemistry. Of course, it left me plenty of time for my studies and my job at Westminster Labs. I needed the extra money for Joey's education. We had scholarships lined up, and we applied for every form of financial assistance and grants we could. Still, I liked to be sure. As it turned out, Joey's scholarships and grants covered his expenses completely." Her gaze rested on the nervous flames in the glowing fireplace. She blinked back unexpected tears. "I was so proud when Joey graduated summa cum laude. It was the greatest moment of my life, greater than any championship game, greater than any other achievement in my life then or ever. It meant that we both beat the system by using the system. We could make a difference. Or we might have . . ."

Head low, hiding her raw emotions, she sniffed. "God, how I miss him."

"If you are from the future, you won't see him here."

The comment stung. "I really am from the future, Ransom. And I won't see Joey there, either. He was killed by a drunk driver two weeks after graduation on his way home from a job interview. But I don't expect you to understand. Henry Ford won't invent the automobile for a while yet. When he does, and he takes his company public, if you're still around, buy stock. That's your Wall Street tip for the day."

She stiffened as his gaze narrowed into a pinpoint on her. The tension between them intensified. Never had she been so aware of the presence of any man as she was of Ransom. The magnetism drawing her closer smacked of danger. Being physically attracted to Ransom filled her with dread. Some potent chemical reactions were colorless, odorless, and lethal.

"I can see you don't believe a word I'm saying, and you've already made up your mind I'm crazy. So, I'll make you a deal. If you don't receive word that Alaska has been purchased by Secretary of State William Seward by the end of 1867, you can lock me up as certifiably crazy. If you do learn of Seward's Folly, as it is dubbed in my history books, then you'll do what you can to help me get back to where I belong."

She leaned forward, enforcing her point. "If it's at all possible, I must return and explain what I've discovered. I may have a cell blocker for at least one type of painful cancer. But I'll need this body. Mine got blown up in the lab when the lightning struck."

"You are my wife, Felicity. True, I thought I was marrying Cassandra and ended up with you, but you're my wife nonetheless." He moved closer, his unwavering gaze rooting her in place. "The only reason I married was to have children who would inherit what I worked for every day of my life since I was seventeen." Less than a handbreadth separated them. The heat he radiated made her tingle with excitement. "The question is *not* whether I'll help you leave, but whether I'll keep you at all."

He loomed over her, his finger tracing, but not touching, the rise of her full breasts above the rose satin neckline generously exposing her creamy skin. Her heart beat rapidly with the threat of his fingers touching her flesh.

"You have one of the most tempting bodies I've seen in a while, but your mind is more than I bargained for. I think I preferred you as a . . . a less imaginative woman."

She eyed him closely and recognized the longing in his gaze as lust.

"It seems we both want Felicity's body for different purposes. From the scant amount I know of the woman, she may not have understood either of us."

"Do you understand what I want in a wife?" His bass voice rumbled with the power of an earthquake. His perfectly arched brows lowered as he pinned her with the intensity of his unwavering stare.

"Yeah—a mute Donna Reed with the patience of Mother Teresa, the sexual appetite of Madonna, and the childbearing fortitude of a rabbit."

"Please repeat yourself, madam. I did not understand your response." He leaned closer, his eyes glittering gemstones behind narrowed slits.

She held fast, refusing to be intimidated by his disturbing masculinity. "I said yes, but I don't know you well enough to consider going to bed with you, let alone having children with you."

"You're my wife. I'll take you to bed whenever it suits me, and I'll do so when and *if* I choose to exercise that right. Knowing me has nothing to do with bedding me."

"Ah, the hooker's motto!" She stood resolute in the face of his ire, her hands balled into tight fists buried in the folds of her skirts. "Never get personal or emotionally involved over the most intimate physical act possible between a man and a woman."

"Madam," he said, leaning even closer, his face darkening, "I want children. All you have to do is have them. I'll take over from there."

She snapped. With all the force she could muster from Felicity's smaller body, she drew back and slapped Ransom. The cracking sound carried sharply across the library and into the turret alcove. "Over our dead body will I give up any children we might have!"

Incensed, she fled, shaken by how powerless women in the nineteenth century were in controlling their lives.

Chapter 7

THE MAN HAD the sensitivity of a piranha. That knowledge instilled more than a little apprehension in Winifred. Four days after her arrival at the Hamilton mansion she sat in her bedroom window seat and replayed the dismal confrontation with Ransom for the hundredth time. What if he insisted upon his marital rights? How hard would she fight him, or would she fall victim to her own attraction for him? The thought of turning a child over to him sent tremors of fear down her spine. Nurturing a child inside her new body for nine months only to have him take the babe away was something she'd never allow. It couldn't come to that. She wouldn't let it.

Although she avoided him except for meals, she'd done so at his whim. Only a comatose woman might miss the way Ransom Hamilton ran his household and everybody in it, including his mother. He couched orders in simple requests or issued a command with a glance. Given her dealings with him, she initially thought fear spawned their eager acquiescence. However, by the third day in residence, she grudgingly admitted they obeyed his commands out of respect. Once he focused those intriguing aquamarine eyes on someone, they relinquished their minds and catered to his every fancy.

Except for her. She refused to do his bidding, not that he presented such a challenge by asking anything of her.

To Winifred's chagrin, Adele expressed open admiration for what she considered Felicity's good fortune for having such a marvelous husband. Considering all the information Win had pumped out of Adele concerning Felicity, her companion's opinion was hardly a surprise. She wondered how sociologists would analyze the household and decided it was a dictatorship. The concept contrasted sharply with her own dysfunctional background where the only leadership came from her. She'd made the ironclad rules by which she and Joey lived, and they'd served them well—until they died.

She pressed her nose against the window. A three-masted schooner tacked with the wind into the harbor.

When all was said and done, Ransom controlled her fate. Recalling his reaction in the library, she thought she might be two steps and one argument away from a one-way trip to an asylum. He hadn't believed her. He hadn't wanted to believe.

Every seedy scene from every movie she'd ever watched depicting an insane asylum haunted her memory. In this time and place, such institutions were probably far worse than anything the filmmakers put on the silver screen. The thought set her shivering with a deep-seated horror. No. She would not go gently into that good night.

Ransom's seething anger and blatant disappointment over her not being Cassandra permeated the room whenever they were together. At times she tried to shrink so he wouldn't notice her. Even the heat of his presence and the blaze of his watchful eyes burned her. The notion of bearing a child and not raising that child deepened her own smoldering anger. But what galled the most was her growing desire for Ransom as a lover. Succumbing was the ultimate self-betrayal and dashed any hope of controlling her own destiny.

Growing up, she had followed her dreams over tremendous obstacles and achieved seemingly impossible goals. Now, even her dreams betrayed her. She woke in the middle of the night expecting to find Ransom beside her, touching her, kissing her, wanting her the way her body wanted him. Maybe she was crazy.

Had Felicity been older, she might have attributed the strange aching in her lower abdomen and the perspiration dampening her nightgown after her dreams to menopause. Unfortunately, she couldn't stretch that physical explanation that far. Twenty was too young for menopause even in the 1860s. Still, she loathed admitting a physical chemistry might exist between her and Ransom. The man affected her on a base, sexual plane.

Ransom captivated her by entering any room she occupied. Despite her determination to avoid him, her traitorous eyes found him with the same lure as a snake charmer exerted on a cobra. Maybe, like the flu, this intrigue would pass and she'd develop an immunity.

She inhaled deeply, tamping down the unreasonable antagonism that rose whenever she dwelled on him. Much as she wished to be back in the 1990s, she was not, and there didn't seem a way to get there. Unless . . . unless the shaman knew of one. Outside the room in which she lamented her plight and fretted over Ransom's decision, Sitka and the Tlingit village awaited. The time for an active role in her destiny lay at hand. Excited by the slender hope, Win sat up a little straighter, then grinned.

Winifred and Adele rode in the phaeton with Caine Tilson driving the matched grays toward town.

A patient man who observed even small nuances with his quixotic hazel eyes, Caine's slender build and thin features made him seem the type of man more likely to grace a university than the counters of Hamilton Traders. His shoulder-length brown hair matched the nondescript color of the clothing he favored. Out of doors, the glasses he wore for close work remained protected in his shirt. Though difficult to gauge his age, Win had learned Caine was only a couple of years older than Ransom.

"Tell me about Sitka," Win requested.

"She's the oldest city in this part of the world. She's the Paris of the Pacific," Caine answered proudly.

"See those two buildings near the waterfront?" Caine pointed them out. "The building with the onion dome is St. Michael's Cathedral. The other is the bishop's house. It belongs to Ivan Veniaminov, the Bishop of Alaska for the Russian Orthodox Church. Veniaminov holds high favor with Czar Alexander II and he's one of the most powerful men in the territory."

The octagonal blockhouse atop Castle Hill stood as the Russian government's silent enforcer for governing and taxing the remote *ostrogs*. The blockhouse overlooked Baranov's magnificent castle that now housed the current territorial governor, Prince Maksoutof, and his family.

"I heard Baron Korinkov is related to the prince," Adele stated. "Or was it the czar?"

Caine chuckled. "Seems to me all the Russians are related to some royal or another, but seldom to anyone of lower rank than themselves."

Before Win could explore that anomaly, Caine pointed at a large structure near the harbor. "That's the iron foundry. At one time, it made bells. Now we make ships. We launched the first steam-powered ship built on the Pacific Coast just a half a dozen years ago."

Winifred noted that Caine proudly touted the shipbuilder and referred to the ownership as a possessive *we,* meaning Ransom Hamilton.

Ships moved through the harbor in an endless parade. Merchants and businesses dotted the streets of Sitka. The fine houses of prosperous traders and the Russian aristocracy sat well away from the harbor. Win studied the town with a cartographer's interest, absorbing every detail for a time she might explore this new place alone.

Adele pointed out the cannons at Redoubt St. Michael and asked Caine questions about their origins. Win noticed that since the "miracle on the dock," as Adele dubbed the otherwise inexplicable event, the pinched lines around Adele's expressive brown eyes had eased and she had a quick, youthful smile.

"Ahead is the Tlingit village." Caine gestured with the reins in his left hand.

"Look at those decorated poles!" Adele nearly came off the seat.

Win nodded. "Totem poles. Each one tells a story." *Thank you, Discovery Channel,* she praised.

A broken row of large plank houses lined the sea well above the double palisade of tree trunks. Notched log stairs stretched from the palisade to the banked walkways running down the front of the buildings. Below, fishing gear and dugout canoes littered the beach. Win estimated the houses as forty feet square. They stood shoulder to shoulder behind their screens of magnificently carved totems, some towering as high as forty feet.

"Notice the markings above the doors," Caine instructed.

Win studied the colorful, intricate decorations.

"Each clan-lineage house displays the crests of its house ancestor. The clans build their houses next to each other." He pointed out the Raven Clan, which was the closest to them. Beyond them was the Eagle, and then the Wolf Clan.

"The interiors of the longhouses are decorated with carvings and painted or carved screens," Caine continued, slowing the phaeton. "There's a big common area and some compartment areas for honored family members and the heads of the house."

"Would you stop so I can get a closer look at that magnificent totem pole?" Win asked. "Look at that one. Is that a trading post? Can we go inside?"

"I guess so," Caine answered reluctantly. He parked the phaeton, then assisted the women.

Win examined the totem in the front of the trading post. The carving of a raven painted white captivated her.

"Felicity," Adele called. "If you wish to see the trading post, come along."

Win obliged and joined Adele inside the trading post. There, she examined a piece of walrus tusk carved into a whale. Feeling a presence beside her, she turned.

"Baron Korinkov," she gasped, delighted to see him again. Although as imposing as Ransom, Ivan Korinkov exuded an easy countenance and was far more generous with his smiles.

"Mrs. Hamilton," he acknowledged, bowing his head and lifting her hand to his lips. "It is so good to see you. We were worried you might not have recovered fully from your accident."

"Oh, I'm quite well." She smiled as Adele joined her.

"Did Ransom accompany you today?" Korinkov's azure eyes swept the small trading post.

"He's at the docks, Baron," Caine Tilson answered as he approached. "Did you learn something about . . ." A glance from the Baron silenced him. "I'm sure he'll be anxious to see you."

"I'm sure he will," Korinkov agreed in a somber tone, then chuckled when he met Win's inquiring gaze.

"Is there something wrong?" she asked, sensing there was more to what the two men were not saying.

"No, nothing for you to worry about." The baron lifted her hand to his lips in a farewell gesture. "Perhaps you and Ransom will join me for dinner soon."

"That would be nice." Having dinner with a man who spoke to her like an intelligent person instead of regarding her as a pariah would indeed be a pleasant change.

She followed the baron out of the store and watched him take his leave, noting the condition of his stressed horse. A dozen questions tumbled through her curious mind. Before he was out of sight, she decided that he might have recognized the phaeton and decided to check for Ransom before going to the docks.

"What could be wrong?" she mused aloud.

"Nothing we need to worry about. Now, come along, dear." Adele ushered her back into the trading post to resume their perusal of skilled workmanship.

At any other time, she'd have enjoyed examining every artifact in the trading post. However, she had to find Spirit Dancer and speak with him alone. Taking advantage of Caine and Adele's interest in the Tlingit's wares and a sudden rush of villagers, Win slipped away. She never gave a thought to her destination. Instinct chose the course at every turn.

She rounded a corner and found the old shaman standing, as if waiting for her. His reed cape billowed gracefully in the sea breeze.

"I knew you would come today." The shaman began walking along the hill above the beach and motioned for her to join him.

"You speak English." Surprise widened her eyes.

He smiled patiently. "When it is necessary. Sometimes it is best to speak through others. It is good for everyone to feel needed. Today, you need me. I am important to you because you have questions."

"Millions of them. I only hope you have the answers I need." She watched his lined face anxiously for the slightest ray of hope.

He shook his head. "For some things the Great Spirits do, human beings have no answers. Only acceptance, thankfulness."

Winifred accompanied him in silence, leaving the Tlingit village behind, knowing she couldn't force answers, merely wait until they were offered. The warmth of the afternoon sun burned away some of her tension. The agitation that tightened her stomach and made her head ache when she thought of Ransom lessened with each step away from Sitka.

At the top of the rise, the shaman sat on one of the weather-smoothed boulders facing the sea. "This is a good thinking place. I come here often. You are unhappy?"

"I want to go home," she answered simply.

The sun glittered on the sapphire ocean and the distant islands rising like mystical phoenixes from the depths. The pristine beauty of the austere rocks and cliffs contrasted with the soft green grasses bowing to the ever-present sea breeze. The blue-gray forest provided a backdrop for Spirit Dancer's special thinking place.

"Ah, you want to leave White Raven." He nodded, but continued staring at the sea.

Hands tightly clasped in prayer and buried in the folds of her skirt, hope shone in her dark blue eyes. "Is there a way?"

The old shaman peered into her eyes as though reading her destiny from a tablet inscribed on her soul. After a long time, he shook his head.

"No going back. Only forward in this place. You learn to live for now. Accept your gift of new life." He lifted a wrinkled, gnarled hand. His forefinger touched the crystal tear running down her cheek. "Not sad, Two Women. The spirits smile on you. They take care of you."

In the days since awakening on the ship, she feared returning was impossible. Whatever had put her here in this body was a force so powerful mere mortals could not change it. In truth, mere mortals could barely believe it, let alone comprehend it. Hearing the one person who knew her dilemma confirm the hopelessness placed a heavy stone on her heart. The finality of having her deepest fears confirmed crushed her earlier optimism. The slender thread of hope woven through her daydreams snapped.

Tears rolled down her cheeks and dripped onto the front of her day dress as she gazed out at the islands dotting the blue sea. Even if she could return, what was there to go back to? Other scientists and researchers would take over her work, especially now that it was in the validation process. They would rediscover the links with the next generation of follow-on drugs. Joey was dead. Alexis and Boyd had each other. And if she could return, who would recognize her? How could she explain the change in her appearance?

Wryly, she knew they were bound to notice she no longer needed glasses. Of course, explaining her ten-inch reduction in height and her drop-dead gorgeous face and hair might be more troublesome. What could she say? That she'd found a hundred-thirty-year-old corpse lying on a Sitka dock? Not even Alexis would buy that story.

Finally, she turned toward the patient shaman. "Thank you. I need a friend who understands who and what I am," she said in a raspy voice, then sniffed and cleared her throat.

"Spirits are your friends." He pointed at a bird soaring on the wind currents. "The eagle watches over you. The raven watches. The wolf watches." He gazed out to sea as though something beyond the whitecaps beckoned.

Caught in the serenity of the moment, she bowed to the irrevocable truth. She was stuck here. Stuck with Ransom Hamilton. Stuck with the guillotine of being sent to an insane asylum hanging over her head and ready to fall on her neck at his whim.

She shivered. Never had she imagined anyone or anything having so much control over her destiny.

Winifred McCanless was dead. Gone. Finito. A two-inch obituary in the *Los Angeles Times*.

Fate had charted a new course for her in another century. Mindlessly watching an eagle play on the air currents, she struggled for acceptance of the painful changes shaping her future.

Gradually her thoughts focused on the present and on Ransom. It might be easier if she wasn't drawn to him the way heroin drew an addict. Just saying no didn't help her any more than it did the addict. The allure was too strong. She considered this weakness a carryover from Felicity's old persona. Winifred McCanless never had a weak moment for a man in her life.

But then, Ransom Hamilton never walked through her door in Los Angeles, either. What if he had?

She giggled at the fantasy. Here, she was as gorgeous as any starlet in Hollywood and Ransom Hamilton didn't want her. The giggle became a laugh. Oh, she would have really turned his head on a basketball court or as the confident Dr. Winifred B. McCanless, up-and-coming research chemist at Westminster Labs.

The laughter died in her throat with the sudden realization that beauty had no bearing on Ransom's aversion. It wasn't who she was; it was who she wasn't. She wasn't his beloved Cassandra. That was what held him back from exercising his so-called marital rights. With a little luck, he'd maintain his distance until she learned enough about Sitka to come up with a plan of escape.

In the meantime, she walked a very fine line. Perhaps in time, his temper would exhaust itself over the loss of Cassandra and he'd take a real look at her.

Her hand flew to her mouth. Where did that thought come from? No matter, it had to go back. That was dangerous thinking. She refused to consider the possibility.

In retrospect, being candid with Ransom had been a mistake. He didn't believe her, which also said he didn't trust her as far as she could throw him.

She drew a weary breath and exhaled slowly. If he told her such an outlandish story in her own time, she probably wouldn't believe him, either. So, why should he believe her? As it stood, if she wanted his trust, she had to earn it. Head shaking in resignation, she wondered if either of them would live that long.

The shaman was right. All she could do was go forward from here and hold onto her memories of another time, a time when Joey was alive. She turned to tell the old Indian of her resolve, but instead she was greeted by Ransom Hamilton's angry face. Instantly, a chill of icy dread slithered up her spine. She tried to speak, but her dry throat closed and her heart began racing.

Chapter 8

"WOULD YOU MIND telling me what the hell you're doing out here all alone?" Ransom asked in a soft, deadly voice that sent the small hairs on the back of Winifred's neck rising in salute.

"I . . . I was talking with the shaman," she managed. As long as she avoided looking him in the eye, her chances of gathering the remnants of her self-control prevailed. She followed his line of sight, then jumped up and scanned the surrounding open space.

Where was the shaman? How long had she been sitting alone? When had he left?

"He was here just a minute ago," she offered, shielding her eyes with her hand and searching southward.

"Miss Clairmont and Caine are beside themselves with worry," Ransom continued as though she hadn't spoken. "I know you're used to being pampered and your every wish indulged, but . . ."

Instantly angry and pinched by more than a bit of guilt for causing Caine and Adele worry, she spun on him. "You

don't know anything about me. You're too pigheaded to ac-
knowledge the truth when you hear it!"

"In the future, you won't be allowed to leave the house
without me," he continued tersely. "You obviously lack even
a hint of common sense." He stood and caught her arm.
"Talking to the shaman. When did you learn to speak Tlingit?"

Winifred glared at the center of his chest and didn't
budge. "Why the hell do you even care? Seems to me that if
some lowlife did away with me while I was out here, he'd
be doing you a big favor." Defiantly, her head snapped up.
She met the fury blazing in his eyes and a ticking muscle
spasm in his cheek. "Your problems would be over."

A vein in his throat pulsed as he visibly restrained his
rage. When he spoke, his voice was barely a whisper. "I've
never been more tempted to strike a woman than I am at this
moment."

"Does the truth hurt?" she goaded, relishing the satisfaction of riling him.

"Truth? Far from it, Felicity. You're my wife, my responsibility. I take *all* of my responsibilities seriously. Especially you."

Heart hammering a jungle tattoo in her ears, she held his
gaze, trying to see beyond his formidable surface. "Then
that's something we have in common, Mr. Hamilton. I take
my responsibilities very seriously, too. The way I see it, I'm
responsible for figuring out how I fit here. It's very apparent
I'll get only scorn, ridicule, and anger from my so-called
husband. At least the shaman understands and offers support
and friendship. A pity Arch Forsythe didn't marry Felicity to
him. It would've solved both of our problems, wouldn't it?"

A harsh snarl curled his lip for a moment. "What? And
give up the luxury in which you've always lived?"

Recalling the grinding poverty and mix of alcohol and
drugs her father's cronies shared in the dingy apartment during her early childhood, she gaped at him. Then she laughed.

Once she started, she couldn't stop. Finally, she sat and held her sides.

Feeling his eyes drilling through her, she struggled for a modicum of composure. "I'm sorry. There's no way you could know how ludicrous that sounded." She drew an unsteady breath. "Oh, Ransom, if it weren't so sad, it really would be funny."

Using both hands, she pushed the tears from her cheeks as she came to her feet. "Felicity was raised in luxury. I'm trying to meld into her background as best I can, but the disparity of who we were and are is far greater than that wrought by a time difference of one hundred and thirty years. Maybe the best way to explain it is to think of everything Felicity was and know that I am the antithesis."

He scowled long enough for her to become stone still and composed.

"In the future, do not inconvenience others while indulging in your fantasies. Is that clear?" The flinty hardness in his expression and his rigid stance bespoke his deep anger.

"Perfectly, Mr Hamilton." She spun on her heel and started toward the Tlingit village.

Caught up in digesting the afternoon's events, she hardly noticed Ransom lead his horse and walk beside her. Somehow or another, she had to convince him of her plight. Dismally, she realized that she couldn't wait for the catalyst of Russia's sale of Alaska. No. By then it would too late. Ransom would have already sent her away or embarked on his quest for an heir.

Her unnerving midnight dreams were filled with visions of Ransom unleashing the intimate passion she'd seen in the movies and on television. She never had a fantasy like this. Life had taught her that dreams often exceeded reality. And she knew no matter what kind of a lover Ransom was, if she became pregnant with a child, he'd take it from her.

Dread sent a shiver through her.

"Cold?" he asked.

After a quick shake of her head, she glanced up. "Do you think we could try to get to know one another before you attempt to put me in an institution or . . . or try exercising what you perceive as your rights to this body?"

Ransom caught himself before stumbling from the impact of her words. Damn. Did she really think her only alternatives were an asylum or violation? Had he been that harsh?

She was right on one score. He didn't understand her. He didn't understand why she had evaded Caine and Adele and set the entire Hamilton household on edge in concern for her whereabouts.

Glancing down, noting the set of her jaw and the hard pace her shorter legs set, he almost believed her. The independent woman she presented in the library a few nights earlier wouldn't anticipate the slightest worry by anyone on her behalf. The idea that they would worry was incomprehensible.

Damn. He wished they were home, but he didn't dare mount the horse and pull her up between his legs. Every time she came near, his body reacted like a stag during rutting season. There was no way of hiding it from her in the close confines of the saddle.

Her fear of him provided an advantage. He wouldn't have to contend with any attempts at seducing him and validating the marriage. What the hell was he thinking? Little Felicity Forsythe seducing him? Where would she learn such things?

But if she wasn't really Felicity, if she was this Winifred person, then he'd best keep his guard up.

He had to stop thinking like that. Of course she couldn't be someone else.

He recalled her wild explanation in the library. When she spoke of her brother, Ransom had needed to shake free of the unreasonable urge to comfort her. He had settled for the safety of disbelief. Felicity had no brother.

At the time, his emotional war had raged and nearly escaped his tight control as he tried reconciling her with the simpleton young woman from San Francisco. Her animation and intelligence as she described her improbable scenario had amazed him. If she wasn't crazy . . . but of course she was delusional. Minds from the future didn't travel through time. However, the vivacious gestures and expressive mood swings that had punctuated her elaborate, yet logical account of future events weren't the product of an impaired mind. Although her monologue had painted an alternately exciting and bleak picture, he couldn't fathom the world she described. Worse, he didn't understand half the wonders she revealed, yet she had made perfect sense in the context in which she had spoken. And she could read with a rapid clarity that matched her glib tongue.

Even more disturbing than her sarcasm had been the underlying logic of her revelations. They had haunted him in the days since. What if she had told the truth? After all, Felicity had appeared quite dead on the dock. Then came the jolting spasm like new life slammed into her body. As an indisputable result, this was no six-year-old mentality beside him.

The war of logic continued playing havoc with his reason. Sometimes, he considered the notion of her driving him mad with her stories and clear descriptions. Already the first strains of dementia had reared its ugly head. He recalled how his heart had lurched when she spoke of leaving for her own time in the same way she might discuss catching a ship for Juneau.

He cleared his throat and mind and addressed the situation at hand. "Baron Korinkov called on me earlier today."

"I suppose he told you he saw me at the trading post," she said. "I don't imagine anyone does anything here without you knowing about it."

He regarded her sharply, wondering how she knew. "Did you notice a black frigate in the harbor this morning?"

"No. The ships look alike except that some have three masts, others have two."

"That black ship is a Russian convict ship. When they dock, they're as likely to dump some of their criminals here as they are to take on the Russian prisoners. Most men prefer death over a Russian prison.

"Last evening, four particularly nasty convicts escaped from the ship. Ivan and a military contingent spent all night finding them."

"Does he report to you after he finishes his jobs?"

"Good Lord, no. Why would you think that?"

"He was looking for you at the trading post and he was in a hurry."

"I told you, he found me."

Curious ocean-blue eyes narrowed on him. "Are you in some kind of trouble?"

"No. Why do you ask?"

Abruptly, she stopped and grabbed his arm. "I'm not an idiot. There may be over a century between us, but I recognize trouble when I see it. And you, Mr. Hamilton, look like the eye of a trouble hurricane. Even Baron Korinkov does your bidding."

"Ivan does no one's bidding except his own and that of the prince and the czar. He's a friend."

"Why was this particular friend so anxious to see you this morning? Certainly not for a little male bonding with lurid tales of recapturing four criminals."

"My business is none of your concern, madam." He rested a hand on her shoulder and started them moving again.

Fighting him every step of the way, she persisted. "None of my concern? I spend a little time alone with the only friend I've got and you feel it necessary to hunt me down like a hound after a fox. You accuse me of upsetting everyone in your household by my actions. Well, if what I did was so reprehensible, maybe you'd better tell me why—and don't give me some story about convicts. You already said they'd been captured *before* I met with Spirit Dancer."

Ransom glowered at her. "Everything will be fine if you act like a proper lady and obey . . ."

"Oh! Wrong word, Ransom. The chances of me blindly obeying your dictates are about as good as getting back to my own time and sleeping in my own bed and going back to work at the job I loved. My job was my life. Through it, I could help save other lives. Lives that . . ." Her hand flew to her mouth and she turned away.

Ransom dropped the reins and spun her around by the shoulders. "Is that why you went to see Spirit Dancer? To play with this fantasy of yours he indulges you in?"

"I . . . I hoped he'd know how I could get back to my own time—where I belong."

The yearning in her voice and the anguish in her sapphire eyes kept him from flinging the acrid retort on the tip of his tongue. "What did he tell you?"

"What do you care? It's not as if you know the White Raven or anything and were being tested by some spirit."

His blood ran cold with apprehension. A scowl reflected his displeasure. "But I do know him," he said softly, watching the play of the sunlight in her windblown hair. "I'm White Raven. Spirit Dancer gave me that name shortly after I came here. What did he say about White Raven?"

For a moment she froze, then she yanked her arm free of his gentle grasp and hoisted her defiant chin a notch higher. Tears pooled on her lower lids. "He said we're stuck with each other. There's no way back for me. There's only here . . . this time . . . this place."

For a second, as he met her watery, unwavering gaze, he believed her entire story. But only for a second. "Caine and Adele are waiting."

Silent, they approached the Tlingit village. The trading post loomed ahead before Ransom spoke again. "In Febru-.ary, someone set my granary on fire. We saved most of the grain, but the fire took a big toll. One of the prisoners, a man convicted of murder during a robbery, admitted setting the fire. He thought he'd be turned over to the Americans. He was wrong. Russians do not release prisoners for lesser crimes."

She slowed her pace. "Did he set the fire?"

"He said he did."

"Why? What did you do to him? I mean, he must have had a reason for setting the fire."

The implications rankled him, but his thin patience persevered. While not comprehending why he'd told her about the fire and the convict, he continued with exacting patience. "He was paid to do it."

Curiosity brightened her narrowing eyes. "By whom? Who is your enemy?"

"He hasn't said. Yet." Ransom saw understanding dawn on her. She caught on more quickly than most men he knew. The contradiction her intelligence presented set him wondering if her impossible story held a grain of truth. Nothing he rationalized explained so great a change. Yet he couldn't accept the impossible.

Watching the gentle sway of her hips as she moved toward the phaeton where Caine and Adele waited, he considered their conversation and began doubting her fear of him. If it wasn't fear, what was it? He would damn sure find out.

"Felicity," he called as Caine assisted her into the phaeton. He waited until she settled and acknowledged him. "I'll see you after dinner in the library. Understand?"

"An understanding of the English language may be the only thing you and I have as a common ground, Ransom. Even so, we may not agree on the precise meaning of some of the words." She dismissed him with a look. "I'm ready to go now," she told Caine.

Ransom mounted his horse and watched the phaeton disappear down the streets of Sitka. He couldn't help grinning. She wasn't afraid of him, which meant she had something else in mind if he backed her into a corner with too many threats.

In the library that evening, Ransom handed Felicity a glass of sherry, then settled into a chair across from her. The way her gaze constantly stroked his body bespoke a fascinated wariness. He hadn't dressed with any special care tonight, merely donned the usual tailored narrow charcoal trousers, white shirt, and a black jacket befitting a casual evening at home.

"Did you find out why the man started the granary fire?"

Her question made him smile. In her naïveté, apparently she expected a discussion of his business. The notion was laughable. No man shared that part of his life with a wife— even a stable one. That wasn't the purpose of marriage. "Not yet. And that's not the reason I asked you here. You expressed a desire for us to know each other. I'll listen to your plan now."

Her gown had an underdress of green grosgrain just long enough to clear the floor with a low corsage. Full forest green sleeves were open all the way down and caught at the elbow and wrist. She wore no jewelry, though the square-cut neckline called for pearls as a minimum. Yet that physical beauty paled in comparison to the fascinating, independent woman she had become.

He relaxed in the chair and swirled brandy in an over-sized snifter while enjoying the way his response flustered her composure. In spite of his resolve for detachment, her unabashed shock enthralled him.

"My plan?"

To his amusement, her eyebrows rose in surprise. "Perhaps I was mistaken. Could it be that you don't have a plan for us to get to know one another? I thought this was important to you." He hid the smile tickling the corners of his mouth. This was wonderful. The woman had no idea of how to mask her emotions.

"Well, it is, but I haven't exactly worked out a plan." She betrayed her unease by picking at the cuticle of her left thumb. "Maybe we could start by asking each other questions. Like, why did your mother name you Ransom?"

Dumbfounded, he stared at her in total disbelief. "How the hell should I know?"

She shrugged, lifting her eyebrows and her shoulders. "It's such an unusual name, didn't you ever wonder?"

"No." The woman asked the strangest questions. He sipped his brandy and started wondering why his mother named him Ransom instead of George or Charles or James, after his father.

"I can't believe it. You were never curious?" she persisted.

"No," he answered sharply, then forced her into silence with his pique over the question. What the hell did his name have to do with getting to know each other, anyway? Still, it did make him wonder. He relaxed slightly, shifting to hide the physical display her presence incited. "Why did you get named Felicity?"

A serene smile heightened the sensuousness of her pink lips. "I suspect the name was for the pleasure Arch and Prudence enjoyed during the creative process. Adele said they loved one another deeply."

He swore under his breath. This conversation wasn't going as intended. He wanted her off balance, but like a cat, she landed on her feet every time he pushed her.

"Have you been married before?" The new direction of her questions broke his brooding silence.

"Me? No. Maybe if I had, I wouldn't have had to do it again, especially the way I did it." Arch's betrayal still grated on his raw emotions. "Do you remember the ceremony?"

Head shaking, she studied her hands. "I wish I did. However, I have none of Felicity's memories, Ransom, only her body."

"I suppose it's too much to expect a conversation without your fantasy world." He relinquished the chair and quickly turned away. The conversation was over. This little game was a mistake, one he paid for with a throbbing in his loins.

He heard the rustle of her skirts as she rose from the leather couch, then the clink of her sherry glass as she placed it on the liquor tray. "Better I talk about it with you than with the townsfolk. Right? Do you want them knowing you married a dimwit or a crazy woman? You can't pack me off to the snake pit without impugning your own reputation. And I won't go quietly."

The nearness of the woman inflamed the need battering his senses. "This discussion is over. Go to your room, Felicity." He kept his back to her and deliberately placed the brandy snifter onto the table so softly that it made no sound.

"No, I don't think you want the town knowing you were outsmarted by an old man who treasured his brain-damaged daughter as highly as your friendship. You owed Arch Forsythe, and I'm the payment. Only you got more than you bargained for."

"Get out of this room," he warned from between clenched teeth. He half-turned to face her, one hand trailing on the edge of the heavy table.

Triumph danced in her eyes and the rebellious tilt of her chin. "All right. Just let me propose a solution to both of our immediate problems. Why don't we get a nice, friendly annulment? You go your way. I'll go mine. Adele and I can go back to San Francisco. I'll be out of your sight and out of your life. You'll never see me again. I assure you, Ransom, I'm an extremely resourceful and capable individual. I'll do fine without you."

At the suggestion of losing her completely, he grabbed her, lifting her off the floor.

She gasped, which was to his advantage as his mouth claimed hers. What began as the possessive, almost brutal kiss of a man starving for a taste of her slowly changed to a tantalizing, teasing seduction with his tongue invading her mouth in exploratory caresses. The honeyed taste of her intoxicated his senses. He made love to her mouth while his hands roamed the small expanse of her narrow waist, the delicate flare of her rib cage, and the deliciously firm sides of her full breasts.

Then she was responding, shyly teasing, dancing with his tongue. His desire raged as she met the sweet plunder of his tongue in wild excitement. Her arms twined around his neck and drew him closer. He felt the subtle changes in her body as she flowed against him and opened herself in submission. The soft mewling sound she emitted into his mouth betrayed her desire. In that instant, he wanted to shout in conquest and plunge his rock-hard manhood into the hot, velvet core of her femininity.

Slowly, sensuously, he let her glide down his body until her toes touched the floor. Through the barrier of her skirts, the movement of her mons and soft stomach over his throbbing erection inflamed his passion. He shifted, holding her against him.

As he reached for the hem of her skirt, a small voice warned that if he sated his desire and made her delicious body his, an annulment moved out of reach. With aching reluctance, he released her skirts and ended the kiss.

Cursing silently at his lack of self-control, he eased her arms from around his neck and set her back on her heels. The shock and raw passion blazing so hot in her blue eyes sent a wave of agony through his already tortured body. He drew back, not really wanting to relinquish her tantalizing nearness.

For a moment, the powerful sensations dazed her and left her visibly shaken. Her unmasked reactions vacillated between exasperation, frustration, and a tinge of fear.

"This is not a game, Felicity. When I tell you to do something, do it!" He grasped her hand and held her open palm and fingers against his erection. "I wasn't thinking about an annulment when I kissed you. Next time I tell you to leave the room, leave. Understand?"

The way her fingers caressed and measured his proud erection corresponded with her widening eyes. When he pulled her hand away, her fingers flew to her open mouth. He groaned as she hurriedly left the library without another word.

Chapter 9

"I'M GOING TO get a job," Winifred announced after dinner when she and Ransom were alone in the dining room.

"A job?" Ransom echoed. Shock and something akin to horror flickered across his features in an unguarded moment.

"Yes. A job. You know, as in work for a living?"

"We're not poverty-stricken. Hell, even if we were, as long as I can earn a living, you don't need a job." The raised arch of his left eyebrow clearly stated that if he questioned her sanity before, her announcement erased all doubt.

"Yes, I do. I have to do something. I can't stand this inactivity." Mentally she reviewed the short slate of possible career choices.

"You cannot seek employment." He rose from his chair slowly. A small tic of irritation in his left cheek replaced his surprise. "Our position in society forbids such nonsense."

"Your position might. Mine doesn't."

"Must I remind you? You're my wife."

"I understood that condition was in the process of being

87

rectified." He'd made his point last night when she lost her head and kissed him back with all the desire howling in her frazzled nerve endings. Seeing him ready for battle, she stood as tall as her diminutive stature permitted.

"Presently, you're my wife."

"I need to be prepared to support myself. I can, you know." The slight tilt of her chin reaffirmed her self-confidence.

"That's not the issue. Nor will it ever be. I've given you my word on the matter."

"You're right. The issue is that I'm going to get a job. I'm not asking you, Ransom, I'm telling you." For her own sanity, she needed to be productive. As the only person in the house without any responsibility, she felt like a spare tire on a motorcycle. Cordelia had all sorts of social activities and responsibilities. Adele was her companion and an occasional nanny for several of Cordelia's friends. All the household staff had defined duties and responsibilities. Only she had nothing to do.

"Please, Ransom, put yourself in my shoes. What if— what if you ended up someplace you didn't expect to be and didn't have anything to do? How long could you stand the idle time weighing on your hands? I've worked all my life. I don't know how to *not* work."

Unconsciously, she held her breath when he didn't respond immediately.

"You cannot seek employment. I forbid it."

"You forbid . . ."

"Furthermore," he continued, warming to the topic, "in the morning I'll put out the word that anyone foolish enough to hire you will no longer do business with me. Do I make myself clear?"

Head shaking in disbelief, she glared at him in disgust. She'd known some men didn't want their wives working, but using his influence to prevent her? Talk about ludicrous! She bit back the angry words on the tip of her tongue. "So much for your reputation as a fair man. To think, I almost believed it."

"I am a fair man, madam."

"You couldn't prove it by me. I certainly wouldn't call your closed-minded, dictatorial actions fair." She tensed with realization. "Or is it just me you have this irrational bias toward?"

Again, he paused as though sorting his words for effect. "Let's suppose, just suppose mind you, that what you've said is true. Let's pretend for the next moment you are from the future. Understand?"

She nodded warily, listening closely for the hinge on the trap she sensed.

"In such circumstances, is it not logical to assume you may not have arrived here with all the information you need to live in this society? Is it not logical that others may know more than you?"

Seeing where he was taking the conversation, she raised a hand in protest. "Yes, but . . ."

"No. It's my turn to speak." He waited until her hand lowered before continuing. "Is it not logical that if you don't heed the advice of those around you that you may do something out of ignorance that might harm you in some way?"

"I suppose so, but . . ."

Some of the hard angles softened around his eyes. "What harms you, harms me as your husband. It harms those who live here. Your walking the streets begging for employment would create a scandal. Women of your station just don't do such things, Felicity."

"Scandal? Or embarrassment for you?"

"Personally, I don't care about that kind of scandal, and I'm damn hard to embarrass. But that's not the case with others in this household. And it would hurt them and you for as long as you remain in Sitka."

The honesty emanating from him both touched a soft chord for his concern and dismayed her. "I need to do something. Can you understand that I have to feel useful?"

He regarded her for a long moment during which she wished she knew the inner workings of his complex mind.

"There are many things this house requires before the end of summer. Half the rooms upstairs need decorating and furniture. Use the catalogs at Hamilton Traders to make selections from. Wallpaper the whole house. Paint it. Turn the ballroom into a greenhouse. I don't care. Just don't touch my library. The rest is yours to do with as you wish. It's your home. You have carte blanche and all the funds you need. Hire as many men as you can find for what you want done. Add a wing to the house, if you want; just make sure they're done by mid-September."

The magnitude of his offer flabbergasted her. She felt the color drain from her cheeks. Recalling her studio apartment that fit into the foyer and the two framed posters she called art, the prospect of decorating a mansion seemed as fantastic as it was funny.

"Will that keep you busy?" Amusement laced his question.

"Why?" she asked, bewildered. Generosity of so great a measure made her suspicious.

"Why what?"

"Why would you let me do this? I mean, it's a bit of overkill as busywork for keeping the little woman out of the mainstream workforce and at home, isn't it?"

"Finishing this house was always going to be my wife's task," he said softly, closing the scant distance between them. "You're my wife. Do it the way it suits you—except for the library."

She searched his face, amazed that he discarded his implacable mask and let sincerity shine in his eyes. Good grief! He was serious.

"Why? I still don't understand. If we're getting an annulment, why would you . . ."

He shrugged casually. "Why not?"

"It seems like an expensive way to, to . . ." His nearness disconcerted her and shattered her train of thought. He smelled of wine and masculinity. She drew a sharp breath, almost tasting him when she inhaled. Her chin tilted higher.

"One of the other rules is that you don't have to concern yourself with the finances. Unless you start buying art from Paris . . ."

"Does that mean I can buy books and set up a room for my own use?"

"Yes," he answered slowly. "What sort of books are you interested in?"

"Chemistry, biology, medical texts. I promise not to do anything . . ." She paused, unwilling to risk his good humor by promising not to make discoveries for which her version of history credited others. "I just want to experiment with a few chemicals, and . . ."

"You want a laboratory, too?"

"Just a small one," she answered quickly, praying she had not pushed too hard. "I'd rather have the books and lab than art from Paris, or even another stick of furniture."

"A choice isn't necessary." He stilled for an instant. "Damn, you're not going to blow yourself up with these experiments, are you?"

Explosive was the reaction of her body to his nearness. His teasing smile banished the flicker of indignation evoked by his question. "I haven't botched an experiment to the point of doing damage for years. Besides, I rather like my short, unathletic self."

"I like it, too."

All thought faded when his mouth brushed hers.

"Do me a favor?"

"Umm?" she responded dreamily, caught in the electricity of the moment. Her lips tingled in anticipation. Just one kiss wouldn't hurt.

"While you're building your lab and library, *and* finishing the house decor, please, don't do the master suite in pink. I detest pink," he breathed, then kissed her lightly.

One buoyant touch fed her craving for a taste of him. Fighting the attraction, she let him kiss her again, then heard him swear under his breath as his warm mouth descended a third time in a masterful possession.

Win stopped thinking, nearly stopped breathing. With a little coaxing from the tip of his tongue, her lips parted. Her blood became lava when he pulled her against him and deepened the kiss. The lingering taste of wine filled her mouth. She inhaled the heady scent of him, a scent that fueled the heat coursing through her body.

His tender, possessive exploration banished the last of her sensibilities. Her hands slipped under his coat, greedy for the closeness the heavy fabric denied. A small cry escaped her when he gripped her buttocks and held her against his arousal. The slow rocking set up a pulse of desire that burned her loins and inflamed her breasts.

Lost in the kiss and the delicious sensations playing havoc with her traitorous body, Win sounded a protest when Ransom ended the sweet torture. Fresh color tinged her cheeks. Immediately, he pulled her hands away from his heated body.

When her muddled brain remembered his request, she laughed nervously. "I don't care for pink, either. How about a Japanese motif with rice mats and wispy flower centerpieces on black lacquered low tables inlaid with mother of pearl, lapis, and garnets set into the dragon's eyes? No bed. Just a painted rice paper screen around the futons. Of course, you'd have to wear a kimono and zoris. In the winter you could wear tabis, too." The image of Ransom in a kimono seated at a small table and scooping rice out of a bowl with chopsticks tickled her.

Ransom retreated, his easy demeanor gone. "How the hell do you know that?"

The last strains of laughter faded when she met his gaze. "What?"

"How the hell do you know how the Japanese live? How they decorate their houses?"

Bowing to the gravity of the questions, her shoulders straightened in a regal posture. "How do you think I know?"

For long minutes he glared at her in silence. Not a trace of the skillful lover who made her burn with his kiss remained. Try as she might to read his thoughts, nothing penetrated his schooled stoicism.

She watched him leave the dining room. Just when she thought she had him figured out, he did something that confused her. The sensitive, generous side of his nature offered great promise. It pleased her to realize that they had shared a few minutes of civil conversation.

"You are a strange man, Ransom Hamilton," she whispered, touching her tingling mouth.

Ransom chose the darkest, quietest corner of his club to brood over his fate in the company of a bottle of fine brandy. During the scant hours of midsummer darkness, most of Sitka slept.

Until Felicity arrived, he had considered one woman pretty much like another. Just as some were tall and others short, some had more common sense than others. He had divided the fairer sex into two categories: those you married and those you enjoyed. Felicity had her own category: those you could enjoy being married to. And, other than the delusion that she was from the future and the possibility she was carrying another man's child, he would have gladly—no, eagerly—consummated the marriage. Christ. What the hell was he thinking of?

Those two problems created impossible obstacles, regardless of how persuasively his body pleaded. In a relatively short time he'd know whether she carried another man's child. But her delusions of being from the future would not be resolved as easily.

Before he pursued an annulment, he had to be sure she wasn't pregnant. If she was, he'd be saddled with her and a stranger's child. Much as he'd like to believe Adele's claim of Felicity's virginity, the changes in her were just too great. Even Adele had admitted she didn't know Felicity anymore.

While part of him doubted the probability of another man, he couldn't ignore the possibility.

He should send her back to San Francisco. There, she could have the child, if such was the case, and be out of his reach, regardless. Yes. She'd be gone. She'd be safe. A bitter sound that might have started as a laugh crossed his lips. He'd be safe.

It would be easy enough to ensconce her in the Forsythe home and have Thomas Nolan oversee her welfare. Child or no, with enough time and money in the right palms, he could have the marriage set aside. He'd be free. But what of her? She'd be a marked woman with a bastard child.

He couldn't allow that, even if it meant claiming the child as his own. But if there was no child, no other man . . . She had to remain in Sitka until he was certain.

He thought of her alone in San Francisco. Hell, she was probably right. The woman living in his home right now didn't need him. She had already discharged Adele as a nurse and changed her duties to those of an occasional companion. He admired Felicity's independent spirit and self-confidence. He doubted she needed anyone.

The thought rocked him. The admission reminded him of how different that woman was from the Felicity Forsythe he knew.

A sour laugh trickled into his raised brandy glass.

Challenged inadequately described the havoc Felicity had wreaked on his life in so short a time. His initial objections for bedding her had dissolved when she first opened her mouth in the ship's cabin. No six-year-old possessed her intelligence or vocabulary. Felicity revealed herself as many things, but she was not feebleminded. Short of her account of being another person from another time, Ransom couldn't find a logical explanation for the change, nor could he refute her story.

The longer he dwelled on the problem, the more certain he was that it didn't matter if she was mad—she was driving him daft. The woman he kissed in the library and the dining room sparkled with sexual curiosity. She was ripe for total submission and melted under his touch. The memory of her lush curves and eager response rekindled his familiar state of arousal.

He poured another drink and rolled the globe of the snifter across his forehead. In truth, he liked her. He admired her persistence and spirit. Hell, he wanted her. No other woman would fill the sharp craving in his gut.

When she fled the library last week, her expression had echoed surprise, not fear that he'd ravish her and bind them together forever in the process. Her responses had been those of a virgin, or at least a very inexperienced maiden. He groaned, his gut knotted with need.

"The headache is supposed to wait until you finish drinking," Ivan Korinkov said, settling in the chair beside Ransom. "Is married life more than you expected?"

Ransom's bitter laugh hung in the air between them.

"I understand there is an adjustment period in all marriages." Ivan splashed brandy into a snifter. "She seems a lively woman with a sharp eye."

"And a sharp mind and a sharp tongue. Felicity possesses a temerity that delights in pushing the limits of my sainted patience." Unwilling to share the condition of her fragile mental state even with Ivan, Ransom regarded him for a long moment. "We're fortunate the weather held and the black ship sailed without leaving us more convicts to keep track of."

"Yes." Ivan sighed. "Our pleas to stop emptying convict ships in the *ostrogs* continue falling on deaf ears in St. Petersburg."

"No offense, Ivan, but some of those men seem more sinned against than sinners. Though you're right; the black ship is a hell of an incentive to mend one's life and find religion."

"Providing one survives to walk upright in the light of day," Ivan added. The controversial topic of convict ships and convict labor was an uncomfortable one for the Russian.

He shifted in his chair. "Speaking of survival—your convict is alive, but barely. The prince's man conducted the interrogation, which I am afraid was more thorough than necessary. The man readily admitted setting the fire. He said he was hired in a Seattle pub by a man sitting behind him who forbade him to turn around. They had several meetings before they struck an agreement and money changed hands. He swears he never saw the man who hired him and he sent the money to his wife and children."

Ransom noted his friend's chagrin for the heavy-handed interrogation in the hard set of Ivan's jaw. But Ransom needed a name, a place to start. Whoever lay behind the rash of mishaps plaguing his operation knew how to cover his tracks. "Did he remember anything unique about the man?"

Puzzled, Ivan nodded. "He said the fellow had an odd proclivity for referring to flowers."

Ransom lifted his head slightly. Flowers . . . His flawless memory battled the brandy fuzz. Gardener. Vance Gardener named everything after flowers or vegetables. Odd, but hardly a solid link—certainly, not criminal.

"An idea?" Ivan asked hopefully.

"Perhaps I should visit Seattle for more reasons than tying up Arch's affairs."

Blue eyes bright with expectation, Ivan leaned onto his forearms. "You do have an idea, don't you?"

Ransom considered what he knew about Vance Gardener, which wasn't much, other than his penchant for equating things and events with garden flowers or plants. Gardener's business practices were questionable. However, Ransom could find no motive for Vance Gardener to sabotage his business operation.

"It's a long shot, but Dirk Riker will help me if I need it." Ransom had known Riker almost as long he had known Ivan. Riker was a solid ally as well as a reliable partner. The lumberjack-turned-businessman had won his friendship early in their association.

Ivan raised his glass in salute at the mention of Ransom's

silent partner in his logging and sawmill operation. "Will you take Felicity with you?"

Hearing Felicity's name ended the momentary respite from her haunting allure. "She doesn't have any idea," Ransom mumbled into his snifter.

"I beg your pardon?"

Ransom emptied his glass. "Felicity. The woman blithely wanders wherever she pleases. There you were chasing down the last of four cold-blooded killers running around on the island and she's strolling along the bluffs as though this was Dover. Mosquitoes have more common sense."

Amused, Ivan's mouth curled into an unwilling smile. "Have you explained the hazards to her?"

"Caine was with her, but she eluded him and Miss Clairmont." Ransom shifted in the chair. "It won't happen again, and I won't take her to Seattle."

"Your wife has agreed to being chaperoned in your absence?" The dimple in Ivan's cheek deepened with his curious smile and Ransom's darkening scowl.

"My wife and I have not agreed on anything, except that the sun rises each day."

Laughing, Ivan set down his snifter. "I don't know whether to envy you or pity you, Ransom."

"Pity me, my friend. For I am truly a man who deserves your pity."

"How much brandy have you had?" he asked, inspecting the nearly empty bottle.

"Not enough. I can still see her when I close my eyes."

Chapter 10

Upon the Malcolms' return to the Forsythe home in San Francisco, the news of Archibald Forsythe's death surprised John and devastated Cassandra. But even before John finished reading the message to Cassandra in the parlor, she fled the room in tears. He couldn't hide his glee. His plans had reached fruition well before predicted. As he comforted his distraught wife, he silently gloated over the good fortune of Arch's death and the bonus of being rid of Felicity in the bargain.

Without the distraction of Felicity and the eagle-eyed vigilance of Adele Clairmont, manipulating Cassandra would be easier. Unfortunately, Cassie hadn't proven as malleable as he anticipated when he set out to meet, woo, and wed this particular heiress. Ah, well, at least she was younger and far more exciting in bed than his previous three wives.

He counted upon the reading of Archibald Forsythe's will in two days to make him a very wealthy man. So short a time, so much to do, so many plans to make. Meanwhile, he'd continue comforting his grieving wife. Well, it was worth the effort. Cassandra was the old man's beneficiary. After all, not even Arch was fool enough to leave an idiot daughter that much money and property, regardless of how much he loved her.

A tall man blessed with startling good looks, perfect teeth, and thick, wavy blond hair, John capitalized on his sensual appeal. In truth, he cut a dashing figure that drew attention whenever he entered a room. John used nature's gifts liberally in making his fortune.

He hit upon his current scheme of marrying heiresses while in New York seven years earlier. Working as a bank clerk, he met Isabelle Merchant, a middle-aged dowager and prime stockholder in the bank. Isabelle had a penchant for young men. At barely twenty-one, John hadn't lost the innocent boyishness Isabelle found so appealing. Her nephew, Vance Gardener, brought John an invitation for an intimate supper with the dowager.

The meal proved very satisfying for Isabelle. Shortly thereafter, John was on her list of afternoon delights. While lavishing clothing and money on him, she taught him the rudiments of social protocol and etiquette. After a time, John demanded that she marry him or forgo the hedonistic pleasures he indulged her with.

Six months into their marriage—with the help of measured doses of arsenic-laced tea—John became a publicly miserable widower. His late wife's only living family, Vance Gardener, grieved with him until they settled the estate. Then Vance bought a ship and went into the slave trading business.

John found green pastures in Chicago, where he courted and married fifty-three-year-old Henrietta Gimaldi. But collecting her estate proved far more difficult. The family demanded a police investigation when Henrietta died after only seven months of marital bliss. Panicked, John fled to Australia. Not until he remarried and committed his third wife to a hospital for her critical lung condition did he learn that Chicago investigators had cleared him of any wrong-doing in Henrietta's death. Flush with the proceeds of the third Mrs. Malcolm's prosperous sheep station, which he sold before leaving Australia, and the accounts from his previous two wives, John sailed for San Francisco. There, he wasted no time researching his next wife. He spent weeks investigating prospects before settling on Cassandra Forsythe.

This time, he had planned long and hard, selecting his quarry carefully by studying the home structure in great detail before placing himself in Cassandra's path. The quick marriages with older women and their tragic ends were dangerous. He needed a woman exciting enough to entertain him and malleable enough to do his bidding. Of course, she also had to be extremely rich. While Cassandra was not wealthy in her own right, Archibald Forsythe had more money than John could spend. There was no telling how quickly he could multiply Arch's fortune once he gained control.

During the days between the Malcolms' return from their honeymoon and the reading of the will, John inventoried all of Arch's known holdings. With the prospective assets tallied, he sent a letter to his trusted friend, Vance Gardener, in Seattle.

On the day scheduled for the reading of the will, John sat ramrod stiff in anticipation of the riches soon to be his. He felt at home in the leather wingback chair in front of Thomas Nolan's massive cherrywood desk. Cassandra continued sniffing into her handkerchief. Faint purple half-moons hung below her thickly lashed violet eyes.

When the tall, distinguished attorney finished reading the will, only Cassandra's occasional sniffles and the rustle of papers sounded in the office.

Surely, there was a mistake! John's numbed senses thawed to painful reality. The old fool hadn't really left everything to his simpleton daughter, had he? His stomach churned in disappointment. All the planning, all the patience he'd shown Cassandra . . . for what?

Then John spoke, his voice strained. "Are you telling me that all Cassie inherits is a paltry trust fund from her mother?"

"It's hardly paltry, Mr. Malcolm. However, that is correct." Thomas Nolan's long, tapered fingers smoothed the folds in the document. Wind-wild strawberry blond hair curled about his tanned face and weathered ears. "This was the original agreement between Arch and Prudence when they married. Perhaps since Cassandra's marriage, Arch didn't feel she required more. He changed his will while you were on your honeymoon. He must have thought highly of your business acumen to entrust you so completely with Cassandra's future."

Thomas Nolan met John's hostile gaze without a flinch. "Of course," Thomas continued, "Cassandra has the timber tracts Arch gave her as a wedding present. Arch was a generous man."

"If he was so generous, why didn't he leave his eldest daughter anything?" John muttered, battling the bitter disappointment. Contesting the will, now registered with the courts, was futile under the circumstances.

"Haven't you been listening, Mr. Malcolm? Cassandra wasn't Arch's daughter. Although he treated her like one, did he not, Cassandra?"

"Oh yes, Mr. Nolan. He always made me feel like his daughter." She sniffed and dabbed the steady stream of tears at the corners of her eyes. "Arch became my father the day Mama married him when I was two. After Mama died . . . we had Felicity, and we took care of her with Adele's help."

John pulled himself together and managed an insincere twitch he hoped passed for a smile. He thanked Thomas Nolan for his time and helped his wife to her feet. "I trust there's no great hurry for us to leave the Forsythe family home?"

"I've not heard from Mr. Hamilton regarding the disposition of the property and the household contents. I doubt he'd object to you living there while you locate another residence." Thomas Nolan addressed Cassandra. "If you prepare a list of furnishings you'd like to keep, I'll see Mr. Hamilton receives it. I'm sure he'll be more than generous with you, Cassandra."

Cassandra managed a faint smile and nodded. "Ransom is a good man. I doubt he'll mind parting with the few pieces I cherish."

John escorted her to the carriage waiting in front of the attorney's office and helped her in. His sullen silence held until they arrived home and he dismissed the servants for the rest of the day.

"You knew!" he shouted at Cassandra as she poured a glass of sherry in the parlor.

Startled, Cassandra glanced up, then replaced the glass stopper in the sherry bottle. "I knew what? That Arch was my stepfather? Of course. Why are you angry?"

"Goddammit! Don't play coy with me, Cassandra! You knew you weren't in his will, didn't you! You knew he was going to disinherit you, didn't you! That's why you married me." Red-faced with fury, he crossed the room and grabbed her arm, sending her sherry into the air. "You knew he'd leave everything to that idiot half-sister of yours, didn't you!"

Paled by his rage, she shook her head. "I married you because I loved you, John, even though I know it dashed my father's dreams. I loved you! Daddy must have changed his will after Felicity married Ransom so she wouldn't be more of a burden than necessary. What difference does it make?" But even before she finished the question, he saw the answer dawn on her.

"Oh, God! That's why *you* married *me,* wasn't it? You thought *I'd* inherit Arch's money and holdings, didn't you?" He tightened his grip when she tried pulling away. "You never loved me. You used me!"

"I used you? You took one look at me and drooled over the prospect of sharing my bed. And what if I hadn't come along? You'd still be waiting for Ransom Hamilton, wouldn't you? Only you'd have a helluva long wait, Cassandra. Arch would have married his *real* daughter to him anyway. I understand Hamilton is as loaded as Arch. Isn't it funny how that idiot sister of yours ended up with it all? Wouldn't you like to have some of it? How about the man? You want Ransom Hamilton, too? Be nice to me and play along and maybe I'll get him for you."

The panic in her violet eyes physically excited him. "What's the matter, Cassandra? Don't you love me anymore?" Cruel fingers dug into the soft flesh of her upper arm and jerked hard, hurling her to the floor at his feet.

Cassandra scrambled away. Cursing, John unleashed his wrath. Even as she screamed, he hauled her against him, then held her at arm's length and backhanded her. Her terror heightened the sexual excitement racing through his veins. Wrapping her arms about her face, she withstood every blow and kick he delivered.

"You'll pay for your deception, Cassandra. The old man is gone, but you're here," he seethed, tugging the buttons of his pants open for his manhood to spring free.

The next morning John visited the bank and transferred the accrued interest of Cassandra's trust fund into his account. Arch had anticipated him, fixing it so neither of them could touch the principal unless specific conditions were met and verified by Thomas Nolan. In other words, if they were destitute.

Cassandra had spirit. John would grant her that much, though she had less today than yesterday. Sometimes it took a few hard knocks to learn the lessons he taught her. Well, she'd obey this time and wait in the house until he returned from Seattle. All traces of yesterday's conflict should have faded from her lovely body by then.

Vance and he would team up again. Together they were unbeatable. Diligent research had already taught John a great deal about their next mark. Grinning, John boarded the Seattle-bound ship, knowing that men like Ransom Hamilton were vulnerable. They spent their lives building an empire, then one day discovered their mortality. Since they hadn't married and sired children, they left no heirs.

At one time, Hamilton had wanted Cassandra. That might be an advantage. How the hell had Hamilton ended up with Felicity? Not that the little dimwit wasn't built like an erotic fantasy. Hell, he'd have lifted her skirts if he could have gotten away with it.

Smug and secure, John watched the California coastline shrink from the deck of the ship. All was not lost. In fact, the stakes had doubled. The game just got a bit more complicated, that's all.

He grinned, eager for the challenge ahead.

Ransom mounted his spirited horse and restrained the animal until he had warmed up before allowing him his head. Regardless of how fast the horse galloped, Ransom's demons and the lingering effects of last night's brandy caught up.

Since kissing Felicity in the library, then again in the dining room, he avoided being home other than for an occasional meal and sleep. Holding her, kissing her, reveling in her innocent, open response proved a grave mistake. Instead of assuaging or tempering his desire, the taste of her inflamed his hunger for examining every intimate detail of her delectable body. Though he loathed admitting it, he enjoyed talking with her and hearing the impossible future she eloquently painted.

He needed to make a decision about his marriage before events overtook them both and the opportunity for an annulment disappeared in a flurry of petticoats and passion. If he spent much more time near her, it would be out of the question.

Felicity was smart and clever. Obviously a quick study, she had learned how the household operated and the pecking order of the servants, their names, and all about their families. Her persistent cheer in the face of Cordelia's stoic silence amazed him and endeared her to the household staff. Her inquisitive nature and cheerful assistance with the smallest task eroded the usual class distinction. Consequently, Meggie MacGregor placed her on a pedestal high enough to scrape the clouds out of a summer sky.

She was decisive. Lord knew, the woman was decisive! Her opinions were never a secret. A small voice admonished him for rejecting her. She possessed all the qualities necessary in a wife.

She drove him to distraction even when he was away from her. Every fiber of his body screamed to possess her wholly.

He rode above the harbor where the daily bustle on the docks continued at a frenetic pace under the watchful eyes and caustic directions of the soaring gulls. Half a dozen languages mingled into a continuous thrum occasionally pierced by shouts or sudden laughter. Everyday sights and sounds bespoke the harbor's prosperity. The midsummer sun shone brightly today. While the light and weather held, men worked. And there was plenty of work in Sitka during the long days of mid-July.

Heavy trapping had gradually diminished the fur seal and otter population. In recent years, Ransom limited his trade in seal and otter pelts to just satisfying his Chinese commitments. While the fur trade had formed the backbone of his business in the early years, he had expanded into ship-building and whaling. During the last few years, he'd concentrated on timber and increasing the size of his shipping fleet. No Hamilton ship sailed without a full cargo hold.

He reined the horse away from the beach and toward the Tlingit village. The shaman stood alone on a rock, waiting, as Ransom expected. Their unlikely friendship had begun the day Ransom arrived in Sitka. Then, too, the old shaman had recognized the vanguard of change.

As a young man of twenty, Ransom's talent for finding a profitable deal where others failed had gained him a reputation and increased the Hamilton fortune that had dwindled during the last few years of his father's life. When James Hamilton died, Ransom assumed command of the family business at the age of seventeen.

He had excelled and quickly established himself as a creditable leader. At seventeen, his few experiences with the fairer sex taught him that he wanted more. For the next three years, he availed himself of everything the interested females of New York, and later, San Francisco, offered, and he gave wholeheartedly of his own experience and considerable bedroom talents.

Everything changed the day he met Archibald Forsythe at a ship auction and heard the older man's colorful descriptions and stories of Seattle and Sitka. A month later, Ransom sailed north.

Ransom's openness for adventure and difference fed his desire to explore everything the northern pockets of civilization offered. His own sense of justice put him on the side of the Tlingit villagers trapping and selling furs to white traders at a fraction of their value. Through Spirit Dancer, he learned their language and earned the trust of the villagers. He became the primary purchaser of their furs and championed their cause with the Russian government. There, he found an unexpected ally in the newly arrived Baron Ivan Korinkov. The friendship they forged and the battles they fought, both political and physical, became the basis of the power each wielded in Sitka today. The legend was carved into the totem pole planted in front of Ransom's brick mansion.

Ransom gave his mystical friend his full attention. The hard lines and angles of his stony expression softened.

"White Raven," the shaman greeted.

"Spirit Dancer."

"You are troubled."

Ransom dismounted and stood on a rock below the old man. "Yes."

The shaman grinned broadly. "Two Women troubles you."

Ransom's head turned sharply toward the shaman. "Two Women?" he asked. "Is that what the Tlingit call her?"

The shaman nodded slowly. "The two women you are married to are in one body. Neither has tasted the fullness of life. Each lived in a narrow tunnel with hard walls. Now, there is only one woman's spirit in another woman's body and no walls. The spirits gave her the body when they took the spirit who lived there. Now, she must learn the joy of her destiny, just as you must, White Raven."

Spirit Dancer's proclamation rocked Ransom into silence. Over the last decade, the two of them had spent countless hours sitting on the boulders where he had discovered Felicity sitting over a week earlier. Experience with the shaman had proven him a man of extraordinary insight and vision.

"It is a test for you, White Raven."

Damn. He had heard her correctly when she mentioned a spiritual test for White Raven. At the moment, the last thing he needed was a Tlingit test, particularly one that distracted him from the half-dozen problems he was juggling. "What kind of test?"

"You will know your own spirit when the time comes. Whether you prove yourself worthy or you do not, the spirits always watch over Two Women. She is special among human beings. There is not another like her. The spirits honor White Raven greatly by placing Two Women in your lodge."

All emotion drained from Ransom as he met the shaman's serene brown eyes. A chill radiated from the core of his being. Surely Spirit Dancer did not believe Felicity's fantastic story. After several minutes, he asked, "Are you telling me there really is a woman from the future living in Felicity's body, and that Felicity drowned?"

The shaman touched Ransom's breast. "What does your heart tell you, White Raven? Why do you ask me? Two Women has spoken the way of things. Remember, life is lived to the fullest when the heart chooses your course."

Disturbed, Ransom watched the shaman walk away.

Accepting what Felicity and Spirit Dancer said required a belief in the impossible. What had she said she would never give him—blind faith? Was that the test? His ability to believe the impossible? He fervently hoped not, since he detested personal failure of any kind.

As it was, his scattered thoughts concerning his wife interfered with the multitude of demands on his time. He mounted his horse and turned toward home.

Distance. That's what he needed. In two days, he'd sail with the *Ompalada* to Seattle and begin consolidating Arch's holdings and addressing some of the persistent problems in his own businesses there.

By the time he returned home, he'd know whether she carried a child and if an annulment was feasible. Then he'd make a decision. Everything would be clearer then. Sure it would.

So why didn't he feel relieved?

Chapter 11

WINIFRED TOOK A swipe at the flour on her cheek with her upper arm, then continued kneading bread dough. Until joining Meggie MacGregor and the Hamilton's round-faced cook, Charlet Mazaka, in the kitchen for morning coffee, she had no idea of the enormous effort running the Hamilton household required.

The dough kneading exertion was worthy of being a pre-game warm-up exercise during her basketball days. Helping make the bread for the entire household gave her a new respect for the food placed on the Hamilton tables.

The heavy kitchen chair creaked when Bull Mazaka stood. Nicknamed for his appearance, he possessed a feline grace that evaporated at the first sign of trouble. In a voice resonating like ocean waves against the rocks during a storm he asked, "Do you want me ta put drain pipes in these here walls? Where do ya want me ta drain 'em to?"

Win folded the dough over and handed it to Charlet. "Have the men finished building the leach field?"

"Yes, ma'am. They did just like you said. I made sure

they followed the plans you drew up." Bull's bushy eyebrows flickered questioningly. His yearly haircut had grown out to let his auburn locks fall around his ears, across the expanse of his forehead, hug his thick neck, and rest in the hollow of his wide shoulders.

"Good. The depth of the leach field should keep it from freezing during the winter. We can get a few of the pipes laid and functional before it gets too cold." She wiped her hands on her apron and winked at Charlet and Bull's eight-year-old son, Bull Jr., who made her wonder if cloning had been possible in the 1860s and the secret lost.

"Run these pipes near the fireplaces, just like on the drawings." A flour-caked finger traced two pipes leading from the bathing room in the master bedroom on the plans Bull held up. "The residual heat of the fireplaces will keep the water from freezing." She winked again at Bull Jr., who eyed her like she was queen of Baranov Island.

"Bull Jr., get three cookies from your mother and take yourself off to school." She watched the beaming youngster take the cookies Charlet offered. "Be sure to ask lots of questions, too."

As soon as Bull Jr. departed, Charlet confronted Felicity. "Why'd you tell that boy to ask questions? You're making trouble for him, Mrs. Hamilton. Mark my words. Trouble."

"Our boy kin handle it," Bull assured his wife. "He's gonna be educated, like Mr. Ransom and Miss Felicity here, Charlet. Don't you worry about little Bull none. He's gotta ask questions ta learn answers. It's the sue-crack-tic teacher."

"I don't make no never mind about anyone named Sue. Mr. Bobbin, he's got his own ways of teaching them kids," Charlet continued, then plopped another bowl of dough upside down in front of Win.

"If Mr. Bobbin is as a good a teacher as I perceive him, he'll welcome questions. The children have to think in order to ask questions, and they're always more interested in answers to their own questions than what some adult tells them they ought to know," Win said, delving into the sweet bread dough.

"Beggin' yer pardon, ma'am, but how do you know so much?" Charlet formed the bread into loaves and dropped them into the pans.

Win nodded at Bull. "I always wanted to be a kid."

"She was a child for so long, it's only natural for her to know how children think," Cordelia Hamilton said as she sailed through the kitchen and out the back door through the mud room.

Felicity beamed in triumph, then winked at Charlet.

"You better watch yer step, Miss Felicity, she's gonna be speakin' to you in no time." Charlet's hazel eyes sparkled over her round, rosy cheeks. "You go ahead and look pleased, but you might be less happy once she does. I've been with the Hamiltons for nigh onto ten years, and I never seen Miss Cordelia in such a state. Whatever did you do to her?"

"Charlet, how dare you ask Mrs. Hamilton a question like that?" Meggie MacGregor chided from the linen bureau.

Charlet blushed and stammered an apology for being out of line.

Win's exuberance faded with the reminder of her station in the house. "It's all right, Charlet." She flipped the dough with a thump. "Especially since you're making my favorite meal tonight."

"Where'd you learn about this here pizza dish, anyway?" Charlet demanded.

"It's an old family recipe."

"I'll be goin', Mrs. Hamilton." Bull tucked the plans under his arm. "I believe they'll have that pipe ready down at the Traders now. Anything else you ladies want while I'm in town?"

After Bull left, Win settled into a comfortable chatter with Charlet, punctuated by Meggie's insights. Initially, both women accepted her assistance with the mundane chores of running the household with reluctance. However, idleness grated on Win's nerves. Within two weeks after Ransom's departure, she had changed the household routine.

First, she turned her attention on practical matters, like running water for bathing on the second floor. With Ransom gone, the master suite became her test site. Then, with Caine's help and Adele's guidance, she had ordered wallpaper and furnishings for two of the upstairs rooms.

The room she selected as a laboratory and personal library required a few modifications. She had those sketched out and waiting for the workmen when they finished the water and drainage system. Under her direction, Bull had already removed the furniture and set two men working on tables and bookcases. Like the items for the rest of the house, the lab and library furnishings were on order through Hamilton Traders.

Last week, she learned of Mr. Bobbin and the school. She insisted that every child of those who worked for Ransom attend classes regularly. Upon hearing of a shortage in slates and paper, she had Caine drive her to Hamilton Traders. There, she loaded several boxes with every available item the children needed in the classroom and ordered the rest. When Caine asked about accounting for the goods, she charged everything to Ransom's household account. Later, Mr. Bobbin informed her that her husband paid his salary and rent, too.

Ransom's loyal employees painted a very different picture of the man she called her pseudohusband. The more she learned about the household staff, the more she learned about Ransom. Gradually, she became aware that he must have been too disappointed or too angry to show her the gentler side of himself for more than a few minutes—or he wanted her to fear him.

All things considered, fear might be safest. However, in the small hours of the night when she relived the kisses, she suspected that if she wasn't careful, she'd want him far too much to remember the consequences.

*   *   *

"Start logging the northern tract along the Snohomish River," Ransom told Dirk Riker. "McArthur will take all we can give him. How much can the men cut in, say, the next three months?"

Dirk stepped onto the muddy Seattle boardwalk and absentmindedly stomped his feet. "With bonuses and good supplies, count on loading a ship of finished lumber a month. Mebbe a fourth in mid to late fall." Dirk pushed back the blond shock of hair crowding his green eyes and adjusted his woolen sea cap.

Reputed as a tough, fair man, Dirk had been Ransom's partner in the logging and sawmill operation for ten years. Uncomfortable in the limelight, Dirk preferred no mention of his ownership. Ransom never questioned his reasons.

"Bonuses are fine by me. If they cut and haul that much timber, they'll earn every penny," Ransom said, delighted by the solution of another problem.

"They like the money. But getting Pancake is the reason they'll do it. I won't ask where the hell you found him or how you convinced him to set up shop in our camp, but I'll tell ya, Pancake is the best damn cook in the Northwest." Dirk's head flew back as he laughed. "There're men who'd work for less wages just to have a decent camp cook."

"Yeah, since they can't have women up there, good grub means a helluva lot. By the way, I'm signing an agreement with a new supplier. His name is Slade Raley. We have an appointment this evening. Hopefully, you'll have a better grade of raw goods for Pancake and the men at the sawmill to work with come next month. If he works out, neither you nor Harris will have any more dealings with Gardener's outfit."

"I was going to mention that." Dirk pushed through the saloon doors and signaled for two of the usual before joining Ransom at a table. Cigar smoke mingled with the sour smell of malt and spilled whiskey. "I started a detailed check of deliveries against invoices after you got here.

They don't usually match. Turns out Harris has been paying just for what we got, not what Gardener invoiced us. Good man, Harris. He said every time he talks to Gardener about the billing mistakes, the man has an excuse. But the bastard's a cheat. Up till now, there hasn't been anyone else to get supplies from. I hope Raley proves trustworthy."

"Seattle is growing. Growth brings competition for Gardener and for us." Ransom waited until the bartender deposited two beers on the table before settling back in the chair and stretching his long legs in front of him on the mudcaked floor. "Did you check on those timber tracts I told you about?"

"Yeah. They're prime. Easy logging. They were Arch Forsythe's, weren't they?" Dirk asked into his beer.

"Not anymore."

Dirk drew back in surprise. "You sold them?"

"No. He gave them to his stepdaughter as a wedding present last year. I wanted your opinion on them. If the opportunity presents itself, I'll bid on buying the land or the logging rights, if you say it's good wood."

"I'd say yes." Dirk nodded, then grinned openly. "Always a step ahead, aren't you, Ransom?"

He grinned back at his partner. "I try like hell. Sometimes . . ." *Sometimes blue-eyed vixens interfered with clear thinking.* "It doesn't always work out."

"I hope you've thought a few steps ahead concerning Gardener. That ol' boy isn't going to like losing a big account like ours. He might take it personal."

"Arm the men and hire as many guards as you need, Dirk."

"I'm not concerned about me or the men. Coming after us is stupid. We don't make those decisions and he knows it. You do," Dirk said softly, lifting his beer and staring at Ransom over the lip of the mug. "Seems to me it's you he's targeting."

Ransom shrugged and finished his beer. "We're sailing

for home with the morning tide. He'll have to hurry if he's got something in store for me this trip." He nodded at Dirk. "We have no proof he hired the man who set the granary fire."

"Shit! I don't have any proof pretty little Karen Taggart can cook unless I catch her in the kitchen of the Blue Whale, either." Dirk quickly looked away, but not before Ransom caught the twinge of longing reflected in his friend's eyes. "Gardener's a strange one. In keeping with his last name, he codes everything by what grows in a garden. If it has the name of a flower or a vegetable, it's Gardener. His ships, his store . . . hell, even his horse is named Tulip. Take it to the bank, Ransom, the man is capable of damn near anything. Watch your back. He doesn't have your scruples about taking a man out, armed or unarmed."

"Thinking and proving are two different things, my friend." Ransom blinked. An image of Felicity's imploring eyes sparkling with truth she couldn't prove and honesty she couldn't hide as she related her impossible story twisted the tight hold she already held on his heart. He cleared his throat and shifted. "Do you know Tom Richards?"

Dirk nodded thoughtfully. "I'd recognize him in a crowd. We've had a few drinks and played a little poker over the years. Why?"

"Tom and I got to know each other in San Francisco before Arch sent him up here to take charge of things. If he comes to you, do whatever he asks regardless of how strange it sounds.

"The story is that I fired him when I consolidated Arch's business with mine. Tom is angry and looking for revenge. He needs a job, but not from you. We're hoping Gardener will exploit the situation and take Tom on.

"Help Tom convince Gardener any way you can. If we're right, Tom may help us prove it. I'm not concerned about a court of law. I just want the right man and an end to the sabotage before it starts costing lives."

"You've got my word on helping Richards. If he runs into trouble, we'll get him on a Hamilton ship bound for Sitka or San Francisco."

"Thanks, Dirk." Ransom stood and extended his hand.

"Any time, partner." Dirk shook Ransom's hand and grinned. "We've been through tougher times."

Ransom met with his new supplier shortly after dinner. Near midnight, he and Slade Raley signed a contract for furnishing the logging camp and sawmill operations with fresh food supplies and staples on a regular basis. Three weeks of hard work had gone into consolidating Arch's holdings with his own, then reshaping them into one solidly constructed business. Fortunately, he'd found a place for every man in both operations.

The *Juliet* sailed in a few hours. To home. To Felicity.

What the hell was he going to do about her? Basically, women were easy creatures to figure out. All wanted something, which wasn't bad, since all men wanted something, too.

He held no illusions of what he wanted from Felicity. He wanted to feel her come undone beneath him. He wanted to savor every inch of her velvet flesh and breathe the rich scent of woman and lilacs surrounding her.

Felicity.

Yes, he knew exactly what he wanted from her. What he didn't know was if he wanted to pay the price for possessing her even once. Whether he had her once or a hundred or even a thousand times, it wouldn't matter. The cost was the same: a sanctioned marriage, a consummated marriage. Forever. No escape.

Although he was hundreds of miles away, the woman's pursuit of his sanity seemed relentless. He wanted to forget her, not think about her in the middle of a conversation or during a quiet moment or amid the mountains of paperwork he had waded through over the last few weeks, but she wouldn't allow him even a moment's peace of mind. Instead, she reached across the ocean and robbed him of sleep. She invaded his dreams even when he worked himself into exhaustion. During the day, he saw her in the guise of other women at the strangest times. Damn. She was everywhere.

He was no closer to a decision than when he had left Sitka a month before. He thought of a thousand reasons why he shouldn't bed her, and one more why he should. Most of the time a war raged between his head and his desire for control of his thinking and, therefore, the rest of their lives. Regardless of his logical arguments, she loomed in his mind's eye, breaching his armor and crawling under his skin, then tying up his nerves.

A man of huge appetites under strict control, he found wanting Felicity as he'd wanted no other woman confounding. She set his blood on fire by being in the same room. Even now, thinking about her aroused him.

His bootheels echoed on the planks as he turned down the wharf where the *Juliet* waited. Fleetingly, he wondered if he'd ever get through a whole day without an erection. After countless hours of self-debate and soul-searching, he acknowledged that if he spent much time around Felicity, he'd bed her. Her submission, followed by her eager response to his kisses, promised a great passion.

He wanted to bask in the warmth of her smile and delight in her laughter. For a moment, he indulged the fantasy of his nightly dreams and envisioned her looking at him with unabashed love in her heart and their child at her breast. A child. The pleasure of the image set him grinning in the darkness. Having a child meant making love with her. Sweet, hot, passionate love. Again and again.

Ransom remembered the way she tasted him, then explored his mouth . . . that sexy little noise she made when he touched the side of her breast . . . the way the contours of her curvaceous body molded against . . .

A pair of arms shot around him from behind and held him in a viselike grip.

Startled, Ransom's instincts took over. He ducked and

swore, angry for allowing thoughts of Felicity to distract him again. With a quick, twisting move, he wrenched free and confronted the menace.

In the shadows cast by cargo awaiting transport off the wharf, two men circled him. One man wielded a knife that caught the glint of the moonlight peeking through the clouds. The other man caressed a heavy length of chain.

A quick glance at his surroundings confirmed that they were alone. His attackers had chosen a spot well out of sight of the *Juliet* and away from any passersby on the wharf.

"What do you want?" Ransom asked, eyes narrowing as he studied their moves.

"You," answered the larger man with the chain.

"What? You don't plan on robbing me?" The man with the knife favored his right leg slightly. The other man kept his head turned as though he saw better with his left eye in the dim moonlight.

"Aye. We'll get our gold soon enough, mate," promised the knife wielder.

All his senses sharp, his reflexes keen, Ransom continued gauging his attackers. The way they played off each other's moves bespoke a long relationship. Each compensated for the other's weakness. This sort of dockside talent made more money hiring out than arbitrarily selecting a chance pigeon in the middle of the night.

Ransom feinted. The knife wielder had quicker reflexes than the chain swinger, in spite of his bad leg. "Then someone must be paying you, because I'm not carrying more than a few bits."

"Aye, and payin' well." The chain rattled, threatening serious damage to anything it embraced.

"Shut up, Zig," snapped the knife wielder.

"Don't listen to him, Zig. This is starting to get interesting. Who's paying you? Vance Gardener?" Ransom watched them closely, moving back and forth, working his way down the dock toward the *Juliet.* "I hope you got paid in advance. He's not one to make good on debts of honor."

"That's enough!" shouted the knife wielder. He started forward, then changed course.

The chain jangled as Zig hurled it overhead in a practiced arc. Just as he prepared for release around his prey's torso and arms, Ransom ducked and scurried away.

Zig swore and slowed the chain.

Ransom's boots slipped on the damp boards, but propelled him toward the *Juliet*. Ducking behind crates and tripping over obstacles cloaked in darkness, he scrambled to keep his feet under him.

Knees bent, arms loose and slightly extended, he checked left, then right, certain they'd rush him when the gap narrowed.

Instead of waiting, Ransom whirled around and scrambled up a line of crates. Holding the high ground, his back against a wall of stacked lumber, he continued toward the *Juliet*, jumping and leaping out of the way of Zig's lethal chain. Determined to stay upright and keep them off balance, he switched direction.

In a calculated leap, he cleared the knife wielder's head and rolled into the middle of the dock before bouncing upright. Immediately, he ducked his head, then dove for the knife wielder's right leg. Ransom's shoulder caught solidly at the side of the knee. In the same motion, he rolled out of reach and popped to his feet.

An agonized scream cut the night, followed by a flurry of curses. The knife wielder staggered against the wall of rough-hewn boxes, grappling for support with his free hand.

Ransom added his own quieter curses. He'd hoped the man would drop the knife or at least ease his guard enough for him to make an attempt for the weapon. Instead, Zig came barreling down on him with the chain singing overhead.

Confident he had at least started evening the odds, Ransom resumed the offensive. He made a dash at the knife wielder and grabbed him from behind. With brute strength, Ransom wrestled him backward, drawing him off balance, angling on his weak right side, kneeing the man's bad knee in the back to heighten the pain. Fingers stretched, he grappled for the knife and watched Zig approach swinging the deadly chain.

Ransom's powerful hand closed on the smaller man's wrist. Slowly, determinedly, he turned the man's hand until the blade pointed at the wielder's chest. Exerting steady pressure, he drew the knife closer and closer, all the while watching Zig and listening as the man shrieked for Zig to do something.

In response, Zig released the chain. It went skittering loudly down the dock. Bellowing incoherently, Zig lowered his head and charged. Ransom lifted his captive off the ground, turning them both toward the rampaging Zig. On impact, the knife went straight through the smaller man's heart. Another bellow tore from Zig's throat when he realized he'd killed his cohort. Still shouting, Zig grabbed the knife hilt with both hands, pulled it free, and began slashing at Ransom.

Stunned, Ransom could only hold the dead man in front of him as a shield until he gained solid footing. Then he hurled the dead weight at Zig.

Zig one-armed his companion aside and pursued Ransom with a crazed gleam in his eye.

Ransom met him. They fought for the knife in Zig's hand with the tensile strength of muscle and sinew. Ransom shifted, throwing his balance on his left leg, sweeping Zig's feet out from under him with his right.

Still, Zig clutched the knife. They rolled toward the water in a death grip, both aware of the consequences of release.

Zig shouted, and with a mighty heave brought the knife down and embedded it in Ransom's right thigh. In a rage, Ransom found a strength he hadn't known he possessed. He slammed the palm of his left hand upward at Zig's nose.

The crunch of contact sounded above the grunts and heavy breathing of the two men. The impact of Ransom's palm sent Zig's nose into his brain.

It took a moment before Ransom realized that Zig no longer moved. Breathing heavily, he used both hands to pry Zig's fingers from the knife, then extracted the blade from his leg.

The pain waited until he was on his feet and hobbling down the dock. All he thought about was the *Juliet*. The fires of self-anger remained temporarily banked, yet glowed and fed his determination to survive the mistake of inattention.

Minutes after he staggered within hailing distance, two of the *Juliet*'s crewmen helped him on board.

"Damn. Get a doctor," Gerald Wagner ordered the first mate. "Take a couple of men."

"No doctor," Ransom hissed. "Just bind it up and let me lie down for a few minutes."

"Goddammit, Ransom! You're bleeding like a stuck pig. You need a doctor," Gerald raged from the doorway of Ransom's cabin.

"Help me get my boots off," Ransom ordered the cabin boy.

The young man's olive complexion visibly paled at the sight of so much blood. He pulled the boots off, then helped Ransom remove his trousers. No sooner had he worried the pants over Ransom's knees than Ransom passed out into Gerald's waiting arms.

John Malcolm withdrew into the deep shadows as three men hurried from the *Juliet*. He had watched with grudging admiration as Ransom Hamilton outwitted and outfought the pair on the wharf.

Vance had touted Liam and Zig as some of the best at taking an unsuspecting man down. Obviously, they weren't good enough. Until seeing how Ransom fought, John had anticipated a far different outcome. Fifty feet away, Zig and Liam lay dead on the damp planks.

It could've been worse, he decided. One of them might have lived and connected him or Vance with the attack. That wouldn't be good. It was imperative that he keep a respectable distance from any seedy undertakings. When he brought Cassandra from San Francisco to sign over the timber tracts, he needed a spotless reputation.

This kind of business required versatility, John thought, moving through the deepest shadows and away from the *Juliet*. Hamilton would either die, or he wouldn't. If he didn't, he'd be slowed down for a while, maybe even permanently crippled.

While Hamilton's death would have cleared the way for assuming Felicity's guardianship, John wasted no time lamenting his fate. The stakes were too high for him to consider failure. Already, the next little annoyance for Hamilton was taking shape. Yes, Carl Owens should be sailing on the *Margaret Elizabeth* by now.

A grin brightened John's serious features. It might be a while before he knew whether Hamilton survived Zig and Liam. If so, the trouble he and Vance unleashed through Carl Owens would deal Hamilton another low blow.

John's grin broadened. The greatest part about all of the trials and problems he and Vance laid at Hamilton's doorstep was the anonymity. Not until John decided the time was right would Hamilton know of his role.

Perhaps he'd tell Hamilton before he killed him. Perhaps not. No point in rushing the fine details at the beginning of the game.

Chapter 12

W<small>INIFRED</small> SURVEYED HER fledgling efforts as a gardener. The warm, clear day coaxed colors from the azaleas she planted along the south side of the house. Nobody would hire her as a landscaper, but Joey would have appreciated the flowers and applauded her naïve efforts. Joey had always noticed when someone went out of their way or did something special.

During the years in Los Angeles, there hadn't been time for growing more than an aloe vera plant for kitchen burns. Now she had all the time in the world and the freedom for dabbling in whatever caught her fancy. Choices and leisure time carried an awesome responsibility.

She had persuaded Caine Tilson to let her work in Ransom's office at Hamilton Traders. The arrangement doubly benefited Caine. He could focus his attention on the business of Hamilton Traders by eliminating the distraction of checking her whereabouts or escorting her on some frivolous excursion.

Winifred learned the rudiments of conducting business in Sitka and the complex details of the trading enterprise in a short time. Gradually, she cajoled Caine into giving her more responsibility. Caine found acquiescence easier than an argument with her. The more she learned, the greater became her hunger to know more.

She discovered a deep interest in the people around her. Every day she greeted Cordelia as though they were on the best of terms. She hoped Cordelia would forget herself and answer.

Meanwhile, she continued gathering the rudiments of her primitive laboratory and anticipated the arrival of enough equipment and raw supplies for constructive endeavors. The only damper on her daily pattern was the sensual man haunting her dreams.

The conflict between seeing Ransom again and dealing with the disturbing sensation of his presence found a fertile battleground in her emotions. She had hoped time and distance would snuff the fire sparked by his kisses. What she suppressed during the day surfaced in nightly dreams with heated clarity.

She put away her gardening tools and went upstairs for a bath. Just as she finished dressing, shouts wound up the staircase from the foyer. Pushing the last pins into her hair, she ran down the hall, then bent over the stairwell and peered into the foyer.

"What's the matter, Adele?"

Four men barged through the front door carrying a fifth man on a makeshift stretcher. They headed toward the stairs. Dr. Branson followed the parade with one of his assistants. It took a moment to realize it was Ransom laid out and pale under the blankets.

Heart hammering in her throat with inexplicable terror, she threw Ransom's bedroom door open and drew back the bedcovers.

"What happened, Gerald?" she demanded, helping the men situate Ransom on the bed.

"He was attacked the night we left Seattle. Took a knife blade in the leg." He checked her reaction before continuing. "It's bad. We got a doctor to sew him up, but it got infected anyway."

"Let's see it." She reached for the bandage.

"Mrs. Hamilton, I don't think . . ." Gerald started.

"Please, Mrs. Hamilton, move out of the way," Dr. Branson demanded, forcing his portly presence to Ransom's side. "Where is Cordelia?"

"Out," Win answered curtly. Heart heavy with dread, she refused to move. She had a greater stake in Ransom's health than any of the men in the room.

"I think you'd better leave while I examine your husband," Dr. Branson said, opening his bag.

"I don't think my leaving has any relevance on your examination, unless you plan on doing something you don't want anyone seeing." Her lip curling in disdain, she eyed the contents of his bag. This was no Marcus Welby or Dr. Kildare. Judging by the condition of the implements, Dr. Branson could easily have been mistaken for the Butcher of Buchenwald. Jack the Ripper and Lizzy Borden used cleaner murder weapons!

Not one of those implements was getting near Ransom's wound until they were sterilized. She closed her eyes. Did they know about germs and sterilization in 1866 Alaska?

Dr. Branson bristled at her. "Then don't faint, Mrs. Hamilton. I won't have time to treat you. I'm on a tight schedule as it is."

Winifred bit off an acrid retort about growing up in the heart of gangland warfare. She didn't like Dr. Branson, even if he was the only available American doctor in town. All her instincts warned her that he was a petty, malicious man.

Branson cut away the bandage around Ransom's leg. The stench of infection permeated the room. Win sucked in her breath at the sight of the putrid hole in Ransom's leg.

"Mr. Wagner! The leg must come off. The wound is already beyond repair," Dr. Branson said. "It's best we do it while he's unconscious. I'll need the board under him. A couple of you men will have to hold him down."

"No. You will *not* take off his leg." Her quiet words carried authority.

"Someone, please remove Mrs. Hamilton from the room. She's interfering with my treatment of Mr. Hamilton," implored Dr. Branson as he looked hopefully from Caine to Gerald.

"No, Dr. Branson. This is my husband and my house. I say who stays and who goes. Understand? You *will* get away from him." Win stared at the wound. It wasn't the first knife wound she'd seen, but it was the most infected. Faint red streaks were already crawling up his thigh and announcing the onset of peritonitis.

"You must leave, Mrs. Hamilton, or one of the gentlemen will escort you out," Dr. Branson stated.

"I said, no. You're not taking his leg. I prefer him in one piece." She met first Caine's, then Gerald's worried gazes. "He's a proud man. I suspect he'd prefer it, too. Besides, there are things we can try *before* amputating."

"Mrs. Hamilton . . ." Dr. Branson started, his puffy face turning crimson.

"I said, no." Again, she sought Caine's then Gerald's pinched faces for consensus, if not open support. "Will you help me?"

"What the hell do you know about doctorin' him? A couple of months ago . . ." Gerald bit back the rest of the words, then asked pointedly, "Do you really think you can save him?"

"Damn right I do," she answered, mentally adding, *He's the best challenge I've ever met,* and realizing how easily the truth slipped out in times of crisis. "Please. You know miracles exist. And there's so much at stake, Gerald. Stand by me in this. I'll tell you if and when the leg has to come off, but I won't allow this man to touch him with those filthy instruments. If the wound doesn't kill him, Dr. Branson's dirty tools will."

"How dare you! Mrs. Hamilton, you can't override my decision. I absolutely won't permit it," Dr. Branson seethed. "The leg must come off right now or I won't be responsible."

She looked him in the eye. "You're not responsible for anything here, Dr. Branson. You're fired. Close up your bag and get out of my house."

"You can't do that!"

"Yes," Caine said, moving beside her, "she can." His head jerked toward Gerald, who reluctantly closed ranks. The three of them stood together, watching everyone else depart.

"I've gone a long way with you, Felicity, and you haven't sold me short yet. But, dammit, woman, you'd better be right on this. We're playing with Ransom's life here," Caine whispered, exhaling.

"If he dies, you'll wish you died instead," Gerald promised. The black eyes glaring at her sent a chill up her spine.

"What do you need?" Caine asked, his fingers combing his shoulder-length brown hair.

She collected herself, ignoring Gerald, then set about dictating a list of things needed from the apothecary. All the while, she examined Ransom's wound. Whatever the doctor in Seattle may have done, his efforts were woefully inadequate. The sutures had burst with the inflammation. She'd have to remove them, then lance the infected mound.

As Caine and Gerald left, Adele knocked on the door, then entered. "Can I help?"

"Yes. Get me hot water, clean towels, Ransom's good brandy, and the sharpest knife in the house. Then get me bread, scalded milk, and a boiled piece of cheesecloth for a poultice." She squeezed Adele's shoulder. "And, Adele?"

"Yes, ma'am?"

"Pray for another miracle."

Adele nodded, then hurried out.

Alone with Ransom, the gravity of his condition settled

heavily. Until a few moments ago, her instincts guided her through the maze of fear and anger. Now she stood beside the man whose life she was responsible for saving.

A tremor of uncertainty rippled through her. Heart beating quickly and feeling overly warm in the cool room, she concentrated on what she had to do.

With a knife from the nightstand drawer, she cut Ransom's dirty clothing from his body. Meanwhile, she battled down fear. Of all the scenarios she conjured for her future in this time and place, not one touched on the possibility of Ransom's death.

If it was humanly possible, she wouldn't let him die. The muffled sounds of someone talking reached her ears. Over and over her lips moved to the litany she was unconscious of praying: "Please don't die. Please don't die. Please, God, don't let him die."

The chant continued in her brain when her mouth turned dry. Adele kept hot, clean water coming from the water and drainage system Bull Mazaka and his men had just finished building in the bathing room.

She wanted Ransom clean enough to at least create the illusion of conquering the infection. Although necessary, the jostling started the wound oozing and bleeding again. She slipped fresh sheets under him once she had him bathed.

"Ransom? Can you hear me?" She cradled his fevered face in both hands. His whiskers were already long and flexible.

He made no response.

Win wrung out a cloth and wrapped it around his cheeks and chin. She overlapped the ends on his forehead.

"Okay, Ransom. It gets tougher now. You have to be strong. You have to want to live. Got that?"

Shallow breathing was his only response.

Catching her bottom lip between her teeth, she focused on his wound. She sterilized the smallest, sharpest knife from the selection Adele had brought in both fire and brandy. Swallowing hard, she knelt beside the bed. The first draw of the blade over a strained stitch cut the thread.

She hadn't realized she was holding her breath until she let it out. One by one, she removed the old stitches, most of which had torn free on one side. Bloody infection seeped into the piles of snowy linen she packed around the sides of his leg.

When the area surrounding the wound was as clean as she could make it, she lanced the infected wound. The stench of decay assaulted her nostrils. Fear made her hands tremble. Rocking back on her heels, she collected herself by adding a new verse to her litany. "Do what we have to and save his leg and life."

When she pushed upright, her lips echoed the silent prayer. Watching Ransom for any sign of reaction, she gingerly pressed the sides of his wound. More of the putrid infection flowed with fresh blood onto the white linen.

Perspiration dampened her dress and pasted loose tendrils of hair against her clammy skin. She put the first of several hot compresses and poultices over his open wound to draw out the poison.

Caine returned and unpacked the items from the apothecary onto the top of the secretary desk in front of the window. "What more can I do, Felicity?" he asked, his eyes fixed on the towel-wrapped face of his friend.

"Pray," she answered, examining the compounds he brought. She gave him the pestle and mortar. "And have Meggie wash these in the strongest soap and hottest water possible. Tell her to let them air dry. No one touches the inside after it's washed."

She saw her own hope, doubt, and fear reflected in Cain's expression. She diverted her attention to the assortment on the desk until she heard Caine close the door behind him.

Looking out the window at the gray clouds weeping softly on the spruce forest, she consciously prayed for the first time since before Joey's death.

Winifred was restitching the wound when Cordelia rushed into the room. She ignored her mother-in-law and tied off the last stitch. Next, she tapped sulfur powder over the area.

"I heard." Cordelia's worried gaze scoured her son's face. His chalky pallor contrasted sharply with the dark stubble forming a soft beard. "Branson's patients don't usually live very long, and he's a trained physician. Do you know what you're doing?"

Win sighed. Any other time, she'd deem a couple of words from Cordelia a triumph. However, she had asked herself the same question a hundred times already. "I hope so, Cordelia. If I'd let that butcher cut off Ransom's leg with his filthy implements, I know we'd be burying him and his leg in a couple of days. As it is . . . I'm praying Ransom is strong enough to make it.

"There are some things I can do for him. They may seem a bit strange, but you'll have to trust me."

"Trust you?" Cordelia snorted. "The way you and my son avoid each other leads me to believe you don't even like him, let alone have his best interests at heart. Why should I trust you?"

Win tucked the end of the bandage and reached for the towel she'd used for bathing Ransom's face. "Why don't you just believe that it is in my best interests to keep Ransom alive and in one piece."

"It might also be in your best interests if my son dies." Cordelia's lips drew into a tight line. Thin worry lines pinched the corners of her mouth and eyes.

Win pressed her wrist against Ransom's forehead. Fever ravaged him without mercy. "Gerald has made the consequences of Ransom's death very clear. Believe me, if I could intimidate or threaten or promise or cajole Ransom into pulling through, I would."

Sadly, she saw the older woman's fear and the worst emotion of all, helplessness. Still, the implication she might not do everything possible for Ransom rankled. "Cordelia, if

I wanted him dead, I'd have left him with Dr. Branson and walked away. By the time that butcher finished, nothing could save him. Infection would've quickly overwhelmed Ransom's weakened immune system."

"What is an immune system? How could you possibly know anything about Dr. Branson and his methods of treatment? What makes you think you know anything about tending his wound?" Distraught and paled by the dire situation confronting her, Cordelia settled into the chair beside Ransom's bed.

"I know a lot more than I have time to explain right now," Win answered as she dried her damp hands on a clean towel. She motioned at the chair Cordelia had appropriated. "If you want to stay, get your own chair, Cordelia. That one is mine."

Cordelia's head shot up, her chin set in outrage. "Why, how dare you . . ."

Feeling the strain of tension in the bunched muscles at her shoulders, Winifred wheeled around. "No, Cordelia. How dare you not speak to me all this time. How dare you denigrate my efforts to keep your son alive, then take my chair. How dare you! I'm not some piece of trash or a lackey you can use as a whipping boy or order around because you and your son didn't get your way. I'm your son's wife. Not Cassandra. Live with it. God knows we're doing the best we can until one of us ends this farce of a marriage. Until then, I'm mistress of his house. Not you. Me.

"I don't want Ransom to die and neither do you or Gerald, or Caine, or Ivan, or . . . or the people who work for him down at Hamilton Traders." Weary, Win sank onto the far side of the oversized down mattress. For several minutes she watched his chest rise and fall, all the while resting her head against the foot poster. "Did you know they think he walks on water?"

Cordelia glowered at her over the expanse of her son's body. "That's absurd. Ransom can't walk on water."

Steeled for the natural fatigue and grouchiness she expected after the initial adrenaline rush of several hours earlier, Win ignored the irritating contradiction. "Perhaps not, but I'll bet he swims with the sharks just fine," she mused.

Cordelia stomped from the room and returned with a second chair. She sat in the corner and remained so silent, Win forgot she was there. Worried, she doted on Ransom. Without modern medicine, his chances weren't good. The days at sea battling the horrendous infection had sapped his strength.

She dripped a rose hips infusion into his mouth, hoping the concentration of vitamin C would fortify him. Before she'd gotten two cups of the liquid into him, her finger turned numb from controlling the flow of the infusion from the top of the glass pipette Caine brought from the apothecary.

Her heart had leaped with joy for the willow bark and salicylic acid Caine wheedled out of the man. As the chemical basis for the original aspirin, willow bark had been used since the days of the Greeks to reduce pain and fever. However, salicylic acid, the active ingredient in willow bark, wasn't synthesized into aspirin until 1853 by a French chemist named Gerhardt. Even now in 1866, aspirin's merits weren't widely recognized and the drug enjoyed very limited distribution. It would be another twenty years before the German pharmaceutical firm of Friedrich Bayer embarked on bringing aspirin to the world.

What she wouldn't give for a modern lab or even for the arrival of her own primitive equipment and supplies. Although crude, she could create life-saving medicines in another couple of months.

During her lonely night vigil, as her mind sifted through the trivia she had gleaned from textbooks, periodicals, and television, she hit upon an idea. "I think I've got it, Ransom!" She beamed at his pale, bearded face in delight. While alone with him, she talked constantly, knowing that people in comas and with fevers heard what took place around them. Sometimes, the sounds pulled them into consciousness.

"Tree moss," she told him proudly. "That's what William Holden told the trooper to keep on his wound in the movie *The Horse Soldiers.* The trooper listened to John Wayne's scorn instead of the good doctor and removed the tree moss from his wound. Later in the movie, William Holden had to cut off the trooper's leg. Who said Hollywood wasn't educational?

"So, what we need is some good tree moss to draw out the infection." She patted the cool cloth against Ransom's forehead. "And I know the right man to tell me the kind of moss I need and where to find it.

"Now, I don't want you thinking I've pinned the future of your leg on an old John Wayne movie. I haven't. Well, not exactly. It just reminded me of something I should have thought about sooner—homeopathic remedies. Who knows more about natural remedies than an Indian shaman from the 1860s? Besides, we're going to start growing some penicillin for you. Just hang in there until it's soup."

She rinsed and wrung the cloth again. "I'm not going to let you die, Ransom. And I'm not going to let that butcher take your leg." She kissed his prickly fevered cheek in reassurance. "I promise."

When Cordelia entered Ransom's room in the morning, Win gave her a few instructions, then left. Regardless of her relationship with her mother-in-law, she knew Cordelia loved her son. She would do anything to keep him alive— even become a temporary ally with her daughter-in-law.

Downstairs, Win gave Charlet very specific instructions on the kind of bread she needed. Charlet embarked on the task immediately. Next, Win sent one of the men at her disposal to hitch up the carriage and act as her driver.

An hour later, she and Spirit Dancer gathered moss in the rain. She listened closely to the shaman's instructions and jotted the answers in the journal she kept. The hard pencil lead cut into the rain-sodden paper.

She returned home with fresh optimism and the knowledge that Spirit Dancer held his own service and offered prayers to the spirits protecting Ransom.

When she opened Ransom's door, Cordelia sobbed and drew another quilt over Ransom.

"Chills?"

"Did you expect him to have chills?" Cordelia asked, sniffing. "If you did, why didn't you say so?"

"I didn't. At least not now. How is he holding up?"

Cordelia turned her stricken, teary-eyed face toward Winifred. "He's dying. Can't you see? He's dying! I thought you were going to save him."

"I'm trying. Believe me, I'm trying everything I know and a few things pulled out of thin air besides." She bit back her own worry and doubts while reassuring Cordelia. She refused to think about Ransom in any way but whole and healthy.

"Just keep him alive. I'll give you anything you want. Just don't let him die," Cordelia pleaded.

Win drew a deep breath and let it out slowly. "Someday, I'd like your friendship. Right now, I'll settle for a little tolerance and help—no questions asked."

Cordelia humbled herself in granting the bitter request. Obviously not trusting her fragile composure enough to speak, she nodded curtly, then left Ransom's side, her head bowed in defeat.

Win sympathized with Cordelia. If they were to be friends in the future, they needed to begin forging the bond now. "Fine. Start feeding him the rose hips tea." Win washed her hands and prepared to remove the bandage covering Ransom's festering wound.

For the rest of the day, Win piled quilts on Ransom when chills rattled his teeth, then pulled them off and bathed him with cool water when the fever climbed. Working against time, she started her "bug soup" of corn syrup liquor and milk sugar. Trouble was, nothing could shorten the hundred hours at seventy-seven degrees needed for the growth cycle. Watching Ransom, she wasn't sure he had that much time.

Long tremors racked Ransom's body, sending his teeth chattering. Win slipped a piece of leather between them to prevent chipping. Only when the chills subsided and the fever spiked could she dribble medicated liquids into his mouth. He burned up the liquids almost as fast as she dripped them in. His fever had to come down. His skin was so hot that it scorched her fingertips to touch him.

During the night, his shivering became so violent she physically restrained him with strips of sheeting.

The next countless hours she spent alone with him, watching, waiting, worrying, listening as he rambled and mumbled, then occasionally shouted nonsensical threats.

For the next three grueling days, Win remained with Ransom. She left only to check on her bug soup with a microscope Caine had produced. She didn't ask where or how he got it, merely hugged him and used the scope as though it was the last one on earth.

The hours blended into one another. Bull Sr. kept a steady supply of wood available for the fire and plenty of hot water in the bathing area just off Ransom's spacious bedroom.

When Caine, Gerald, Ivan, Cordelia, or Adele checked on her and Ransom, she ignored them. Win had neither the energy nor the patience for conversation. Ransom's condition spoke for itself. Adele feared that if she didn't rest, she'd expire before Ransom recovered. Win ignored everyone except Ransom.

During the worst of the fever, Winifred listened as he hallucinated on a hundred topics. She cringed when he spoke her name with a deadly venom and smiled wistfully when he uttered the same word with the longing of a tender lover in the throes of passion.

Damn him! He couldn't die. There was too much left unsettled between them. Even weakened and fever-ravaged, he felt big and solid.

Regardless of their discord, he had sworn to care for her

whether she needed it or not and regardless of the state of their marriage. The realization that she was the beneficiary of such total commitment both awed and unsettled her. It had always been she who protected. She knew the level of commitment such a responsibility engendered. What her instincts proclaimed as truth, the people close to him avowed in action and attitude. Ransom Hamilton was a man of his word—a rarity in any age.

He muttered incoherently for nearly an hour the fourth night. She'd given him two doses of her penicillin "bug soup," and prayed it cured rather than killed him. Small restless movements of his arms and legs sent her hunting for the restraining strips.

"Felicity," he whispered plaintively, freezing her in her tracks.

Hopeful, she crawled onto the bed and leaned against the headboard. When she cradled his head against her breasts, he quieted. Stroking his fever-dampened hair, she smoothed a cool cloth over his forehead and sang every soothing song she knew.

By dawn, his skin felt a bit cooler. His eyes opened briefly and she thought he might have smiled as he burrowed his face against her breasts.

Her arms tightened around his head and shoulders. "Sleep now and heal up," she whispered before placing a tender kiss on his brow. Exhausted, she started to leave.

"Don't go," he whispered. "Please."

"I'll stay for a little while. You won't be alone. I'd never leave you alone."

A strangled sound escaped him. "I know. You never leave me alone."

In moments, he was sleeping soundly. However, Winifred didn't move to the rocking chair and nap for another hour.

On the fifth day, Ransom's fever broke.

"You must eat something, Felicity." Cordelia held a full tray and closed the door behind her with a nudge of her shoulder. "I swear, you haven't eaten two meals since they brought him home. Now, unless you want me to summon Dr. Branson to treat you when you collapse . . ."

Winifred raised an eyebrow and managed a tired smile. Every muscle in her body ached and screamed for respite. "You've learned which button to push, haven't you, Cordelia?" She sat on the chair and smoothed the stained, wrinkled skirt across her lap to receive the tray. The food did smell good. Her stomach growled. "It seems my appetite has returned. Thank you."

Win speared a succulent piece of crab. "Tell me about Ransom. I'll bet he was a handful as a child."

A faint laugh softened Cordelia's features. "He was. I encouraged it, too, until he was eight." The laugh lines faded with a distant memory. "It was a game we played. He was the model of perfect behavior in public and during social occasions. Otherwise, I let him run wild. He learned to read from the books I read his nighttime stories from. Even as a four-year-old his memory was perfect. He never forgot anything." Cordelia's eyebrow lifted in warning. "He's much sharper now."

"What happened when he was eight?" She stole a glance at the silent, bearded man lying so still amid the sheets. What she'd learned about him promised that he was still capable of duality.

"James, his father, oversaw his education. When he realized how bright Ransom was, Ransom's childhood ended. He lived in the offices of Hamilton Shippers. By the time he was fifteen, there wasn't anything Ransom didn't know or couldn't do in the business.

"He took the whole thing over when James died. Ransom had a streak of wanderlust. He grew tired of New York." Cordelia shrugged. "We talked. We decided to go to San Francisco and see how the other side of the country lived. Ransom sold Hamilton Shippers to his cousin. We sailed the day he closed the deal.

"He brought me to Sitka for a visit ten years ago. I've been here since. Given a choice, I'd die here. I love this island and her people."

Cordelia sighed heavily and turned in the chair beside Win. "He's going to make it because of you, Felicity—with his leg. Thank you."

"Yeah, well," she conceded, swallowing a bite of crab, "he won't be running any marathons soon."

"Marathons?" Cordelia knitted her brows in question.

Knowing she had slipped again, Win racked her sluggish brain. She bought time by taking another bite of food. "The Greeks. The ancient Greeks ran a set route of twenty-six miles."

"Oh." Cordelia settled back but continued staring.

By the time Win finished eating, her discomfort found new heights under Cordelia's relentless perusal. Exhausted, Win vowed to take more care in what she said.

"What?" Seeing Cordelia's doubt, she turned away.

"Who are you?"

The urgent whisper raised the hairs on the back of Win's neck. She gripped her fork a little tighter and tried to calm the quickening of her pulse. "Felicity Forsythe Hamilton." Her eyes pleaded a halt of the questions whose answers bred additional questions of a more serious consequence. With her defenses as depleted as her physical reserves, silence was the only safe course available.

Cordelia shook her head. "I met Felicity a little over two years ago in San Francisco. You're not her. Oh, you look like her right down to the mole on your neck beneath your right ear. But you're not her. Who are you? How did you fool Adele?" Cordelia shook her head and glanced at Ransom. "Cassandra couldn't have done as much for him and she has a cool head. The Felicity I met could barely hold the same thought for two minutes."

Cordelia retrieved Win's journal from the floor. "You write in this book as though writing down everything you do is as natural as breathing. Sometimes, when you're writing and talking to me at the same time, you have a vocabulary I struggle to keep up with. Felicity could neither read nor write, nor could she speak more than simple sentences. Who are you?"

Winifred grew very still and remained silent. Revealing her history to Ransom was very different from sharing her secret with Cordelia. Finally, she stood. "I am Felicity Forsythe Hamilton," she repeated succinctly, feeling as convincing as a tin robot in a 1950s science fiction movie. "I am the miracle on the dock. Just ask Adele."

She set the tray on the chair and lifted the quilts around Ransom's leg. With trembling hands she changed the dressing. All the while, Cordelia's gaze bored into her. When she tucked the quilts around Ransom then stood and massaged the ache in her lower back, Cordelia grabbed her and hugged her fiercely. She felt the quiet sobs racking her mother-in-law's body.

After a moment, Cordelia pushed away, wiping the tears with the back of her hand. "You may be the miracle on the dock to Adele, but you're an angel to me. Thank you for my son, Felicity. I am forever in your debt."

Stunned, her mind struggling from a lack of sleep over the last five days, Winifred's mouth opened, but no words poured forth. Relief swept through her.

"Go. Get a bath. Get some sleep. You've been at his side since they brought him home. I'll take care of him. You've done the most difficult part," Cordelia said softly. "Now that his fever is broken, he'll be fine. If anything changes, I'll come and get you."

Dead on her feet, Win nodded, pausing to check Ransom once more before departing.

As she fingered a stray lock of his raven hair from his forehead, she couldn't help smiling. He was stubborn. Ornery. Determined. And strong.

Then she was looking into bright aquamarine eyes that had been chilling so often in the past, but now bored into hers with an icy regard that made all previous looks seem like nothing in comparison. The stormy shards bespoke a monumental anger. She drew in her breath with an audible gasp.

Finally, he closed his eyes and released her from the spot where she had been riveted. Heart beating wildly, she fled the room, wondering what she had done to infuriate him this time.

Chapter 13

Ransom battled his way out of a pain-fogged sleep. The knife fight replayed in his memory. Damn. If he'd been concentrating on the business at hand instead of daydreaming about Felicity, they'd never have taken him by surprise.

While wandering through the limbo between light and sweet, dark oblivion, Felicity's face mixed with Spirit Dancer's words. In the delirium images of his fever, he saw her laughing, frowning, biting on her lower lip, and trying not to say more than she thought proper and bursting to say it. Regardless of the expression, she haunted him. A dark, exciting fire burned in her, one he suspected rivaled his own rapacious passions. Should those flames ever ignite in concert, the heat would consume them.

Damn her anyway, whoever she was. She enticed him on every level from her strange speech and dry wit to the way her emotions lay exposed in a look or a word. Unpretentious and easily awed, she brightened the world around her.

Recalling the feel and taste of her kiss summoned him into consciousness. By God, he wasn't giving her that much power over him! Letting his thoughts wander had nearly cost his life. He had to stop thinking about her. Yet breathing underwater might be easier than quelling thoughts about his mysterious, possibly crazy, wife. Swearing silently, angry with himself and her for being so damned invasive, he opened his eyes.

There she was, gazing down at him. Only this wasn't the same soft, deliciously desirable woman he'd left in Sitka. She appeared gaunt. Her hair dangled in streamers from a disheveled bun sliding down the back of her neck. Strain scrubbed the color from her cheeks and lips. Dark lavender half-circles stained the hollows beneath her eyes.

My God! What's happened to her? He closed his eyes. Anger melted into sorrow. The rock sitting on his heart grew heavier as he drifted into a sleep marred by guilty dreams.

When he woke hours later, Felicity slept in the chair beside his bed. She looked fresher, or at least her hair wasn't quite as wild as it had been earlier. If not for the dark rings beneath her eyes, he might have convinced himself that he dreamed her gaunt specter.

How long had she been sitting there? For that matter, how long had he been in his own bed? The last thing he recalled was the incredible pain in his leg and the rough sea bouncing the *Juliet* home.

Panic seized him. His leg! Had they taken his leg?

Reflexively, he sat up, then bit back a shout at the pain shooting up his leg. To his great relief, two feet tented the quilts at the end of the bed. He gritted his teeth and wiggled his toes. White-hot agony shot up his right thigh, assuring him the foot was connected and functioning.

For several minutes, pain rendered him motionless. Hell, he could barely breathe. With what seemed like the speed of a melting glacier, the pain ebbed to a steady, roaring throb thundering in both his leg and his head. He found a glass of water on top of the nightstand.

He drank it in one gulp. Still thirsty, he fetched the water pitcher one-handed. He drank his fill, then gritted his teeth and lay back, breathing hard from the exertion. He clutched the water pitcher in the cradle of his right arm and let the waves of pain run their course.

He closed his eyes, then opened them, cursing. Felicity was painted on the inside of his eyelids. Vaguely, he remembered her cradling his head against her breasts and the sweet peace that followed.

What was he going to do with her? If he believed Spirit Dancer, she spoke the truth. She represented a living, breathing impossibility. The trouble was, the more he considered her actions, the more logical the impossible became.

Her anger over having his child flitted across his memory. Having the child hadn't angered her; the idea she couldn't raise it did. She had as much said that if she couldn't raise the child, she wouldn't have one.

Despite the pain in his leg, the notion of begetting a child with her stroked the fires of his desire. A child. Christ. What if his impression in the library was wrong? What if she was already carrying a child? She'd know by now. Regardless, bedding her meant binding them forever. When he stripped everything else away, he knew it couldn't be otherwise. Commitment was commitment. He either made it, or walked away, or in this case, sent her away. But sending her away seemed a more difficult option each time he ran around in this endless circle.

What if he consummated the marriage and she reverted to the old Felicity? The prospect made him shiver. Could he stand a lifetime with a mindless wife? For that matter, could he tolerate a lifetime with a woman who thought she'd traveled through time and possessed another woman's body?

In the hopscotch of random thoughts, he considered the ramifications of the United States purchasing Alaska from the Russians. If Felicity was right, which she couldn't possibly be, because no one could know the future unless they come from the future . . . If by some fluke, she'd heard about it in San Francisco . . . *How would she know the date and price if it weren't a fait accompli?*

Well, he would see. He would hold out and see. Even if it killed him, which it damn well might, he wouldn't consummate the marriage until . . . until what?

Christ, what if she's really from the future? What if she's right?

Head spinning with the paradox, Ransom hugged the water pitcher and succumbed to the oblivion of sleep.

"Can't you put something on it to reduce the itching?" Ransom asked as his hand disappeared under the quilts.

Winifred poked her fingertips into a nerve junction in his shoulder, effectively paralyzing his arm. "Keep those hands above the covers. No scratching. The only thing you can do is hurt yourself."

"Damn, but you're a harridan," he hissed. A line of daggers shot from the sharp glance he cast her way. "And a goddamn torturer." He rubbed his shoulder where her fingertips froze his nerve endings. "Who taught you how to do that?" He turned away before she answered. "I'll thank you to keep your hands off of me in the future."

"Keep my hands off of you?" Winifred spun around, her cheeks brightening at his veiled accusation. "Of all the things you might accuse me of, Ransom Hamilton, putting my hands on you in any but a medicinal way is the most absurd."

He squirmed, ignoring her denial, then pushed higher on the pillows. "What did you put on my leg to make it itch?"

Exhausted by too much worry and too little rest, she glowered down at him. "Nothing. However, I assure you, if I come across something to make it itch, burn, or twitch, you'll be the second to know and the first I'd try it on."

"Pain-inflicting witch," he mumbled.

In a blatant effort for self-control, she straightened her shoulders. "Itching is a good sign, Ransom. That means you're healing. The combination of penicillin and Spirit Dancer's medication is fighting off the infection. The stitches are holding. The swelling is down. If you weren't such a big, complaining baby, I'd put a couple of stitches across the drainage hole I left. But I wouldn't want you to faint at the sight of the needle."

Ransom unleashed a stream of invective that questioned not only her parentage and her sanity but her ability to find a chamber pot in broad daylight with all the furniture removed from the room.

Seething, Winifred gnawed on her lower lip and held her silence for a full thirty seconds. Eyes narrowed, hands fisted and pressed against her hips, she leaned toward her disgruntled husband. Danger flashed in her blue eyes. "The next time I die, I'm going to heaven. And you know why, Ransom? Because of the tremendous patience I am exhibiting even as we speak. You are the most self-centered, whining, puerile, immature ingrate I have ever had the misfortune of knowing."

Having said her piece, she started for the door. "The only way, and I do mean *only* way, this could be worse is if this marriage were real. Thank heaven there is still a glimmer of hope for me on the horizon. And as soon as you get out of that bed, I'll expect you to carry through with the annulment so we can both get on with our lives. Do I make myself clear?"

"Who the hell are you to tell me what I'm going to do when I get out of this bed? The way you're torturing me, I'll be lucky to walk again."

She snatched the spare pillow from the rocking chair beside the door and began fluffing it. "If that Dr. Branson you admire so damn much had worked on you, that's one worry you wouldn't have right now, since you'd only have one leg—if you were still alive, which I seriously doubt."

"I'm not so sure . . ."

Felicity threw the pillow at the headboard beside Ransom. It hit with a resounding smack. He yelped in surprise, then unleashed a stream of curses.

"I am! Damn it, if there's one thing I do know, it's how infections and disease start and how they kill. Every time that man uses one of his unsterilized instruments on a patient, he runs the risk of killing him. You couldn't have withstood the consequences of him cutting off your leg, Ransom." Her voice softened into a lethal whisper that held his full attention. "No, my dear husband, I'd be a widow by now and you'd be six feet under, buried beside your leg. If you never believe anything else in your life, believe that."

She stomped out of the room and slammed the door so hard, the wall rattled. "Cordelia! Your little boy needs his nose wiped!"

Two hours later, she pronounced him out of danger, provided he follow her simple directives, and turned his care over to Cordelia before retiring. His surly attitude was more than her sleep-deprived nerves could tolerate.

Staying close in case Cordelia needed her, Winifred had Caine bring the Hamilton Traders and shipyard receipts and ledgers to the house. She took up residence in the library. First Caine, then Gerald, brought her bookkeeping. Neither man understood Ransom's accounting methodology, nor dared ask, fearing Ransom might rush his recovery.

The books weren't based on the twentieth-century accounting principles she'd learned in college, but the system was logical. It would have been easier with a computer. Her second choice would have been a calculator. She settled for the abacus decorating a library shelf. During the next two weeks, she worked undisturbed and caught up the books for all his businesses. Her last batch of bug soup was nearly gone and she wasn't distilling more.

It took a bit of discreet questioning of the household staff and Cordelia's cooperation to decipher the accounts entered in what at first glance appeared a jumble of numbers and letters. The regularity of the entries set her mind on unraveling the mystery. Judging from the size of the entries, Ransom was a philanthropist who specialized in sending young, promising men to college. From the appearance of the correspondence found in his big desk, the candidates came from a half-dozen orphanages. Each institution had a jumbled account number entered into the books of the business supporting it. The ship-building operation funded the majority of the scholarships, with Hamilton Traders challenging for the lead. Even the fledgling packing plant had a cause in San Francisco.

She had nearly finished posting the weekly accounts for Hamilton Traders when the massive library doors banged open. Startled, her head shot up. Ransom leaned heavily on a cane and limped toward her. The first thing she noticed was his clean-shaven cheeks and the glistening ebony mustache he kept. The second thing was the foreboding scowl etched into his angular features.

All traces of restraint faded when he saw the ledgers. "What in seven hells are you doing with my books?"

Maintaining her dignity, she smiled sweetly. "Posting the week's accounts. What do you think I'm doing? Checking the spelling and addition?" Sensing he considered this a major trespass into his sacred territory, she tucked a receipt into the ledger and closed it. "But now that you're capable of making it down the stairs, I'm sure you're ready to resume this task."

"God damn it, Felicity . . ."

"Oh, no need to thank me." She hurried around the table, staying well out of his reach. "I'm sure it would break every bone in your body to do so, and you've got enough to mend as it is."

"Where the hell do you think you're going?"

She paused at the library door, pressing her shaking hands into the voluminous folds of her skirt. "Why, for my riding lesson." Why not? The heroine in the single romance novel she'd read rode masterfully with her hair flying in the wind in graceful splendor. Come to think of it, she did just about everything masterfully.

"God damn it, Felicity!"

Ransom's earth-shaking bellow followed her through the front door. She wouldn't return and endure his rage. Absolutely not. Two hours of his black silence or acrid comments in the morning and two more in the late afternoon were more than sufficient for any dutiful wife awaiting an annulment.

Seeing the horses near the stables, she doubted her horsemanship would achieve a masterful level in this lifetime. All things considered, she preferred a four-cylinder Mustang over a four-legged one. But she wasn't going to be confined to the house.

"I'm not chattel. This is 1866 Sitka, Ransom," she seethed. "There's a salmon in every pot and a horse in every barn."

The stables were empty. Staring at the saddles and harnesses, she realized that not only didn't she know how to ride, she didn't know how to saddle a horse. A few minutes later, she located the groundskeeper and persuaded him to take her into town. She needed a few hours to reclaim the illusion of independence.

Sauntering down the street leading to the ocean with no particular destination, she breathed the damp air deeply. After the passing rain, everything smelled and looked scrubbed and healthy. She didn't want to think about Ransom or any of the problems waiting at home.

At the edge of town, she ventured out onto the rocks and gazed across the expanse of blue water sparkling with the morning sunshine to the smoky emerald islands reaching for the sky. Gentle waves curled and foamed about the piers and scatterings of rocks on the beach. Here and there gulls glided through the wind currents and cried out to the unfortunate land-bound creatures below. The only clouds in view were puffy white cotton balls hovering around the majestic peaks rising behind the odd conglomeration of buildings comprising Sitka.

The scene eased the tension coiled in her shoulders. If the winter wasn't too bleak, she'd love this place. A raw, wild beauty lurked beneath the deceptive cloak of verdant trees and grasses.

Remaining in Sitka was out of the equation unless she and Ransom came to terms. This morning's little display in the library dashed any hope of that possibility. Heavy-hearted, she admitted she didn't really want to leave Ransom. However, his actions offered a poor incentive for staying.

When she had walked into his room without knocking early that morning, she had been unprepared for the sight of him hobbling around with the help of a cane. The only covering on his magnificent body had been the bandage around his thigh.

Although she had immediately excused herself and ducked back into the hall, her heart thundered, her face flushed, and her hands itched to touch him in ways far more carnal than she'd ever imagined.

She closed her eyes and remembered all the details of his body. While the fever raged, she had bathed every inch of him and never thought twice about it. Now, she remembered the way his thick mat of black hair flared across his chest then tapered at his hard belly to a thin arrow pointing at his abundant sex.

Walking along the boardwalk, remembering the erotic sensations he conveyed in those fleeting seconds when he saw her at the door this morning, her pace slackened.

She had never expected a man to say "I love you" any more than she had expected to say those words. She'd had to die and assume another woman's body before anyone, including herself, thought her pretty. Even then, it didn't matter. She still needed to be someone else for the husband she inherited to say a kind word. She'd have to be Cassandra to receive that reward.

"Hey, come 'ere. I got somethin' ta make ya happy," came a slurred masculine voice from behind.

Jolted into the present, she glanced around. She had wandered into the seedier quarters of Sitka. She picked up her pace. The time had come to go home.

"I said, come 'ere, girlie!" the man shouted. "I wanna see what's under them fancy skirts."

"Drop dead," she muttered, hurrying toward the next cross street.

A filthy hand snaked around her arm, spinning her around. She peered into the gap-toothed grin of a middle-aged sailor who sailed more ale schooners than sea schooners. Looming over her, he grinned, exhaling a stench of decaying teeth and rotgut whiskey that nearly knocked her over.

"Come on, l'il missy. I'll put a smile on your sour puss." He laughed, swaying back and forth. "I'll make both pusses smile." Then he reached for her.

"Don't even think of touching me again," she warned, backing toward an alley, her hands rising in front of her.

"How am I gonna make ya smile lessen I touch ya?" He followed, grinning.

The light pattern changed. Winifred glanced around her, then swore quietly. In that instant he reached out. His filthy hands closed on her upper arms, shoving her deeper into the alley.

Dimly, she heard someone call her name, but it didn't matter. She lunged, driving her heel into the top of his foot. Hearing the bones snap, she twisted, freeing her arms. Next, she gripped his ears and slammed his face hard onto her up-swinging knee. When he grabbed at her to keep from going down, she got anxious. In a flurry of motion, she lifted her skirt, shoved him back, and kicked him squarely in the chest. He crumpled just as quickly as her skirts fell back into place.

She brushed her hands together, then smoothed her hair as she exited the mouth of the alley and walked straight into her husband.

"Damn," she muttered, realizing he wasn't going to let her go around him. She didn't have to look up and see his fury; she felt it radiating from him.

"Damn is right." The menace of his voice inspired more

anxiety than the drunken sailor. "Where did you learn how to do that?"

Squaring her shoulders, she lifted her chin until she met his icy gaze. Suddenly finding the humor in her situation, a faint smile brightened her troubled features. "At the East L.A. Karate Dojo. Charley Fong was my *sensei.*" She executed a perfect one-legged crane position.

"What are you doing?" he asked after a moment.

"Other than lamenting *The Karate Kid* hasn't made it to your neighborhood? How about praying you'll go away and leave me alone?" Her arms dropped and her shoulders slumped. She was tired of fighting, tired of waiting for him to do something about their marriage. All her life she'd made things happen. This waiting and allowing someone else control of her future was over.

"I'm done arguing with you, Ransom. I'm bone-damn-tired of walking on eggs and trying to convince you of something you'll never believe. Patience is not one of my strong suits. So let's draw the line in the sand right now.

"If you want this marriage annulled, do it and shut up about it. I'll take Adele and head for San Francisco. It might be enjoyable. Certainly, I'll have a better time than I'm having here. And this time around, Ransom, I'm going to learn how to have *fun.* I'm going to smell the roses and walk barefoot on the beach and eat chocolate until I turn brown.

"If you plan on committing me to a nuthouse, give it your best shot. I promise you the fight of your life.

"If you want to give this marriage business a go, I'll consider it under certain conditions. The first and foremost is that you never—and I mean *never*—try separating me from any children we may have." She stood a bit taller and met his gaze.

"I wouldn't hurt anyone out of hate, and I wouldn't hurt anyone out of anger or revenge. But make no mistake, I *would* kill for love. And if I ever have a child, you can bet your bippy I'll love that child with all my heart and every drop of strength in this body. I won't let you or anyone take him or her away. Be warned, Mr. Hamilton. I'll kill anyone, even you, who tries taking my children away. Those are my terms."

"I think you've finally said something I believe," Ransom said slowly.

Her gaze never wavered and her voice held an undeniable conviction when she spoke. "Oh, you'd better believe me. I've seen my share of misery and violence, Ransom, even if it is a life you deny existed. I've lived with the consequences of being an 'oops, I'm pregnant.' I won't have children just to gratify your ego or some perverted need you have for rearing them alone. Life's hard. I want my children to have both parents."

Chapter 14

THE ANGER IN Ransom fled. In its wake remained genuine admiration. While he muddled with acceptance, she had found some measure of herself. She had moved on and left him behind as nothing more than an option for discarding or exercising. Watching her, Ransom saw her sincerity. Her emotions were transparent and deep.

He hadn't known he was lonely until he went to Seattle. He missed her fire, her willingness to take him on in any arena. She made him yearn for the future about which he had dreamed for years.

For days he'd lain in the prison of his bed, desperate to hold her and angry because he wanted to. The courage it took for her to speak for him and stand her ground in the face of Doc Branson won his respect and an undying gratitude. How had she known what choice he would have made?

Mentally, he shrugged, certain she'd have done anything necessary to save his life. And he wondered why, considering the way he treated her. Even after the success of her diligent efforts, he hadn't been civil. Every time she came near, his senses took flight. The woman was definitely in his blood.

Seeing the drunken tar accost her had sent him into a fearful rage. Heart thumping, his brain screaming for speed, his injured leg couldn't move fast enough to keep the miserable cur's hands from touching her delicate flesh.

What he hadn't expected was the manner in which she protected herself against a man twice her size. Even more disturbing was her strange attitude. It made him think she'd suffered the misfortune of previously encountering such a distasteful situation.

If nothing else convinced him of the validity of her impossible story, the man lying in a heap against the wall did. Felicity could never have defended herself.

"Would you get on the wagon with me?" he asked. "Please."

Win nodded curtly, then climbed onto the wagon seat. A serenity settled over her. She had spoken her heart. She had warned him. The next move was his. She hated playing games and never considered them her forte. If he rejected her terms, the only option left was San Francisco.

The thought of leaving Ransom saddened her. Grudgingly, she admitted she cared for him deeply. Lord knew why, but she did. Of course, the reactions he evoked from her body might have some bearing, but it was more than that. He had the fight, strength, and stamina of a survivor. She understood and respected the price of survival. Despite his attempts to hide it, she had glimpsed his soft, tender side.

"Where are we going?" she asked when he drove by the turn leading home.

"Someplace nice." He clucked at the horses, urging them on.

They rode in silence for a few miles before Ransom stopped at the top of a hill with a panorama of Sitka, the sea, and the emerald islands beyond. Winifred glanced over her shoulder at the breathtaking view, then climbed down.

"Oh, Ransom. This is a beautiful place."

He struggled down from the wagon, keeping his weight on his left leg. When he stood beside her, he tilted her face toward him and kissed her forehead.

"What?" she asked warily.

"Thank you for my leg. Thank you for my life. Thank you for pulling me through when others would have given up," he said softly. "I won't say I understand you. And I can't profess unquestioning belief that you're a woman from the future in Felicity's body. I'm just not as predisposed to disbelieve it.

"Felicity couldn't read, write, do mathematics, or tend a wound." He thumbed away a lock of hair the wind blew over her cheek. "And you can do it all, can't you? And do it well, I might add, judging by the work you've been doing on the ledgers. I suspect Caine has taken advantage of you."

"You'd be wrong again." Like a sunflower following the day, her face moved of its own accord to the motion of his hand. She relished the heated feel of his fingers on her skin. Shimmering waves of excitement coursed downward, making her nipples harden and her lower abdomen contract.

"It seems I'm wrong a lot where you're concerned—in your opinion." When he smiled, she thought she could look at him for the rest of the day and maybe most of next month.

She blinked hard, trying to clear her mind of tingling fuzz.

He retrieved a blanket from beneath the wagon seat and motioned to a spot under a tree affording a panorama of the town and the sea. Win spread the blanket, then helped Ransom ease down onto it. His stoic exterior masked the price he paid for stretching the flesh around the wound.

"Don't you dare open your leg up, Ransom. I know stressing it like you are hurts, so go ahead and complain," she encouraged, settling down beside him. "You're very good at it."

"My leg is fine." Ignoring the barb, he patted the space beside him. "Come sit beside me and tell me who you are."

When she reluctantly complied, he caught her chin on the edge of his knuckles and lifted.

Wary, she met his kind gaze with resignation.

"This time, I'll listen with an open mind."

"Why?" Much as she wanted to trust him, she couldn't. Not yet. "Are you looking for a way for me to incriminate myself and make it easier to send me to the funny farm?"

"Funny farm?" he asked, puzzled. "I've never considered farming funny."

"Don't try distracting me. Why do you suddenly want to know about me?"

"You're not going to make this easy, are you?"

"I already tried direct and easy with you, Ransom. I didn't get very far. You prefer obtuse and difficult, as I recall."

"Try again," he suggested. "Please."

"What's the deal here? Did Cordelia give you a manners lesson? All of a sudden you're saying please and thank you when you wouldn't give me the time of day before."

Ransom laughed. It was a deep, rich sound that vibrated over the crest of the hill and into the blue-gray trees.

She held her silence while waiting until he exhausted his amusement.

"Yes, as a matter of fact, she did, right after she verbally boxed my ears." His confession lacked contrition and she knew he must have been a devil of a child.

"You needed it." She turned her back, hugged her knees, and watched a cotton ball cloud dance with the sunlight.

"Please," he repeated.

She studied him, searching for any sign of mockery.

Hesitant at first, she began relating the highlights of her past twenty-nine years. The sun slipped lower on the horizon and she talked, pouring her heart into his accepting silence. As she spoke of things Ransom would never know and people she wouldn't see again, she started feeling uncomfortable. At first, she couldn't pinpoint the source of her unease. However, as her monologue continued, she realized her memory wasn't clear and sharp on some things. Maybe it was nothing more than the strain she had been under.

She shook off the nagging sensation when speaking of Joey. Tears rolled down her cheeks as she recounted Joey's death and the tremendous sense of his presence the night she died in the twentieth century.

Exactly when she moved into the circle of his arms, she wasn't sure. The next thing she knew, Ransom was tenderly kissing her and intoxicating her with his nearness.

The kiss started as a gentle surprise. Win's parted lips responded timidly to the pressure of his mouth. The textures of his invading tongue and the resulting burst of flame surging through her veins evoked a moan of amazement. No physical or mental defenses withstood the blossoming desire he kindled. He was intense and vital, brimming with sense-shattering excitement and heat. She merely held on and rode the waves of desire cresting one after another as he fully explored her mouth. The growing blaze sweeping her body left her restraining her own sensual response. A shiver of ecstasy rippled from her head to her toes and coalesced in her breasts.

He exuded a potent masculinity far beyond the hard muscle gliding beneath his heated skin and cool white shirt. Suddenly she was lying beside him on the blanket, his powerful hands drawing her so close she practically melted into him. The feel of his arousal against her mons sent spasms of excitement pooling through her lower abdomen.

He gripped her buttocks and held her firmly against his manhood. Slowly, he began the primal rhythm as old as the stars and as hot as the heat that gave them light. A small entreaty escaped the back of her throat. Every fiber in her body cried out in surrender.

She freed his shirttails, then slid her hand underneath. The sensation of hot satin flesh urged her quest onward. Her greedy fingers on his heated flesh hurled the kiss into a richer, more consuming passion. She explored him, hungry for the feel of his flesh and finding that there was nothing soft on him. He was breathing, molten granite under her touch. Her fingers glided along his ribs, over his back, and toward his shoulders until the stretch of his coat denied her.

The barrier brought her back to her senses. She fought against her own raging desires and reluctantly yielded the fiery luxury of his flesh. Her breathing was ragged and her senses all but destroyed by the conflict raging inside her when she ended their kiss.

For long minutes she gazed into aquamarine eyes tempering a burning desire. Gradually, Ransom's breathing steadied. As it did, Win's turmoil settled into familiar pragmatism.

"Some things never change," she whispered, stroking his cheek with the back of her trembling hand. "People have always let their hormones rule their heads, then lived with the consequences."

He managed a quick, pained smile. "Would the consequences be so bad? And what are hormones?"

The questions unnerved the scant composure restraining the wild desire to know him in the most intimate way possible. Gentle as he was, the consequences might destroy the slender threads of reserve that kept her from making a complete fool of herself.

She had vowed never to bed a man without the promise of marriage. Now, for all intents and purposes, she was married. Lord knew she wanted more than a kiss from him. But there were consequences. There were always consequences.

He brushed his lips and mustache across the back of her hand. "Let's go home. Our first time should be in a bed with clean sheets and a warm fire. When the time comes, we'll create our own world and explore it and each other slowly. I want to savor every second.

"I want you naked in the middle of the bed with your hair down. I want to touch you everywhere and feel your hands on me until neither one of us can stand it, and you come undone with me buried inside of you. Damn, but I want you,

Liss. And I want to please you and make you glad you're here."

A hitch in her breathing betrayed the effect of his word pictures on her vivid imagination. The way he called her Liss felt like an intimate caress. With great attention to his wounded leg, she inched away.

For a moment she couldn't believe what he was saying. Did he actually *want* this marriage? Did he want her?

In dreams, he whispered words of love and promised his heart while giving his body. But this was not a dream. The image he painted meant a real marriage. The secret part of her where stubborn dreams lingered cried out with joy. Unwilling to betray the new, tender hope singing in her heart, she straightened her clothing with an unconsciously sexy shimmy of her shoulders. On her feet, she offered his cane and a hand.

He accepted both, then gifted her with a dazzling grin as he tucked his shirt in and she turned away blushing. He hauled her against his chest and held her fast. "Don't be embarrassed. Good Lord, woman, I'd like nothing better than to feel your hands on every inch of me, just the way I want to explore you," he whispered, his voice husky with desire.

"I-I've already touched you most places." Remembering how freely she had ministered his body during his fever, she risked a guilty glance up. "Only not with . . . with *that* kind of touching in mind."

"What kind of touching?"

The sun caught the golden highlights in her hair as she lifted her head and looked him squarely in the eye. An impish grin lit her blue eyes. "Lust."

Surprised, Ransom threw his head back and bellowed his delight. "Good Lord, woman, there is so much more to you than a pretty face."

"Right." She pushed away and retrieved the blanket. Regardless of how often she gazed in the mirror, she couldn't consciously think of herself as pretty. "I've got an appetite, too. I missed lunch." Patching up her dignity, she folded the blanket and placed it under the wagon seat.

He caught her again and pulled her close. All traces of mirth had vanished. "I have to ask you something."

She watched as he searched her face. "What?"

"Are you pregnant?"

Frowning, she blinked twice, sure she hadn't heard correctly. "What?"

"Is Felicity pregnant?" This time, he pronounced every word succinctly.

She met the guarded probe of his unwavering eyes. "Is that what you feared? Another deception? Another unexpected *bonus,* shall we say?"

"I have to know." For an awkward moment, they locked gazes, each measuring the implications of an answer in a different light.

Win hesitated, realizing the difficulty of asking and the importance of the answer. His possessive stance promised protection regardless of the outcome. "If it's as you fear?"

A crooked smile softened his features and portrayed a sincerity that charmed her. He drew a deep breath and exhaled slowly before answering. "I've asked myself that question a thousand times in the last couple of months."

"Did you find an answer?" What turmoil his fears created. His struggle for answers had been no easier than hers.

"Yes." He tucked her head under his chin and stroked her shoulders. "I'll claim the child as mine. The babe didn't ask for the circumstances of its conception. Having a child on the way removes the option of an annulment. Our marriage would be real even if you never shared my bed."

She slipped her arms around him as the magnitude of his decision settled. How many demons chased this man? How many of them were real? The realization of how important a direct lineage of children was to a man in this time jolted her, making her flinch. She knew from hushed conversations at the Traders that Ransom had his pick of women and had selectively chosen more than a few to share his bed over the years, but he possessed a deep sense of honor and commitment. And he was fair. Regardless of the cost to his plans for an heir among the house full of children he wanted, he'd accept another's bastard as his own.

Leaning back, seeing the tenderness of his patient gaze, she understood the hostility he so freely showered on her since regaining enough strength to speak. Judging from his response today, he, too, experienced the chemical reaction between them. She almost smiled at her new understanding of chemical dependency. The depth of his gaze tugged at her heart. "Maybe you aren't so bad after all."

A mirthless chuckle barely reached her ears. "Then again, maybe I am. I would hope for a girl."

Suppressing an understanding smile, she ran her fingers along his jaw. Captivated by the coarse feel of his whiskers, she swept her thumb over the side of his silken mustache. "It was a noble decision only an honorable man could reach, but it isn't necessary. If there is ever a child, it will be ours—yours and mine, Ransom."

There was no sign of regret or relief. "In that case, there are still options." He kissed the palm of her hand.

"We have company." Ransom inclined his head toward two figures standing at the edge of the treeline. "No telling how long Spirit Dancer and Cloud Chaser have been there."

She relaxed her hold and let her arm loiter around his waist, then waved at Spirit Dancer. The old Tlingit lifted a hand in response, then the two men disappeared into the trees.

"He's watching over you," Ransom told her.

At the wagon, he lifted her effortlessly onto the wheel. His hands lingered at the flare of her hips before reluctantly releasing her.

"I know," she answered quietly. "I've never had anyone look out for me. It sort of a nice, uncomfortable feeling that's difficult to explain."

Ransom climbed into the wagon and settled beside her. He tilted her chin and placed a kiss on the tip of her nose. "I hope you'll get used to it."

Her eyes narrowed suspiciously. "Why are you being so nice to me? Cordelia may have read you the riot act on manners, but on her best day, she couldn't begin to move you into any line you resisted." Curious and cautious, she wondered how long this enjoyable side of him would last.

He pulled on a pair of fine leather gloves, released the brake on the wagon, and slapped the reins against the traces. They were halfway home before he looked down at her for several long moments, then answered. "Cordelia had nothing to do with this. The truth is, you've haunted me day and night since the morning I fetched you from the *Ompalada*. Damn, when Adele opened the cabin door and you were standing there staring at me like you had seen a ghost, you looked like an angel in that blue dress. Your eyes were shining. All I could think about was what a sod I was for wanting to bed a woman with the mind of a six-year-old." A sudden grin changed his seriousness to a teasing expression. "Then you opened your mouth."

When he remained silent, she started giggling, caught in the spell of his sparkling eyes as changing as the ocean currents. "That usually does it for most people. But did you ever stop to think maybe some part of your mind you're not conscious of was aware of the change?"

"No," he stated simply. "Something that deep would have required me to believe you in the library that evening when you told me what happened."

"But you didn't believe me, did you." She quickly dropped her gaze.

"No."

"Do you now?" She held her breath. So much of her future rested on his answer.

He considered the question carefully. "I'm not the kind of man who operates on blind faith, but I have been known to believe in divine revelation upon occasion. Accepting is the hard part." He cuddled her delicate shoulders and pulled her against him. "Be patient with me, Liss. I'm trying like hell to accept what I can't disbelieve."

She nodded, content for the moment. He was trying. That was more than she hoped for when she got up this morning.

He squeezed her shoulders as they neared the house. "You must have some questions. Given the abysmal way I've acted, you probably have a few doubts about spending the rest of your life with me. With your permission, I'd like to court you, Liss—until we're both sure we want this marriage."

"Neither one of us may live that long," she said softly.

He laughed. "Lord, I hope you're wrong. Celibacy is not only difficult, it's downright painful at times."

According to what she'd read and overheard at Hamilton Traders, the code of gentlemanly conduct was conveniently loose. Puzzled, her brow knit with a frown. "I thought sophisticated men of the 1860s took their pleasure . . ."

He halted the horses in front of the stable before turning slightly in the seat. "My word is my bond. When I signed the marriage papers, I was bound. It doesn't matter if the circumstances changed. I gave my word. You better know now, I don't believe in divorce. If we go forward, it's until one of us dies. So think about it long and hard, Felicity.

"I won't promise you love, but I do promise you protection, loyalty, respect, and fidelity. I'll be your friend, and I want you to be mine. If we're blessed with children, we'll raise them together. I understand a great deal after listening this afternoon. You have a rare quality: loyalty. If we go forward, I'd expect loyalty from you. And most important, I think you'd make one helluva mother.

"You wanted plain, direct talk; there it is, Liss. Now my cards are on the table, too. Think about your next bet before you raise the stakes or call the hand, all right?"

Emotion choked the words in her throat. Feeling as passionate as he did about the commitment both of them would be undertaking, she recalled his decision concerning a child not of his loins. How he must have struggled with the decision. That he considered it at all bespoke a chink in the granite wall of his self-assurance and the pragmatic nature of a fatalist. He wouldn't promise love, but he did promise honesty. All she could do was touch his face and nod. Why was this happening now when she was starting to question the stability of her mind?

For the next two weeks, Win accompanied Ransom on his daily excursions. She marveled at the speed of his recuperation and identified with the way he pushed himself. In the quiet moments of night, she delighted in his notion of courtship.

Instead of flowers, he brought her science books. Instead of candy, he found carpenters to finish her laboratory and library. And instead of a sailing sojourn, he arranged an afternoon with the apothecary, who had some interesting ideas of his own concerning drugs and treatments.

Always the perfect gentleman, he'd maintained a physical distance, not so much as indulging her with the kisses she craved. The surly barriers guarding his private self disappeared. The man she discovered confirmed Adele's proclamation that she was indeed fortunate he was her husband. This morning as Win had dressed, she knew she wanted the marriage. More than that, she wanted to be part of his life.

The squeak of Ransom's office door at Hamilton Traders drew her attention. She glanced up from behind the desk, expecting Ransom. Instead, Gerald approached.

"You're looking pleased with yourself this afternoon, Gerald. Did you stop by the house and visit with Adele already?"

"Not much escapes you, does it, Mrs. Hamilton?" Gerald settled into the chair across the desk from her.

"I wish that was true." She sat back in the oversized chair built for Ransom's dimensions and waited to hear the purpose of this rare social visit.

"First, I figure it's high time I apologized for doubting you when we brought Ransom home."

"You stood with me when it counted. I don't think I

thanked you for that. As for doubting my ability . . ." She shrugged and smiled. "So did I, and I know me. You had more reasons than any to question. You knew Arch. And you knew how it was in San Francisco." The implications of the drastic changes in Felicity's personality and abilities hung between them. "It was a lot to ask of you."

"Maybe. Caine trusted you. I trust Caine. Still, I shouldn't have threatened you," he continued.

"Forget it. I have." She stood and reached across the desk. "Friends?"

Gerald took her hand in both of his. "Friends, Mrs. Hamilton."

"My friends call me Felicity." The name came naturally to Win's lips.

When she saw him start to balk, she added, "At least in private, Gerald."

He nodded and sat when she did. "I'll be taking Adele as my wife before winter sets in. We're hoping that sits well with you. We aren't getting any younger and can't afford to waste any more time."

"I, ah, I may need her for a little while in San Francisco, depending on how some other plans work out. But I promise, I wouldn't keep her any longer than necessary and I'd make sure she had good accommodations back to Sitka." Just thinking about living so far away from Ransom twisted her heart.

"I see. When will you know?" he asked, thoughtfully rubbing his cleanly shaven chin.

"It isn't my decision alone." She spoke so softly he leaned forward.

"I see. Well, come what may, Adele and I are getting married in the fall and spending the winter together whether it be in Sitka or San Francisco. I hope you have no objections."

She managed a smile for his determination. "I don't think it would matter, would it? But no, I don't. And thank you."

He winked at her and rose as the office door crashed open.

"We got big trouble on the docks," Caine called out, then rushed off, shouting orders at the man behind the counter.

"I'm going with you," Win said, scurrying around the desk.

"You ought to stay here. Ransom . . ."

"Ransom can . . ."

"Ransom can what?" Ransom closed the distance from the opposite corner of the store. His cocked eyebrow served a warning she recognized instantly.

"Can take me with him," she continued without hesitation. "Or I'll go by myself."

"Damn, but you might try, too." Ransom took her hand and led her through the store.

"Where's your cane?"

"Got it," he said, snagging it from beside the door. "You will stay out the way, won't you?"

"Of course." She pulled her summer cloak around her to ward off the chill lingering from the storm.

The phaeton waited in the street. Without a word, Ransom handed her into the carriage, then hit the side with his cane. "I'll see you for dinner. Wait for me where it's safe."

Realizing he was sending her home, she started to stand up. The rocking of the carriage on the rutted road slammed her back into the seat. "You blew it, Ransom! You were doing so well with this courtship action, and now you blew it! I mean big time, too."

She turned to petition the driver. Seeing Caine holding the reins, she knew the futility of appeal. Ransom owned his loyalty. Besides, Caine would never intentionally incur Ransom's wrath. Only she tested and braved her husband's temper. Sitting back, she knew dinner might be an eventful affair after this little ruse.

Chapter 15

THE RUSSIAN FLAG and Baron Korinkov's crest fluttered in the breeze atop the *Nadia*'s main mast. The dock beside the whaler buzzed with Russian and American activity. Ivan introduced Ransom and the ship's captain, Uri Shemitov. The captain spoke Russian as his crew carried off the survivors of Ransom's whaler, the *Margaret Elizabeth*. Captain Shemitov visibly relaxed when Ransom responded in flawless Russian.

Ivan directed them away from the activity to a stack of new rope coils.

Captain Shemitov tamped tobacco into the bowl of his pipe. "We sighted the *Margaret Elizabeth* along the island chain. *Nadia,* she is a small vessel for a whaler, but quick. We had room for another kill," the captain explained in Russian, his restless eyes darting between his pipe, Ransom, and the baron.

"The *Margaret Elizabeth* had a whale. They were pulling her boats up when we saw her. Captain Fergeson and me, we bested each other many times. Ten years, we worked these waters. When I saw him, I shouted across the water. He shouted back." Captain Shemitov cast Ransom a sorrowful glance, cleared his throat, then lit his pipe. "All was well then."

Ransom held his silence, familiar with the rivalry and camaraderie among the proud American and Russian whalers.

"We made a kill the next morning. When we were secured, we made sail for Sitka. I thought to see the *Margaret Elizabeth* following the whales. We did not.

"We have our own work to do. Three days ago, we weathered a big storm. In the morning, our lookout spotted a dory in the current. I sent men to take them aboard.

"We laid on heavy sail and made for port," Captain Shemitov concluded, then drew heavily on his pipe. "We had to try to save them."

"Can you venture a guess on what sank her, Captain?" Ransom asked, sickened by the loss of so many men.

Shemitov shrugged and shook his head. "No. Fergie, he was good captain. Expert with the whales. He was the best for reading currents and weather. My lookouts saw no icebergs. No other ships.

"The *Margaret Elizabeth* sat well in the water when we last saw her. She had no time for another kill. We would have seen her. I am sorry, Mr. Hamilton. I do not guess the cause for the ship to go down." Shemitov shrugged hopelessly. "Perhaps one of her crew can tell you. If they live."

"Are you satisfied, Ransom?" Ivan asked, thoughtfully staring off at the *Nadia*.

"Yes." He extended his hand to Captain Shemitov. "Thank you, sir, for bringing the *Margaret Elizabeth*'s crew home so quickly. I realize it put a strain on your vessel and I'm in your debt."

Captain Shemitov shook Ransom's hand. "Fergie was a comrade at sea. He would do the same for my crew." He caught a nod of dismissal from Baron Korinkov and started to leave, then paused. "Mr. Hamilton, the whale boat had sooty marks on it, but she wasn't burned. If you find out what happened . . ."

"I'll let you know personally, Captain Shemitov. You can count on it," promised the baron. "A friend is hard to find and harder to lose."

The two men exchanged silent nods, then Captain Shemitov headed for his ship.

Ransom stared at the water. He trusted the old sea dog's instincts. Confirmation of the captain's muted suspicions lay with the *Margaret Elizabeth*'s survivors.

Ivan's words about friendship echoed in his mind. Fortunately, Ivan held the distinction of being one of the few men Ransom regarded as a trusted friend. The baron had a reputation for taking an enemy head-on, staring him in the eye, then unleashing a lethal arsenal intent on obliteration. Only in the political arena did Ivan Korinkov pick an opponent apart piece by niggling piece.

"I don't know what the hell's happening or why, Ivan. I've got two more damaged ships, both from suspicious causes. Hell, the *Estelle* had her main mast sawed halfway through. I'd call that sabotage, wouldn't you?"

No answer was expected, nor did Ivan offer one.

The losses of the last few of months hardened Ransom's already foreboding mien. Although the possibilities seemed endless, considering the attitude of the Russians and their possessiveness of Baranov Island in general and Sitka in particular, he couldn't find the culprit among the major traders. He counted several as friends and had amicable relationships with the rest.

Besides, for the last twelve years, the fur trade with China that created his business had diminished every year. The Russian government had closed the Chinese market to all their citizens. There was little genuine hostility or competition for whales and the fishing trade. Both were plentiful.

He pondered who might profit by causing him trouble, who he might have unknowingly slighted or offended to create such a ruthless, cunning enemy. And why? Without a doubt, his enemy was a dangerous man. He had already demonstrated how cheaply he held the lives of the *Margaret Elizabeth*'s crew. The questions nagged at him. If he knew why these things were happening, he might figure out the identity of the man behind them.

Given the targets and the ease of infiltrating the island's prosperous operations, he calculated the probability of the source of his trouble originating outside Sitka. An inner eye focused on Vance Gardener. All his instincts assured him of Gardener's involvement. This time of year, when everyone needed sailors, trappers, whalers, and tanners, made him vulnerable to an outsider with mayhem in mind.

"Who is after you, Ransom? Who wants to hurt you, to see you fail?" Ivan mused. "Is this Vance Gardener you suspect so powerful? So clever?"

"The only one I've eliminated is you," Ransom answered. "I have a few suspicions, but nothing I can rely on. As for Vance Gardener, he's capable of almost anything, but I don't understand what he'd gain by the deaths of so many. Nor can I imagine what would motivate him to do this. Remember, I didn't change my Seattle supplier until the night I left."

"Unless the deaths do not bother him, my friend, in which case he believes he has relieved you of yet another whaler at the height of the whaling season."

Ransom considered the possibility before responding. "You're right. But I'd trade the ship for the crew any time. Still . . . Gardener wouldn't have had time to find the *Margaret Elizabeth* . . . Unless he made his plans before then and knew . . ." Ransom shook his head. Although the logical conclusions sounded right, they felt wrong. "No one knows exactly where the whales run in advance."

Ransom shoved away from the rope coils and tried to shake the morose pall that dwelling on unanswered questions carried. "Let's see about moving the *Margaret Eliza-*

beth's survivors home, then you can join us for dinner, if you have no other plans."

The baron grinned in open amusement, having caught the little play in front of Hamilton Traders when Ransom sent Felicity packing. "She has changed you, Ransom. Maybe you think about her too much. It is a husband's duty to guide his wife in the ways of the world. But you indulge her and even encourage her to play a man's role at your trading store. Is her temper so severe you hate denying her anything or facing her alone?"

"Felicity?" He chuckled at the good-natured jibes. "She flashes but she doesn't stay angry. And she knows how I feel about her being down on the docks. The Hamilton Traders building is as much of a concession as I'm willing to make."

"I thought you were marrying her sister, Cassandra; or would you prefer I mind my own business?" Ivan asked guardedly, measuring his gait to Ransom's slower pace.

Ransom sighed and tried walking without the cane. "Originally that was my plan; however, things change. This may turn out better than what I anticipated with Cassandra. Felicity has an unexpected depth, spirit, grit . . ."

Ivan clapped him on the back. "Ah-h-h. I understand, my friend. The woman saved your leg—and your life. It is only natural that you have strong feelings about her. Of course, she is also a joy to the eyes, but I'm sure such a small thing would not influence you in the slightest."

They were nearly at Hamilton Traders when Ransom slowed further. "That doesn't have a damn thing to do with how I feel about her." The revelation surprised him, too.

Ivan chuckled, shaking his head. "I will not attempt to understand what is between you and your wife. Come. Let's check on your survivors. Perhaps we can get them home before dinner."

Three hours later, Ivan, Caine, and Gerald sat in the elegant dining room with the rest of the Hamilton household. Despite her best wheedling techniques, all Win learned about the *Margaret Elizabeth*'s survivors was that they were very ill and Ransom wanted them cared for at his home. He'd had the empty storage room off the kitchen cleaned and cots set up.

As soon as the men adjourned to the library for cigars and brandy, Cordelia rushed upstairs. She returned shortly with Win's medical journal and a satchel filled with the medicines Win had concocted for Ransom.

"If those men are to have a chance, you must help them, Felicity. Come along. There's no time to waste," Cordelia insisted.

"Cordelia, I don't know anything about treating them," Winifred protested.

"You seem to know what they don't need. 'Tis truly a miracle, this knowledge of yours, Felicity," Adele chimed in. "Dr. Branson arrived a short while ago. The first thing he'll be wanting ta do is bleed them. Should he be doin' that? Before, you said you wouldna bleed Mr. Ransom because . . ."

"Damn," Winifred seethed. Dr. Branson would kill all three men out of ignorance. "All right, you've convinced me."

Much to the women's relief, Dr. Branson and his assistant were just finishing a piece of Charlet's prized carrot cake and coffee in the kitchen.

"I understood that there were three survivors," Win inquired of the man inside the sickroom.

"Aye, ma'am, there were. One o' the men died shortly after we carried him off the *Nadia,*" the taller of the two guards explained.

"That narrows our efforts," Dr. Branson said, ignoring the women. "Jeffrey, bring around the washbowl from the stand near the stove. These men need to be bled."

"No, they do not," Win insisted. "Bleeding only increases the difficulty of overcoming their injuries. They need liquids. Lots of liquids. Rose hips tea. Vegetable broth. Liquids high in nutrients and vitamins."

"Mrs. Hamilton, is it your intention to take over my practice?" Dr. Branson asked icily.

"No, I'm not a trained physician, but there are some things I know that can help them. You can't bleed these men." Win approached the two survivors. Exposure and the battering they took from the hail didn't account for all their injuries.

"See those bruises, Mrs. Hamilton? That's bad blood. These men must be bled. Now, my patience is at an end. Please, leave and allow me to do my job," Dr. Branson insisted.

"I'll not let you bleed them." Winifred rose to the challenge, fortified by Adele's and Cordelia's presence beside her.

"And I'll not tolerate your constant interference. Your husband's company engaged my services for the welfare of these men. That is exactly what I intend."

"At the moment, you're the only American doctor in Sitka. Who else would he summon? But that doesn't make you competent. You would see to their welfare like you would have seen to Ransom's by unnecessarily cutting off his leg?" Cordelia demanded.

Branson bristled and eyed her coldly. "That might have been an error," he admitted quietly. "But he would have lived."

"He did live. With his leg," Cordelia pressed, genuinely angry at how close Ransom had come to losing his leg—and his life.

"Mrs. Hamilton, I have no desire to argue with you. Please, take your daughter-in-law into the parlor."

"No. If Felicity says these men won't be bled, they won't be. They are Hamilton men and this the home of the Hamiltons. If anyone goes, it'll be you, Dr. Branson," Cordelia countered, closing in on the man.

"You there, sitting at the table," Dr. Branson called into the kitchen. "Go get Mr. Hamilton." He retreated and nodded at his assistant. "He'll take his womenfolk out of our hair, Jeffrey."

When the guard left, Win started brewing several kinds of teas from leaves Spirit Dancer had given her and her own concoctions from her incomplete lab. She wished circumstances had not dictated this situation and another confrontation with Ransom so soon, but there seemed no way of avoiding it. If she left the men with Dr. Branson, he'd bleed them. The younger, blond man gasped shallow, ragged breaths.

"Let's get busy on this one," Dr. Branson told Jeffrey. "The other one won't see the rising sun."

"Now, you wait one minute," Cordelia started, insinuating herself between the patient and Dr. Branson. "You sent for my son. He'll be here in a moment. Why not wait until he arrives and hear what he wants done?"

"You're interfering with Dr. Branson. Get out of the way!" shouted Jeffrey as he pushed Cordelia, knocking her down. Cordelia's head hit the side of the door with a resounding thud. Still, Jeffrey continued advancing.

Adele screamed and covered her face with her hands.

Win darted toward Jeffrey. With a calculated kick, she sent him flying across the room and into the far wall. Redfaced, Win followed in hot pursuit. "How dare you touch my mother-in-law! How dare you inflict violence on her!"

A stunned Jeffrey stumbled, wide-eyed, and stared at her in disbelief. "You kicked me," he said incredulously. "You kicked me." Doubled over, he clutched at his chest.

"And I'll do it again if you don't leave immediately. You'd better hurry, because my husband will do more than kick you, you barbarian bully." She whirled around, her eyes snapping with anger. "Dr. Branson! Pack your bag and get out!"

Win knelt beside Cordelia. "Are you all right? Can you sit up if I help you?"

Dazed from the blow, Cordelia nodded. "I can't believe he knocked me down." Bewildered, she grasped Win's hands and allowed herself to be guided into the closest chair. "I-I'll be all right, Felicity. Maybe Adele can get me some water."

"Oh, yes ma'am," Adele said, eyeing Win with new respect.

In a flurry of curses, Dr. Branson snapped his bag closed and hastily departed through the back door with Jeffrey in tow.

Adele brought a pitcher of water and a cup for Cordelia. Next, Win sent her upstairs for laudanum.

Ransom and Ivan quietly entered the kitchen. "Felicity? You had to see for yourself, didn't you. What the hell happened this time?"

She ignored the question, affording only a glance at Cordelia. "I think we can save this man, Ransom. But not if Dr. Branson bleeds him. I know it's standard medical practice," Win continued, pleading her case more with her eyes and the words she didn't say. "But it's wrong. It weakens the patient. This man isn't strong enough to fight for his life with the injuries he has and try to make more blood. He needs liquids to help his body replace the blood he's lost and recover from dehydration."

Win dripped rose hips tea into the older man's mouth and massaged his throat to help him swallow.

Ransom nodded his assent, thereby closing the subject and further discussion.

"What's this Charlet said about someone hurting you, Mother?" He approached Cordelia and gently took her by the shoulders. When he saw the black and blue bruise forming above Cordelia's left eye, instant anger descended with a chilling tension that permeated the small room. "He's a dead man," Ransom seethed.

"No. Please, Ransom, I'm fine." She gripped his forearms with steely fingers. "Felicity took care of it," she whispered. "Leave it be. Please. All you can do now is raise questions you cannot answer and she refuses to."

Ivan slipped out of the room.

"Help me, Ransom," Win ordered from her patient's side, giving Ransom no time to think. "I need this man propped up into almost a sitting position so fluid won't fill his lungs. If he gets pneumonia, I doubt we can save him without a purer form of penicillin or some other broad-spectrum antibiotic."

"Can we get some of that in time?" Cordelia asked hopefully. She followed Ransom to the pallet and looked on anxiously.

Realizing she had spoken out loud, Win paled as her worried eyes darted from Ransom's angry gaze to Cordelia's concerned one, then back. "No," she said simply.

Cordelia nodded, accepting the curt answer. Ransom wouldn't be dismissed as easily. "Why not?" he whispered, his face inches from hers over the injured man. "We can buy . . ."

"I can make some, but it takes a hundred hours to cure. He'll be dead or recovered by then. What we need won't be invented for another seventy or eighty years. Penicillin didn't come onto the mass market until World War II in the 1940s," she answered in an urgent hiss.

"I shouldn't have asked."

"How will you get answers if you don't ask questions?"

"Forget it. I'll lift him. You put pillows behind him." He knelt beside the cot and lifted the unconscious man. "Damn, he's got a high fever."

"Yes, he does. I can't find any infected wounds or broken bones. His injuries must be internal." Win built a ramp of pillows and folded blankets to elevate her patient's head and torso.

"Where did Ivan go?" Cordelia asked.

Winifred shrugged, not caring for anything but her patients and the laudanum Adele handed to her. "I'm afraid Dr. Branson was right about this young man," Win whispered, kneeling down between Cordelia and the young blond man. "At least we can ease his suffering. Maybe he'll breathe easier, too."

Win dripped a laudanum and water mixture into his mouth. After several minutes, he quieted and breathed a little deeper. Cordelia squeezed Win's shoulder in a show of confidence.

Ivan returned a short while later accompanied by two men. "Tell them what to do, and they will do it, Mrs. Hamilton. Phillippe and Boris have taken care of many of my injured sailors."

The two young men gaped in wonder at Win, ignoring everyone else in the room.

"You see?" Ivan admonished them. "You see how small she is? How could a tiny woman like Mrs. Hamilton kick a man in the chest or send him across the room? The coward lied to lessen his own crime. Any man who strikes a woman has no decency and even less credibility. Believe your eyes, not that spawn of a slug."

His attention refocused on the incident with his mother, Ransom immediately started for the door.

Ivan gripped Ransom's shoulder and unleashed a barrage in Russian, which restrained Ransom. He switched to English and addressed Win. "Now, Mrs. Hamilton, if you please, tell Phillippe and Boris how you want these men cared for tonight."

Dark-haired Phillippe and sandy-haired Boris regarded her with wary brown eyes that never wavered as she explained their duties. After a moment, they relaxed and began asking questions about her methods.

Half an hour later, Ransom towered over her, effectively ending the treatment comparisons that could wait until tomorrow. "There will be two men stationed near the kitchen. If you have need for anything, ask, and they'll get it for you," Ransom assured them.

Win gazed into Ransom's unreadable eyes, wondering about his real feelings concerning her interference with Dr. Branson's patients. She battled down the incredible urge to stand on her tiptoes, reach up, and pull his head down until her lips touched his. She yearned for his hard body against hers just to make sure her midnight dreams were not exaggerated fantasies.

He said nothing, merely smiled, then left with Baron Korinkov. She suspected he had unfinished business to attend to before visiting his club with the baron.

"To a job well done," John Malcolm toasted, lifting his brandy glass toward Vance Gardener.

"Aye," Vance agreed less enthusiastically. "Sinkin' a ship is bad luck, John. I hope you know that. But sink her, we did—with the help of Mr. Carl Owens, late of San Francisco through Seattle." He tilted his beer stein against the fragile crystal in John's well-manicured hand.

Both men drank and settled into the comfortable parlor chairs close to the warmth of the small fire taking the chill from Vance Gardener's fashionable home.

"You're one convincing son of a bitch," John said, saluting Vance with his glass. "Owens must have believed you'd be there to pick him up."

"Aye. He did," Vance said, his bushy eyebrows drawn over his brown eyes in serious contemplation. "What do we do next?"

"Wait for the next door to open on opportunity. Hamilton is cautious now. He's been attacked personally, so he'll be careful. He'll select crews more judiciously."

They chuckled, knowing the folly of trying to check the history of a seaman who didn't want it known. It wasn't as though the trading companies could be choosy.

"We'll let him think he's safe for a while." John admired the shine on the toes of his new boots. "Eventually, it will be time for me to make my dear brother-in-law's acquaintance and oversee the welfare of my wife's sister—and her fortune."

Vance nodded thoughtfully. "I'd rather not sink any more ships. It's bad luck."

"Are you superstitious?" John asked in genuine interest.

"I was a man of the sea. We're all superstitious. If you

stay at sea long enough, you learn to accept the whims of the devil."

John regarded him, realizing that Vance embraced such silly superstitions. "All right. We'll refrain from sinking any more ships—unless we absolutely must."

"It ain't the ships, John. A murdered crew has been known to rise up from the depths. If you see them, you know you're going to die that day. They're the ones who don't rest easy until they give you a dose of bad luck."

"A quick mind can outmaneuver bad luck any day, Vance. Don't worry about it. We've got Hamilton on the defensive now. We'll let him think he's safe for a while."

"Aye," Vance agreed.

"Yes, my friend," John continued, his brown eyes twinkling with delight, "soon we'll have more money than we can spend in a lifetime."

Chapter 16

Restless, Winifred slipped out of bed and donned a heavy, modest wrapper. The night's activities and her concern for the two unconscious men in the kitchen storeroom kept her mind moving at a rapid pace. She decided to alleviate her concern by checking on the men and making some warm milk with honey to help her sleep.

Regardless of her pressing concern for the men's welfare, her thoughts strayed to Ransom. What was wrong with her, anyway? Here she was, allowing some chauvinist man to determine her future. Worse, she placidly bided her time while he reached a decision.

Padding silently down the steps, she grimaced at the darkness beyond the halo of her small candle. What would Alexis say if she knew?

She'd say, "You're in big trouble, girl. Get a grip on yourself and get a life!" Win nearly laughed aloud, while stoking the firebox embers in the kitchen stove. The pieces of dry kindling she added caught fire quickly.

"Would you men like a pot of coffee?" she asked the four

covertly watching her from various parts of the kitchen and sickroom.

"Yes, ma'am," answered one of the guards.

She went about fixing it, then checked the concoctions steeping on the back of the stove before setting the milk on to warm.

"I am very worried about this one." Boris spoke slowly in precise English from beside the young man's cot. "It pains him to breathe."

Win stroked the young man's forehead, saddened by the loss of years he'd never know. "Give him as much laudanum as you think he can stand," she answered, meeting Boris's inquisitive brown eyes. "If we can't save him, for God's sake the least we can do is ease his dying."

Understanding flickered at the corners of Boris's mouth. In that moment, he appeared as young as his charge. "Yah, Mrs. Hamilton. We can do that."

She checked with Phillippe, who was more encouraged by his charge's condition. "If he makes it through the night, he may live," the young Russian told her. "I think you are right. No bleeding. Give liquids. Much liquids."

"There should be enough on the stove to last the night. I'll be down in the morning and show you how to make them, if you like."

"Oh, yah. I would like," Phillippe answered, exchanging nods with Boris. "We both like."

Assured there was nothing more she could do at the moment, she poured the milk and checked the progress of the coffee. Upon leaving the kitchen, her thoughts returned to Ransom.

In truth, somewhere along the line, she'd fallen into the trap dooming women since the beginning of time. She had started caring about the man. She stopped short, rocked by the realization. Warm milk sloshed over the lip of the cup. It was true. She loved him. Why else would she let him surround her with uncertainty?

The only thing worse than Ransom owning her heart would be the devastation of his rejection. Despair-laced fear shot up from her toes, leaving an oppressive wake that held her in place on the stairs. What a consummate disaster.

Her vision shimmered at the thought of Ransom turning his back on her. Lord, she couldn't bear his nearness without knowing the fullness of the promise he radiated. Even if he freed himself with an annulment, she'd never be free of him. He'd haunt her dreams and fill her fantasies despite the futility of making them real.

Dismally, she realized his rejection meant the loss of hope. The slender thread at which she dangled on the bottom and he held at the top, twitched and danced. When he dropped it, she'd fall into a lonely, inescapable pit.

What else could she expect? Why wouldn't he want his freedom? He'd never chosen her as a wife. She wasn't Cassandra. The crushing depression of facing the future without him made her knees weak. She drew a steadying breath designed to cleanse the dark thoughts from her mind.

Forget pride, she told herself. Forget holding the upper hand and hiding her emotions for fear of being hurt. If he rejected her, it would hurt. But to hell with this silent suffering and uncertainty! She had to know where she stood. She needed to hear him reject her. Then she'd leave. Forever. She didn't think she could bear seeing him afterward.

On the other hand, maybe, just maybe, he wouldn't reject her. He had said he couldn't promise love. He didn't say he *wouldn't* or *couldn't* love her. Maybe he would . . . eventually. In time, he might love her. Maybe a little bit? Stranger things happened.

If the universe embraced all things as possible, maybe Ransom would love her someday. Maybe . . .

"Ah, hope dies hard in some of us fools, Alexis. That's why I let him call the shots, and pray he chooses me. I know I'll never be first in his affections. Cassandra is. But maybe second won't be so bad. Surely it will be better than having no part of him," she whispered.

How much she had changed since arriving in Sitka! She'd never willingly settled for second before. And she wasn't settling now. Not exactly. If he chose a real marriage with her, she'd be the only woman in his bed. He'd promised fidelity and he was a man of his word.

Heavyhearted, unconvinced by her last stab at optimism, she climbed the stairs. As she turned down the hall toward her room, she saw light streaming through Ransom's open door. Drawn by an irresistible power, she paused at the threshold. Her heart beat a little faster with the daring of her trespass.

Ransom closed the chiffonier. As though sensing her presence, he turned. Standing motionless in his close-fitting trousers and half-opened shirt, he studied her for several long minutes.

A sea of doubt battered the fragile shores of hope. Being so close, yet so far away from the man she loved heightened the fear of being rejected. How would she endure the years of wanting and loving him, and never seeing him again?

He crossed the room in half a dozen deliberate strides, then stood before her. Waiting.

What felt like a wad of cotton in her throat kept her mute. Her trembling fingers tightened around the mug to keep the contents from spilling.

"Liss," he whispered, his voice resonant with soulful longing. The untempered need shining in his aquamarine eyes nearly stole her breath.

One by one, he unwrapped her fingers from the heavy cup. His gaze never left her face as he placed the mug on the corner of a table. He extended his hand to her.

Heart quickening in excitement, her gaze roamed from his hand to his inviting eyes, then back. The fear of rejection splintered like a shattered glass. If she accepted, the marriage became real. He would be hers.

Hardly believing the anguish she'd endured moments earlier was all for naught, she blinked. He was still there, offering everything she wanted. Slowly, she lifted her hand

and placed it in his, amazed by the contrasts of large and small, callused and smooth. His eyes drew hers as he raised her fingers to his lips. Holding his gaze and captivated by the emotions playing across his expressive features, she watched in warm fascination as he kissed each knuckle slowly before turning her hand over and sensuously kissing her open palm.

"Are you sure, Liss?"

"Yes. Are you?"

"Yes."

"I'm not Cassandra."

He smiled, his eyes twinkling with a secret delight. "No. You definitely are not Cassandra." He kissed the back of her hand, then turned it over and traced her open palm with the tip of his tongue, savoring every line and crease. Each touch, each movement, inflamed the need for an indefinable something blossoming inside her.

"Liss?"

"Hm-m-m-m?" The spell he wove snared her in a web of delicious heat.

"I'm not Larry Bird, either."

She stopped breathing.

He regarded her from under an arched brow.

"Oh, no, Ransom," she said sincerely, a playful smile tugging at the corners of her pink lips. "You're not a young Larry Bird." The smile faded as her eyes widened. "You—you're real." Then Ransom did something with his tongue and she forgot all about the mock fantasy she'd conjured in the library.

Erotic sensations shot up her arm and lodged in her tingling breasts and tightening abdomen, leaving her speechless and hungry for more. Unconsciously, she licked her lower lip, wishing it was her mouth instead of her hand enjoying the intimate touch of his lips and the silken feel of his mustache on her skin.

Slowly, allowing her plenty of time to change her mind, he removed the cotton wrapper and revealed her sheer lawn nightgown. Win remained motionless, wallowing in the sensuous spell he cast with a look, a touch. In a single, fluid motion, Ransom swept her up and kicked the door shut.

Eyes squeezed shut, Win locked her arms around his neck, afraid he might drop her. Then he was holding her with one arm, relying on her iron grip to secure her against him.

With a small cry of protest, she pressed herself into his shoulder. Some part of her mind still disbelieved her small proportions.

"I won't let you fall, Liss." His arms embraced her again and she breathed a little easier. "Open your eyes. Look at me."

Reluctantly, she obeyed, her heart hammering with anxiety.

"I'd never let you fall. I'll never hurt you or allow you to be hurt if I can prevent it."

The honesty shining in his eyes made her believe him. She managed a slight nod and eased the death grip on his neck.

"Kiss me," Ransom ordered, his voice husky, his head lowering.

She met his mouth, knowing they were beyond the point of turning back, her fear of falling forgotten.

The slight trembling she felt against her body uncurled a familiar heat. Ransom's kiss ignited the embers of desire glowing in her heart. Awed by the flood of passion sweeping through her, she whispered his name.

His lips closed on hers again. This time his tongue darted into her mouth for an intimate taste.

Any further words caught in her throat with a quick intake of breath. The gliding caress of his tongue along the inside of her lips enthralled her. Though his touch was as gentle as a hummingbird's wing, she sensed the banked heat of his rapacious desire.

His tender kiss flared passionately. The surge of need it evoked tightened her embrace. She gave way to it, then gradually tempered the tide when he gentled the tempo of the kiss.

"Touch me," he whispered against her mouth. As he lowered her legs to the bed so she knelt against him, his hard contours inflamed her sensitive body.

With uncertain hands, she slipped the last few buttons of his shirt, ever so careful not to brush his skin with her fingers, but only skim the black, silken hair glistening in the lamplight. "I want to touch you everywhere, Ransom, all at once. I want to feel your skin against mine, and know the beat of your heart against my breast. I want to feel all the places where you're hard and I'm soft. I want to learn every freckle and mark on your body and all the places in between."

The heavy rise and fall of his chest as his breathing quickened should have warned her how close to the edge of control he skated. She eased the shirt down his left arm, then removed it from his right.

When she looked up, his long, black eyelashes rested on his cheeks. Perspiration beaded his forehead. She ran splayed fingers up his chest, savoring the hot, smooth textures of his skin, burying them in the thick mat of silky hair, then paused, uncertain when he didn't open his eyes. Her fingertips moved back and forth over the hardening nub of his nipple. The patterns of silken hair across the breadth of his chest were marvelously intriguing. Touching his naked skin heightened the exquisite pleasure vibrating through her.

A tremor rippled under his skin. She rested her forehead against his chest, then turned slightly and kissed his bare skin. "You are magnificent, Ransom." Her breath was a heated whisper against his chest.

Her timid tongue caressed his skin, sampling the male taste of him and exploring the changing textures. He groaned; his whole body tensed in response.

She stiffened, startled, when he grabbed the back of her nighgown and tore it in half, then pressed her smooth body against his chest for a long moment, neither moving nor allowing her to move. Part of her would be content to hold him like this for the rest of her life.

Slowly, his hand slid into her loosely braided hair. In seconds the long tresses flowed in a golden-brown glory down her back and tickled at her waist. She met his glittering aqua gaze and let him slide the tattered nighgown from her arms. It joined his shirt on the floor.

His hands felt hot on her neck and cheeks as he tipped her face upward. His mouth descended on her parted lips. The delicious feel of his explorations fueled the fire raging inside her.

His tongue grew more insistent, prowling the edges of her mouth thoroughly before delving into the hot darkness beyond. The rhythmic pulse of his tongue sliding in and out of her mouth was an erotic promise she eagerly accepted. She clung to his shoulders, feeling her world change as he lowered her onto the bed. His powerful body covered but did not crush her as he rolled them onto their sides before breaking the kiss.

A small sound of disappointment escaped Win. Never had she imagined the tumult, the tenderness, or the physical yearning that sweetly assaulted her senses. Her hands curled in his dark hair and drew his mouth down. The desperate search of her tongue for his made him wild. He kissed her deeply, drawing her into him as he rocked her against his arousal. Her fervent response wrung a groan from him and he pulled her even closer. *Oh, yes,* her heart cried out, longing to be one with him, to know the glory of the promise he made with his body.

When he began to break the kiss, her arms flew around his neck and held him while their tongues engaged in a sensual duel. He rolled her on top of him. The delicious pressure of her full breasts against his chest sent her squirming.

Slowly, sensuously, he consumed her with his heated forays along the fullness of her breasts arching into his chest, over her ribs, and into the valley of her narrow waist, down along the flowing swell of her hips. He filled his hands with her buttocks, squeezing, molding them in a delicious rhythm to his pulsing hips. The sensations colliding in all her sensitive, secret places left her lost in the kiss. Each touch fueled the pagan she was becoming, clamoring for more carnal delights even as she relished and savored every new impression. Her heart swelled with love for the acceptance he tenderly showered. He wanted her for tonight, tomorrow, and forever.

Winifred relinquished his mouth and pushed back to look into his eyes, then trembled at what she saw. Without a word, she sat on her heels and began unfastening his trousers. All the while, her trusting eyes never left his. Only the sounds of their ragged breathing broke the silence. She slid his trousers down far enough for him to kick them off.

Finally, she snapped the invisible tether holding her gaze and regarded his body in open admiration and blatant yearning. She laid her palms on his chest. The thunder of his powerful heart and the fire of desire beneath the shiny pelt of hair and passion-heated skin made her hands tingle. She traced the pattern of his hair where it narrowed on his flat belly, following it to his fully aroused sex.

She blinked, realizing how large his erection had grown and how small she was. Sure her eyes played tricks on her, she ran the tip of her index finger down the length of him, then lower, over the twin sacs of his manhood.

The sharp intake of breath hissing through Ransom's teeth drew her attention. "Did I hurt you?"

"You're killin' me, Liss," came his raspy reply. Lightning quick, he pulled her down beside him and covered her mouth with a sense-stealing kiss that betrayed his voracious need. The intensity might have frightened her had her own hunger been less. She needed him in far more than a physical sense. Only by loving him fully could she hope to gain his affection. And she wanted all of him in every sense.

A trail of tender tickles from his mustache, lips, and tongue moved along her cheek. Her head arched back, exposing the tender skin ahead of the path he traveled. He nibbled and nipped her earlobe. Lord, how his kiss inflamed her everywhere he touched! The amorous journey continued around her slender neck to the hollow at her throat where her pulse beat a strong, fast tattoo. His lips left fiery trails on her skin, his breath a steam that cooled her when it touched.

The heavenly experience of his hands on her breasts and his mouth at her throat hurled Win into a whirlwind. Unbidden, her back arched and her pebble-hard nipples rose in anticipation. The shards of pleasure his fingers and thumbs created with her nipples set her squirming from the heat searing her womanhood. When his mouth unexpectedly claimed her breast, the sensation became so overwhelming she cried his name in ecstasy.

He tasted the other breast, then held both in his hands, teasing, tickling the nipples with his mustache, grinning in delight of her uninhibited response. His fingertips closed on the pink flesh and distended nipples. With deliberate slowness he rolled the silky flesh and hardened nipples lightly, tugging sensuously and matching the rhythm of the sinuous movement of his erection against her thigh. Win thought she was very close to heaven, yet her body screamed there was more.

"My God, you're responsive," he breathed, then suckled her again. "You're like liquid fire. You burn so sweetly."

Her fingers dug into his thick raven hair, urging him toward her upthrust breast. "Don't stop, Ransom. Please."

"Not if my life depended on it," he hissed, then captured a tantalizing pink crest and drew it into the moist heat of his mouth for a moment. "I need to be inside you more than I need to breathe," he rasped. His hand followed the contour of her soft belly, lingering at her sensitive navel, before exploring the lush auburn curls protecting her womanhood.

Feeling him at the door of her most intimate place gave her pause. She met his smoldering gaze and relaxed, trusting him. His fingers tenderly parted the tight, velvet petals of her flesh, opening her for his intimate touch. The delicious promise tested her mercilessly.

With a keening cry of pleasure, Win writhed under his caress. The strain coiled in her threatened to erupt and scatter her in all directions. Needing the anchor of his hot flesh, her hands took on a life of their own. The hard sinew of his shoulders rippled under her fingers. The fine sheen of perspiration coating his body let her hands glide over the hard ridges and hollows in his back and onto the flare of his tight buttocks, where she dug her fingers into his flesh, wanting him closer.

The way his fingers teased, lingered, then teased again, revealed the marvelous delights of his masterful touch and the depth of her desire for him. The inexplicable need building inside her grew until she thought she might scream.

"Oh, yes. Give in to it," he murmured.

As soon as she did, a sudden surge of pleasure shot through her being.

She cried out when he abandoned her breast, then met him greedily when he claimed her mouth in a hungry kiss. The kiss was deep and powerful. The urgency of their rhythm and mutual need to join grew stronger with each frantic heartbeat.

The fire he created sent her hips undulating against his hand, seeking something else, something more. He slipped a finger inside her moist, hot femininity and groaned at her tightness.

Tiny contractions grew stronger as he slipped a second finger in and pressed deeper until encountering the barrier of her maidenhead. He moved between her thighs, spreading them wider, and guided himself to the edge of her womanhood. Only then did he stop kissing her and draw back. Supporting the bulk of his weight on his elbows, she felt the luscious pressure of his entry into her tight, moist passage. She whimpered, disappointed when he deliberately and reluctantly withdrew from the promise of paradise.

"It will hurt the first time." He swept a damp tendril of hair from her cheek with the back of his hand.

"I'm afraid it will hurt more if you don't do this . . .

soon," she panted. The slow, sensual glide of her hands down his ribs to his hips, and the pull corresponding with her upthrusting hips conveyed her demand. He penetrated the depth of her woman's heart in one swift motion, then held still while she adjusted to the invasion.

"Are you all right?" he asked.

Her eyes remained closed for a long minute as the only reaction she allowed for the loss of her maidenhead. He was hers in a oneness that filled her body and sent her heart singing with joy. When she opened her eyes, she saw his concern, then smiled. "I need you . . . I need you to . . . make this feeling inside me go away." The violence of the hunger passing over Ransom's face promised he understood.

"Liss . . ." He moved slowly, nearly withdrawing before penetrating deeply again and again. She burned for him, growing hotter as he fueled her fire. Passion drove her hips upward, demanding more.

In the frenzy of desire, the pace quickened, each questing for fulfillment, their gazes never wavering.

"Wrap your legs around my waist," he told her.

She obeyed, then drew a ragged breath. "God . . ." she breathed, reveling in the sensations he created by moving his hips in small, quick circles, moving deeper and faster into the core of her with every stroke.

"Ransom!" she cried out, feeling the irrevocable building of something so powerful she couldn't stop it.

"Don't fight it. Ride it! You're mine!" He plunged into her, giving her all of him, finding the depth of her. Each time she took all he gave and drew even tighter around him. The deep strokes carried them ever closer to the pinnacle of paradise.

"Now, Liss! Now!" he ground out between clenched teeth. Again, he plunged deeply into her. Her incoherent cry shattered them both. Wrapping his big hands over the tops of her small shoulders, he braced her as he wildly drove into her once more, calling her name when he poured his seed into her womb.

Winifred held Ransom tightly, never wanting to let him go. The afterquakes of her release left her dazed. In her wildest fantasies, she'd never imagined anything so beautiful that it shone in every cell in her body.

After an indeterminable time, Ransom rolled them onto their sides and kissed her tenderly.

Win kissed his shoulder. "I had no idea people practiced such self-discipline on so grand a scale." Fingering away a lock of damp hair dangling over his left eye, she smiled.

"What do you mean?"

"I'd live in bed with you until neither one of us could walk, if you were agreeable." Her smile faded and her hand stilled. "I had no idea I could feel so . . ." Lost for words, she shrugged.

"I know," he answered softly. "Very few people are fortunate enough to experience what we did tonight. I can't explain it, but I know it's true."

"You mean, it was a fluke? An aberration?" Her eyes widened with uncertainty.

He grinned, already hardening inside her. "Would you like to try it again and see?"

She grinned back, then laughed lightly. "Want some candy, big boy?"

"Yes," he answered, burying his hands in her hair and drawing her mouth closer. "I want everything."

Chapter 17

Humming "Sweet Mystery of Life" and recalling Madeline Kahn's drastic change in *Young Frankenstein,* Win skipped down the stairs. Nothing in any century rivaled the magic she and Ransom had created last night. The couple of hours of sleep she caught after dawn more than vanquished her weariness. Today, she was too happy to be tired.

Earlier, Ransom had awakened her with gentle, intimate loveplay that quickly blossomed into raging passion.

Content and smiling, she had snuggled deep in the quilts when he abandoned their bed. She had dozed until a tub of deliciously hot water was ready in the bathing room. Fresh towels and soap had awaited her beside the steaming tub. Not until she sank into the lilac-scented water had she discovered how tender their lovemaking had left her.

Win entered the dining room where Cordelia sipped a steaming cup of chocolate. A familiar motion brought Meggie with an additional cup of chocolate and pastries.

"You look well this morning, Felicity," Cordelia said knowingly. "It's been years since I've seen Ransom so cheerful in the morning. I trust the two of you reached an agreement?"

An agreement? While not all their differences were settled, they had found a satisfying, common ground on a physical plane. It would have to be enough to begin their marriage. There was no undoing last night. Nor did Win wish to. Regardless of what the future held, she'd never regret the spontaneous passion that consumed them.

"It seems we have—for the time being," Win answered carefully. The aroma of the hot chocolate made her mouth water. The night's activity sparked her appetite.

Win blushed under the knowing sweep of Cordelia's wise green eyes. They had forged a tenuous bond since the crisis of Ransom's fever when his life hung by a thread. At times, Winifred deemed her an ally. Then some unguarded word or unplanned event changed Cordelia's demeanor and made Win wonder exactly where she stood with her mother-in-law.

"He won't be able to set you aside easily," Cordelia continued.

"You mean an annulment?" Win selected a pastry from the silver platter sitting between her and Cordelia.

"Among other things."

Win wondered which role Cordelia played today: ally or adversary. "No, Cordelia. There can't be an annulment. We each made our choice in that regard last night." She sipped at her chocolate, wishing for eggs, hash browns, toast, and ham instead of fruit-filled pastry and baked apples.

Cordelia inclined her head with the trace of a smile turning the corners of her mouth. "He allowed you a say?"

"Of course. Why wouldn't he?" She selected a baked apple and placed it on her plate.

Cordelia's pleasant laughter lilted through the dining room. She clasped her hands together and rubbed her palms back and forth.

"What do you find so amusing?" Win bit back the urge to join the infectious mirth.

"I'm delighted he allowed you a say."

"Well, I don't see where he had a choice. I mean . . ."

Again, Cordelia's contagious laughter rang out. She pushed away from the table and regarded Win through tear-sparkling eyes. The merriment gave her the appearance of a much younger woman. "You have a great deal to learn, Felicity."

"I don't doubt that for a moment." Win speared a piece of cinnamon baked apple with her fork.

Cordelia allowed her to eat before continuing. "He didn't have to give you a say, Felicity. Very, very few husbands allow their wives a voice in anything."

Win speared a second apple as she weighed this new bit of information. "Other than the fact I didn't give him the choice of excluding my opinion, why do you think he allowed me to have a say?"

"I was hoping you'd tell me. Ransom is not a hard man, though he gives the appearance of being so. Is he in love with you?"

The soft hope lacing the question surprised Win. She met Cordelia's optimistic gaze, then shook her head. According to the romance novel, people seldom married for love during the 1800s. Many marriages were arranged like twentieth-century mergers, like the one Ransom thought he had with Cassandra. It seemed an insensitive but widely accepted practice.

Her eyes narrowed in contemplation on Cordelia.

Arch Forsythe had allowed Cassandra her own choices. She had chosen John Malcolm rather than wait for Ransom. But Arch took care of Felicity, too, in a manner that altered Ransom's choices and his future.

"Maybe he didn't like not having a say in the way Arch Forsythe arranged things. Maybe he didn't like having someone else determine his future and make crucial decisions that changed his life without asking his opinion," Win said slowly. "Until I drowned, or almost drowned, there hadn't been a lot of choices . . ." Her words faded into silent thoughts.

"Please, Felicity, tell me what happened on the dock." Cordelia's green eyes sparkled with a plea for understanding.

Her sincerity touched Win and she almost answered her out of reflex. At the last instant, she shook her head regretfully. "I don't really know. I agree with Adele. It was a miracle. There is no scientific explanation."

Cordelia leaned forward. "There. You use terms like 'scientific explanation' that Felicity wouldn't have known. That room of yours with its beakers and those chemistry books go beyond the bounds of eccentricity. You know what you're doing in there. You *know* things. I can't believe Ransom pulled you out of the water and you not only recovered from a brain injury the doctors said was irreversible, but you ended up knowing things none of us do. Yet, for all your wisdom, you lack the knowledge of the basic rules of social conduct. Reconciling those differences is very difficult."

Cordelia's candid assessment commanded Win's full attention. Heart beating a little faster with mounting anxiety and breakfast turning into a lump in her stomach, she regarded Cordelia for a long, silent minute. "Don't stop now, Cordelia. If you've given it this much consideration, you must have an opinion. I'd like to hear it."

"Oh, I would so like to hear *your* explanation, Felicity."

Winifred held Cordelia's gaze as her heart skipped a beat. "Believe me when I tell you, Adele has aptly termed it a miracle and she is correct."

"You can trust me, Felicity." Sincerity blazed in Cordelia's green eyes. "Who are you?"

"Who do I appear to be?"

"We both know you are not who you appear to be. Are you a mirror relative? Someone identical in appearance?"

"No," Win whispered. "I am Felicity Hamilton and that's who I will be for as long as I live." This time, she believed it, too. Lately, she thought of herself often as Felicity, perhaps because that was what everyone called her.

"Were you someone else? I mean . . . I don't know what I mean, but . . ." Confused, Cordelia shook her head.

Win straightened her shoulders. "Cordelia, anything I say about the past I remember can only pose a burden to those who know. I won't place that burden on your shoulders."

The reluctance playing across Cordelia's face made Win relax further. An impasse was far better than speculation in this case. The older woman averted her eyes in acceptance.

Relief swept though Winifred. "I need to check on the *Margaret Elizabeth*'s survivors. Come with me?" Besides wanting Cordelia's company, the suggestion was the best peace offering she could think of at the moment.

Cordelia smiled tightly as she rose. "Yes. I'm sure Phillippe and Boris would like to be relieved. I made sure they had a full breakfast earlier."

The young blond sailor had died shortly after sunrise. Boris had overseen the removal of his body before the household awakened. The two shipmates would be buried later in the day. Win turned her attentions on the last and eldest of the three men.

The care from the Russians had brought his fever down, but all efforts to rouse him were futile.

"What's wrong with him?" Cordelia wondered aloud as she bent over him.

"I think he's in a coma." Win brewed more tea from her nearly depleted supply of leaves and herbs. Soon, she'd visit Spirit Dancer and replenish her cache.

"How do we get him out of it?"

Sinking onto the edge of the chair, Win massaged her temples. Didn't she know something about comas? Weren't comas caused by a chemical imbalance? Or was that depression? Damn. She should know.

Cold dread knotted her stomach. How could she forget such basic stuff? How did she know it was basic? Little pieces of her memory faded in and out when her attention focused elsewhere.

She couldn't dwell on it now. Then she heard herself answering Cordelia. "He has to bring himself out of it. It will help if we talk to him. He might even remember some of what we say when he wakes up."

The coil of fear around her heart loosened. The answers still breathed in her memory. Her thoughts had been so filled with the daily routine of this foreign place she now called home, she must have merely put aside that part of her knowledge.

"Since we don't know him, why don't we read to him," she suggested. "Does anyone know if he speaks English?"

"Who?" Ransom asked as he entered the sickroom, his sparkling gaze devouring his wife. He was dressed in knee-high heavy boots, close-fitting pants, and a warm blue flannel shirt open at the neck. A tuft of the silken thatch patterned on his chest peeked through the open vee of his shirt beneath a soft deerskin jacket.

"Our patient," Cordelia answered, watching her son shower his wife with his complete attention.

"His name is Patrick Feeny and he speaks English with a bit of an Irish lilt," Ransom answered. "Come." He held out his hand.

Drawn like a moth to a flame, Winifred placed her hand in his and accompanied him into the library. He closed the doors behind them.

"Kiss me," she whispered when he stood so close his warm breath caressed her hair. She tilted her face toward him. Excitement mingling with sweet anticipation flowed through her.

Ransom inclined his head and kissed her chastely once. Twice. A third time, slower, leisurely. A fourth time, tasting the slightly parted seam of her lips with the tip of his tongue.

"Ransom—" She slipped her arms around his neck and molded her body against his.

Her plea was all the encouragement he needed. He re-

warded her with a groan and a searing, fiery kiss that left no
doubt what he wanted to do with the erection straining his
pants and throbbing against her belly.

When the kiss ended, she held him, weak-kneed and
shaking. "It scares me." Her cheek slid over the soft flannel
shirt covering his chest. How quickly her entire body responded to him. Even now, her heart beat frantically and her
arms and legs tingled with expectation.

"What scares you enough to make you tremble, Liss?"

"I didn't think I'd ever want you as badly as I did last
night."

She felt his heart accelerate against her cheek as though
he, too, was remembering their passion.

"And?" he prompted when she did not continue.

She gazed up into his smiling aquamarine eyes and almost forgot what she was saying. "And . . . and I want you
more right now than I did then. When does it go away?"

"Hopefully, never." He kissed her again.

It seemed months instead of mere hours since they last
made love. A voracious hunger to touch, feel, and explore
claimed her reason. Her unbridled desire and lack of restraint fueled the heady sensation as she found his lips.

Breathing raggedly, he broke the kiss and tucked her
head against his chest. "If we don't stop now, Liss, I swear
I'll lift your skirts and take you right here, and to hell with
anyone who happens through those doors."

She pressed her cheek against him, feeling a trembling,
not sure if it was him, her, or both of them. "If you don't
think discovery would be considered an unforgivable breech
of etiquette or cause scandalous gossip in the elite social
strata, I'd love to accommodate you," she said shakily. "I'm
always glad to perform my wifely responsibilities, you
know."

Ransom's laughter rumbled deep in his chest. "A regular
paragon of wifely virtue, aren't you?"

She peeked up at him through the curtain of heavy lashes,
and whispered, "I try." She gave him her most innocent ex-

pression so he wouldn't notice her hand move until she ran her fingernails up the length of his erection.

The sharp, hissing intake of a breath vanquished his laughter. "Maybe we should consider tending your patient." Ransom's powerful fingers closed on her tiny wrist and drew it up to his chest.

"Which patient?" An impish smile flirted across her kiss-swollen lips.

"If I take you upstairs, Liss, we won't be down until tomorrow. That's a promise."

A shiver of excitement heated her. She drew a long, deep breath, clearing her head. She had never thought herself capable of such brazen behavior. But then, she had never wanted anything the way she wanted Ransom touching her, holding her, loving her . . . making love with her.

The library door opened. "Bull recommended a book called *Moby-Dick*. I believe I saw it in here," Cordelia said cheerfully, ignoring the suggestion of impropriety at the desk. "He said it's about a whale. I hope it has a happy ending."

Ransom's warm lips grazed over Win's forehead with a promise. "I'll be home for dinner. And I'll want to retire very early."

His expression made her wonder just what was on the menu.

"Caine brought over the books, receipts, and invoices from the shipyard. They're in a stack beside the desk. If you have the time and inclination to do them, fine. If not, Caine or I will," he said from the library doorway.

He afforded Cordelia a glance, then shook his head. "I don't think *Moby-Dick* is appropriate, Cordelia. There's a copy of *The House of the Seven Gables* in the bookcase beside the turret."

Win lingered for a few moments after Ransom and Cordelia departed the library. "What is happening to me?" she whispered. Never had she lost control of herself or a situation to the extent she just had with Ransom. Had he not stopped them, she might have let him take her without considering who might see them. Shaking herself, she bit her bottom lip and sauntered away from the desk. Gradually, the color in her cheeks faded, but the sting of disbelief for her lack of self-control persisted. No one, absolutely no one, had ever affected her the way Ransom did. Never had she allowed anyone that much control over her in any form. Yet she could hardly wait for the next time they were alone.

The air in the room cooled perceptibly. She glanced around, feeling a familiar presence. "Joey?" she whispered, turning in a circle. Some of her agitation faded. As long as she had Joey, she had an anchor.

Fortified, she returned to the sickroom.

As she gazed at the pallid features of the unconscious man, the frailty of life struck her anew. The new life she led in this time was a gift, one to be lived to the fullest. She would fill her days—and her nights—with Ransom. He made her feel vital in a way she had never dreamed possible. He made her feel feminine and beautiful inside and out. Being so electrifyingly alive was addictive.

This emotional part of her life hadn't existed before Sitka. The marvelous colors Ransom showed her last night and this morning awed her with their soul-stirring beauty. Lord, how she loved him.

Chapter 18

Ransom and Winifred entered the converted sickroom off the kitchen. Attended by Phillippe, Patrick Feeny rested in a propped position on his cot. The sailor sipped broth from a floral-patterned china cup cradled in his callused, shaky hands. Bruises in various stages of discoloration and swelling gave his skin a mottled texture. His blue eyes widened and his sipping halted self-consciously at the sight of Winifred.

Ransom seated Win, who smiled in approval at Phillippe and Boris, then took a stand behind her beside Baron Korinkov. "Are you in any pain, Mr. Feeny?"

"No, sir, not exactly, so long as I don't breathe too deep," Patrick Feeny answered, touching his ribs gingerly. "I'll not be fit for haulin' much sail for a couple o' days."

"I'll fix something for your discomfort after we've finished talking, Mr. Feeny. It will make you sleep, too," Win promised.

Patrick Feeny shrugged his uncertainty. "At least when I'm hurtin' I'm knowin' I'm alive, Mrs. Hamilton."

Ransom met the injured man's gaze and nodded knowingly. In a calm, captivating bass tone, he told Feeny of Captain Uri Shemitov and the *Nadia*'s role in his rescue, then introduced Baron Korinkov. "Are you up to telling us what happened on the *Margaret Elizabeth*?" Ransom asked softly.

Blue eyes measured each of the listeners. "I was first mate on the *Margaret Elizabeth,* Mr. Hamilton," the sailor said with a hint of Irish brogue, then stared into the innocuous cup of broth. "I been sailin' with Captain Fergeson for nigh onto a decade. Ain't wanted to sail for none other. He runs a good, tight ship. He's a right fair man, Mr. Hamilton. He dint deserve ta lose the *Meggie E.*"

Patrick sipped the golden broth before continuing. "We had us a run o' luck goin' and a good crew. With our belly full, we were heavy in the water and turnin' fer home when the trouble happened.

"I was relieving Mr. Chalmers at the helm for a spell. 'Twas a clear night. The smell of a big storm rode the wind. We knowed we was in fer it come the dawn. Captain Fergeson, he already warned us of the way of it. He always read the weather, Mr. Hamilton. He knew the weather's moods like 'e knew his own daughter's name—her name being the same as the ship, o' course."

He paused, toying with the cup. The reluctance to relive the harrowing event and the emotional aftermath nearly got the better of him.

"We weren't expectin' no trouble, mind ya. The crew was bedded for the night and we were running smartly with the wind. Curt Harken was on deck, too." He caught a glimpse of the folded cot leaning against the wall, then studied his hands.

"I'm sorry, Mr. Feeny. Neither Mr. Harken nor the other crew member pulled through," Win said softly, taking his cup and handing it to Charlet for a refill.

"Young Curt, he was like a brother an' a son ta me. He dint have no one else, 'cept me and the *Meggie E.*" Tears hugged the lower lids of Feeny's bloodshot eyes when they homed in on Ransom. "He was a good man, Mr. Hamilton. A damn fine sailor. Carl kilt him. Aye, he did. Just like he kilt the rest o' the crew and the *Meggie E.*"

He accepted the refilled cup of broth from Win and stared into it for a moment before taking a sip.

"He blew a hole in the *Meggie E.* below the waterline. We was heavy, Mr. Hamilton and running good sail to catch the winds in front of the storm. But when the explosion came, everythin' went ta hell." He cast a guilty glance at Win. "Sorry, ma'am."

"Don't worry about how you tell your story, Mr. Feeny. Just tell it the best you can. I know this is difficult for you." She laid a gentle hand on his shoulder and gave him an encouraging squeeze. "At your own pace, Mr. Feeny. Right now, our first concern is your recovery."

Patrick Feeny's bloodshot eyes gazed upon her as though she was a vision of the Blessed Mother bestowing grace upon his tortured soul. "Aye-aye, ma'am. I thank ye.

"The *Meggie E.* went under so quick there wasn't time ta whisper a prayer. She burst into flame and listed hard to port. Then the main mast snapped and brought down the wrath o' God. I dint know what happened till later. All I knew then was how hard it was ta get clear o' the riggin' as she slipped into the water on her side.

"It beat the tar out o' me afore I got free. I cut the lines on two of the whaleboats before losing me footing and gettin' caught up in the mess. I thought I was goin' down fer sure, but St. Elmo protected me, Mr. Hamilton. He must have freed me, 'cause that's the only way I coulda gotten into the water clean.

"When I looked around fer the ship, she was gone. Just like that. Damn near as quick. Gone. I was in the water with the pain in my ribs, tryin' ta breathe and swim. I swum into the side of one of the *Meggie E.*'s whaleboats. I heard Curt's voice and couldna believe our good luck.

"Curt, he was arguing with Carl. Carl dint want me to get inta the boat. Curt, he wouldn't have it no other way. I caught me a wave swell and got me leg over the side. Curt helped me in. All three of us was in bad shape. Me and Curt called out for the other men. Twice, we heard voices. Me and Curt, we rowed ta the spot we thought they were, but when we got there, there was only water."

Pained by the memory, he drained the cup and swallowed his reluctance to continue.

"Finally, we dint hear no more voices. Afore dawn, the storm blew in on top o' us. The rain, it was cold. So was the wind. It found every warm spot we had, but it wasn't the worst. The hail beat on us like Satan's own fist. At first, I had a spot o' shelter under one of the benches. Curt and Carl, they was too big ta fit. They had ta protect themselves as best they could.

"When the storm was over, we couldn't hardly move we was so cold and hurtin'. It took the rest o' our strength ta row the boat inta the current where we'd have the best chance of being spotted. Alls we could do after that was pray. Pray and listen ta Carl Owens confess his sins, may his black soul rot in hell fer all eternity." Feeny crossed himself solemnly, then continued. "He come out o' his head, Carl did. The lad started rantin' and ravin', sayin' how he's ta plant charges o' black powder below the *Meggie E.*'s waterline.

"Curt wanted ta toss the traitor overboard, but I dint allow it." He cast a guilty glance at Win. "'Twas thinkin' two ways that refused the lad. If Carl lived and we was rescued, I knowed Mr. Hamilton would be wantin' to know the way of it. But truth be told, I dint think we'd be rescued. I dint want Carl dyin' any easier than us. 'Sides, I dint think the two of us could've hoisted Carl over the side we were hurtin' so badly.

"I wanted Carl to tell us why he turned on his mates," Patrick concluded softly, staring into the empty cup in his hands.

Ransom gave the man a moment before asking, "Did you find out?"

"Aye. I did." Patrick shook his head. "'Tis a sad day

when a man scuttles his ship and mates for gold coin, but that's what 'e did."

"Did he say who paid him?" Ransom pressed.

"Nay, Mr. Hamilton. He dint, though I asked." Patrick's pain-filled eyes found Ransom. "I'm sorry. He only talked about a gardener in Seattle who was suppose ta be awaitin' him on some damn flower. He made no sense a'tall. There ain't no flowers floatin' in the sea and there sure aren't no gardeners, not even wee leprechaun ones, growing a thing on a ship, 'specially not a fine whaler the likes of the *Meggie E.*"

Ransom became so still that Win glanced up and checked his breathing. With forced patience, Ransom coerced Patrick Feeny into recounting every word Carl Owens uttered, but learned nothing more from Feeny's effort. Finally, he took the empty cup from Feeny and left with Ivan.

Win prepared a tisane laced with a few drops of laudanum and waited while Feeny downed the drink. All the while she sorted through her patient's story of the role Carl Owens played in the *Margaret Elizabeth*'s demise. The far-reaching implications sent a shiver along her spine.

Apprehension grew into worrisome dread by the time she turned the knobs on the library doors. Closing them behind her, she met the two serious gazes turned toward her.

She crossed the expanse and accepted the glass of brandy Ransom offered. Sipping it, her gaze still locked with Ransom's, she became dazed by the sudden realization she could lose him to an assassin.

"I believe the time has come to lay the rest of the cards on the table." Chin lifted, she approached him. "Who is this gardener? What is the flower Mr. Feeny mentioned? A ship? And who tried to kill you in Seattle? Why?"

"I wish I knew. I'm going back to Seattle for those answers, Felicity. Right now, there are only suspicions and many, many questions. I'm as eager as you to learn who scuttled the *Margaret Elizabeth* at the cost of her crew."

"I'm going with you," she told him. A glitter Win recognized as dangerous danced brightly in Ransom's eyes. His implacable expression kept her from reading more.

"I'll miss you; however, it's best that you remain here."

"Why? If you think you can disappear for another couple of months while I twiddle my thumbs up here, think again. We both know I can take care of myself—and you." A movement from Ivan reminded her they weren't alone.

"I'm touched by your desire to protect me, despite the implied insult that I'm incapable of taking care of myself. Put your mind at ease, Felicity. Ivan will accompany me," Ransom assured her. "We've watched each other's backs in the past when the wharves were rougher."

"I promise you, Mrs. Hamilton, I'll not return without Ransom in as good a condition as when we leave Sitka." The seriousness of Ivan's pledge set off her alarm signals.

Ivan placed his glass beside the brandy bottle and bowed to her, then to Ransom. "I have a few things to arrange tonight, so if you'll excuse me, I'll be going."

After bidding Ivan good night, Win pressed her concerns. "Please, tell me what this is all about. Tell me what's going on." The hushed stories she caught bits and pieces of from around the stove at Hamilton Traders always silenced when she neared. "Maybe another opinion would help."

Ransom shook his head. "I don't want you worrying about this. There's nothing you can do, except stay here, where you're safe and comfortable." He reached for her.

Winifred spun away, setting the brandy snifter down hard on the library table. "Be seen and not heard? I seriously don't think so. What you're asking is out of the question."

"I'm not asking."

Win drew a steady breath and ignored the obvious implications. "That's wise of you. I thought we were beyond the point of unreasonable demands—both ways." She waited for the secondary meaning concerning his acceptance of her true identity and past to settle in. "Sometimes, what we can conjure is far worse than reality. You can't expect me to sit here and worry about what sort of demons are chasing you in Seattle—demons evil enough to sink the *Margaret Elizabeth* and annihilate her crew—without knowing the whole of it.

"Let's face it, Ransom, anyone who tried to kill you in Seattle, then sank one of your ships, is more than mildly upset. He or she isn't going away." She snatched up the brandy and settled onto the leather couch. "Now, tell me the rest. I already know about the granary fire."

She watched his features tighten, hiding all traces of emotion, then continued undaunted. "I know about the sawed main mast and the series of so-called accidents on two of the big whaling ships, and the cut nets on the fishing trawler. I do the account books for all your businesses, remember? So I know what the lost cargoes and the repairs cost. It seems the only area you haven't had any misfortune in is the fur trapping the Tlingit do for you. Why do you suppose that is, Ransom?"

Ransom leaned against the table and met her probing gaze. "It sounds as though you already know my business, madam. There is nothing more to tell."

"Who is this gardener?"

"I have no . . ."

"Bull! I *felt* your reaction when Patrick Feeny mentioned Carl's reference to a gardener. I *felt* it, Ransom! It was so strong you couldn't hide your physical response, though your face yielded nothing. The mask is perfect, have no fear. But you don't need it here. And for heaven's sake, don't tell me you don't have a clue.

"Give me a little trust and give me the truth. Believe me, what I can conjure with my imagination can be pretty gruesome. I mean, what if the Hillside Strangler got sent back to Seattle in this time frame?" She shivered at the thought of those maniacal eyes turning his way.

"Hillside Strangler? Never mind. I understand the point." He studied her determination for a long moment. Decisive, he pushed away from the table and joined her on the couch.

"Gardener is his name, not his occupation. Vance Gardener. He runs a supply and dry goods operation in Seattle, and he has four ships named after flowers. A couple of years ago he tried expanding into the trapping business. I heard he went down to a few of the southern islands to do business with the Tlingit and the Haida. His terms robbed them blind. Consequently, they wouldn't sell to him." He spread her fingers against his palm. The contrast in sizes caught her attention briefly.

"I suspect Vance Gardener was behind the attempt on the pier, Liss, but I can't prove anything. I keep asking myself, why? What is in it for him? What motive does he have that I'm unaware of?" He covered her hand with his.

"In truth, I've never liked Mr. Gardener, so it's hard to be objective. How much easier it is to blame those we dislike than to keep seeking the truth."

"And how dangerous," she whispered, relishing the tender way he stroked her hand. Electrical pulses rippled up her arm and warmed the rest of her body.

Ransom nodded. "He's an old sea dog. Sailors in general are a superstitious lot. While it's hard to believe he'd blow up a ship and ever set sail again, he'd also know where to set a charge like the one Patrick Feeny said sank the *Margaret Elizabeth.*

"At any rate, I'm working with suppositions. I prefer you to remain here. If I'm right about Gardener, Ivan and I will take steps to ensure our continued good health." He kissed her fingertips. "Besides, I couldn't tolerate recuperating from another life-threatening injury without you by my side."

"You mean, if I don't summon Doc Branson when you show up on a stretcher again?" She shuddered, remembering his close call.

"Exactly," he whispered, drawing her across his lap. He murmured her name and began removing the hairpins. "Will you stay here and take care of yourself for me?" He brushed his lips against hers. "Will you ease my mind by remaining in our home so I can concentrate on getting to the bottom of this?"

"Does this mean you're giving me a choice?" She traced his ear with her tongue and lips, then smiled as his whole body tightened.

"Yes," he breathed into the crook of her neck.

"Then I'll do as you ask and stay if you answer all my questions before you leave. Even so, I won't like it." She arched into him, savoring his nearness.

"If I give you an option, will you always do as I want?" He spread her hair over her shoulders and began loosening the buttons at the back of her neck.

"No." She blazed a trail of titillating, delicate kisses along her lower lip, then nuzzled her cheek against his silken mustache. "I believe you're trying to change the subject . . . and I'm going to let you. For now."

"Good, because I'm going to make love to you, Liss. The only option you have is whether it's here or upstairs." Two more buttons at the back of her dress popped free.

"Upstairs."

His mouth stifled her shriek when he scooped her up from the couch and carried her to their room.

"I'll miss you," Win murmured.

"I won't be gone longer than necessary. Not more than a couple of months. If I don't have it resolved by then, I'll come home." Ransom watched her bite her lower lip in the mirror while he undressed. Damn, but she was the most naturally sensuous woman he'd known.

Drawn by her allure, he crossed the room and caught her in his arms. Her delightful laughter and the feel of her satin skin against him teased his appetite. Her newly found trust in him not to drop her pleased him immensely. Though a tiny thing, she often acted as if she had the strength and size of a man.

Tonight, he carried her to the thick bed of furs spread in front of the fire. He knelt, then slowly lowered her legs until

she knelt in front of him, their naked bodies pressed together.

The heated glow of the fire cast a golden-red aura around
her hair. Enthralled, he lifted a handful of silken tresses, then
let the gossamer strands spill off his fingertips. "You're like
your hair—strong, soft, and flexible. You have as many
facets to your personality as your hair has colors." He
caught another curling tress and showed her how it hugged
his fingers. "Your body fits mine the same way."

She built his desire with the touch of her lips at the center of his chest and the slow, tantalizing way her open hands
glided along the outside of his thighs, over the hard swell of
his buttocks, and into the narrow vee of his waist.

"Every night, you touch me in exciting ways until you
own my soul," she whispered, laying a trail of kisses in a
widening arc across his chest.

"You like my touch." Ransom inhaled the perfume of her
hair and relished the feel of her lips and fingers on his body.

"Oh, I do." The tip of her tongue teased the hardened nub
of his nipple and sent him to a higher level of need. A subtle intake of breath betrayed his pleasure in her tormenting.
Then she drew the nub into her mouth and teased him with
her teeth and tongue much the same way he had pleasured
her until she begged for more that morning.

"Making love with you is addictive," she murmured.

The sensation of her hands sliding over his skin and
defining the hollows where his muscles connected created a
heady sensation that made him feel like a god. But he was
also a slave to the pleasure she gave so willingly. There was
nothing he wouldn't do for her or the gratification of her
touch. Eyes closed, he reveled in the burgeoning need she
generated as her hands molded his shoulders, his biceps,
then outlined the crooks of his elbows. When she leaned
back and laced her fingers in his, he opened his eyes.

"Do you want to kiss me, Ransom?" She arched, her nipples grazing the tender part of his flat belly. Absently, he
licked his lips, hungry for the tantalizing peaks.

He grinned, enjoying her seductive game. "Yes." The sensation of her aroused nipples sliding over his belly inflamed his desire. "I want to kiss your delicious mouth until you're gasping for breath. Then I want your beautiful breasts . . . Why are you shaking your head?"

"It's my turn." Breathless, she caught her bottom lip, seemingly unaware of how close he was to grabbing her and making his words true. His fingers alternately pressed into her hands and pulsed. She found his other nipple. He let her toy with her power over him, build his need, and tease him.

His heart thudded against his rib cage in anticipation of tasting her sweetness. He fought his smoldering desire as her lips and tongue burned a trail down the center of his chest and belly.

When she reached his navel, she untwined her fingers from his. Slowly, she ringed the indentation with her tongue. A series of quick forays into the hollow in his tight stomach brought Ransom's hands closing on her shoulders. He lifted her and sank onto his heels, drawing her against him.

"You're playing with fire, Liss."

His mouth claimed hers in a fierce, possessive kiss that left no doubt about the effect she had on him. He explored her sweet depths while his hands cherished her full breasts and hardened nipples. Her moan and the arch of her back to further fill his hands with her creamy breasts deepened his ardor.

Unexpectedly, she pulled away from his ravenous mouth. Startled, his hands stilled.

She sat back on her heels between his legs and gazed up at him with emotion-filled eyes as blue as a deep, summer sea.

"What is it, Liss?"

"It's, it's still my turn," she answered in a raspy whisper.

A generous lover, he drew a ragged breath that sent his chest heaving and wondered at her carnal intent. "What do you want to do? We'll do it."

Win showered her attention on the throbbing shaft and

twin globes her fingers deftly teased and tested. The electrifying pleasure she created nearly robbed Ransom of his sanity.

"I . . . I want to . . . to kiss you here."

He stilled for a few heartbeats, anticipating her next erotic exploration.

"Would you like it?" Holding him firmly, she slid her hand up and down the length of him. His desire pulsed against her fingers and palm, his breathing quickened as his need for release screamed in his veins.

"Yes," he hissed. "If you don't . . ." He never finished the words or the thought of her not liking what he burned for. His heart nearly stopped when her warm, wet mouth closed around the most sensitive part of his manhood. What began as a timid exploration quickly turned into wild enthusiasm.

Her bold quest frayed his control. She stroked him with her mouth and fingers. Small moans of appreciation and desire escaped from low in her throat.

He whispered her name in warning, lost in the stunning vision and ecstasy of his wife pleasuring him. Her hair blanketed his thighs and glistened in the firelight. His manhood stood ready to erupt into her sweet, seductive mouth. Barely restraining his climax, he picked her up by the shoulders, groaning at the forced abandonment of her ardent passion.

"I'm not done." Panting, she frantically searched his face for a sign that she had done something wrong.

"Yes, love, you are, or I will be." He eased her onto her back. The realization that she enjoyed pleasuring him as much as he had enjoyed her doing it severely tested the last shreds of his control.

"I wanted you to . . . to . . . " she managed, wide-eyed.

Ransom swore and apologized in the same breath. The urgency hammering at every fiber of his being sent him plunging inside her with a loud groan of pain and ecstasy. She was so damn moist and tight and sweet. Just the thought of the pleasure she bestowed sent him teetering over the edge.

"Yes, Ransom," Winifred cried, her body moving in concert with each full penetration of his throbbing manhood. She lifted her legs, but before she locked them around his waist, he pulled them up to his shoulders.

"Liss." His eyes told her he couldn't wait.

"Yes."

Each thrust drove harder and faster and deeper into her woman's heart. Every time her hips met his demanding penetration, he absorbed a little more of her essence and unknowingly left her another tiny chunk of his heart. He was sure he was touching her soul when ecstasy carried them into their special paradise.

Her cry of release faded into Ransom's groan as he buried himself in her all the way, then held himself there and soared with her.

Moments later, he tenderly guided her legs down around his waist, then braced on his elbows and held her until they breathed normally. He was thoroughly satisfied.

When he raised his head, he kissed the rapidly beating pulse point in the hollow of her throat. Such a big spirit lived in her small body. And she was his. She made him forget everything except her.

He frowned. Somehow, that wasn't a comforting realization. Since returning to Sitka, it had become impossible to maintain any real distance between them. He found that he couldn't make love to her and then go about his duties without giving her a second thought. On the contrary, she invaded his thoughts constantly.

For a selfish moment, he considered taking her with him. Then he swore silently. He couldn't expose her to the dangers waiting in Seattle. Leaving Caine and Gerald as protectors eased his mind somewhat. He didn't plan on telling her about the other men he had posted. Even so, Gerald and Caine were the ones he trusted with her safety.

"What's the matter?" Her brow knit with concern over his dark expression.

"I'm going to miss you."

She smiled knowingly and cradled his face in her hands, her thumbs tracing his lower lip. "You're not getting soft on me, are you?"

He shook his head slightly, savoring the feel of her delicate hands on him. "What do you mean?" His face moved against the smoothness of her hands and drank in her tenderness. His mustache tickled where she traced it along his upper lip with her thumbs.

"You're not doing anything crazy like falling in love with me, are you, Ransom?" Her thumbs stopped moving as she searched his face for the answer she craved as much as she feared. Avoiding the risk, she pressed her fingers to his lips.

She bent her head and touched her lips to his. The kiss carried a sadness that gradually melted as Ransom hardened inside of her. The urgency looming over them promised little sleep before he left at dawn for Seattle.

Win stood on the widow's walk until the ship disappeared among the cloud-shrouded islands dotting the harbor. Earlier that morning, she had sat in bed and sipped coffee while watching Ransom dress. He had asked her a question, a very simple one, but even now, the answer eluded her.

"Will Seattle become a state?" he had asked while pulling on his boots.

"It will become an international city, the largest city in the state of Washington," she had answered, admiring the way his trousers hugged his thighs.

"It will be the capital someday?" He had shrugged into his coat, then joined her when she didn't answer.

"No," she had said slowly, wondering what city became the capital of Washington. It wasn't Seattle, but what was it? Why didn't she know?

Now, watching the ship disappear into the horizon, she realized that there were a number of states she no longer knew the capitals of, some other W state . . . what? Wyoming! Yes. Wyoming. The burning certainty that she'd known the names of the capitals at one time built her perturbation. What other state capitals had she forgotten? For that matter, what states?

She hurried inside and made a list of all the states she remembered. Only when she couldn't recall how many states were in the Union did she start feeling bone-chillingly frightened.

The more she explored the gaps in her memory, the greater her fear grew. "Oh, don't be gone too long, Ransom," she whispered, staring out the window at the sea. "Please."

Storm clouds as ominous as the dread clutching her heart crept over the ocean, turning it gray and frothy.

Chapter 19

Aᴛᴛᴇʀ sɪx ᴡᴇᴇᴋs in Seattle disappointment, dead ends, and a deepening loneliness were all Ransom had found. He had been sure Patrick Feeny's reference to a gardener was a direct link with Vance Gardener. It didn't take a genius to deduce Gardener's unscrupulous nature. However, Gardener had carefully thrown sand over his own slime trail. After six weeks, Ransom was no closer to discovering why Gardener wanted to harm him than he was to proving his involvement in the sinking of the *Margaret Elizabeth*.

The investigative agents Ransom had engaged while recovering from his wound in Sitka had provided a few details of Gardener's background.

Gardener's years of slave trading in some of the seedier ports and pits of the world had ended four years earlier when the Yankees boarded his ship off the Virginia coast. Vance had escaped during the ensuing fight, but he had lost his ship. Those of his crew who had survived the battle received the reward of a Yankee prison. The chance of survival in such places was not good.

A year later, Gardener sailed into Seattle and soon became the main dry goods and foodstuff supplier. His general store prospered. However, Gardener wasn't content as a land-bound merchant with a small, aging fleet of ships.

According to Tom Richards, who had landed a job at Gardener's store, an Easterner made several sporadic after-hours visits. Thus far, Richards hadn't learned the fashionably dressed gentleman's name, although he provided a detailed description. Richards relayed the whispered rumor that the man was from San Francisco.

On one of the last hectic days in Seattle, Dirk Riker requested Ransom's presence during a routine negotiation. While not certain, Riker thought their prospective client's name had once been linked with Vance Gardener.

The timber buyer waiting in Dirk Riker's office was a dapper man in his forties named Jeff Mecham. Mecham focused his attention on Ransom as they seated themselves at a finely finished cherrywood table completely out of place amid the unfinished wooden walls of the sawmill office. After introductions, the trio settled into a discussion of the business climate.

"This is my second venture to Seattle. My first visit was a bit over a year ago, and I must say, the town is certainly growing rapidly, as no doubt are the business opportunities for an entrepreneurial-minded man." Mecham accepted the steaming coffee from Dirk.

"Perhaps you'll meet with the same measure of success this time as you enjoyed on your last visit," Riker prodded.

"Oh, I'll do far better," Mecham responded with a laugh. "Last time, I came on business that held great promise at the outset. Unfortunately, it didn't work out."

Riker shrugged as he sat across the table. "Ransom and I know nearly everybody in Seattle, or at least the old-timers. We've been in business here for over ten years. What was your man's name?"

"Gardener. Vance Gardener."

With that revelation, Jeff Mecham commanded Ransom's

complete interest. "I hope the arrangement didn't affect you too adversely?" Ransom asked casually.

Mecham smiled wistfully. "No," he said simply. "However, the reason I mention him at all stems from a blatant and embarrassing curiosity on my part to know what became of Mr. Gardener. He was quite irate when last I saw him. I feared he'd be stricken with apoplexy."

Ransom studied the man for several long minutes. He needed answers and he needed them yesterday since he was sailing for home in two days.

"Dirk, I'd like a moment alone with Mr. Mecham." Ransom watched Mecham's brow rise ever so slightly at the odd request.

Once Dirk departed and closed the door, Ransom addressed the Californian. "Mr. Mecham, I'm running out of time, so I'm going to be direct. Tell me everything you know about Vance Gardener."

"I'm not sure that . . ."

"Please, bear with me. The reason I asked Dirk to leave is not because I don't trust him. Dirk and I have been partners for years. He left so you'd be assured that anything you say rests between us."

Jeff Mecham openly studied the man on the other side of the table. "Why do you want to know about Vance Gardener?"

"My reasons are more serious than curiosity, Mr. Mecham. I can't prove it, but I believe he's behind the sinking of the *Margaret Elizabeth,* one of my whalers. Her first mate survived only because a Russian whaler found him adrift. There wasn't supposed to be a survivor."

Ransom related Patrick Feeny's tale. By the time he finished and added a few other incidents, including the episode on the dock that nearly cost him his life during his last visit, Mecham was nodding thoughtfully.

"Technically, Mr. Gardener isn't a client," Mecham mused. "Money never exchanged hands, nor did we have a contract. So I wouldn't be breaching any professional ethics."

Mecham continued nodding pensively as he relaxed in the chair. "One of the things I do is put together trading agreements between buyers and sellers. Vance Gardener was interested in negotiating a trade agreement with the Chinese for seal and otter pelts. I understand he contacted some of the local tribes—or is it clans here?—to do the actual trapping.

"Initially, the match with Gardener appeared promising to the Chinese. However, it fell apart after the Chinese tong I was dealing with asked questions Mr. Gardener hadn't expected.

"The Chinese tongs are very thorough in checking their trading partners. They have high standards and, bluntly speaking, Mr. Gardener didn't measure up. I don't think his former occupation as a slave trader bothered them. The Chinese have no aversion to bartering in the flesh trade. What disturbed them was how he attempted to satisfy his greed. To them, getting caught and losing his ship as a consequence was stupid. He barely escaped with his life. His crew wasn't that fortunate. Gardener takes shortcuts. They don't like that and judged him unsuitable.

"In the end, it became a moot point. The Chinese renewed their agreement with their previous trading partner. I understand he is an American who had been on the verge of getting out of the business. I also understand they respected the American partner enough to offer him an inducement to continue supplying them for the next several years. Very unusual for the Chinese, I must add."

Ransom tented his fingers under his chin. The key puzzle piece dropped into place. The picture took form. At long last he had Gardener's motive. The granary fire had occurred almost six months after he accepted the new deal with the Chinese. Rubbing his jaw, he calculated the time it logically took for such information to reach the trading communities.

The timing fit perfectly. He shifted, uncomfortable with the mounting anxiety.

"Now I'll ask you, Mr. Hamilton, were you the mysterious American partner who insisted on anonymity the Chinese preferred?"

Ransom rubbed his chin over the pyramid of his fingertips. "Damn." He understood revenge. He understood anger, even bitterness over losing out on the lucrative Chinese agreements. But he didn't understand why a man sabotaged an operation and indiscriminately took the lives of men who had no influence over the real target of his vengeance.

Now that he had a possible motive and corroboration, he'd begin tightening the screws on Gardener. If he disliked being beat out of the fur trade agreements with the Chinese, he'd detest Ransom's plans for him now.

Ransom and Jeff Mecham spoke a while longer before Dirk returned and they negotiated a very favorable deal for Mr. Mecham's client, which meant a hefty bonus for Jeff Mecham.

The Blue Whale Restaurant offered the most sophisticated cuisine in Seattle. Mack Taggart ran the business his sister, Karen, owned with him. She planned the menus, supervised the cooking, and made at least one specialty dish a day. Ivan led Ransom into the restaurant. Delicious cooking aromas teased their appetites.

"Baron Korinkov, Mr. Hamilton," Mack greeted, checking his pocket watch, "your table is ready."

"What is Karen's special tonight, Mack?" Ransom asked, threading his way through the tables cloaked in finely starched linen and decorated with a bud vase containing a wildflower and a sprig of evergreen. He pulled back a chair at the table he and Ivan guaranteed with a healthy tip nightly.

"A tender pork roast smothered in apple-raisin gravy," Mack said over his shoulder.

"Sounds delicious," Ivan said, seating himself.

"Ransom? Ransom Hamilton?" came an inquisitive feminine voice from behind him.

The interest glittering in Ivan's eyes told him the woman was attractive. Ransom turned in his chair slowly, then stood, astounded by the sight of his sister-in-law.

"Cassie? What are you doing in Seattle? I thought you were in San Francisco or going around the world on your honeymoon." He clasped her offered hand in both of his. Cassandra Malcolm was as beautiful as he remembered, golden blond, delicate, with clear violet eyes and flawless ivory skin.

"We arrived from San Francisco a couple of days ago. John, my husband, is checking on the timber tracts Father gave me as a wedding present." Tiny distress lines pinched a furrow across her forehead. "I'm surprised you're in Seattle, Ransom. How is Felicity? Is she here? And Adele?"

Ransom surveyed the watching restaurant patrons uncomfortably. "Where's your husband?"

Distress deepened Cassandra's frown. "He's late. Something important must have detained him at the last minute."

After hearing Ivan clear his throat a second time in as many minutes, Ransom performed the introductions, then invited Cassandra to join them while she waited for her husband. Before he could seat her, Ivan assumed the duty.

Cassandra shyly nodded a thank you at Ivan for his courtesy. "Please tell me, how is Felicity?"

"She is well, as is Adele, who by now has married Gerald Wagner. Sitka agrees with both of them." The less said about Felicity, the better. The Felicity that Cassandra mentioned was very different from the one Ivan knew as his wife.

Although her eyes sought Ivan, who gazed steadily at her, Cassandra continued addressing Ransom. She glanced over her shoulder, then leaned closer. "Keep her there, Ransom. Let her be happy there. Please," Cassandra pleaded in a whisper, worry knitting her brow.

"Cassandra, I assure you, Felicity is quite content and

very healthy. I intend for her to stay that way." His gaze narrowed on Cassandra. A dark shadow hovered around her troubled eyes. "Is something amiss? Something I should know about? If you need help or you're having second thoughts about . . ."

"No. No, Ransom. Nothing is wrong," she answered hurriedly. "I just miss Felicity, I guess. I know you'll take excellent care of her." She closed the topic by diverting her attention to Ivan.

Ransom barely listened to their conversation, but he watched them. The mention of Felicity's name deepened a familiar longing haunting him. Carnal memories of their lovemaking besieged his restless dreams. He woke in the middle of the night with a raging need to hold her and an unreasonable fear she might slip into the icy fog of oblivion.

Maybe she was right. He was going soft on her. If that meant spending far too much time thinking about her and having blood rush to his loins every time he did, then he definitely was going soft on his wife.

He had expected to miss their passionate bedtimes. He hadn't expected to miss her smile, her wit, her peculiar way of speaking and viewing the world. It caught him by surprise when his heart pleaded for their reunion.

An occurrence the day before he left Sitka filled his memory. He had returned home from helping the men at the shipyard move a new boiler into place. Grimy from the labor, he went to bathe. Stripped down to his pants, he had just finished filling the tub when the bedroom door banged open.

"She's gonna show you I'm not making it up, Tommy. Water really can go up and down and disappear straight into the ground without a trace," came Bull Jr.'s proud voice.

"Uh, we believe you," came a second young, although tentative, voice.

"Seeing is believing," he heard Felicity say. "Come on, boys. Let Bull Jr. show you what a fine job he and his father did putting the water and drainage pipes up here," Felicity urged in a tone that gave no option.

She swept the bathing room drapery aside. Ransom stood beside the tub, arms akimbo and unable to suppress the grin lighting his face. Felicity, flanked by three boys as tall as she, halted in her tracks.

"I . . . I didn't realize you were home."

"Please, continue with your demonstration. I'll wait." He swept an arm toward the water pump beside the fireplace, his grin spreading in open amusement.

Slightly flushed, she gave him a curt nod, then herded the boys into the bathing room. Her eyes kept wandering as she explained the engineering, the purpose of a leach field, and the need for placing the pipes near the chimney. Upon concluding the explanation, she accompanied the boys from the room.

Just as he finished bathing, she returned and locked the bedroom door behind her. She had eagerly explained how the argument between Bull Jr. and Tommy had been escalating toward a physical confrontation when she discovered them outside the kitchen door. As she explained, she removed her clothing. By the time he took her in his arms, she had only her chemise and pantalets remaining.

He broke off the memory and focused on the present. A slow smile grew as he watched his friend succumb to Cassandra Malcolm's captivating charm. Strange that he should only feel amusement instead of jealousy or bitterness or keen disappointment for having lost the woman. When he looked at Cassandra, he felt nothing. This, too, surprised him, albeit pleasantly. For two years he had wooed her with letters she never received and prepared a home for her as his wife. But she belonged to another man now. Despite the circumstances, she had chosen John Malcolm.

Still, had things turned out differently, he might have been content with Cassie. She wouldn't have given him a moment's worry.

On the other hand, Felicity gave him plenty of worry.

During the years he had planned his future, he never dreamed his wife would rule his thoughts, increase his worries, or spark his emotions the way she did. Brighter and of quicker intelligence than most men, she constantly surprised him with her keen insight and unusual opinions. A man could live half a dozen lifetimes with her and never grow bored. Even now, she filled voids in his being with sunshine where he had known only darkness. He ached to rush home and hear what mayhem she'd caused or what new building project she had started, or how the world would change.

Watching Cassie, he noticed tiny worry lines on her forehead. Even though she smiled, enthralled by Ivan's company, something seemed amiss.

He reviewed her strange conversation before she curtailed it. If Cassandra missed Felicity, which he didn't doubt, why did she think it so important that Felicity remain in Sitka? For a fleeting instant, he wondered if her husband figured into her odd statements.

As Ransom contemplated Arch's warnings about Cassandra's husband in his letter of explanation, Malcolm joined them.

Irritation rippled down John's perfectly postured spine when he saw his wife in rapt discussion with a distinguished man who was devouring her with his eyes. After Cassandra performed the introductions, John graciously joined the Russian baron and Ransom Hamilton for dinner. Fortune had provided a marvelous opportunity for learning more about his quarry.

John seated Cassandra beside Baron Korinkov. Let them flirt and drool over each other, he decided while bestowing a dazzling smile in her direction. Cassandra would pay for her outrageous conduct later.

"I've heard a great deal about you," John told Ransom. "Arch sang your praises. So has my wife." He glanced at Cassandra with a look that wilted her smile like a rose cast into a flame.

"I've known the Forsythe family a long time." Ransom poured wine into John's glass. "You're fortunate to be a part of it."

John studied the man closely, surprised by Ransom's sincerity. How could Hamilton consider himself fortunate when he was married to Felicity? Short of a quick tumble under her skirts, what was the dim-witted chit good for? Maybe Hamilton wasn't as smart as his reputation suggested.

Recalling the scene he'd witnessed from a safe distance in the dark of night on the dock, John reconsidered. Hamilton had weaknesses. All men did. Even so, John surmised that underestimating Hamilton the way Liam and Zig had was a serious mistake. He'd keep that in mind. If Hamilton hadn't been smart as well as strong and quick, Liam and Zig would have killed him instead of dying on the dock and leaving the job undone.

"Cassandra said you're checking on some timberland." Ransom topped off John's wineglass. "Are those the tracts north of here Arch acquired several years ago?"

"I don't know when he bought them," John answered. "But, yes, they're north. Are you familiar with the area?"

"Yes. If you're thinking of selling them, you might want to reconsider," Ransom said quietly.

The way Hamilton's strangely colored eyes stared without blinking made John uncomfortable. "I've had several offers," John replied cautiously. What was Hamilton's game? He had spoken with several logging operations. Generally, they agreed with Vance's assessment of the land's worth.

Ransom shrugged indifferently. "If you want to sell and they offer a price you like, sell. If you hold out a few years, the timberland will escalate in price. Already, there is speculation of building a railroad."

Briefly, John considered offering Hamilton the land, then discarded the notion. He didn't want Hamilton suspecting how close to the line he lived. A financial gamble he took in San Francisco just before bringing Cassandra north had proven disastrous. Instead of doubling his fortune, it had cost him dearly and heavily dented his liquid assets. Access to the Forsythe estate had become imperative.

The botched attempt on the docks had left Hamilton with a small limp and a healthy caution. Time was running out. Winter rode the wind. Once it settled in, ships wouldn't sail as regularly between Seattle and Sitka. Already, a new idea whirled in the back of John's mind.

During dinner, John probed Hamilton's interests in Seattle and Sitka. It annoyed him that whenever he mentioned Felicity's name, Cassandra's attention wandered from the baron. By dessert, he determined that Hamilton genuinely cared for simpleminded Felicity.

"Cassandra and I were wondering if you planned on keeping the house in San Francisco for Felicity. I suppose Thomas Nolan informed you that we've been staying there when we're in San Francisco," John said, sitting back in his chair and examining the clarity of the brandy he held against a warming candle in the center of the table.

"I hadn't given it much consideration," Ransom answered cautiously. The alarm on Cassandra's face gave him pause.

John nodded thoughtfully. "Felicity may wish to return. She's comfortable in familiar surroundings."

"Why would Felicity leave Sitka without Ransom?" Cassandra ventured, her violet eyes darting between her husband and Ransom. "Ransom has always preferred Sitka over San Francisco."

John cast a tolerant glance in her direction. She froze into silence while he sipped his brandy. "You know Felicity's delicate health, Cassandra. It might be best for her to live in a milder climate than Sitka during the winter. It would be good for her to spend some time with us, her family, again. I'm sure she has missed you in her own way, just as much as you've missed her."

"I have missed her." Cassandra kept her thick, black lashes lowered, avoiding all three pairs of eyes trained on her.

"Felicity won't be leaving Sitka," Ransom announced. The instant relief he saw when Cassandra lifted her long lashes and met his gaze stunned him. "I prefer keeping her close."

"Take good care of her," Cassandra whispered, her intense gaze never wavering.

"That's a promise." Ransom lifted his brandy in salute.

A dark shadow passed over John's handsome face. He thanked Ransom for the meal and held his wife's chair while exchanging parting pleasantries. He was furious with Cassandra for interfering with his invitation to bring Felicity to San Francisco.

Ransom watched the Malcolms depart the restaurant. Ivan ordered another round of brandy. The two men sat in silence, each lost in his own thoughts for several long minutes before Ivan spoke. "I wish I had met your Cassandra before she married him and became afraid of men. She would have been worth any price or sacrifice. It is best she stay away from Sitka, Ransom. I fear if I saw her unhappy, I would take her away from her husband. He doesn't deserve her. Nor does she deserve him.

"She's afraid of him, Ransom. I have seen that look in other women—women whose husbands beat them regularly. If she would say such a thing happened to her, I'd hunt him down and beat him to death with my bare hands. Then I'd take her home, where she would live like a princess—my princess—and treat her as the royalty she is."

Stunned by Ivan's emotional declaration, Ransom held his silence. Ivan had just expressed more tender feeling for Cassandra after knowing her an hour than he had felt for her in all the time they had known each other.

Chapter 20

DESPERATION FORGED DRAMATIC changes in Win's behavior during Ransom's two-month absence. Driven by a terror that alternately paralyzed and generated frenetic energy, she methodically cataloged the changes in her memory. The scant amount of weight she had gained since arriving in Sitka melted from her bones.

Cloistered in her sparsely equipped laboratory every afternoon and evening, Win wrote in one journal after another until very late at night. Fearing the knowledge acquired over her lifetime was slipping into a black, timeless abyss, she logically categorized her memories and experiences.

Her test tubes and beakers gathered dust. The newly arrived chemistry tomes remained untouched on the bookshelves. The more memory gaps she uncovered, the faster she wrote. Exhausted, the muscles in her right arm and shoulder knotted and cramping, she carried her journals to the bedroom where she fell into bed in the small hours of the morning.

When she slept, she dreamed of making love with Ransom; of him watching her in that special way he had of

concentrating all his energy on her; Ransom in danger from
an unseen nemesis; Ransom fading out of her life as a
misty, gray fog of forgetfulness swallowed her. The last
dream always woke her with a scream of protest lodged in
her dry throat and her body coated in perspiration. The
stench of fear filled the room after the fog dream. Icy panic
gripped her heart when she considered the possibility of
losing the precious feelings and emotions Ransom had
brought to life.

Even as the tide of memory ebbed and flowed with some
of its vitality fading, she was certain she'd never feel for another human being the way she felt about Ransom.

And what of him? How would he react? Oh, he might
miss her if she slipped away entirely. But whether because
of his sense of obligation or because he genuinely cared, she
didn't know. A realist, she suspected the former. After all,
she wasn't Cassandra. She hadn't been his first choice. Hell,
she hadn't been his choice at all.

If her mind slipped over the edge, he would send her
away . . . divorce her . . . marry another woman to bear and
nurture his children. Would she know when it happened?

Winifred shuddered, torn between the absolution of
oblivion and the sweet torment of memory. Regardless of
the fate of her memories, she'd never forget making love
with Ransom. Who could forget heaven?

Winifred snuggled in warm, comforting bathwater nearly
filling Ransom's oversized tub. She arranged a damp, folded
cloth over her eyes, then concentrated on relaxing the knotted muscles in her shoulders and twitching right forearm.
The steamy warmth of the bathing room mingled with the
scent of lilacs.

During the strenuous ordeal of documenting Winifred's
memories, she became detached and began thinking of herself as Felicity. Not the Felicity that Adele recalled in conversation, but a new woman who embodied the physical
and intellectual properties of all she was. Like the dominant
personalities of a schizophrenic blending into singularity,

she *was* Winifred McCanless of Los Angeles, Felicity Hamilton of Sitka, and Liss, the woman in love with her husband.

The melding of identities had crept into her awareness with the stealth of a rising pond fed by an unseen source. The gradual intrusion lapped at the shores of conscious thought in comfortable evolution. When she gazed at herself in the mirror, she saw the Felicity she was now. As her memories of all that Winifred achieved in a place that grew more distant and vague with each passing day, the comfort of a solidified identity provided a stable island in the rising pond of uncertainty.

The days grew shorter than the nights at the end of September. Idly, Win speculated on how cold it got during a Sitka winter. Sinking deeper into the hot water, she wondered if October was too late in the year to build a sauna. Lord knew there was enough lumber. She ruminated over insulation materials, then pictured the hot sauna in the heart of a dark winter evening with her and Ransom languishing on the benches.

Just thinking of his hands on her body sent a wave of anticipation across her skin and puckered her nipples. Had she written about saunas in her journals? She couldn't remember. With a disheartened sigh, she settled back and wished for Ransom's return.

"You're just like a cop, Ransom Hamilton," she told the cloth covering her face. "Not around when I need you."

"What do you need me for?" came his teasing voice from the other side of the heavy curtain isolating the bathing room from their bedroom.

Win bolted upright so quickly that water went sloshing over the sides of the tub onto the brightly tiled floor. The facecloth fell onto her breasts. "You're home!" Sheer joy sent her spirits soaring. He was home! Her mind was still intact. She had a little more time in his arms.

The curtain parted. "I'm home," he repeated, grinning, removing his clothes as quickly as possible.

"When?" She scrambled, tucking her feet under her on the slippery surface. The overpowering need to touch him cast a pink glow over her wet skin.

"We docked less than half an hour ago." He hopped on one foot and pulled his boot off, then switched. His smoldering gaze never left the vision of loveliness rising out of the water like a glistening phoenix. "Did you miss me?"

"Is the Pope Polish?" Win climbed out of the tub and grabbed a towel. Her eyes feasted on him and her heart raced in exultation.

Confused, Ransom faltered, then dropped his boot. It landed with a resounding thud. "No. Of course not. He's Italian."

"He is?" Damn, where did that come from? Wrapping the towel around her to stem the water sluicing down her body, she approached. "I missed you, Ransom. I missed you terribly." She released the towel and busied her fingers on his trouser fastenings. The delicious hardness of his arousal throbbing against the backs of her fingers sent her grinning in anticipation. Obviously, he missed her, too.

She had forgotten what a beautiful, powerful figure he presented: tall, dangerous looking, with an erection that made her breath catch in her throat. She had forgotten how large he was *all* over. And he was real—not a dream or a wishful figment of her imagination.

When she gazed into his fascinating eyes, a thrill coursed through her body. His eyes were bright and glittering with an urgency that reflected hers.

Win caught her breath, awed and delighted by his blatant need and that she could affect him so. She kissed the center of his chest, relishing the way the whorls of black hair tickled her face. The familiar masculine scent and heat radiating from the wall of muscle consumed her senses.

Her fingertips trailed lower, along his belly, then closed around his aching manhood. Ransom groaned and threw his shirt behind him.

Caught in the power of his presence, she arched her

neck and leaned farther forward, pressing her breasts against his heated skin. Now that he was here, she hungered for all of him. "I missed you so much that if I don't have you inside me in the next two minutes, I may dry up and blow away."

With a growl, he shucked his trousers. There was no thought, no illusion of tenderness in their demands on one another, only need. He lifted her, treasuring her softness against his chest, tasting the sweetness of her hungry mouth, then he lowered her, filling her with himself as her legs clamped tightly around his waist.

In the mindless moments that followed, she was wet and wild and ravenous. She clung, wanting all of him inside her, drawing his tongue deeper into her mouth. And he fed her with a fierce abandon that drove him to his knees, and still she couldn't get enough of him.

She met every deep thrust, her need soaring out of control. There was no thinking, only feeling: feeling the rightness of their joining . . . the fullness of her body and soul with him inside her . . . the raging need to claim him when he released his seed.

She tore her mouth from his and sought his gaze. The need and the hunger she saw in his smoldering aqua eyes were her undoing.

"I can't . . ." The rest of the words died as she started the final soar toward paradise. Dimly, she heard him say her name. Then he was holding her hips and buttocks tightly in his big hands. Each stroke of his manhood plunged deeper and faster and harder, until he followed her into ecstasy with a sweetly tortured groan.

For a long time they held each other in trembling arms, neither willing to release the other, both suffering from the sensual deprivation of separation. Gradually, their ragged breathing normalized, and still they held one another.

"God, how I missed you," she breathed, then laid a trail of kisses along his shoulder.

He wanted to tell her how much he missed her, how he

thought of her constantly from the time he left. He wanted to tell her how much he needed her while he was in Seattle, how it felt like he'd had this particular erection since the morning they parted. He wanted to tell her how much she meant to him, how he'd discovered his good fortune of being married to her instead of Cassandra.

But the fear that there was something gravely wrong held him back. Saying the words might make the dark specter hanging over them more real.

Cordelia had waylaid him when he entered the house. Her sincere concern for the time Felicity spent sequestered in her special room or their bedroom, writing in the growing mounds of journals during his absence, tugged at his mind. Felicity's haunted features conveyed an even a darker tale. Her gaunt expression and the shadows of secret demons under her troubled blue eyes chilled him. The desperation with which she made love transcended physical need.

"Goddamn! I missed you, too, Liss." He buried his face in her hair and breathed her rich woman's scent. "Hold on." Unwilling to release her even long enough to stand, he brought them upright with her clinging to him, her head pressed into his shoulder as she laughed in delight.

A few heartbeats later, he settled them in the tub. "Now, where were you before I interrupted?"

She pushed back, giggling as he became even harder inside of her. "Lying here alone and having erotic fantasies about you, and wishing you were here so we could live them together."

His soapy hand closed on her breast, capturing her nipple between his thumb and forefinger. "I'm here now. Show me. Tell me. I want to pleasure you in every way possible."

*   *   *

Long past midnight they exhausted themselves into immobility. Though physically spent and sexually sated beyond his wildest expectations, sleep eluded Ransom.

He tucked the quilts around Felicity's shoulders, believing her the most amorous, responsive woman he had known. She was made for him. Her uninhibited adventures in the carnal delights they gifted one another with challenged his own appetite.

Draping his arm over his forehead, he stared at the ceiling and recalled the scene in the foyer when he returned. Cordelia had been adamant about speaking with him *before* he saw Felicity. He knew his mother's moods too well to think of avoiding her.

"Help her," Cordelia had begged while holding his arm in a death grip. "For God's sake, help her with whatever is driving her. She won't tell me. Ransom, she's going to kill herself before spring if she doesn't stop this foolishness. I'd help her any way possible, but she won't talk about what happened on the dock. She refuses to speak about this obsession of hers to write, write, write."

Cordelia had captured his interest with the mention of the dock. A perceptive, intelligent woman, Cordelia realized Felicity was far more than she should be. Of course Cordelia questioned the drastic change. Curiosity was as much a part of his mother's nature as breathing. It amazed him that she had accepted Felicity as she was now without continually pressuring for answers. Part of him marveled that Felicity had won Cordelia's friendship without telling her anything.

At best, his mother had been reluctantly willing to tolerate his wife. He didn't know why she had been hostile toward the idea of an arranged marriage. After all, her own had been arranged and seemed an excellent relationship. Cordelia had not looked at another man since James Hamilton's death some fifteen years ago.

Before Felicity's arrival, Cordelia had considered going to Boston, or perhaps San Francisco, once his bride assumed the duties of running the household. But neither had mentioned her leaving. Cordelia and Felicity had developed a relationship that went beyond that of in-laws. Just today, his mother had pleaded for his help with her friend—his wife.

He had listened attentively as Cordelia explained how Felicity spent hours and hours writing in a growing stack of journals since the day he left. Caine and Gerald still brought the business accounts, which she worked on in the mornings. She had all but abandoned everything and everyone else.

Then she strolled, sometimes for hours, alone. Occasionally, Spirit Dancer accompanied her. Daily, she locked herself in their room or her lab and wrote in the journals until the small hours of the morning.

Watching the steady rise and fall of Felicity's breast under the quilts, he knew she slept soundly. Careful not to disturb her, Ransom slid from the warm bed into the chilly room. He pulled on a pair of trousers before feeding the fire.

Felicity's journals stood in a neat stack on the floor beside the writing desk near the window. He picked up the top three and carried them to the fire.

For the next two hours he read about her childhood and Joey, the glory days on something called a basketball court, and pages of gibberish she labeled chemical formulas, compounds, and structures.

Finally, he replaced the journals, banked the fire, and crawled into bed. Watching her sleep, he knew beyond the shadow of a doubt that the woman sleeping beside him was Dr. Winifred Beatrice McCanless of Los Angeles, California, circa 1996, living in Felicity's body in 1866.

Chapter 21

"YOU MUST TAKE me to Sitka," Cassandra demanded, her exasperation apparent to the discerning eye of her husband. "Read this! Ransom wouldn't have sent for me if Felicity wasn't very ill."

John casually crossed his ankles, waved off the letter thrust at him, and examined the fine brandy in his glass. Cassandra was most fascinating when her highly spirited nature surfaced. "I don't have to take you anywhere, my dear. I find your inconsequential demands most wearisome."

"Inconsequential demands? Inconsequential demands! I've never asked you for anything, let alone made inconsequential demands. Rather, it's you who makes demands.

"For God's sake, John, she's the only living relative I have! She needs me. I'm going, whether you accompany me or not."

"I see. And did you plan on bartering your delectable body and the little bedroom tricks I've taught you in exchange for your passage?" Malcolm tilted his golden head curiously. He restrained his smile in the face of the determination blazing in her lovely violet eyes. Even now, the way those unusual eyes snapped and shone intrigued him.

"You are vile, John. I've only to present this letter and myself at any Hamilton ship bound for Sitka and they'll *give* me first-class passage." Red-faced with indignation and outrage, she crossed her arms under her ample breasts.

"Do you enjoy pushing me, Cassandra?"

"No. But I have to get to Sitka. Felicity needs me. Ransom would never have sent word otherwise."

John inclined his head thoughtfully, hoping Felicity meant as much to Cassandra as he'd counted on when he forged the message. During the planning stage, he surmised that nothing short of her own death would keep Cassandra from her precious little sister's side in a time of need. He held his silence, waiting for her resolve to crumble. When it did not, he knew he had judged the situation correctly. "So you think Ransom Hamilton still loves you enough to provide you with passage on any of his ships," John goaded. He knew her Achilles' heel.

"He doesn't love me, John. He never has. Besides, this has nothing to do with anyone except Felicity," she insisted. "Ransom had this message sent over this morning. Obviously, he wants me to come. He'd surely guarantee my passage to Sitka."

John bristled in feigned indignation, enjoying the display of urgency battering at her fragile self-control. "And what about me? You think I should allow my wife to answer the summons of her former lover? The man she once loved? The man she hoped would marry her?" He kept prodding, probing for another weak spot for sinking his next hook. Damn, but she was fun to antagonize. The more indignant she became, the harder his erection grew.

Cassandra faced her husband in open defiance. "Unfortunately, I have loved only one man in my life. To my great shame and sorrow, he married me for what he thought I might bring him when my father died. Arch, thank God, saw through you, John, even though I didn't. But you weren't

courting Arch, were you? You were so sure he had no choice
but to leave his wealth to you through me. You have no idea
of how glad I am you miscalculated."

His finger stilled on the lip of the brandy snifter it was
circling. Anger dashed his ebullient mood. The blond bitch
had gone too far—again. His normally intense brown eyes
turned on her in a flat, unemotional stare as he rose from his
chair and set the snifter aside.

Reflexively, Cassandra retreated a step, then defiantly
held her ground. "I promise you, John, if you lay a finger on
me, I'll scream at the top of my lungs. Every man, woman,
and child in this hotel will know John Malcolm beats his
wife. And tomorrow, if I'm still alive, I'll tell them why.
What will they think of you then?"

John regarded her for a silent moment. Cassandra's problem was her mouth. It kept moving. She didn't know when
to shut it. Hell, she just might scream this time. He didn't
dare mark her face. The bruises would be too difficult to explain, and she bruised so easily. No. He'd let her slide
tonight. She was right, and it galled him. He needed an im-
peccable reputation in Seattle. That was why Vance handled
all the shady work.

He glowered down at her, then grinned in satisfaction at
the terror and determination she exuded. Her unblinking violet eyes remained pinned on him. Both knew he'd collect a
pound of flesh from her later.

Slowly, deliberately, he lifted his hand and brushed the
back of his fingers across her cheek. "Is it the Russian baron
or your sister whose company you seek in Sitka? Would you
like the big Russian baron under your skirts as much as he'd
like to be there?"

She glared at him, not dignifying his accusation with a
response. After a tense moment, she spoke. "What do you
want, John?"

"What makes you think I want something?"

"You always want something for anything you do. What
is the price for taking me to Sitka?" Loathing narrowed her

eyes. Resignation laced her voice. He'd conquered her again, but then, he had known he would.

"Ah, well, if he means that much to you, I suppose I could indulge you," he taunted. "Yes, for a price." His grin broadened when she shivered.

"What is the price?" she asked in a whisper.

"Sign the timber tracts over to me." He raised his eyebrows and lowered his chin. "Your unwillingness to part with them is creating problems. I dislike problems, Cassandra. I like my life enjoyable and smooth and exciting."

She sighed. "I should have known that's what you wanted." She nodded slightly. "I'll sign them after you've booked passage for me and have me on board a ship bound for Sitka."

"My, my. We are getting dictatorial these days, aren't we?"

"You haven't exactly earned my unquestioning trust, John," she said sarcastically. "Those are the terms. I'll rot in hell before I sign them under any other conditions."

He smiled for a moment in silent forbearance, his eyes hard and cold and never leaving her face. "Very well."

"Then you'll book passage tomorrow?" Cassandra appeared hopeful, yet very afraid. It was a mood he'd cultivated in his young wife.

"Yes. If you meet my other condition." Ah, the game wasn't as near the end as she obviously hoped. His erection throbbed in anticipation.

Instantly wary, she studied him for a moment before asking what it was. He smiled, then opened his pants and pointed at the spot where he wanted her to kneel. "Make it sweet and long for me. Take your time, Cassie, and show me how loving and grateful a dutiful wife should be. Oh, no hurry to accommodate me. Take your clothes off first. I'd like you naked, in case I want to touch you. You're so much more desirable when you're vulnerable."

He watched her swallow hard, then begin disrobing.

"Yes, my faithful wife, move slowly. I enjoy watching your armor disappear."

"How much longer until we arrive in Sitka?"

John followed Cassandra's gaze across the choppy water to the tree- and cloud-shrouded islands punctuating the coastline.

"It's taking us so long to get there."

John sighed with forced patience. "My dear, the ship is going as fast as it can."

"I'm sure it is," she mumbled into the chilled wind. "How could you delay booking passage for three days, knowing Felicity is ill? If we had done it my way and found the first Hamilton ship bound for Sitka, we'd be there by now. I'd be with my sister. I don't understand why you waited for this crumbling relic to sail, other than to prove how miserable you can make me."

Why did she complain all the time? "If you can't be civil, go below. I'll not tolerate you airing our minor differences in public." John seized her arm in an iron grip, then guided her from the rail in the strict manner reserved for subduing a recalcitrant child.

At their cabin, he released her. "You wait here quietly, Cassandra. Not a sound. Understand?"

Satisfied that Cassandra would obey, John locked the cabin door and joined Vance at the ship's rail. Gardener dressed like the rest of his crew for the venture and showed no discomfort in the face of the biting wind.

"Is everything in readiness? Do your men know what to do?" John glanced around, a bit uncertain of the trustworthiness of a few of Vance's men. If anything went wrong, there would be no escape. The stakes were so very high this time. Ah, what adventure this game offered. What excitement!

"Aye. I picked the lads carefully. They know what we're expecting. Makes no never mind what happens, they'll hold to the story." Vance lifted his sea cap and scratched his stubby fingers through his salt-and-pepper wavy hair, then replaced the cap. His luminous brown eyes were set close together over a long, crooked nose that had been broken at least twice. His thick, graying beard and mustache hid a thin-lipped mouth and strong jawline. Heavy whiskers served as the best disguise against those from Seattle who might easily recognize him.

"There's nothin' to worry about, John. First, we'll get rid of Hamilton, then that snippy wife of yours, and make it look like they run off together on the *Rose of the Waves*. By the time we're done talkin' up the scandal, you'll appear the aggrieved husband brought to Sitka on false pretenses.

"Cassandra will appear the tainted rose more interested in gettin' into her sister's husband's pants than takin' care of her sister." Vance stuck a cigar in his mouth and took his time lighting it. All the while, John bore Vance's scrutiny, his polished, polite expression never varying.

"All we need to do is lure Hamilton away from Sitka." John met Vance's twinkling eyes. "I trust your three men can handle a small, female dullard. I don't want her harmed. If she suffers any trauma, it will be difficult gaining her trust once Hamilton and Cassandra are out of the way. I'll need to win Felicity over long enough to gain control of Hamilton's accounts and her guardianship.

"Hamilton's friend, the Russian baron, may be an obstacle, but there's nothing he can do. Legally, I'm family."

"We don't want trouble with the Russians. Your plan will work, John. The men know what to do. We went over everything again this morning. Tommy knows that island. He made some maps for you. My men are ready. They'll go to work as soon as we drop anchor."

John examined the gray horizon. "Good."

"Yes, sir. By the time we finish in Sitka, even Cordelia Hamilton will believe her son ran off with Cassandra. Too bad the lovers' ship will sink." Vance laughed into the wind.

"Your wife would be excellent trade goods with her blond hair in some of the Mideastern harems. To them, she'd be a lotus flower. Pity we'll have to drop her off before the

Rose changes her identity." Vance took a hard drag from his cigar, then examined the ash. "I believe the *Rose of the Waves* might become a *Morning Violet*."

"You'll be well compensated when I assume guardianship for Felicity," John assured him.

"Oh, I've no worry on that score, m'boy. None a'tall. Anyone who can convince his wife to beg for a trip he wanted to take and sign over the timberland she didn't want to part with to boot can coax maple syrup from a sycamore tree. The note you wrote and signed Hamilton's name to was pure genius." The admiration in Vance's tone was genuine. "You've done well since New York. Very well. I wouldn't miss watching the master at work, particularly against Ransom Hamilton."

"I plan to do even better once he's out of the way. After this little escapade, I'm retiring." He reached into his coat and withdrew a gold cigar case that he had found among Arch's possessions in the San Francisco house. "There's nothing to spoil a man on the idea of marriage like four or five wives by the time he's thirty." He winked at Vance, and they both laughed loudly.

Chapter 22

IT WASN'T FAIR. Win had to tell Ransom what was happening. She dreaded it. He seemed happy with the way things were. So why tell him? Why share the misery? Besides, what could he do about it? Nothing. Absolutely, positively nothing.

The internal battle had raged since Ransom's return. The strain of perpetual conflict turned her stomach into an acid pit. Absently, she rubbed circles over her tummy. Just what she needed, an ulcer. With her free hand, she shut her journal and placed it on the top of the stack beside the secretary in the bedroom.

Long ago, she'd learned that everything had a price. There were no exceptions. But she hadn't counted on the cost of falling in love. Oh, the price was becoming greater than anything imaginable. Try as she might, there was no way of changing what she felt for Ransom nor stopping her love from growing.

Early on, she thought absence might diminish her feelings and replenish the expanding gaps in her memory. Instead, her love deepened each day of the eight weeks Ransom spent away from Sitka.

During the month since his return, they made love every way she imagined possible and a few that caught her by surprise. Each time he claimed her body, she lost a little bit more of herself. Not just her heart. She had already given him her heart. She lost something even more precious: her soul, her identity, her past. The past wasn't hers alone. It belonged to Joey, too. Someone had to remember Joey!

She folded her arms on the desk and rested her cheek atop them. Years of training and discipline had helped her analyze a logical string of events and possible causes and effects. With no outside body of evidence supporting her theories, she had carefully documented the reasoning behind her conclusions.

The initial panic of losing her mind and reverting to the simple creature Felicity had been before falling from the *Ompalada* had diminished since Ransom's return. Her greatest comfort lay in the remembrance of everything since awakening on the *Ompalada*. That fact bolstered a tenuous assurance of her continued lucidity. In dark moments, she prayed it was so.

Now, instead of making endless entries in the journals, she began analyzing the writings and comparing them against what remained of her memory. The greatest loss was her ready knowledge of advanced chemistry and technology. Her early notes referenced things like electron microscopes and gene splitters. Today, she no longer comprehended their purpose.

"I thought you would be in bed. Are you tired?" Ransom placed a kiss on her upturned cheek. "Have I been too demanding?"

It was time. She had to tell him. She drew a shaky breath as she slowly straightened. For a long minute, she gazed at the precious face of her love that filled the great voids of her fading memory. Futility, desire, despair, and excitement warred on the battlefield of her tattered emotions.

"What is it, Liss?" Concerned, he dropped onto his haunches.

"I don't want to love you." The words scorched her agony-riddled heart. Tears surged into her eyes, threatening to spill with the next thought or word. "No. Please. Don't touch me," she begged, stilling his hand in midair.

"Like hell! You're my wife. I'll touch you any damn time I want." But he didn't touch her. When he spoke again, his voice carried a quiet, threatening edge. "I never asked you to love me. I never promised you love. What's this all about?"

"I—I love you, and I don't want to. The price is too high," she whispered. Fear rattled her confidence. Sorrow tethered her courage. Telling him was more difficult than she had imagined.

"Wh-what did you say?"

Desperate for understanding, she pounded the desk with her fists in frustration. "I said, the price is too high!"

"Before that," he urged softly, caressing her shoulders, then turning her until her teary eyes met his.

"What? That I love you?" The fragile fabric of her control unraveled. "Is that what you want to hear? That I love you?" His expression softened further as she repeated the words.

"Why . . ."

Exasperated, she shrugged. "How the hell should I know why I love you? I kept thinking it would pass, like the flu or a craving for chocolate or if we made love just one more time, but it doesn't go away. It just gets stronger and things keep getting worse." Tears of futility spilled down her cheeks.

Ransom plucked her from behind the desk and carried her to the big chair by the fire, where he settled and adjusted her on his lap. "The flu?" he inquired with a sad smile. "Is loving me so terrible?"

Through her own pain, she sensed his. She touched his cheek, then ran her finger along his jaw. "Loving you is the easiest thing I've ever done. It just happened. I didn't plan it or schedule it or decide to give two hoots for you."

Using his handkerchief, he dabbed the tears from her cheeks. "Tell me why loving me makes you so unhappy."

A fresh flood of tears spilled over the dam of her thick lashes. "I'm selfish."

He cocked an eyebrow and waited for an explanation. After a moment of emotion-filled silence, he spoke. "I've discovered many qualities and traits in you, Liss. However, selfish isn't one of them."

"I *am* selfish. I don't want to pay the price for loving you."

"What price could there be for loving me? I've promised you fidelity, protection, comfort, and participation in raising our children, should we be fortunate to have a half-dozen or so." The hope she heard in his voice softened the last edge of harshness from his features.

Tension blossomed between them for the long minutes it took for Win to muster the courage for an answer. Her heart thudded in a steady, apprehensive rhythm. She garnered her best presentation behavior and straightened her shoulders.

"I've examined what's happening to me from every imaginable angle. I've written down everything I can remember." She stole a glance at the fifteen large journals stacked beside the secretary desk. "But I've already forgotten so much."

"If you've forgotten, how do you know you . . ."

"Just listen. Please." She struggled to keep from jumping off his lap and running from the room. Seeing him nod, she pressed on. "I know because of the gaps. At first, I rationalized them away. For example, when you found me in town and took me to the top of the hill overlooking the harbor and asked me to tell you who I was, some things were fuzzy, things that shouldn't have been.

"Later, the morning you left for Seattle, I couldn't remember the capital of whatever state Seattle becomes a part of."

"You said Washington at the time," he reminded softly.

Her hands flew up in resignation. All pretense of hiding her frantic turmoil fell away. "You see? Now I can't even remember the name of the state. I can't remember what I used to do or . . . Even some of my research notes no longer make sense, and I wrote them!

"I'm losing my past! It'll be like I never lived. Like I never knew Joey." Head shaking, she shoved herself away from his chest. "Oh, no, Ransom. I can't afford loving you. You cost way more than I can pay." A fresh sheet of tears gushed down her cheeks.

"I can't even remember the complete periodic table of elements, for God's sake! I knew that better than my own name!" Sniffing, she snatched up the handkerchief.

"But you remember Joey?" He pulled her closer.

"Yes," she sobbed, "I remember Joey."

"Everything about Joey?" He leaned back and tucked her head under his chin.

She thought hard on the question. Strangely, she did remember everything about Joey. But the surroundings faded into nothingness. All that remained was Joey, like someone had selectively erased some of the rudimentary elements of each setting with an eraser a cartoon artist might use to alter the background. "I remember Joey," she agreed, taking hope that Joey would continue to live in her memory.

"Who else did you love?"

"Alexis. She was my friend. And Uncle Hiram. He never wanted anyone to know he cared about me and Joey. But everything he did for us said so. He took us in after my mother left us."

"And your childhood? Do you remember it?"

Languishing in the shell of serenity Ransom built around them, she closed her eyes and thought about her years growing up in East Los Angeles. Faces and names came easily. Oh, yes, she still owned those memories in sharp, clear, living color and vivid detail.

"I still have the important parts," she answered thoughtfully. "What I'm losing is the future. I remember eating toasted bread, but not how I made it. I remember going places, but not how I got there. I remember the feel of the politics, but none of the names. I remember some of the states in the Union and their capitals and not others. Oh, Ransom, this is hell."

"Sh-h-h-h-h." He held her tighter and kissed her hair. "Tell me the states you remember."

After a brief hesitation, she complied with a recitation.

The small lines around Ransom's eyes softened. "I'd ask you about the others, but Washington is the only one I know."

She sniffed as a response.

"Would you feel better if I told you that you just named every state of the Union as of today?" he asked.

She shook her head. "You don't understand. I remembered everything until I started caring about you, started loving you. But I can't figure out how to unlove you, and even if I did, I don't know if my memories would come back."

His eyes closed and he swallowed hard. "I'm the one who is selfish, Liss," he whispered. "I never want to do anything that might cost me that dearly. Your mind is so quick, undoubtedly you would have found a way to unlove me, if one existed."

She sagged against him in resignation. "My research is gone. Anything to do with technology . . ." The words faded into a ragged breath exhaling in defeat.

"You mean, all the advances between this time and Winifred's are fading?"

"It seems that way. Everything I worked for my whole life is vanishing into a mist revolving around you, Ransom." She shook her bowed head. "When I met you on the *Ompalada,* all I could think of was Handsome Ransom Hamilton. I haven't been able to get you out of my mind since the first time I saw you."

"Your memories aren't completely lost, Liss. You have your journals, and you have me. Tell me what you can.

Later, if you forget, I'll remind you. Since I want to know everything about you, your telling serves two purposes."

The continued movements of the back of his nails over her nipple hardened it to a prominent pout and set her squirming on his lap. The insatiable need for him hovering just below the surface flared to life.

He nudged her head back with his chin, then bent close to her mouth. "You're extremely competent at anything you attempt."

"No, not without . . ." she protested, her breath already thready with anticipation.

"Yes, you are. I'm as hard as a rock. I need you to make it go away." He traced the outline of her lips so lightly with the tip of his tongue that she had to stretch to keep him in reach. "And I know you're extremely competent at handling that task when it arises."

The threat of her problems retreated into the mist swirling around him. "Make love to me, Ransom. Slow, beautiful, erotic love. Make me glad I love you. Please."

Slowly, his lips slanted on hers in a kiss brimming with restrained passion. The first tremors of desire shook her. The steel hardness of his arousal against her hip served notice of her effect on him. He shifted, adjusting them both by lifting his hips and thrusting his engorged manhood against her.

Sheltered from stark reality by his embrace, her heart heard the kiss silently speak of his passion, then leaped in anticipation as his expert fingers loosened the multitude of buttons running down the front of her dress.

When she began opening his shirt, he broke the kiss and smiled, his left eyebrow arched mischievously as he captured her hands in his, then kissed them. Confused, she looked questioningly at his quixotic expression. He answered by kissing her trembling fingertips.

"I want to touch you." She searched his face with loving expectation. Her fingers tingled for the feel of his naked flesh.

"You are touching me." He folded her hands in her lap

and lowered his head until his lips barely brushed hers. With a slow, deliberate motion, he kissed the corners of her expectant mouth. All the while, she felt the buttons on her dress fall prey to his nimble fingers.

"You're touching me everywhere I touch you."

"Ransom," she breathed, stretching toward the promise his mouth offered.

"I'm going to make love to you, Liss. Slow, beautiful love," he promised, freeing the series of buttons at her waist. She gasped when he breached the sturdy fabric of her gray woolen day dress. His splayed fingers became tiny bolts of lightning charging her body until they rested lightly over her rapidly beating heart. "For a little while, I'm going to make you glad you love me. I want to make you happy you're my wife."

Right now, she was very glad she was his wife and would not trade the bliss he showed her for anything. The sorrow of loss crept farther into the shadows of her memory.

Ransom brushed his mouth over hers, his hand drifting lower, then caressing her breast. Reflexively, she arched, thrusting her aroused nipple forward in search of his palm. He cupped the full globe, his fingers flexing in a slow, sensuous rhythm, touching everywhere except her proud nipple as her need for intimate attention built.

When his mouth closed on hers, Win allowed him to taste her for a moment. The excitement of his thumb and forefinger rolling her nipple back and forth with a small plucking motion sent a shiver of need from her tingling breast to her heated loins. The urgency of her kiss reflected her desire. Quickly, she tempered the impulse to embrace him and hold his tenderness close. Her hands formed a knot of interlaced white-knuckled fingers in her lap, her thumbs rubbing slow circles against each other.

"You're a magnificent woman, Liss." Ransom's smoldering gaze led his gentle fingers across her cheek. She kissed his palm, then let her tongue trace down his wrist when he brushed back the lock of hair wandering across her forehead. If she lived to be a hundred, she knew she'd never forget the delicious taste of him.

Slowly, taking great pains to save all the hairpins, he freed her lush mane and spread handfuls of curling tresses over her shoulders. "You're my queen, Liss. There is nothing I wouldn't do to make you happy."

His proclamation sparked every nerve into a silent celebration. She watched, spellbound with sensual delight, as the tip of his finger traced a path of fire along her shoulder, over and around her breast, down to her waist, then up the center of her ribs and between her breasts. When it curled under her chin, she lifted her gaze and found him watching her.

"I could look at you all night, you're so beautiful. You make me the envy of every man in Sitka. But it isn't the outside beauty they see that I prize. Your real beauty belongs to the woman inside this body, to Winifred McCanless Hamilton. She's the one who shines like a beacon in a stormy night. I treasure her beauty. It transcends the physical world and is far greater than I thought possible for any human being to possess."

Love and pure joy surged through her at the sound of her name from his lips. In that instant, she experienced a happiness missing since Joey's death. Peace settled over her troubled heart. His gift of faith made love flourish. Brimming with inexpressible emotions, she met his mouth.

He tempered their kiss. The soft, almost sad touch of his lips on her temple sent her following his lips.

"You taste of salt, of crying. It breaks my heart when you cry, Liss," he whispered in her ear.

"No crying," she promised, captivated by his masterful seduction of her senses.

Her dress fell free. She held perfectly still while he slipped it down her arms and let it pool at her waist. She watched the intensity of his desire grow with the amount of her flesh he revealed. As though answering the plea she radiated from the depths of her being, he gave her his mouth.

Hungry to share the joy his words bestowed, she delved the depths of his mouth, savoring his taste and textures. The slight stiffening of his chest emboldened her. She almost smiled and broke the kiss when his nimble fingers released the ties on her petticoats and drawers.

But it was Ransom who reluctantly ended the kiss and drew back slightly to steel his breathing into a slower rhythm. "I'd cross the frozen sea for your kiss. Your touch alone sets me on fire."

"Chemistry can be very powerful," she whispered, stilling her hands midway on their journey to capture his face and drink the nectar of his lips again.

"More than chemistry," he answered huskily, sliding his hand behind her knee and lifting her leg to remove her shoe.

With his gaze locked on hers, the simple removal of her stockings turned into serious love play. The touch of his fingers sent tingles along her skin as he rolled her stockings down her legs in sensuous motions, kneading her warm flesh, caressing every part of her thighs and calves. Never had she experienced such tender feelings for another human being. Her trusting eyes filled with love and countless emotions reflected from her soul.

"Nothing will ever be as precious to me as you or your love, my sweet wife."

"I want to love your body, to touch you." Her voice was an aching, raspy whisper. How she yearned to return the pleasure of his touch.

"Soon, Liss, soon." He embraced her with his left arm and buried his face in the volumes of hair at the crook of her neck and shoulder. His heated breath against her sensitive skin fired the growing ache in her lower abdomen. Cooler air rushed below her ear when he deeply inhaled her scent, then held it in his lungs for a moment before slowly releasing it and nibbling at the hollow of her neck as though testing to see if she tasted as good as she smelled.

The gentle pressure traveling the sensational pathway up her inner thigh spread pleasurable ripples from the crown of her head to her toes. Searching, his agile fingers sorted the fabric of her drawers and found her heated feminine flower as his mouth claimed hers. The center of her being quaked in anticipation as her legs parted, giving him more freedom.

A small cry escaped her when his fingers found her sensitive nub. His slow, delicious teasing stoked her desire white-hot with the need burning between them. Lost in the sensation of pleasure and the heady excitement of his ministrations, conscious thought fled.

"God, but you're soft and sweet," he breathed, then resumed the kiss.

The heated magic flared brightly. The world of wondrous sensation he created captivated her. For the moment, she no longer controlled her existence. He became her sole reason for breathing. He possessed her heart and captivated her soul. She squirmed, following the titillation of his expert fingers bringing her higher and higher. She couldn't get enough of him or his kiss. Lost in the building tension and promise of rapture, her arms moved over his shoulders and twined around his neck. Thick, raven hair filled the hands holding his mouth to hers.

A temporary fulfillment lay a few heated touches away. Just when she thought it was hers, he stretched the play a moment longer. A small protest from the back of her throat escaped.

He gifted her by slipping two fingers into the heart of her need. She moved with him, as he glided in and out of her heated depths, invading, teasing, then retreating. Hot, inexpressible urgency built inside of her, sending her arching and straining against his hand. Still, he drew it out, not allowing her to move too quickly toward the heavenly flight, pacing her until she cried out against his mouth. Again, his fingers slipped all the way inside and quickly fluttered back and forth. Rapture twinkled within her reach.

This time, it was his groan that took them to the next

precipice. He rapidly fluttered his fingers in deliberate, short motions, helping her reach the promised ecstasy, then sending her soaring with a gasping, incoherent cry.

Her cheek pressed against his shoulder, she embraced him, wanting to hold him forever, and be a part of him, and feel his rapidly tripping heart beat against her sensitive breast. When he held her, made love with her, the price for loving him didn't seem quite as high.

"Hold on, Liss," he whispered. Her arms locked around his neck as he stood up. He stripped away her garments into a puddle on the floor. Only her chemise remained when he sat her on the bed. In seconds, it, too, disappeared.

She scrambled under the heavy quilts and watched him remove his jacket, then toss it in the vicinity of the chair. Next his boots hit the floor with a thud. She loved the sinuous glide of his muscles in the shadowy aura cast by the golden firelight. He was all potent male, and he was hers.

For a long moment, they watched each other as she wiggled into the center of the bed with the quilts bunched around her. Waves of golden brown hair fanned across her shoulders and the quilts mounded just below her full breasts. Her nipples hardened under his slow, smoldering gaze.

"Are you going to take off the rest of your clothes?" she asked, puzzled over his immobility.

He shook his head. "No."

An impish grin lit her face. "May I undress you?"

Again, he shook his head. "No."

He drew the covers away. The intensity of his gaze set her skin ablaze. "You're my queen, Liss, this bed your throne." As he trailed the back of his hand along her calf and inner thigh, gooseflesh rose in its wake. Her thighs parted in welcome.

"If I am your queen in this fantasy, will you do as I ask?"

"Quite possibly," he agreed, a small smile easing some of the strain cast by their play.

"Let me take off your clothes," she whispered.

"Nay, fair queen. 'Tis ill-fitting for a lady of your station to remove the unworthy threads of your servant." Now he did grin, then winked at her.

Win laughed in delight. "Then I request that you take off your shirt. Let my eyes feast on at least that much of you."

He complied with madding slowness, his gaze devouring her, lingering at her breasts, searing her flesh with hunger.

Irrepressible, unrestrained passion crackled in the warm air between them, drawing them nearer, closing the distance. They came together on their knees, their mouths fusing. She moved into his tight embrace, loving the way his arousal throbbed against her belly through his straining trousers.

Her splayed fingers pressed into the hard muscles of his round buttocks as though it was possible to get closer to him. Everywhere he touched her, he lit a fire. Meanwhile, their tongues wove and danced in an intricate tempo with ever-changing leads.

Secure in Ransom's arms, Win melted against him as he laid her back on the big eiderdown pillows. As he cupped her breast in his hand and teased its peak into pebble hardness with his thumb and forefinger, Win writhed in abandon with the heavenly torment he created.

His mouth claimed her breast in a bridled passion that intensified her pleasure. She *felt* like a queen under his expert worship. For long minutes he made love to her breasts with his mouth, mustache, and hands, driving her to the brink of screaming her need. All the while, his manhood remained out of her needy reach.

He swept a pillow from the top of the bed, lifted her hips, and slid it beneath her. A small cry of surprise escaped.

"Your pedestal, my queen," he said, then bowed his head.

Win laughed, loving his antics. Her mirth faded as a devilish grin that she recognized promised much stole over his face. She whispered his name as he settled amid the warmth of her thighs.

To her delight, he plundered her belly button with his

tongue, then tickled her soft, velvety skin with his mustache until she squirmed and giggled.

Murmuring praise for the perfection of her femininity, he spread the petals protecting her most sensitive spot, then bent his head for a taste. His tongue felt like a branding iron forged by the fire of promised fulfillment. She barely caught her breath before he nuzzled the auburn triangle nestled between her thighs. The feather glide of his hot tongue around her inflamed nub sent waves of pleasure flowing through her body. The delicious sensations shot fire through her veins. As she yielded to the erotic glory, he carried her to another height and still continued delighting and tantalizing her.

She savored each minute stimulation, each thrill of titillation. Just when she thought she'd go wild with wanting, his fingers slipped inside and he began suckling her sensitive nub. The rhythm of his ministrations sent exquisite tremors through her body. She moaned his name over and over. In mere minutes, the special magic he worked sent her ascending toward the sparkling colors of bliss. She cried out, her fingers clutching the sheets to hold her to the ground.

When she floated back to earth, Ransom awaited, naked, braced on his elbows over her. "I'll never get enough of you, Liss. I won't let you stop loving me. I won't let you leave me. I'll pull you back," he promised, kissing her lightly.

As though to prove both him and his words real, her hands explored his broad shoulders and roamed down the knotted muscles of his back. Lava-heated bare skin seared her fingertips when she reached his buttocks.

"I want you inside me, Ransom," she breathed against his lips. She ran the tip of her tongue over his bottom lip and tasted a trace of herself. "I'm whole when you're part of me. It's so good, what you do to me, but it's not the same." God, how she loved him. Her love flourished in the afterglow of the tender way he worshiped her body with every glance, every touch.

"I know, Liss. God. I know."

Strong fingers curled over her shoulders. His arms tightened, holding her in place. With a quick movement of his hips, his manhood stood poised at the entrance to heaven. "I know," he ground out between clenched teeth. The pillow tilted her hips toward him invitingly.

"Come home," she whispered, thrusting her hips at him, then let out a cry when he responded by burying himself all the way inside her.

With those two words of undeniable invitation, he plunged into her sweetness, closed his eyes, and abandoned all control of his existence to the compelling need to give himself to her and claim her heart in return.

"Are you sorry you love me?" His mouth waited a breath away from hers.

"No. Never sorry." She cradled his face in her hands and kissed him as proof of her words.

"I want you to be glad . . . for a little while . . . to be happy." Against his firm intent, his body sharpened the thrusts, making them quicker and harder.

"I am, Ransom . . . I love you. I can't change it." Her legs locked even tighter around his waist as her hands glided over his shoulders. "And if you don't take me soon, I may dry up . . . "

"And blow away?" Then he could wait no longer. The rapacious dragon breathing fire through his veins conquered his restraint. Hot, blazing desire claimed his senses. All that mattered was that they were together. They were one. They met each other again and again, each thrust deeper, more desperate, more penetrating than the previous one.

"Liss," he hissed from between his teeth.

"God. Yes!" Her fingers sank into his hard-muscled buttocks and pulled him to her as though she could take his entire being within her woman's heart and hold him there forever.

"Yes!" she cried again.

His right arm swooped down around her lower back and

lifted her. He held her there as he surged into her, then stretched that last tiny bit right before spilling his seed. The frenzy of their passion swept them into an ecstasy of shimmering bliss beyond the bounds of the earth.

The afterquakes of their potent climax kept them silent and holding one another in a trembling embrace. Both wished to preserve the powerful aftermath of euphoria settling peacefully over their world.

Finally, she opened her eyes. He gazed down at her, feeling her love and wanting to hold her against his heart forever. There was nothing he wouldn't do to have her beside him for the rest of his life. She made him feel complete and that all things were as they should be when they were together.

"I'll never regret loving you," she promised, touching the place on his cheek that spasmed into a tic when he became distraught. She belonged to him. She loved him.

"I'll never let you. You're mine." He placed a gentle kiss on her forehead and rolled them onto their sides, not yet willing to separate from her. He tucked her head under his chin and held her close as he drew the quilts over them. She fell into a calm sleep within minutes.

Ransom lay awake into the small hours of the morning. Somehow, he wasn't surprised that Fate would try stealing Felicity. It seemed the only thing he was successful at was making money. That, of course, was easy. It required a little hard work, some planning, and a willingness to learn.

Intimacy. Now that was something difficult. For the life of him, he couldn't understand why he hadn't told her he loved her. Then, recalling the few words he had spoken, he thought that perhaps he had.

Chapter 23

WIN WOKE ENERGIZED by optimism. With the help of Ransom's excellent memory, she wouldn't lose all of her past. As a repository, he'd hold her memories in trust and bring them alive when her own memory failed. And she had the journals.

Ransom slept soundly beside her. The heavy growth of his beard cast dark, seductive shadows on his face. For a long time, she watched him breathe and the flutter of his eyes when he dreamed. A wave of love swept through her.

She smiled tenderly, then touched the edge of his mustache over lips that had loved her so artistically hours earlier. The man had lips as talented and masterful as his hands. Sleep eased the hard edges that sharpened his features while he was awake. Here, he was vulnerable, open—hers without conditions. Her lips hovered over his. Warm breath caressed her cheeks. She placed a kiss on his mouth, then slid away, careful not to disturb him.

Ransom continued snoring softly without so much as a twitch.

Just before drifting into sleep earlier, she'd decided upon the errand that might provide the confirmation she sought. Excitement grew as she laid a fire against the growing chill in the room.

Thirty minutes later, washed and dressed for the cold out of doors, she joined Cordelia for a quick cup of chocolate. She bolted down a pastry on the way out of the dining room, promising Cordelia she'd eat a real breakfast with Ransom later.

For now, she had something very different in mind. The soul-baring conversation she had with Ransom segued her thinking into a different direction. Perhaps things were not quite as bleak as she had speculated previously.

Pulling the heavy, fur-lined cloak, which Ransom had given her upon his return from Seattle, tightly around her shoulders, she set off for the Tlingit village. The day brightened with a late, gray dawn. A stiff, cold wind blew steadily from the north. Churning clouds dipped low with a heavy burden of snow. This morning, even the threat of foul weather couldn't dim her ebullient mood.

Spirit Dancer would give her the confirmation she needed, or he would say she was wrong. *Please, God, don't let me be wrong.*

She prayed that her loss of memory was confined to the technological and historical events between now and her time. As painful as parting with the knowledge she had spent so many years acquiring and mastering was, she judged it a favorable trade for Ransom in this time. "Ya can't have it all, kiddo," she whispered, bending her head into the brisk wind.

Ransom filled a void her career had never touched. A future with him glowed more brightly than anything technology promised or her Ph.D. delivered.

As long as she retained her personal past and the cherished memories of those she loved, the essence of her identity remained intact. And she had Ransom. He hadn't come right out and said he loved her, but last night he had showed her faith, tenderness, and understanding. He had laid the deepest feelings of his heart bare.

She thought Ransom wore his ferocious mask to keep people at a distance. If he allowed them too close, they might see what lay behind the aura of danger enveloping him. Ransom had a handful of trusted friends: those he would do anything for or give anything to help. He had even fewer real enemies, none of whom remained in Sitka.

Not surprisingly, his complex nature appealed to her and made him easier to love. He was the most honorable man she'd ever known, a man she trusted to keep his word. And he'd given his word to be her husband in all things, except love. He couldn't make himself love her any more than she could keep herself from loving him.

Turning down the faint path worn into the sparse, brown grass, she quickened her step. She planned on being home in time for breakfast with Ransom. Tonight, she'd tell him the rest of what he must know. Imagining his reaction at learning he'd be a father brought a smile. Before telling him the news, she'd speak with Spirit Dancer and learn the extent of the memory changes. If anyone could tell her, the shaman could. The fate of their entire future depended upon it. If all she lost was her memory of the future, she'd be able to raise their child and have more children with Ransom. The critical parts of her past would remain. She'd always remember love.

Unexpectedly, something clamped around her arms. She reacted instinctively, but with too little force. A thick rope pinned her upper arms against her sides even as she fought the restraint. Still, she lashed out with her hands to protect herself. Reflexively, she sidestepped and swung around, her booted foot raised.

She connected with a leg and felt it give before jumping back. A muted curse escaped the attacker as he faltered, but he remained on his feet. His two companions continued circling.

In less than a few frantic heartbeats they rushed her, effectively ending her resistance. One man jerked a smelly sack over her head and yanked it down. The other two held her, then lifted her and bound her feet. Before she could scream, they wrapped the rope pinning her arms around her body and legs, pulling her skirts and cloak tightly against her body.

"This is a big mistake. Let me go. Ransom . . ." she pleaded, seeing and smelling only dirty burlap.

"You wanna be gagged, bitch?" threatened a voice from behind her.

Adrenaline released by the fear-filled confrontation thundered through her veins. "No," she answered, shaking her head inside the bag, cringing from the scratchy fibers and fighting the fear blossoming in her chest.

"Keep yer damn mouth shut. We already know who ya are an' who yer damn husband is. Make another sound and I'll gag ya without takin' the bag off yer head. Got it?"

Bile rose in her throat even before she was aware of it. The musty folds of burlap prickling her face and the ropes tightly binding her arms created a claustrophobic panic. She battled the waves of blackness summoning her to a gentler place. She could not throw up!

Cold terror pounced on her thoughts. She nodded, wondering if they meant to kill her. However, the time for contemplating their intentions passed before she finished the thought. One of the men picked her up and slung her over his shoulder. Blood rushed to her head, making her dizzy. Who would do this? Why?

Then she was falling, with no way of stopping herself and no time to scream. She hit the ground headfirst.

The next thing she knew, the pounding in her head forced her into grim reality. Bound and blinded, she turned her thundering head toward the wind, forcing the steely fibers of the burlap into her sensitive cheeks. The flow of almost breathable cold air cleared some of the vertigo swirling through her senses.

One of the men untied her feet, threw her onto a horse, then lashed her onto the saddle. This was a horrible nightmare: on a horse with a bag over her head. At least they had done a good job of securing her atop the beast. The way her head throbbed, another good fall would keep her from worrying about anything for the rest of her life.

Icy wind tore at the edges of her skirts and whipped around her legs and feet as the horse galloped toward some unknown destination. She lost track of time during the bruising ride that stretched into an infinite torture.

When they pulled her off the horse and dumped her onto what felt like a pile of furs, the pounding in her head had beaten her into resignation. The cold penetrated her clothing and her awareness. She shivered uncontrollably.

The roar of the ocean assaulted her ears. Tiny beads of icy dampness on the foul burlap pricked her skin when the wind beat the fabric against her face. The tang of salty spray stung her nostrils. Her hopes for the end of the journey died when the boat surged precariously into the thrashing water. *Oh, God! They are going to go out on that unforgiving, angry sea. I'm going to die again!*

Trussed in coils of rope and buried under layers of furs, panic seized her. She could barely breathe beneath all the layers. The boat rose and fell with the waves. She strained to hear the terse conversations around her. Gradually, she realized that the high gunwales and skill of the sailors kept the waves from swamping them.

Somewhere beyond panic, beyond futility, she found a hysterical calm. All she could think about was Ransom. Would she ever see him again? Then he, too, faded as darkness claimed her.

"Where the hell did she go? There's a Northern blowing down," Ransom ranted at his mother.

"I don't know, but she should have been back by now. She said she'd join you for breakfast." Drawing the heavy drape away from the window, Cordelia peered outside anxiously. Ransom glanced over her shoulder at the growing maelstrom. Fine, grainy snowflakes scurried across the ground. "The only place she might go within walking distance is the Tlingit village."

Dressed for the fury of the storm, he left the house and mounted his waiting horse. Why the hell didn't she wake him? If she wanted to see Spirit Dancer, he'd have gladly taken her.

Urging the reluctant horse into the teeth of the growing storm, a nagging voice expressed his deepest fear. Surely she wouldn't leave him voluntarily. Not after last night. No. She would not.

He shouted her name into the wind as he followed her usual route to the village. Only the howling wind answered his call.

The more time passed, the more dire became her circumstances. Dressed as she was, she couldn't survive the storm even if she found shelter from the wind. The rapidly dropping temperature sucked the warmth from any exposed part of a body. Soon, a man who hadn't protected his mouth and nose from the frigid wind would freeze his lungs by breathing.

With diligent thoroughness, he scoured the trail. No one roamed the areas around the longhouses. Ransom tethered his horse in the lee side of Spirit Dancer's dwelling, then went inside.

The shaman greeted him stoically and motioned Ransom over to the fire. Ransom shook his head. "Has she been here?"

"No. She has been taken," Spirit Dancer answered, staring at the flames.

An invisible fist hammered into his gut. Ransom's steps faltered. *She's been taken back. Gone forever?* A future without Felicity yawned before him as a gaping, black void. He had not really considered her returning to her time before today. But he knew he should have. What Fate gave, Fate could also take away. No, she said she couldn't go back . . . but what if she was wrong?

She couldn't be gone. She wouldn't leave him willingly.

She loved him, didn't she? Remembering the beatific confusion of her admission last night, his doubts melted. She loved him. "Where?" he managed.

"Enemies took her." Spirit Dancer's voice sounded thin and distant, his concentration intent upon the flames. "Right now, she is very cold, White Raven. Terror holds her heart in its hand. The land is testing her. I see no shelter for her. The enemies do not let her speak of the cold."

"Where?" Rage chilled his voice. Fists balled at his side, he approached Spirit Dancer, looming over him in desperation, willing the old shaman to conjure a vision he could share.

"I will find her," Spirit Dancer promised. "The spirits protect her. But she is near the next world. Get what you need. Take no horses. The spirits will show the way if you are on the land." The shaman turned back to the flames. "You must hurry, White Raven. Hurry."

Were he to put his faith in anyone, it was Spirit Dancer. The old Tlingit revered Felicity as just a step this side of the spirit world and his gods. He had acknowledged her specialness the moment she stepped off the *Ompalada*.

Over the years, the mystical powers Spirit Dancer quietly displayed during their close friendship were beyond question. How he tapped into the spirit world, Ransom had no idea, yet he did not doubt the shaman's genuine ability. Spirit Dancer's mystic power now became the only link Ransom had to finding his wife. And he would find her. And those who took her would know his wrath.

The vigilant Tlingit parted, forming a path to the longhouse door. Ransom hastened outside and mounted his horse.

A short time later he had a heavy pack stuffed with the necessities for his trek. In the kitchen, he waited impatiently as Charlet wrapped the last of the provisions he had requested.

"Tell Gerald and Caine what's happened. Have them scour the town. We can't take any chances," he told Cordelia while stuffing a slab of venison jerky into a bag. "Send word to Ivan. Tell him I don't want any ship sailing without having been searched thoroughly for Felicity. Ivan is creative. He'll think of a way to search the ships."

"We won't leave anything unchecked. But you'll find her, Ransom." Cordelia wrung her white-knuckled hands. "You must find her." Tears pooled in her green eyes. In that moment, she looked all of her fifty-three years.

The worry-riddled response he might have made stuck in his throat. The chasm of anxiety gaped under his tightly strung emotions. Focusing only on preparing to survive the ferocity of the storm, he held everything else at bay. The only certainty lay in the death of whoever had taken Felicity.

He'd promised her safety. He'd promised her protection. He'd failed miserably by being unaware of the danger. He'd let her down, and in the process, he'd let himself down, and jeopardized the gentle woman dearest to his heart, the person essential to his happiness.

He stuffed the last of the provisions into his pack, then fastened his heavy polar bear coat.

Cordelia braced his pack on the kitchen worktable long enough for him to slip it on. She handed his gloves over one at a time. Then, just as she had when he was a child building snow castles in New York, she arranged a muffler around his neck. Before she wrapped it over his face, she reached up and put her arms around her son as far as they would reach.

"She loves you, son. So do I," Cordelia said in a shaky voice, fighting back tears.

"I know. I love you, too." He kissed her cheek and pulled away. With the muffler looped around his face until only his eyes were visible, he secured his hat. Flexing his hands in his gloves, he crossed the mud room and left the house.

Outside, two Tlingit with traveling packs approached. Beneath the layers of fur, Ransom recognized Cloud Chaser, the shaman's apprentice, and Raven Wing, the clan's fiercest warrior. Ransom nodded at the pair and fell in behind them after Cloud Chaser pointed their direction.

In a daze of semi-consciousness, Win fantasized that she was on a massage table in an Eddie Bauer dressing room. A kindly masseuse with Inga embroidered on her crisp, white coat used golden hands to rub Ben-Gay into her aching muscles. Another part of her was trying on sub-Arctic clothing. Of particular interest were the electric socks. Brightly colored and deliciously thick, they promised to keep her toes warm as long as a pink bunny beat on a bass drum.

The horse stumbled, jolting her from her reverie. All things considered, she preferred this to the bobbing longboat. True, she had been protected from the icy teeth of the north wind while on the boat, but being consumed by the angry sea while trussed in burlap and rope promised a dismal finality. This time, no one would pull her from the sea, place her in a warm bed, rub feeling into her limbs, and feed her brandy. Remembering the suffocating fear and helplessness under the layers of damp fur as she lay in the boat sent her whispering a prayer of gratitude that her captors had sense enough to abandon the idea.

When she heard the horses again, she had protested the cold on her legs and feet. The furs they tied around her legs and hips barely protected her from frostbite. Matters took a turn for the worse when they gagged her before fastening another heavy fur over her head and shoulders. They then started climbing what seemed the tallest mountain in the world.

Eyes closed against the climb and the thunder in her head, she considered the real possibility of dying tied to this horse. With no idea of whether it was dark or light or how many hours they had traveled, she faded in and out of consciousness.

If she survived this, she swore she'd never ride a horse again. If she survived this, she'd never bemoan the exchange of the learning and technology of her past for the glowing future with Ransom and the child she carried.

Ransom dominated her consciousness. She relaxed as much as possible into the bonds holding her to the saddle as they ascended a mountain high enough to touch the moon. With a wistful sigh, she drifted into a fantasy world where she made love with her husband with slow, seductive movements, and where heat abounded.

The brutal wind howled in the distance. The horse stopped amid the jostling sounds of men dismounting. Win braced herself against the rough treatment she expected.

With the layers of fur peeled away, she stood only in her cloak, which, regardless of its warmth, couldn't protect her from the incredible cold.

A man held each arm and half-dragged, half-pushed her forward. Had she been able to speak, she would have asked them to remove the bag over her head so she might navigate herself. She walked as fast as her stumbling, numb legs and throbbing head allowed.

The tallest of the three men removed the filthy gag, then asked if she needed to relieve herself. He had to remove the fetid burlap bag from her head so she could see where he wanted her to go.

Win squinted into the torchlight flickering in front of her and drew a clean breath. The foul taste in her mouth lingered, regardless of how many times she scrubbed her tongue against the roof of her mouth, then swallowed. It felt warmer in the dark enclosure where they stood. The first thing she noticed were the jagged walls and ceiling. They were in a big cave that sheltered them from the screaming, icy storm. The wind barely reached this part of the cavern.

She extended her hands in the hope they'd untie her.

"No," was all the taller of the two men accompanying her said. He pointed at a black spot on the roughly textured lava wall, then pushed her toward it. "Go. Take care of yer needs."

The dark patch turned out to be a branch of the tunnel

maze. Surely he was not going to watch! She shrugged. It didn't matter. Even pride couldn't refuse her the opportunity for relief.

He stuck the torch in the ground, then motioned her behind a corner where the light barely reached. Win obeyed, grateful for the modicum of privacy. She used the time to collect her thoughts and survey the strange area. Cold as it was, eluding her captors by slipping into the darkness was sheer folly. At the moment, everything seemed stacked against her.

The texture of the pocked walls was sharp. Lava steam and gases or some other volcanic cataclysm had formed the caves a long time ago. With the loss of so much of her memory, she seldom found substantive reasons for what she thought she knew. But she relied on those revelations the same way she trusted her instincts.

Her captors didn't bother with the bag or gag when they resumed their trek into the heart of the caverns. Shrewdly, Win examined her surroundings in the dancing torchlight. When they passed another narrow offshoot, she noted a musty odor and trickles of steam rolling over oddly shaped icicles on the ceiling before disappearing down another branch into an ominous blackness.

"Is that a hot spring?" she asked, keeping her eyes straight ahead.

"Yeah. Too hot ta put yer hand in," answered the tall man on her right. "Can't camp there. It's damp. We'd freeze when we came out here."

After a couple more twists and turns, they entered a large domed cavern. The big man hurled his burden of furs in front of her. "Sit," he ordered, then pushed her at the furs when she didn't comply fast enough.

Holding her throbbing head, she glared up at him, barely able to make out his features. Her heart quickened with anxiety. She gritted her teeth against the waves of nausea her pounding head created.

"You cook?" he asked.

She stared vacantly, for the moment not understanding what he wanted. Then it registered. He wanted her to fix a meal. Not only didn't she cook much beyond coffee, hot milk, and scrambled eggs, but she wouldn't cook for these cretins. Let them starve! The emotional agitation sent her headache into high gear.

"Shit, Sug! She's feebleminded. How the hell she gonna know how ta cook?" asked the shorter man. He punched Sug in the arm. "C'mon. Let's git a fire goin'. Tommy'll be hungry when he's done with the horses."

Win stared at the dirty patch covering the smaller man's left eye without really seeing it. The easy acceptance of her inability to do anything registered. At that moment, she decided to say as little as possible. If they thought her the simpleminded creature Felicity had been before the "miracle on the dock," let them harbor those beliefs. Perhaps they wouldn't watch her as closely. Considering her plight, she'd take every thread of surprise or advantage available.

The aroma of coffee, biscuits, and salmon teased Win's stomach into a growl. She ate when they called her, but said nothing during the course of the meal. When she finished, Sug demanded her boots.

Again, she offered her hands for release, but he shook his head. She struggled to remove the boots with her hands tied. Leering and bending close to her, the man with the patch, whom the others called Ralph, pulled her boots off. His dirty fingers groped and glided up and down the inside of her legs. She fought back the nausea of revulsion. The way things were, she'd need all her strength very soon.

Sharp rock edges dug into her feet through the thick woolen socks. Gingerly, she picked her way toward the pile of furs Sug indicated. Lamenting the loss of her boots, she settled into the warm layers, knowing her plight could be worse.

She'd have to ask for her boots to go anywhere or do anything in the cavern. Without foot protection, any hope of escape evaporated like smoke. The lava would shred her socks, then her feet, before she reached the outside, where she would freeze.

Resigned, she hunkered into the furs in search of warmth and waited for her head to stop throbbing. A few feet away, the three men huddled around the fire and watched her.

Chapter 24

THE WIND'S ICY fingers bullied Ransom and clutched at his heavy pack. Like a woman too angry to cry, the storm launched a wild fury but held back the heavy tears of snow for a saner moment.

The last rays of light faded quickly in the storm. An angry sea thundered fifty feet below the three men who dared the slippery heights. Cloud Chaser pushed onward, climbing the narrow trail etched into the weather-sculpted rock face towering over the sea. Ransom followed, trusting the Tlingit apprentice because he was the only hope of finding Felicity.

As darkness wrapped a hostile fist around the freezing land, the wind raged with a howl that called to the heart of the loneliest wolf.

The trio measured progress in inches and feet along the narrow ledge. To stop was to die. There was no rest until they scaled the jut and descended the other side.

Pretending sleep, Win listened as the hushed voices anxiously discussed the arrival of a fourth man. No doubt, he was the one who told them she was simpleminded.

It seemed unlikely that anyone outside of Sitka considered her in any other light. And no one in Sitka considered her intellectually impaired—a bit eccentric perhaps, but not simpleminded.

Having none of Felicity's memories, she wouldn't recognize the mastermind of this heinous deed when he arrived, but she'd find out without betraying her intellect. How difficult would playing the role of forgetful simpleton be? After all, that's what they expected. Even Adele hadn't shown the slightest surprise when she couldn't remember her own name on the *Ompalada*.

Her captors huddled around the blazing fire and laughed over something she couldn't hear, then grew quiet for a moment. She peeked over the furs and watched them through squinting eyelids.

"She's dead ta th' world," Ralph said.

"Somethin' don't make a lotta sense, here," Sug said pensively.

"Whaddaya mean?" Tommy poured a cup of coffee.

"Why'd a man like Mr. Hamilton go an' marry some girl what couldn't think straight?" Sug asked. "He don't seem the sort that'd marry jest fer a tumble. Hell, I heard every skirt in Seattle was after him. So why'd he marry her if he coulda had all a them? Don't make no sense. He's already got a ton a money."

"It don't really matter none," Ralph answered. "Mebbe he likes humpin' a broad who don't talk back. Thing is, he's what we want. He'll pay the ransom ta git her back. That's all we cares 'bout."

"Hey," Tommy said, grinning from ear to ear. "Ain't that a ransom from Ransom? Get it? That's his name."

The three of them enjoyed a good laugh over the play on words. The volume of Tommy's laughter made it obvious he considered himself the intellectual giant of the group for making the connection.

Win's stomach churned in queasy anger. So that was it. Kidnapping. Extortion. They wanted money. The concept carried a familiar ring.

Then they were talking loudly enough for her to hear again. She swallowed her ire and strained to catch as much as possible.

"Are we gonna kill him after he brings the money?" Tommy asked hopefully.

"Uh-huh," Ralph said, nodding. "By summer, there won't be much left o' him. Nobody comes here except mebbe Indians. They ain't gonna say nothin' about some old bones. We're suppose ta leave the dimwit with the dandy."

"Do we git to have her a'fore we gotta give her over? Seems like a waste not ta," Tommy speculated eagerly. "I ain't had me a fine lookin' woman for a long time."

"You ain't ever had a fine lookin' woman in yer life," Sug countered.

"Yeah, I did. Mebbe not as fine as that one there, but I had me a good-lookin' woman once, and I didn't have ta pay, neither," Tommy defended.

"Was she alive?" Sug taunted.

" 'Course she were. Ya don't think I'd hump no dead woman, do ya?"

"I've seen the women you put it to. Some were hard ta tell," Sug stated.

"But iffen he's gonna kill her later, cain't see how it'd hurt to have a little fun first. 'Sides, I'd bet she'd like it," Ralph said. "We'd be doin' her a favor."

Distraught by the awful vision of her and Ransom's futures, she shuddered. Since they planned on killing her anyway, she'd fight them on the rape. How many times could a woman die? With fresh vigor, she worked on the rope bindings with her teeth. The rough hemp cut into her wrists and opened the scabs on her chapped lips. The taste of blood fueled her efforts.

"Ah don't like killin' a woman," Sug said a while later. "It's bad luck."

"Sug's right," Tommy agreed.

"I don't fancy it none, myself," Ralph said. "Mebbe we could just hump her 'til we cain't no more, then tell the dandy we wants her back when he's done with her. I ain't got no problem killin' her husband. You know how them widow women needs a good man or two. Hell, we deserve her fer capturin' her and gettin' through this here storm."

"He ain't gonna let us stick around after we're done with her husband," Ralph mused. "I hear tell she's worth a lot of gold to him."

"Ta who? Her husband?" Tommy asked, interested.

"Yeah, and ta the boss's partner. I heard him tellin' the boss he planned on havin' it all and her. He 'n the boss are gonna make it look like Hamilton and the dandy's lady run off together, but they'll both be dead. Pretty good plan, eh?"

In the silence hanging onto the end of Sug's speculation, Ralph began moving around. "Ya did a good job fixin' up this here cave for us, Tommy. Real good. Ah don't figure we gotta set up a watch tonight. Ain't nobody coming through this storm and th' only ones who know we're here is the boss an' his dandy partner."

"Ah gotta feed the fire ta keep the horses warm," Tommy said. The sound of his bootheels on the rough lava stilled Win's efforts with the ropes. Tommy passed inches beyond her feet, then faded into the distance.

Motionless, she listened while Sug and Ralph settled into their furs. It wasn't likely any of the three Neanderthals would rape her tonight. They were tired. Besides, rape sounded like a group activity with these three.

Whoever planned her abduction knew a great deal about her husband. The sophisticated tale he apparently concocted to cover the deaths of Ransom, some unknown woman, and eventually herself would have to be very convincing. The one person Win counted on to raise hell if Ransom disappeared was Cordelia. The woman was a bulldog. She'd mobilize all of Sitka to find her son and his killer. But justice wouldn't do her, Ransom, or the other woman any good. They'd be beyond caring.

Her stomach churned at the thought of harm coming to Ransom. There were so many things left unsaid. Her heart lurched at the prospect of him becoming a father. Did he suspect? In six months they would be parents—if they lived that long.

After Tommy returned and settled in beside the blazing fire, she waited until long after she heard three discernible snores before working on her blood- and saliva-soaked ropes. Raw abrasions burned her mouth with every bite and tug on the foul, rough hemp. The first knot loosened. Her head still pounded. Dried blood matted the hair around the painfully swollen cut on her crown.

Because of the storm, travel to the caves would be impossible. She believed Ralph on that score. What if the storm blew over by morning? They might not attack her until after Ransom delivered the money. When he did, they would take it and his life. She couldn't allow that.

Using her swollen lips and tongue, she wormed a gap in the final set of knots. Her wrists pressed together, creating slack. She bit hard and pulled.

The end of the rope slipped through the knot. With another tug, her hands slid free. For several long minutes, she listened and gathered her daring. First, she needed her boots. Slowly, she shoved the furs away and crouched, then stood. Once she had her boots, she'd collect the furs. Next, she'd find the horses, saddle one, then take the rest with her. If they found their way back to Sitka, she swore never to denigrate one of the beasts again.

It was a lousy plan, promising only a small chance of survival in the storm, but it was the only one she had, and it was better than staying and being the lure for Ransom's death. She rubbed her temples, hoping for a better scheme once her head cleared.

She caught the back hem of her skirt, brought it through her legs, and tucked it into the waistband. Her eyes intent on the boots outlined by the blazing fire, she inhaled deeply, then exhaled. Ears tuned to the sleep sounds of her captors, she approached the fire. Her heart thundered. Her head throbbed. The voice of reason pleaded for caution.

With each step nearer the boots standing between Sug's feet and Ralph's head, her heart beat faster.

One of the men emitted a loud snore that stopped his breathing. She froze. Waiting. When he snuffled like a great walrus, she closed her eyes in relief. She waited until all three were snoring before moving again.

Three feet. Two feet. She reached out. Her hand closed on the top of her boots and she lifted.

Ralph rolled over.

She froze with the boots a foot off the ground.

Then his hand closed on her ankle and jerked her feet out from under her, pitching her sideways. She went spinning on top of Sug. In his drowsy state, Sug batted her toward the fire as though she was an annoying fly. She landed hard on her back.

Ralph jumped onto her chest, knocking the wind from her lungs. Terrified, gasping for air, she gaped into his leering face made even more malevolent by his single eye gleaming in the flickering light.

"Goin' somewhere, Missy?"

She cringed, desperate for escape, pinned against the rock by Ralph's considerable weight. Lava points cut into her flesh. She felt a pop along the left side of her rib cage when he bounced on her. What felt like the last air in her lungs gushed out.

"Git offa her," Sug ordered irritably. "She cain't breathe. We ain't suppose ta hurt her."

As soon as Sug dragged Ralph from her chest, the agony of breathing set her lungs on fire. After a few breaths, the pain around the rib that made a popping noise intensified. She wanted to curl into a ball and die quietly, but Ralph held his booted heel on her ankle.

"I asked you a question, girl. Answer me." He ground his boot into her ankle. Lava shredded her sock and cut into her heel and calf. A slow smile stretched his twisted mouth.

She cried out, reflexively trying to sit up and push him away. The pain in her rib only allowed her to reach out.

"Best answer him," Tommy warned from beside Ralph. "Where'd you think you was going?"

Ralph removed his foot from her ankle. The instant relief dazed her until he crouched beside her and leaned into her face. His foul breath was a poison robbing her of what little air she had managed to gasp. He grabbed a handful of hair from the top of her head and yanked.

Her brief scream echoed in the cavern. The cut on the crown of her head started throbbing and bleeding again. Everything before her eyes began swimming. Then she wanted to faint, to hurry up and get this over with, but all she could do was tremble and wait for the next onslaught of pain.

"Damnit, Ralph! Give her time ta answer. Ya scairt her half ta death. She ain't normal. Ya gotta remember that." Tommy grabbed Ralph by the shoulder and jerked him away.

She breathed a little easier without Ralph looming over her.

"Where were ya going?" Sug asked softly.

Wild-eyed, her gaze darted from Ralph to Sug and back. "N-n-n-necessary," she managed.

"Necessary?" Sug asked.

"Damn. She's just wantin' to take care of her needs, Ralph, and you went and scared her." Tommy shoved Ralph away and picked up her boots. "Get up!"

Vision swimming, head and ribs shrieking with agony, she tried to sit. If she didn't obey, Ralph would hurt her again. Looking into his partially illuminated face, she realized he delighted in inflicting pain. The more helpless the victim, the greater his enjoyment.

Determined to deny him further pleasure, she sat up. The impact of her boots being thrown against her chest sent the air whooshing from her lungs again. She rolled onto her side and gathered her precious boots, then clutched them against her fiery chest as though they were a golden treasure. They'd have to kill her before she gave them back.

"Put 'em on and go do what ya gotta. Then git back on them furs. There ain't nowhere ta go and no way ta git there, girl. Understand?" Tommy demanded.

Mutely, she nodded, then steeled herself for the growing agony of putting on her boots. The lava cuts along the heel and calf of her left leg were already swelling. Once she got the boot on, she'd have to cut it off.

While the men settled down again, she pushed upright, then staggered into the darkness.

"I'll follow her," Ralph announced, throwing back his blankets and furs.

"No," Tommy said. "I will. I'll check the horses while I'm at it."

Too soon, Tommy caught up and took her arm in a death grip. Win felt the familiar nausea start churning her stomach. She didn't trust Tommy any more than she did Ralph. They both radiated a ruthless quality she recognized from the street bullies of her youth.

When he pulled her close, his gap-toothed grin bespoke his intent. He wanted her for himself, before Ralph or Sug realized what he was about. An icy calm blanketed her emotions. The pain running from head to toe faded. Her shattered nerves stopped functioning. She'd do whatever was necessary to preserve the life growing inside her womb.

Chapter 25

RANSOM FOLLOWED CLOUD Chaser into the hollow of a rock outcropping. The three men huddled in the darkness and formed a barrier against the swirling wind. They laid wood for a small fire. The flame wasn't intended for warmth in the glacial night; it augmented the medium binding Cloud Chaser with Spirit Dancer.

Ransom stared into the fire and saw only flames. Obviously, Cloud Chaser divined far more from the wind-twisted pyre. His head bobbed in understanding as though engaged in a mute conversation with a spirit housed in the tongues of flame.

After a while, Cloud Chaser relaxed. When the ritual ended, the strain of communicating with Spirit Dancer's vision deepened the lines the cold pinched around his eyes. "We eat. Drink. Then we go," he told them.

Ransom bit back the urge to prod Cloud Chaser. All three were tired from battling the storm's fury. Once the snow started flying, traveling would be almost impossible. Ransom focused on the trek ahead. Thinking on a deeper level was dangerous. He burned too much energy with his anger and burgeoning hatred for the vermin who'd kidnapped his wife and cast her into harm's way. Fear for her plight made him warm. Frozen perspiration killed just as surely as insufficient clothing.

Felicity was so vulnerable in this hostile storm. The winter cloak he'd given her was no protection against the teeth of a freezing blow such as this one. The cloak had been intended for warmth in the closed carriage during the short ride into town.

He swore retribution on her abductors. She had to be afraid. Terrified. Spirit Dancer had said she was cold. The northern freeze forgave nothing and no one. It spread its lethal punishment on everything within reach. Its insidious effects became most evident after the friendly touch of warmth. Then came the pain of frostbite and burn of skin chilled beyond revival.

A shiver of dismay shook Ransom. He ate without tasting and drank without quenching his thirst. His haunted eyes peered into the darkness in search of a path. The dread of living without her gnawed at the raw edges of his heart. Nothing would hold meaning without her. Who would ever love him so dearly? Who would ever sacrifice so much of herself as a price for loving him?

Anxious, he shoved the rest of his venison jerky into his pocket.

"We go," Cloud Chaser finally said. Outside the meager shelter, the wind and fine granules of swirling snow blasted them. The storm pounced into the recess and claimed the fire's life.

Connected by a sturdy rope, the trio bent into the growing tempest. The two followers relied solely on Cloud Chaser's vision as guidance through the frozen darkness screeching and twisting in the wind's fury. Cold gnawed at every piece of exposed skin it could sink its needlelike fangs into, then opened wider and bit harder.

In the bitter, black cold, time stood still. Just when Ransom thought they had walked the length of the island, Cloud Chaser tugged on the rope and led them out of the wind.

Raven Wing pulled off a glove with his teeth, then rummaged in Ransom's pack for the stash of candles. In the light cast by one protected candle flame, they moved slowly, single-file into the lava tubes and caverns, staying close to the walls.

As they rounded a sharp curve, horses nickered. The animals were a welcome surprise. They examined the horses and warmed themselves at the dying fire Ransom eagerly fed into blazing life. Whoever had cared for the horses had rubbed them down and provided plenty of feed and water. Ransom scowled at the provisions barrels against the far wall. The abduction had been well planned by someone familiar with the harsh, volatile weather of Baranov Island.

Raven Wing examined the mounts closely. "They are better rested than we." He ran his hand down the flank of the barrel-chested bay. "We will take them when we leave."

Shrugging out of his pack, Ransom nodded. He and Cloud Chaser squatted near the fire. The apprentice drew a map of the caverns in the ashes and indicated the place his powerful vision from Spirit Dancer promised they would find Two Women.

Ransom laid out the heavy fur garments he'd brought for Felicity. It didn't matter if they were too big. They could tie the excess together. Next, he found a fresh candle and lit it with an ember from the fire.

"I will go with you," Raven Wing said softly.

Ransom shook his head. "If all does not go well, I won't be coming back and I don't want any of the Tlingit harmed for the help you've given me and Two Women."

"Will you kill them?"

Ransom took his time answering. "If they've harmed her, I'll kill them tonight. But I need answers before they feel the death I have planned." After a final glance at the map in the ashes, he checked his pistol and holstered it. Preferring the lethal silence of the blade, he withdrew his hunting knife from its scabbard and silently moved into the tunnel.

He hadn't gone far when he heard someone approaching. He snuffed the candle. Seconds later, a shadow-dancing torch illuminated the walls. When the man rounded the corner, Ransom hurled the full impact of his fist into the man's gut.

Tommy doubled over, dropping the torch.

Ransom sent another fist into Tommy's jaw, effectively silencing him.

Tommy flew backward, hit the wall with a cracking sound, then slid down.

Poised for battle, Ransom watched him, his heart beating hard. His opponent didn't move. Cautiously, Ransom checked the odd angle of the man's neck. Upon closer inspection, he saw it was broken.

Cursing silently, Ransom grabbed the man by the collar and dragged him a good thirty feet into the total darkness of an offshoot tunnel. Hidden so far inside the smaller passage, he wouldn't be found quickly.

Raven Wing waited beside the torch stuck into the ground and burning as a marker in the main tunnel. "I am a warrior. I go for Two Women."

Ransom nodded in resignation.

A few minutes later, they made their way through the twisting maze. Ransom snuffed the torch before entering the inky corridor. Soon, a faint glow flickered off the walls. They were close. Very close.

Holding their knives ready and bent low, Ransom and Raven Wing crept into the domed room. Ransom's keen eyes scoured the chamber. Ahead, on their left lay a bundle of furs. Closer to the fire, two figures slept.

Ransom circled right. Raven Wing moved into the gyrating shadows on the left. Only the soothing crackle of the warming fire sounded in the cavern. Crouched to spring at anything moving in the shadows, they approached the two figures buried in layers of furs and blankets near the fire.

Ransom and Raven Wing communicated with a series of gestures. Each took the closest form, figuring a fifty-fifty chance it was Felicity.

Ransom bent onto one knee, his knife ready, and leaned over the mound of blankets. No amount of furs could make Felicity so large.

A man surged out of the pelts with near blinding speed. A knife blade glinted in the firelight, slashing toward Ransom.

Ransom caught his wrist and started down with his own blade. Instantly, the big man's hand gripped Ransom's knife-wielding wrist. Locked in combat, the test of brute strength remained a silent battle punctuated by an occasional grunt.

They rolled near the fire, each trying to gain advantage or dislodge the other. Ransom stretched the big man's arm toward the flames. The stench of burning hair and flesh wafted between them.

Abruptly, Sug released the knife into the flames and bucked, pulling his wrist from Ransom's grasp. He grabbed for the knife in Ransom's hand and caught his wrist.

Their eyes locked. Ransom released his fury from its mental cage, then grinned menacingly when surprise turned to fear in Sug's eyes. With a mighty shove, he embedded the knife into the big man's heart, holding it there until astonishment became a permanent feature.

Ransom withdrew his knife and wiped the blade clean on the Sug's shirt, then checked with Raven Wing.

"Is he dead?"

"Almost," Raven Wing answered, holding his blade at Ralph's throat.

"Ahhh! God! Don't let 'em kill me!" Ralph pleaded.

Ransom scoured the remaining blankets and furs, his fear mounting when he found Felicity's cape, but not her. He stormed back and hauled the injured man up by his hair. "Where is she?" His demand reverberated off the walls.

"Tommy took 'er. Don't . . . don't kill me! Please. Help

me. I'm jest doin' what I'm told." Ralph tried to double over and stem the blood spilling from the wound in his side.

"Who told you to take my wife?" The ice in Ransom's question matched the cold gripping the island.

"Oh, God! Hamilton." Ralph groaned and clutched at his side. "If I tell you, he'll kill me."

"If you don't, I'll kill you. Slowly. Painfully. You'll wish yourself dead a thousand times before I finish. Now, you tell me who."

"Vance Gardener an' his partner. They said she wouldn't be hurt none. I told ya. Now ya gotta help me."

"Who's his partner?" When Ralph's eyes started rolling toward the back of his head, Ransom shook him. "Dammit! Who is Gardener's partner?"

Ralph roused for a moment. "Don't know 'is name . . . a fancy . . . dandy . . . slick." Ralph passed out and Ransom dropped him onto his furs.

"Leave him. We must find Felicity. Christ, she's not even wearing her cloak. She'll freeze." He and Raven Wing snatched up the torches lying near the fire and lit them.

They started down the tunnel leading to the horses, Raven Wing exploring the offshoots on the left, Ransom taking the right.

"Felicity! It's Ransom. Where are you?" he called.

"Two Women. You are safe. The spirits have sent us to you," shouted Raven Wing.

Their calls ranged between booming echoes and muted cries. From a corridor halfway down the tunnel, Ransom summoned Raven Wing. When the Tlingit joined him, he gestured at a torn strip of fabric hanging on a jagged out-crop.

"She's in there." Ransom indicated slushy footprints icing over at the entrance of the tunnel housing the hot spring pool, then lifted the woolen strip from the rock and examined the dark stain by torchlight. "Blood. She's hurt." Steam billowed from the opening and roiled along the ici-cles on the ceiling. "I'm going in." Ransom began removing his clothing, starting with his heavy coat. The only safe way of entering and later exiting the steam cave was naked. If his clothing became steam-saturated, it would freeze solid on him as soon as he hit the subzero air.

"I'll get clothes. Blankets to dry," Raven Wing said, propping his spare torch on the wall. "You stay there till I come back. I bring Cloud Chaser, too."

Ransom nodded, too busy undressing to answer. Holding a torch at waist level, he entered the tunnel, calling Felicity's name and identifying himself.

He ducked through the ice ring forming around the entry to a bubble cave lodging the hot spring. Steam wafted upward through a hole he knew would freeze over by the end of the night. The rising vapor swirled with his movements and continued its ascent. The dense moisture muted the splattering of boiling water in the pool. When the spring belched a great bubble, the sulfur burned his nostrils and sent steam through the tunnel by which he entered.

His breath caught in his throat at the sight of Felicity's damp form curled into a ball and resting against the dripping wall.

"Oh, God, Liss," he murmured, angered and agonized by her condition. Her blood-matted hair hung in snarls caught on the rocks. The way she clutched her middle provoked vile images of the cruelest possibilities he knew a woman could endure.

Gingerly, he cupped her chin and turned her face toward him. A rush of protectiveness so strong it was staggering washed through him. She didn't deserve this. And he shouldered a lion's share of the blame for not protecting her as he promised.

"Liss? Can you hear me?" he asked, gently moving the wet tangles of hair from over her eyes.

At first she gave no sign of recognition. She stared with vacant eyes and blinked several times.

"Liss? It's me, honey. Ransom. God, please say something."

"Ransom?"

A flicker of relief eased the knot tying up his gut. "Yes, sweetheart. It's me. I've come to take you back."

"Back?" A small shake of her head denied him. "We can't. We'll die if we leave. We'll freeze. And it's so warm in here. We can sleep. He won't come in."

"No, Liss. He won't ever come in and he's not waiting for you anymore. I'm here now. You're safe." His heart ached when she shook her head.

"Safe is an illusion." She rested her forehead on her knees, her head still shaking. "I didn't want to die, but I made the wrong turn and . . . and I had to come in here or . . . or . . . I couldn't fight anymore."

Damn, but the helpless feeling was back and there was no way to alleviate her pain. If she'd argue or scream or yell, he'd know she was all right. Seeing the physically and mentally beaten woman who had fought and won more battles in her life than any three old men, he knew she wasn't all right.

"We must leave. Can you walk? Or should I carry you?"

"No. No! Please, don't touch me." Her head shot up. A mixture of pain and terror filled her teary blue eyes.

Ransom cupped her chin. "Liss. You're safe. Please, trust me."

She stared without blinking. Gradually, a spark of life flickered in her eyes. A tremulous hand reached out and touched his cheek. "You're real."

"I'm real, sweetheart. Will you come with me? Will you let me take you out of here?" A smile of relief twitched at the corners of his mouth.

"Yes." She stroked his face for reassurance.

"Are you hurt badly?"

"I have a concussion . . . a cracked rib on my left side, and . . . and I need to cut my boot off my left foot pretty soon. I could use a few stitches in the top of my head, too. Everything else is . . . is tolerable."

Ransom issued a string of dock curses as the misery of her injuries settled in. "Take my hands. We're going to stand up and get you out of those clothes."

"I'll freeze . . ."

"Don't worry. I'll take care of everything else, including keeping you from freezing." He took her hands and carefully drew her up against his chest.

"It's okay, Ransom," she whispered dreamily. "I had worse on the basketball court, only not all at once."

"What did you say?" he asked, unable to understand her muted words.

"Huh? I didn't say anything." She blinked hard as though trying to keep him in focus. "Did I?"

He had her stripped and sitting on her clothes in minutes. He left the torch and felt his way to the steam riddled entrance where Raven Wing and Cloud Chaser waited at a safe distance. He dashed into the freezing cold and grabbed a fresh torch, a clean shirt, and his knife.

The black violence simmering behind his calm facade almost erupted when the angle of his torchlight revealed the bruises and scrapes on her body. Holding himself in check, he cut the boot from her foot. With a clean shirt, he bathed her wounds with the healing waters of the bubbling mineral spring.

His heart swelled with love when she posed no objection at being carried out of the cavern and turned over to Cloud Chaser and Raven Wing for drying and dressing.

She groaned and held her rib. "Okay. Now we're both ready, but I really *do* have a headache tonight."

In the muted light of the torch, he caught the glint in her eyes. The temptation to hug her was immense, but he overcame it. Instead, he laughed in open relief, thankful to have her back.

Shivering uncontrollably as Cloud Chaser and Raven Wing dried her, Win had no time for embarrassment. The insidious cold penetrated every cell in her being. With Cloud Chaser's support and soft-spoken instructions, she donned the strange clothing. Although heavy and bulky, the layers held the cold at bay. She loved her new outfit.

Ransom carried her to the fire where the horses waited. There, he wrapped her ribs and made her comfortable while her hair dried. She pulled clusters over her shoulder and worked through the snarls with her fingers.

She hadn't realized Raven Wing remained behind until he joined them, toting a pile of furs and blankets formerly owned by her captors. The thought of the three cretins coming after her again plunged a shard of fear into her heart. She trembled, recalling Tommy's attempt to get under her skirts.

Tommy's methods of persuading an unwilling woman proved more subtle than Ralph's. Tommy coerced his victims by pinching and quiet intimidation. Had she not anticipated an attack, he might have succeeded with his first attempt. She used the element of surprise by tromping on his instep and following that with a solid knee into his groin. She'd never run so hard, fast, and blindly in her life.

The advantage had switched. Tommy had a torch and cornered her. The choice became him or the hot spring. She chose the hot spring.

"Are they all dead?" She stared at the furs and blankets Raven Wing sorted.

Raven Wing's nod served as a sad balm that uncoiled the tension tightening her bruised body. Her hands dropped into her lap as her eyes sought Ransom. "They were going to extort money, gold I think, for my return. When you brought it, they were going to kill you." She shivered at the gruesome memory.

"Another man is coming here. I don't know when. He's the one who wants you dead. I wasn't supposed to die right away." Eyes closed, she shook her head, struggling for the words her tired brain wished to ignore.

As an escape from the frightful thoughts, she concentrated on Ransom's meal preparations.

"Two things about this country, Felicity. You must drink plenty of water and you must eat. Of the two, water is the most important, so drink up." He gestured at the cup beside her.

Cloud Chaser rearranged her damp hair. "Almost dry."

She drained the cup and set it down. "Do we have to stay here until the storm dies?"

"We go soon," Cloud Chaser said, settling onto a rock near the fire. "Too many evil spirits here. When winter is done, we will purify these caves and make them safe again. Now we will eat. Dry your hair. Then we go."

"It will be good to be home where I can sleep for about a week." Had she ever been so tired? At the moment, she was almost too weary to feel pain. Since Ransom bound her ribs, they ached less.

"You aren't going home. I'm leaving you with Spirit Dancer."

A wave of panic lanced her being. "Not going home? Why? I didn't do anything wrong. I think I would've died before I let those three . . ."

Wiping his hands, he hastened to her side. "Sh-h-h-h-h. No, sweetheart. You've misunderstood. I want you safe. The only way I can do that is to find out who's behind this, then deal with them. We can't wait for our man here. We have to get you back where those cuts on your leg and back can be treated. Remember what you told me about infection?"

She remembered very clearly, and she knew he was right. The first signs were evident in her calf.

"With you at the village, no one will know I've found you. If they think you're missing, they'll have to change their plans. They'll make mistakes.

"Vance Gardener is involved with the man you mentioned. They're playing a deadly game and I want you out of their reach. Right now, we have an edge, we have you back. So, we take no chances. We can't risk anyone knowing I've found you. You'll be safe in the longhouse. Raven Wing will watch over you, too."

The back of his hand stroking her cheek soothed her. "You're the target," she said. "And there's another woman they're going to kill, too. It's supposed to look like you ran away together.

"Ransom . . ." She took his hand while searching his eyes. "They didn't know . . ."

"What? What didn't they know?" he encouraged.

"About me. About the . . . That I'm Two Women. They thought I was, well, like Felicity used to be."

As he rocked back on his heels, his eyes brightened. "What else did you learn?"

The tempered urgency he emanated bespoke the importance of telling him everything that had happened since leaving the house. She called upon an inner reserve and found a logical detachment while relaying the events. By the time she finished, she had consumed the water, jerky, and biscuits Cloud Chaser routinely handed to her.

The telling left her exhausted and Ransom pensive. Weary, she closed her eyes against her perpetual headache just for a moment. The next thing she knew, Ransom was tying off the legs and sleeves of her fur clothing. Too tired to worry or move, secure in the safety of his care, she let him bundle her up without protest.

She came fully awake when Raven Wing lifted her and handed her to Ransom. The feel of the skittish horse beneath her set off an alarm.

"You know I won't let you fall," Ransom assured her. "Get comfortable and sleep if you can."

The security of his arms quelled her apprehension. She snuggled against him and let her eyes drift shut. Even the pounding in her head lost its power.

She awakened briefly when they rested the horses. The screaming storm no longer seemed real. The three of them found her in the caverns; they'd find their way home.

They traveled through the daylight hours without stopping. The wind and blowing snow buffeted them. Ransom roused her to drink from canteens they kept inside their coats. They refilled their canteens with snow.

The last rays of dusk were fading from the clouds by the time they caught sight of the Tlingit village. Her head still throbbed, but with less intensity, for which she was grateful.

Ransom carried her into the longhouse. All the while, she muttered, "I am never getting on another horse. It's cruel, brutal punishment."

"The horse didn't seem to mind." Ransom settled her near the fire, then untied the ends of her sleeves and pant legs and rolled them up. He examined the scabs and red rope burns around her wrists.

"I wasn't talking about the horse." Her mood softened when she gazed into eyes filled with worry. "When will I see you?"

"Tomorrow or the next day. When it's safe."

"How long will I be here?"

"I don't know. Until it's safe."

"How are you defining safe?"

"Safe is when Vance Gardener and his partner are no longer a threat," he replied evenly.

She wondered if that meant when they were dead. The question hung on the tip of her tongue, but she didn't want to hear the answer. For the first time, she truly understood how dangerous her husband was and the ferocity with which he protected his own.

"The spirits smiled on you both," Spirit Dancer told them. "Raven Wing speaks highly of your courage, Two Women. You are brave."

Tears filled her eyes at the sight of the shaman who now looked twice his great years. He awed her. He'd known where she was and guided Cloud Chaser in the storm. Truly, he had powerful spirits directing him. She recalled his assurances that those same spirits watched over her. Now she believed him. "I thank you and Cloud Chaser and Raven Wing for your friendship and courage to guide Ransom to the caverns, Spirit Dancer."

The shaman smiled at her before turning his attention to Ransom. "Go now, White Raven. We will care for her. She will mend whole and well. You must rest, too. The battle is not over. You will need your strength."

Ransom nodded at the old man, his debt of gratitude, more than he could repay in a lifetime, evident in his shining eyes.

He touched Felicity's cracked and swollen lips with his thumb, then placed a tender kiss on her forehead.

"Thank you for coming after me," she whispered. *Thank you for loving me.*

"You're mine, Liss. I take care of what's mine." He kissed her softly on the lips.

She watched him leave, feeling a blister form on her heart. For a while she had deluded herself that his love for her had sent him into the storm. Why else would he have risked his life? But it wasn't love. She was a possession and Ransom Hamilton cared for his possessions. No one stole something of his and kept it.

Chapter 26

"FOOD, A HOT bath, and bed," Ransom answered from the mud room off the back of the kitchen where he removed his storm gear.

A few minutes later, he entered the kitchen and washed up. "Damn, but it's cold out there. We're going to wake up with a foot of snow."

Cordelia tossed a towel at him, then poured two steaming cups of coffee. "Sit," she ordered, pointing to a chair at the worktable.

The bowl of venison stew and fresh bread, butter, and preserves she placed before him carried a command of "Eat." She waited until he complied before taking a seat across the table.

"Will you continue searching at first light?"

"No. The storm is growing worse, and I need sleep."

Cordelia wrung her hands as she studied her son's face. "She's not dead, Ransom. I know it. I just know it. Actually, I didn't think you'd come home without her. "

Ransom's spoon paused midway between his bowl and

his mouth. The temptation to tell her that Felicity was safe nearly won out. Then he reminded himself that the smallest slip, regardless of how unintentional, could jeopardize Felicity's safety. This time, he'd protect her at all costs. He held his silence.

She waited until he finished the stew before speaking again. "There's something I must tell you." She toyed with the rim of her coffee cup. "I know you're tired and this isn't an opportune time for discussing this, but there's never a convenient time for confessions."

Ransom glanced up from his meal. "What?" he asked, reaching for another piece of bread.

"The letters you wrote Cassandra Forsythe weren't delivered because of me. I never posted them. I intercepted the letters she wrote you when I picked up the mail. I burned them all." The painful disclosure pinched tiny lines into Cordelia's smooth face.

Ransom stopped chewing and gaped at her in disbelief. Surely he had heard wrong. "You what?"

"I didn't want you to marry without love, Ransom. You didn't love her. She didn't love you." Cordelia lifted her head high, her hands flat on the table. "You *both* deserved better than that."

"Who the hell were you to decide what we deserved?" Christ, first Arch's betrayal, now his mother's confession of betrayal. Who next?

Instead of cowering or charging back, Cordelia met her son's hurt, angry glare. "Do you love Felicity?" Her palms lifted slightly and her fingers began curling on the wooden surface.

"Why? Are you going to sit in judgment of whether or not I deserve her or she deserves me?" He didn't want to know this—not now.

"Do you love her?" Cordelia shouted, her hands balled into fists on either side of her coffee cup.

"It's none of your damn business." His appetite gone, he batted the bowl away and left it spinning on the edge of the table. "Why? Why did you betray me? What did I do to *deserve* that?"

"Do you love her?" she demanded in a stony voice, her emerald eyes as determined and unrelenting as his. Her knuckles turned white from the tight fists pressed against the table.

"Yes! God damn it! I do!" His fist hit the table hard and sent the dishes jumping and the coffee sloshing from the cups. "Satisfied?"

"Yes," she answered softly, relaxing her hands, then pushing away from the table. "Yes. And it will be worth your wrath for the rest of my life to hear that answer from your lips." She stood. The scraping sound of the chair legs on the wooden floor grated with finality. "When this is over and you've found her, as I know you will if you haven't already, I'll book passage on the next ship for San Francisco."

Head high, Cordelia folded her hands in front of her and turned to leave.

"Why, Ma? Why?" The anguish in his voice hung in the space between them.

Shoulders set, she paused at the kitchen door, but didn't turn around. "Because I love you, son."

"Saying you love me is an excuse, not a reason. You owe me an explanation." With a sigh, he softened his harsh tones. "I want to understand why you did this . . . why you betrayed my trust in you . . . and, damn, why are you telling me now of all times?"

"I know that if you love her, you'll turn this island inside out and you'll find her." She drew a long, deep breath. "I know you, son. You wouldn't have come home without her. There will be no arguments or questions from me. You'll do what you think is best for Felicity, which is as it should be.

"As for the other . . . Some things are best left alone." Shoulders drooping, Cordelia remained poised at the kitchen door with her back an unyielding wall.

Tired as he was, her statements carried no surprise. She

knew him better than anyone. Rubbing his whiskered jaw, a question Felicity had raised popped into his mind. He'd been meaning to ask Cordelia for weeks. Now his instincts deemed it relevant. Glaring at her tension-stiffened back, he asked, "Does it have anything to do with my name?" She visibly flinched and Ransom leaned back, confident he'd struck a nerve.

Silence swam in the gulf between them for several minutes. "Felicity asked me about my name once. Before then, I never gave any thought as to why you named me Ransom instead of after my father or some other traditional name. Now I'm asking. Why did you name me Ransom?"

After another long silence, Cordelia faced him, her green eyes dry, the pain of old emotions readily apparent. "I was angry." Her right hand laid in the palm of her left, she presented the picture of composure.

They had spent too many years under the same roof not to know the ways in which to extract information from one another. Ransom set aside the hurt of her betrayal and concentrated on discovering her motives. "So why didn't you name me Angry?"

In spite of the seriousness of the topic, the right corner of Cordelia's mouth twitched. Her fingers flexed, revealing a rigid tension. "That might have been too obvious, though it crossed my mind."

His brows shot up in surprise. "Really? You would have named me Angry?" Now it was his turn to soften. "Angry Hamilton?" A small smile eased some of the agitation filling the space between them. "I can see it now in the London drawing rooms and the social parlors of Boston and New York when I was growing up." His voice rose an octave. "May I present Mr. and Mrs. James Hamilton and their son Angry."

The mockery had them both at ease for a moment before the strain of the circumstances returned.

"Tell me, Mother. Tell me why," he pleaded, the need to understand blazing clearly in his tortured eyes.

Cordelia winced at the distress stamped on her son's angular features made harsh by fatigue and disappointment. She sighed in resignation. "I was barely nineteen, and I was in love," Cordelia confessed, resuming her place at the table.

"Ulf Voss was a Norwegian sea captain building his own shipping fleet. He had two ships when I met him, though he was a young man of only twenty-three. He was a hard worker. To me, Ulf was a golden Viking whom I wanted to spend the rest of my life loving and being loved by.

"We wanted to be married, so we went to my father. Ulf asked him for my hand. But my father said no. He said he'd signed papers to wed me to James Hamilton.

"At the time, James seemed ancient. I was nineteen and he was forty, more than twice my age. I protested." She shrugged. "Father locked me in my room and promised he'd call the law if Ulf tried seeing me. I cried. I threatened to run away. I managed to sneak out to see Ulf twice with the help of my maid. Ulf and I were going to flee on one of his ships and be married somewhere else. But the night we were to leave, James caught us at the dock."

Ransom poured them coffee, his attention riveted on the sudden coldness of his mother's eyes and the hardness in her voice.

"Your father didn't mince words or spare anyone's feelings. He wanted me because I was young and he thought me beautiful. I'd be a pretty bauble on his arm. After all, I was trained in the ways of high society and had been running our household since my mother's death when I was but twelve.

"And he wanted an heir." A tired hand swept a cluster of silver-threaded raven hair toward her otherwise perfect bun.

"To that end, he'd bought my father's gambling debts. Father gambled for as long as I can remember, but he'd kept his wagers small. However, his habits must have undergone a change because he owed James Hamilton a considerable fortune. The debts amounted to more than my father had. The payment of those debts was to be my bride price. If they weren't paid, my family would be disgraced and left penniless. I was the oldest of three girls. The thought of my sisters living in the streets was painful, but I admit, Ransom, I was willing to let them do it and leave with Ulf."

Cordelia's mouth twisted in a calculated smile. "I'd been the dutiful daughter and taken care of everything for my father and sisters for almost seven years. I deserved my freedom. Or so I thought at the time. I didn't make the gambling debts, but I was being asked to pay them with my future, my heart—with Ulf.

"You may have wondered why I'm not close to my sisters. James told them I didn't care if they lived in the streets. He told them how selfish I was in preferring to run away with my Norwegian sea captain. I could hardly deny it. It was true. I didn't care what happened to anyone except Ulf.

"Ulf was my weakness and James used it. He asked me if I knew what happened to the crew of a ship attacked by pirates and burned to the waterline." Cordelia's fingers laced around her coffee cup. The distant look in her eyes said she was far away reliving the pain of a memory.

"I knew then that choice was merely an illusion. I had no choice. I had to marry James. So I made the best deal I could. In the process, I shamed and humiliated Ulf. I told James I'd marry him and stay married as long as Ulf remained healthy. If anything happened to Ulf or his ships, I'd divorce him and create a scandal they'd talk about in society drawing rooms and parlors for years." She flashed Ransom a knowing look. "Your father hated scandal, which always made me wonder what he'd been caught at and by whom."

Cordelia sipped her coffee, her expression more in tune with the present. "Eventually you were born. I named you Ransom because that's what you were to me at the time. Oh, I loved you with all my heart. But you should have been Ulf's son. You were so beautiful and so good, you should have been born out of love, not coercion and underhanded agreements."

"I noticed that you didn't cry at his funeral," Ransom remarked, mulling over the revelations.

"No. In spite of the circumstances of our marriage, I was a good wife to your father. I denied him nothing. I upheld my end of the pact, and so did he. Although I did all that was asked and expected, I couldn't prostitute myself any further by shedding a single tear when he died."

In the silence that followed, his curiosity got the better of him. "What happened to Ulf Voss?"

"I don't know. I no longer received newspaper clippings on him or his business to prove he was alive after James died. I suppose during the last thirty-four years Ulf found another princess to love and married her and lived happily ever after." She smiled sadly at her own assessment. "You cannot turn back the hands of time, Ransom. That's why, at the risk of incurring your undying wrath, I couldn't let you go forward with Cassandra. You wouldn't listen when I spoke of marrying for love. I guess it was like describing fine chocolate to someone who has never tasted it.

"But I must ask, now that you've had a taste of love in your marriage, would you willingly settle for less?" With the question, her eyes locked on his. Cordelia nodded, contentment easing the strain. "Hopefully, you'll encourage your children to marry for love."

While she cleared the table, Ransom weighed her story. So many things about his childhood and the oh-so-formal relationship of his parents now made sense.

The banging of the back door distracted them.

"It's colder 'n hell out there!" came Caine Tilson's shivering voice.

Ransom fetched another cup and poured coffee while Caine shucked his heavy outer gear. "I know. Here. This will warm you." He uncorked a bottle of fine Scotch whiskey and poured a shot into his and Caine's cups. Cordelia cleared her throat and pointed at her coffee cup with a soapy hand. He poured a healthy slug into her cup, too, and they exchanged a knowing look. It had already been a hard night.

"When did you get back?" Caine asked. He glanced around the kitchen, then lifted his eyes to the ceiling. "Is she home?"

"No. She isn't here," Cordelia answered softly.

Ransom caught her eye, then slightly nodded a thank you for her unquestioning support. "I got back an hour or so ago. The storm is building into a real fury," Ransom told Caine. "Is everything secure at the shipbuilders and on the wharf?"

"Aye. It's fine, all battened down and shipshape. We've nothing to worry about on the wharf at the moment, either." He picked a chair at the table near the stove and wrapped his long fingers around the cup to leach the warmth from the coffee he sipped.

"I've grown quite fond of your young wife, Ransom. I've been praying you'd find her, but I guess it wasn't too likely in this storm." Using two fingers, he fished a letter out of his shirt pocket and put it on the table. "Maybe this will give us a clue. Someone left it on the counter shortly before I closed up tonight. I brought it by in case you had returned."

They stared at the envelope with Ransom's name neatly printed on it. Ransom reluctantly dragged it closer and opened it. He read for a moment, then read it a second time before tossing it at Cordelia and Caine.

"Someone is counting heavily on you wanting her back," Cordelia said slowly, pointing at the amount of the demand.

Ransom retrieved the letter and smoothed it on the tabletop. Right now, he needed a clear head, but three days without sleep blunted his senses. He reread the letter aloud, then hunched over it and stared at the paper.

Felicity had warned of an extortion attempt. With the storm raging, no doubt the man her abductors awaited still enjoyed the illusion of having his golden bargaining chip safely stashed in the caverns.

"The penmanship is legible but not distinctive. I don't recognize it, so I probably haven't seen it before. The writer is well-educated; at least he can spell. The sentence construction is English or American. Russians write English in a different style. Consequently, we can eliminate most of the Americans in Sitka since they have a tendency to do the same."

"What about the man you suspected in Seattle? Vance Gardener?" Caine asked eagerly. "Could he write this?"

Ransom shook his head, then drained his cup. "Gardener's expertise with a pen doesn't stretch this far. Besides, I've seen his handwriting, and this isn't it, but he's involved." Recalling Felicity's account of the trio's conversation, they were waiting for Gardener's partner. Most likely, his partner had written the letter.

"Two of the men from the *Juliet* told me this afternoon they saw Vance Gardener on the wharf. He's grown a heavy beard and dresses like a common sailor," Caine mused. "You scared the *Juliet*'s crew something fierce when you went aboard her bleeding from that knife fight. Not a one of them holds any kindness for Vance Gardener, even if you can't prove he hired your attackers."

Ransom shrugged. The scant amount of whiskey relaxed him. The strain of the last few of days crept over him. He gave his head a small shake to clear it. Gardener was involved, but he lacked the patience and planning abilities evident in the caverns. Gardener was far more likely to think about things like provisions after the fact. This smacked of another style, one more sophisticated and insidious than Gardener's.

"Tomorrow, when I can think straight, I'll work on this," Ransom said, pushing to his feet. "Right now, I need a bath and some sleep."

Later, he lay in bed, listening to the storm rage and wondering if Felicity's headache had abated. Was she resting? Was it normal for her to sleep so much after a blow to the head? But nothing about what she experienced was normal. Damn, but he missed her.

With the weight of worry over her safety a lighter burden on his shoulders, he dared to examine the terrifying emotions roiling below the surface during his search.

While he could plan many things in life, he couldn't plan everything. He hadn't planned on her loving him, and he certainly hadn't planned on loving Felicity Forsythe Hamilton *or* Winifred Beatrice McCanless.

Staring blindly at the ceiling, his eyes stung. The tumult of emotion he'd repressed during the search crashed through. His entire body trembled with the thought of losing her forever. He couldn't make it stop. Had he ever been so afraid as he had been then?

His eyes closed, and still he saw her vacant stare from the steam cavern. She had looked like the Felicity he knew in San Francisco. God, what would he do if she reverted? Or he lost her completely?

He drew a ragged breath that sounded like a sob.

For however long she enriched his life with her presence, he'd cherish her. The happiness she gave him outstripped anything he had believed possible.

He recalled holding her while she spoke of Joey. Although time had lessened the anguish of losing her brother, she told him there would always be a hole in her heart, but that she'd never wish she hadn't known him in order to avoid the pain of his loss. She had said the world would be a poorer place without Joey's generous heart, his laugher, his friendship, and his cheer.

Tears stung Ransom's eyes when he recalled her turning to him in the faint firelight casting long shadows across their bed and asking who she could have loved all that time and who would have loved her, if not Joey. Tonight, he understood completely.

Cordelia was right. Now that he loved her, he could never settle for less.

Ransom woke to a clear sky glittering with familiar stars. Sleep sharpened the disquiet in his heart. With Felicity hidden among the Tlingit, his world remained fragmented. Until this mess with her kidnappers ended, the separation was a necessity. That galled him and destroyed what little good humor lingered from ensuring her safety. Her health lay in more capable hands than his. Given her injuries, the combination of Spirit Dancer and Felicity's healing arts was more effective than anything else on the island. Even so, he ached to oversee her recovery.

Determined to end this threat, Ransom dressed and hurried downstairs. Before he finished his morning coffee, Baron Korinkov arrived.

"It seems I'm in time for breakfast." Ivan took a plate and helped himself to the fare spread on the sideboard.

"Do join me." Ransom spread blackberry preserves over the stack of pancakes on his plate. "If you'd like something else . . . "

"Oh, no. My intention was to talk, not eat, however . . . " His smiling blue eyes met his friend's knowingly. "I am glad you have returned. How is Felicity?"

Ransom scowled. When had his feelings for his wife become so transparent that those closest to him knew he wouldn't rest until he found her? "She isn't here."

Ivan's ebullient mood melted into chagrin. He settled at the table and asked Meggie for a cup of coffee. Once he had it, he went about consuming his breakfast.

"Close the doors on your way out, please," Ransom requested of Meggie. When they were alone, he withdrew the ransom note from his inside jacket pocket.

"Unless you're starving, read this between bites." He ate while Ivan studied the demand.

Neither spoke until they adjourned behind the closed door of the library. "All my men are searching or watching for any sign of her. She'll not leave the island through Sitka," Ivan promised solemnly. With the storm gone, the men on the island had been mobilized to search for Felicity before the next piece of foul weather blew down from the top of the world.

Ransom pulled the drape back from the ice-frosted window and stared out at the pristine snow. "You were correct in assuming I wouldn't return without Felicity. She's safe."

Ivan regarded his friend with open speculation and growing relief. "Little you do surprises me anymore, Ransom. Yet, I worried when you said she was not here. Is she, well?"

"She's injured, but she'll recover. She's with Spirit Dancer." He released the drapery.

"What have you in mind?" Ivan selected a cigar from the humidor on the shelf beside the library table. He lit the end and watched the blue-gray smoke drift toward Ransom. "Do you plan on keeping Felicity hidden?"

"Yes. Other than the Tlingit, only you know she's there. I want it kept that way."

"Cordelia?" The Baron arched a finely sculpted eyebrow.

"She suspects but will hold her silence. She, too, wants Felicity's safety assured and knows she can't let slip what she doesn't know." The soft tightness of Ransom's voice closed the subject. "Cordelia won't ask." The wound of her betrayal gnawed at his tender feelings for his mother. Regardless of her motives, her actions violated a lifelong trust.

"They cannot expect payment for someone they no longer have. What will you do?"

The twinkle in Ransom's eyes revealed an intrigue with the game at hand. "They don't know that I know they don't have her," he told Ivan slowly. "If they're more greedy than smart, they'll try bluffing or finessing for the gold. If not, we won't hear from them until they learn she's alive and perhaps make another attempt. Let's hope they are greedy."

Ransom explained where he'd found Felicity and the fate of her three abductors.

"Caine received reports of Vance Gardener's presence here. Most convenient. It seems only he knows the identity of the fourth man Felicity's abductors awaited. He was to meet them at the cavern, but we don't know when. Let's hope he becomes desperate or arrogant enough to make a mistake."

"Would you know Mr. Gardener's handwriting?" Ivan fingered the note on the table.

Ransom nodded. "Gardener didn't write the letter." The knuckle of his index finger rapped sharply against the wood under the paper. "The handwriting, like the plan, is the work of another man."

"Or woman," Ivan said thoughtfully.

"Or woman," Ransom agreed slowly. His mind leaped back to Seattle and Cassandra's pleas for Felicity's safety.

"Cassandra," Ransom hissed. "Or . . ." Hearing his friend draw a sharp breath, Ransom glanced at Ivan's reddening face.

"Or what?" Ivan asked.

"Or her husband." The two men gazed at one another for several long, silent minutes, each exploring new possibilities.

Ransom fingered the letter. "What would the Malcolms be doing with Vance Gardener? He's not the kind of man one would seek out as a trusted friend or even an acquaintance from their social level."

Considering the warnings in Arch's letter, Ransom reevaluated whether or not the two men shared a common ground. If indeed that was the case, it might explain a few things.

"Vance Gardener is a greedy bastard who'd sell his own children. Since he's here, he must stand to gain something substantial, or he's being paid very well for overseeing a delicate task personally."

Ivan's thoughtful azure eyes followed the smoke swirling from his cigar. "We agree on Mr. Gardener's sterling character qualities. Perhaps his task is taking Felicity from you?"

"If so, his partner will be unhappy when he can't deliver. From what Felicity overheard, the man her abductors awaited was Gardener's very silent partner."

"Regardless, Gardener will be looking for her once they discover she is gone."

Ransom's head dipped in an almost imperceptible nod. "I've no doubt they'll look hard for her then. But a white man is easily noticed among the Tlingit. Raven Wing won't allow anyone, other than me and perhaps you, in sight of Felicity."

Ivan stubbed out the cigar. "Now that the storm is over, the fourth man will soon discover what you left in the caverns." He approached his friend. "They'll search for her, and they'll watch you."

"I know. And I'll spot them. They'll see nothing." The steel in Ransom's tone left no doubt.

"And you'll find out who put Gardener up to this?"

"Oh, yes." Although spoken casually, iron ice could have formed in the corners of the room from the chill of his confident promise.

"And if it is Malcolm?"

"I am beginning to suspect that it is John Malcolm. He undoubtedly knows that I planned on marrying Cassandra. It would take some convincing, but he might make a believable case for me disappearing with Cassandra. In fact, we'd be dead. I've thought long and hard over what Malcolm would gain."

"And?"

"Control. Guardianship of Felicity."

"Felicity hardly needs a guardian. She's the most independent, capable woman I've had the pleasure of knowing."

"Malcolm doesn't share your opinion. I believe he is here, and so is Cassandra. The questions are where . . . and why, since they haven't paid a social call to this side of the family."

The two men shared a knowing look for several long moments.

"Cassandra may be involved, too, either as an accomplice or as one of the intended victims or both. She is his wife," Ransom said evenly. He hoped she wasn't involved. There was no way of knowing how her love for Malcolm influenced the changes in her life. He was learning how strangely people acted and how faulty their judgment became when their emotions were involved.

"You are right to be suspicious, Ransom. Nevertheless, I tell you, you're wrong if you suspect Cassandra's involvement. The woman I met in Seattle is incapable of harming her sister. Nor would she be a willing party to such a deed."

He wished he shared Ivan's unquestioning belief in Cassandra's loyalty. In truth, Ivan probably knew her better from the hour they had spent at dinner at the Blue Whale than he ever had.

Ransom watched his friend pace and identified with the restlessness eroding his peace of mind and preventing him from lighting in one place for more than a few minutes. "I would believe that of the Cassandra I knew in San Francisco. But she has changed, Ivan. Even so, I doubt she'd willingly or knowingly act against Felicity.

"But Felicity was abducted, brutalized, and damn near frozen to death by those two-legged vermin. I'm suspicious of everyone remotely associated with Malcolm and Gardener." He shivered, recalling Felicity in the steam cavern. "God knows what would have happened if I'd waited for the weather to clear."

Anger pinched his features with grim speculation. "If Malcolm is behind this, I'll have retribution. I'll have justice."

"Call it what it is, Ransom. You'll have your vengeance. I would expect nothing else, for it's what I'd do."

"Yes," Ransom agreed with lethal softness. "I won't tolerate anyone jeopardizing Felicity's safety or happiness." Again, the sun-brightened snow beckoned through the window. He'd wait until late at night before risking a visit to Felicity.

Chapter 27

TOMMY MIGHT NOT have been the most literate seaman, but his cartography talents stood second to none. John
Malcolm had no trouble following the crusty seaman's
map. A second map detailing the twists and turns inside the
caverns proved equally accurate. Uncomfortable in the
eerie, total darkness, John had carried two torches through
the tunnels.

John had returned from the Baranov Island wilderness a
disturbed man. Beneath the deceptive snowfall, in the bowels of the lava tubes and convoluted caves, frozen death had
awaited. Finding Ralph and Sug sprawled beside the ashes
of a long-burned-out fire shook him.

Distance calmed his rattled nerves. He assessed what
he'd seen in the cavern. Clearer thinking brought a new confusion and a multitude of questions. Where in the hell was
Tommy, and what had he done with Felicity Hamilton? Had
Tommy taken her for himself? Had the three of them fought
over her? Or had Tommy killed Sug and Ralph while they
slept, then taken her? If so, where was he keeping her?

"This is a goddamn island. He can't go far," John mumbled, pacing back and forth in the kitchen of the house Vance had rented for him.

All John's instincts shouted to abandon the scheme and set sail for San Francisco. This recent turn of events made the game very dangerous. Too dangerous. The critical elements were falling apart, and the game was still young.

The stakes might be high, but so were the risks, and if he couldn't pull it off, the consequences were disastrous.

Ah, but the rewards were so tantalizing. Two fortunes glittered on the horizon, his for the taking. The lure of such great wealth overrode the voices nagging at him like some itch in the middle of his brain he couldn't scratch.

Getting Ransom Hamilton out of the way and gaining control of Felicity shouldn't have been difficult, he lamented. Now it would be, given the uncertainty of Felicity's whereabouts. Damn Tommy, anyway.

The plan had seemed foolproof in its simplicity when they came ashore at Sitka. Sug, Ralph, and Tommy were to watch for Felicity, then abduct her at the first opportunity. Once she was secured and Hamilton arrived with the price of her release, they'd shoot him. The gold was critical for the believability of the plan. No one left everything behind to run away with a woman.

All they had needed to do was sit in the well-stocked caverns and wait for Hamilton and the gold. The trio wasn't the brightest, but they were loyal, or at least John had considered them so until he went to rendezvous with them.

Cassandra's glowing praises of Hamilton promised that he'd recoup his wife because it was his duty. After meeting Hamilton in Seattle, his own assessment of Hamilton's weaknesses matched Cassandra's unwitting commendation. John had to admit that few people incited a man's protective instincts like Felicity.

But now, things had changed. John spent the rest of the day weighing the pros and cons of playing it safe.

Perhaps retreat was best. If they left now, no one would

know of their visit. He'd fight for the golden prize another day under more favorable circumstances.

However, there was so much money at stake. Enough that he could spend lavishly and do whatever he wanted for a long, long time, even after deducting Gardener's exorbitant share. Certainly such great reward warranted an equal risk.

Late that night, he sat with Vance and devised another plan. The opportunity of having it all had disappeared with Felicity. More than likely, she had died in the frigid storm. Tommy wouldn't drag her along once he finished using her. He had his own escape from the island to worry about. With all the searching Hamilton's men organized, John needed to move fast, before they discovered her body or stumbled across her and Tommy.

Still, John might get at least a piece of the Hamilton/Forsythe fortune if he played the new game well. Grinning, he recalled tales of the gaming clubs in London. Perhaps England would be a nice place to live after this bit of business ended.

The easy acceptance of the Tlingit made Win comfortable in the midst of an unfamiliar culture. Children needed feeding, washing, and dressing, and willing hands always found a task. Time moved faster while she was busy working or learning the language.

Spirit Dancer had treated her wounds, which responded well. Gradually, her headache ebbed and the occasional bouts of double vision disappeared. Her greatest concern was the child in her womb. As the days passed, she slept less and grew stronger. When all seemed well with the babe, she began to relax.

On Ransom's third late visit in a week, he sat with her near the fire in the longhouse. Most of the inhabitants were asleep.

"Spirit Dancer says we were correct: I'll lose all my memories of technology and the advances between now and my own time. There is no going back. There is just here and you and home." She sighed, still mourning the loss of a large part of her identity. "How much longer until I can go home?"

"Is there nothing we can do to keep your memories?" Ransom asked quietly.

"No. I guess I just have to accept it as a done deal."

"I'm sorry," he whispered into her hair.

"Don't be. It's not your fault any more than it was your choice," she said, touched by his sorrow for her loss.

"Nor was it yours, Liss." Ransom smiled slightly and raised an eyebrow. "Do you miss me?"

Win kept her head bowed so her hair hid her face. He could read her too well. "Parts of you."

"Oh? And what would those parts be, madam?"

She leaned against him, settling her head against his chest, carefully interlacing her fingers over her pulled-up knee. "I miss your hands and the feel of them moving over my body. And your fingers. Ah, your magic fingers create the most heavenly and exciting sensations I've ever known. You take me to paradise with your artistic touch.

"I miss your mouth." She risked a quick glance and saw passion blazing in his eyes. "You have the most amazing, talented mouth. I'm absolutely fascinated by what you do with your lips, your teeth, and your tongue, Ransom. I didn't know a human being could create fire with the touch of his mouth on mere flesh."

Ransom sat very still, enthralled by the way she made love with words.

"I miss your eyes, the way you look at me when we're hungry for each other, the way you seem to see inside of me and know my deepest desires and most private thoughts. Have I ever told you I could look into your eyes for days? You have the most beautiful eyes, Ransom. They speak to me from behind the stony mask you wear to protect yourself from the world. Yes, I do miss your eyes.

"And I miss the comfort and strength of your arms around

me. When you hold me, I know nothing bad can happen. I feel safe. I feel at home, like I belong there, in your arms."

The bulge in his breeches forced him to shift. He held her a little tighter against him.

"You are the most exquisitely built man I've ever seen. You're so much bigger and more powerful than I, but you're also gentle and tender with your strength. Even when we're burning for that ultimate piece of heaven from each other, you never hurt me. You drive me wild! Sometimes you move so hard and quick in the frenzy of our passion I can barely meet you, and still, you never hurt me. So, yes, I miss your beautiful body and the way you claim mine and give yours in return.

"I miss your voice and the way you whisper my name when we're making love and the sounds you can't hold in when we soar together. I even miss the sound of the orders you give." She laughed softly. "You make polite requests or suggestions, but everyone in the house knows an order when they hear it.

"Most of all, I miss your mind. Without your marvelous mind, the rest is nothing. I miss the way you make the world yours. And I love the way you make me the center of your world when we make love.

"I never thought it was possible to feel as strongly about another person as I do you. Sometimes, I wake up in the night frightened by the intensity of what I feel and the possibility of losing all of it in a heartbeat. So, yes, I miss you, Ransom. I miss you a great deal."

He gathered her tightly in his arms and held her fiercely against his heart. Then he was kissing her with love and passion that defied words.

"I'll never stop wanting you," he breathed against her mouth. "I need you. And I promise you, this will be over soon and you'll be home with me where you belong."

Raven Wing chose that moment to tap Ransom on the shoulder. He nodded at the door of the longhouse where Ivan waited. Ransom motioned the big Russian closer.

Reluctantly, Ransom released his wife and brought them both to their feet.

Ivan bowed his head to Win and addressed Ransom. "We found Vance Gardener. You were right. John Malcolm is here, too. Cassandra hasn't been seen in Sitka, but one of Caine's men heard a couple of sailors talking about making the voyage with her, Gardener, and Malcolm."

Ransom nodded. "We'd better move and keep track of them."

Win stood motionless as he kissed her on the forehead and promised he'd return when he could. "It will be over soon."

She watched him pull on his gloves as he hurried toward the door, her mind spinning. He said he wanted her. He said he needed her. But he never mentioned love. Two out of three wasn't so bad in most things. Had he told Cassandra all three? Was that why he was so eager to leave? Would he search for Cassandra with the same zeal he had searched for her? And when he found her, what then?

She imagined the reunion of the two lovers. Cassandra had been his first and only choice for a wife. A small voice reminded her of the ease in which marriages were set aside. She wasn't naive enough to believe herself exempt from such heartache. On the contrary. Her entire life had prepared her for it with one lesson in vulnerability after another, starting with her father's abandonment of the family.

Nor would she live with a man, even one she loved with all her being, when another woman owned his heart. Her stomach churned with the revolting vision of discord such an arrangement fostered.

Contemplating the need for making harsh decisions soon, she stared at the door long after Ransom and Ivan left. She never doubted that Ransom desired her. The possessiveness and responsibility he displayed on her behalf ran deep. But they weren't love.

The uncertainty of her future with Ransom never seemed greater. As much as she loved him, she didn't believe she could share him with Cassandra, even if Cassandra left Sitka. She'd be a ghost in their bed.

She needed time for him to discover the extent of what he felt for her. She wondered if he'd ever love her. Many of his actions offered a promise of unspoken love, but she couldn't be sure. Instinctively, her hands spread over her flat stomach.

"I need the words, Ransom," she whispered. "I won't give up until I'm sure you can't love me or that you do love her."

If Ransom wanted Cassandra, he'd have her and only her. Nothing Win could do would change what Ransom wanted. In that regard, she understood him as well as she understood herself. Survivor that she was, she would fight the best battle possible and accept the results, then make the necessary painful adjustments and continue with her life. And painful they would be, too.

She would have their child alone. He wouldn't know until after he set the marriage aside, if he chose to do so. No. She'd never yield the care of her child to anyone as long as there was breath in this body. Not even to Ransom.

A firm hand shook Win awake. Around her, people slept peacefully through the small morning hours. Alarmed, she rolled onto her back and peered up into the Spirit Dancer's dark eyes. She obeyed his concise hand signals and dressed warmly, then followed him outside.

Crisp night air stole her warm breath in great plumes of steam. She wrapped her muffler around her lower face as Ransom had shown her to protect herself from the cold.

By the light of a full moon playing hide-and-seek with high clouds warning of an approaching storm, Spirit Dancer led her away from the village. Raven Wing waited at the cluster of rocks on the bluff Win considered her meditation place. A familiar apprehension prickled a warning that gelled in dread as frigid as the night.

"What has happened? Where are we going?" Win implored in broken Tlingit.

"They search for you," Spirit Dancer said as she mounted the horse snorting steamy plumes in the cold air. "Raven Wing keeps you safe."

With growing alarm, she gazed into the shaman's dark eyes. The resignation she saw charged her trepidation. For an instant, she froze with the realization the nightmare hadn't ended in the caverns. It reached out and ensnared her and the generous people who protected her. A dozen questions formed and died in silence when Spirit Dancer laid his hand on her thigh, then patted her in assurance.

"Go quietly, Two Women," he told her. "Men come to the village. The spirits will protect us all."

Before she could voice her fear-filled concerns for the Tlingit's welfare, Raven Wing snatched up the lead rein and urged her horse forward. She wanted him to wait while she asked her questions. The urgency with which he spurred his horse denied her.

Raven Wing headed across the open ground on a northeastern course. Over her shoulder, Win saw Spirit Dancer returning to the village. A lump formed in her throat. Although he had powers beyond anything she dreamed possible, he now appeared old and shrunken against the white snow sparkling in the moonlight. A strong wind rose, blowing snow in their tracks and creating new drifts against the rocks.

She whispered a prayer for the safety of the old shaman and the kind people who had given her shelter and friendship.

As they crested the next hill, she glanced back at Spirit Dancer and the village. For a moment she thought she saw lights bobbing on the far side of the village. Distance and the refracting cold distorted her vision. Her instincts and Spirit Dancer's actions warned her of a narrow escape.

Healthy resolve filled her with energy. Regardless of what happened, she would do what was necessary for survival. The future lay in the child growing inside her. She would allow nothing and no one to harm him. Head bent, she urged the horse into the teeth of the wind.

If men were willing to risk the wrath of the Russian government by raiding the peaceful Tlingit in the dead of night, something had gone terribly wrong. Neither Ransom nor Ivan would allow such an intrusion. Rather, Ivan had steadfastly used his political power to support the sanctity of the village.

Her worries mounted as she wondered about the invasion and the consequences facing those who befriended her.

"What the hell do you mean, a search party went through the Tlingit village this morning?" Ransom shouted at Ivan. "You told me you'd keep your men away from there. Don't you have some sort of noninvasive treaty with the Tlingit?" Helplessness fueled his outrage.

"They weren't Russian. The men came from the taverns on the wharf and were quite drunk at the time. I would wager Gardener and his minions instigated the search. They have to be sure Felicity is not here before they meet with you today. The village was the only place searchers had not turned inside out to find her." Ivan led Ransom into the study of his opulent home and closed the doors. "I checked on the Tlingit as soon as I learned of the raid. Felicity was not in the village. I was hoping you had brought her home."

Shoulders rigid with apprehension, Ransom turned around slowly. If she no longer hid in the village, where was she? "Spirit Dancer?"

"I'm sorry, Ransom. Cloud Chaser refused to let me talk with him. The old man was knocked around during the skirmish. He was in a healing trance. Cloud Chaser assured me Felicity wasn't in the village." Ivan poured a pair of stiff drinks. The early-morning hour meant nothing more than the promise of a long, difficult day.

The practiced calm that had been so great an asset during the years Ransom built his business empire insinuated itself as a blanket over the tumult churning at a lower, primordial level. His heart demanded knowing Felicity's fate.

"Did anyone see the raiders take Felicity?" Ransom downed half the whiskey in his glass.

Ivan shook his head. "According to those in Spirit Dancer's longhouse, Felicity had assisted in preparing the evening meal, but no one saw her when the men came from town.

"Fortunately, the searchers created more fear and mayhem than injury."

Ransom unleashed a fulminating stream of curses at the world. Rage turned his aquamarine eyes the color of old glacier ice and his gaze was as chill. If she had been taken, he hated to imagine how harshly she might suffer in the hands of drunkards who believed her of diminished mental capacity and unable to recall what happened to her. Felicity would fight them. Furiously. And be overpowered and hurt again. Ultimately, they'd use her.

He was at fault. He should have protected her better. A husband's primary duty to his wife was protection. He had promised her that, and failed miserably. Again.

He recalled sitting with her at the fire in the longhouse and her admission of how safe she felt in his arms. The memory launched razor-sharp arrows wounding him in countless invisible places. At that moment, he would give anything to have Felicity in his arms where she felt at home and his world was complete.

No amount of self-recrimination altered the situation. In four hours, he'd meet the demands of Felicity's abductors without knowing her fate. For the first time since the ordeal began, he hoped Vance Gardener's men had her.

This close to the time of the exchange, they were less likely to harm her. Filled with steely resolve, he tamped down his fury and guilt. After he had Felicity safely at home and he delivered his brand of justice, they would never threaten his wife again.

"Caine and some of my men will seize Gardener's ship

while we confront the bastards." Ransom's voice was calm, quiet, lethal. "They will not leave Sitka."

Ivan raised an eyebrow as though an echo in the ornately decorated study added the word *alive*. "As you know, my friend, Russian justice can be blind as well as swift. Prince Maksoutof owes me favors."

Ransom understood perfectly what Ivan implied. There were whispers about the fate of enemies to the czar and the Russian state. Rumor said they were destroyed, sometimes at leisure, when a public trial proved inconvenient or embarrassing to a well-placed official. The ribbons of power his host held so comfortably in his capable hands stretched back to St. Petersburg. With Ivan's governmental power and prestige, it would only take a word in the right ear to mete out whatever justice he favored.

The hard expression chiseling Ransom's features created doubt that Felicity's abductors would live that long. "I care little about any man's justice, save my own. If they've harmed one hair on my wife's head . . ." The warning hung in the air with a reminder of the men whose remains lay frozen in a cavern across the island.

John glanced away from his pathetic wife. How had he managed to stay married to her so long? She bruised so easily that he practically had to shut his eyes and let his hands define her supple curves to sustain an erection.

"Why don't you kill me and get it over with?" Cassandra asked from the edge of the bed, her head hanging.

"Have I told you how much I enjoy hearing you whine?"

"I didn't know it was possible for a man to hate the way you do. Why? Arch's money?" Reflexively, she shrank from his raised hand, her violet eyes resigned to the inevitable blow. Instead of hitting her, he laughed.

"You had better pray all goes well today with your former lover. If it does, you'll be free soon enough." John considered the benefits of the events about to make him a very wealthy man. He'd rid himself of Cassandra, too. Damn, but she had become a tiresome bitch.

"It appears your former love is a widower. Felicity wandered away during the storm and hasn't been found. They've searched everywhere—even the Indian village."

Cassandra screamed in despair.

John cocked his head and smiled benignly at her. "Perhaps it's possible your brilliant little sister survived the storm?" The horror in her ashen face coaxed a harsh laugh from him. "No? I didn't think so either."

"What have you done?" Cassandra pushed off the edge of the bunk and stood tall in the small ship's cabin. "Where is she? Felicity would never have . . . "

"Unfortunately, I have done nothing to Felicity. Things would be far simpler for me if I did have her. In my hands, Felicity is worth a great deal of money." He selected a dress from the armoire and threw it at her. "Put this on. I'm taking you off the ship today."

He didn't like the way she came to life at the mention of leaving the ship. "Don't get any stupid ideas." John ran his open fingers down the sides of her discolored arms. "I'll be at my loving wife's side every step of the way. After all, we vowed for better or worse, till death do us part."

The fear making her shiver quickened his blood. If he had a little more time, it might be worth pursuing. He checked his pocket watch, then shrugged. Maybe later.

He watched her trembling fingers fumble with the buttons on her sturdy woolen traveling outfit. Yes, definitely later. It would be a pity to miss a final sampling of her talents. She performed so well when frightened. Perhaps it was the way her chin quivered.

Cassandra slipped her cloak around her shoulders and ran a brush through her hair.

A short time later, under a graying sky and equally gray water ruffled by a cold, raw wind, John and Cassandra took their places in a small boat. He watched placidly as she gripped the side while they lowered the boat onto the choppy ocean.

"Relax, my dear. It will all be over very soon." He smiled at her. Too bad she had turned into such an ungrateful, uncompromising bitch.

Win dozed fitfully in the cozy cave where Raven Wing had made their camp until they received word that the danger had passed. At the back of the shelter, the horses rested and nibbled at their feed. Outside, loose snow swirled against the lofty trees whispering secrets to the late, gray dawn.

She stood and gingerly stretched her aching ribs. Cloud Chaser had joined them and warmed himself by the fire. "We go soon," he told her. His patient brown eyes followed her as she adjusted her heavy, fur-lined boots.

"Is it safe?" She straightened the furry garb fastened with a series of knots and pliable leather ties. Although modified for her smaller frame, Ransom's clothing hung on her, but she refused to part with it. Having something of his so close made him feel nearer.

"Yes. It is safe."

Relief coursed through her with a sigh. "I'll be glad to get back to the village. I've been so worried about what may have happened there. Is everyone well? Were the children . . . "

Cloud Chaser shook his head. "We do not go to the village."

Distressed, she paused double-checking the makeshift suspenders on her pants. "Where? What's happened?"

"Soon, you join White Raven." He spoke the words softly, but she heard them in every cell in her body.

"Home? I'm going home? Why now? What's happened at the village?" She shrugged into the heavy coat that reached her knees, then fastened it and wrapped thongs around each of her wrists, tying them off with her teeth.

"What's wrong, Cloud Chaser? What's happened that you aren't telling me?" She pulled the ends of her muffler out of the collar of the coat and wrapped her face. Next, she secured her hat. The only visible part of her face was her eyes.

"Spirit Dancer was hurt when the men came looking for you." Cloud Chaser nodded at Raven Wing as the warrior approached with the saddled horses. "He will not mend this time. Soon, I fear he will join the Spirit World. I am not ready for him to go."

The news stunned her. Tears stung her eyes. She reached out and clasped Cloud Chaser's hand. "Oh, Cloud Chaser, I'm not ready for him to leave, either. Is there anything we can do to keep him with us?"

A hint of resignation softened Cloud Chaser's thin-lipped mouth. "You and I, we will not be ready for him to leave until we draw our final breath, Two Women. But Spirit Dancer will go. When he hears the spirits call his name, he will go." The young man patted her hand and pushed to his feet. "Now, we go."

She pulled on her gloves and dutifully led her horse from the shelter of the warm cave. Instantly, the obnoxious wind pestered her clothing, searching for a weak closure to harass.

"Please, can we go to Spirit Dancer first?" she asked, her eyes searching Cloud Chaser and Raven Wing. "Do we have time? Will he . . . "

"No. We go to White Raven. Spirit Dancer says to wait five days. He will see you then. The children are calm. None were seriously hurt." Cloud Chaser fell into line behind her. "Spirit Dancer is well enough, Two Women. His concern is for you."

Torn between her desire to be with Ransom and assuring herself of Spirit Dancer's condition, she gnawed on her lower lip and followed Raven Wing.

An hour later, they dismounted in the trees at the edge of a small clearing in the blue spruce forest behind Sitka. The blowing snow and wind bending the sturdy branches of the trees sang an eerie song of warning, danger, and death.

Moments later, Ransom, Ivan, and Gerald rode into the clearing. The long shadows of the southern sun conferred an ominous pall on the chill wind bullying the clouds around the sky.

When Win started toward the treeline and Ransom, Cloud Chaser drew her back. "We wait here. Spirit Dancer has told me the way of it."

Unsure why Spirit Dancer wished her to wait in the trees and hold a distance from Ransom, but trusting the message and Cloud Chaser completely, she retreated. The Tlingit closed ranks behind her as a windbreak.

"White Raven does not know you are here. This is as Spirit Dancer wishes. Now, we wait for your enemy," Cloud Chaser said very quietly, his head cocked as though listening to a voice riding the wind.

She watched, her thoughts in turmoil. Without a doubt, she loved the man waiting in the clearing and flanked by his friends. Something about him seemed indestructible and forceful enough to move mountains.

Never had she believed she'd love any man with the depth of being that she loved Ransom. Never had she expected to be loved that way. Nor did she believe herself to be now. Perhaps after today they would talk and sort out what kind of future awaited them. She didn't want to leave him, but she knew she couldn't settle for being second in his life.

Chapter 28

THE SOUND OF horses and troika bells grew louder, drawing the charged attention of those in the clearing and the three watchers in the trees.

Four heavily armed men flanked a horse-drawn sleigh carrying two people through the forest facing the clearing.

The sleigh stopped a dozen paces from Ransom. A man climbed down and approached the center of the small distance. Three of the four armed horsemen nudged their mounts closer. Rifle barrels sighted Ransom from their elevated vantage points.

"You brought the money, Mr. Hamilton? In gold?"

"Yes, Malcolm. I brought it. Now, where the hell is my wife?" Ransom's wrath stilled the wind. His bass voice boomed into the trees. It seemed that the heat of his anger would melt the snow around them.

Malcolm picked an imaginary piece of debris off the sleeve of his finely tailored woolen coat and dismissed Ransom's demand. "I'll see the color of your gold."

Ransom cast a telling glance at the saddlebags nearly buried in the snow between them.

"It's all there. Where's my wife?"

"Patience, my friend, patience." Malcolm bent to the task of checking the contents of the saddlebags.

"I'm not your friend, and I've run out of patience," Ransom bristled. His hands balled into fists, ready to club Malcolm into a mass of oozing flesh and broken bones. Without a doubt, he knew Felicity wasn't here. The figure bundled in the troika sat too tall. He scoured the riders. *"Where the hell is she?"*

Malcolm ignored the potent ire and took his time examining the contents of each pouch. When satisfied they contained the promised gold, he picked up a saddlebag and summoned the nearest rider.

Ransom's hand shot out and grabbed Malcolm by the coat, nearly lifting him off the ground, oblivious to the telltale warnings of cocking rifles and the jangle of nervous horses. "The gold is in exchange for my wife. It isn't yours until I have Felicity. Understand? Now, where the hell is my wife?"

Malcolm pointedly gazed at Ransom, then at the hand holding him. When Ransom released, he hastily stepped out of reach and straightened his coat. "You are fortunate my men didn't shoot you."

The bitter laughter rolling from Ransom's mouth halted the wind as though something more formidable possessed the air currents and sent the horses dancing. Great plumes of steam snorted from their distended nostrils. "You won't kill me. Not here. Look around you, Malcolm. These are my woods. This is my island. Most of the men here have worked for me or the baron at one time or another. If you think you could leave after killing me, then your stupidity exceeds your arrogant greed.

"The game is over. Where the hell is my wife? I want her now! I'll make it simple. No Felicity, no gold. Am I making myself understood?" His fiery aquamarine eyes bored into

Malcolm. His savage wrath lay a word away from being un-leashed.

In the ensuing silence, snow fell from the upper branches of a tall spruce behind Ransom. Nothing else moved. Even the wind paused to listen.

Malcolm cleared his throat and squared his shoulders, his eyes pensive as he studied the fury towering before him. "I have another proposition, a better one. Oh, yes, Hamilton, what I have to offer you is far better than the half-wit you married. Most of the time, one woman is like another. Some are younger, some older. All perform the same functions to varying degrees. What I offer you is a woman expertly trained in pleasing a man. For the most part, she is beautiful, educated, and well-mannered."

Ransom's eyes narrowed. "The only woman I want is my wife." The lethal softness of his words barely reached Malcolm. However, their effect sent the horsemen back another step.

"Why? The woman is feebleminded. She's a burden, a millstone shackled around your neck for the rest of your life. Think of it. Eventually you'll get tired of humping that sweet-looking little thing. She'll get old and worn out and still be a half-wit. Having her out of the way merely frees you up. Her dying is a favor to you."

With lightning swiftness, Ransom clutched Malcolm by the lapels of his fine coat with both hands and lifted him off the ground. Malcolm came nose to nose with the raging beast of Ransom's fury and trembled.

"You killed her? You killed my wife?"

The horsemen separated in search of positions offering a clear shot at Ransom.

"No! No! I haven't seen her since last year. Since San Francisco. I swear it!" he gushed. "Let go of me."

Ransom hurled him away, suddenly relieved. Through the fog of seething rage, he saw the fear in Malcolm's face and felt the impulse of truth. If Malcolm and Gardener hadn't taken her from the village, perhaps she'd slipped away and hid until it was safe. Hope bloomed on the arid soil of his emotions and he clung to the sweet scent. By now, every man on the wharf knew what kind of hell awaited anyone who harmed his wife. Besides his own might and reputation, he had the support of the most powerful of the Russian barons on the island. There would be no escaping the awesome consequences awaiting any who touched his wife in other than a helpful manner.

Hope also restored his dignity. He became all business. "If you don't have my wife to trade, you don't get the gold. It's very simple." As far as he was concerned, the meeting was over. He bent and snagged a set of saddlebags.

"Not so fast, Hamilton. I still have something you want. Something you'll gladly pay well for. Easily as much as you were going to pay for that . . ."

"Do not insult my wife again," Ransom warned through clenched teeth.

Malcolm inclined his head in patient indulgence. "Very well. You'll pay easily as much for what I offer as you would have for Felicity."

"I don't think so. There isn't anything in the world worth as much to me as Felicity," came a soft, deadly hiss from Ransom. A crimson flush warmed his neck.

"What about the woman who should have been your wife? The one I understand you wanted to marry but didn't ask for in time?"

Ransom was aware of the sudden shift in Ivan's stance beside him. "What about her?" He glimpsed two men escorting the troika's other passenger toward them.

"It's simple. You want Cassandra. I want money. We'll trade. If Felicity is indeed dead, you're free to marry her."

"I'm afraid it isn't that simple, unless I kill you and make Cassandra a widow." The audacity of the man's nefarious plans fueled Ransom's loathing.

"Ah, not so. You see, I'm afraid my previous wife isn't exactly deceased. Or she wasn't when Cassandra and I were married. A slight oversight on my part, I'm afraid. So you see, the marriage lacked a certain, shall we say, validity?"

Cassandra's bowed head snapped up, her violet eyes coming alive with rage. "You were married? All this time you were married to someone else?" She screamed in effrontery. "You cad! I've been shackled to you through lies and deceit and I was free all the time? You used me. You abused me. You . . . you . . . liar!"

Wild with unrepressed emotion, her violet eyes raked the men surrounding her. "Somebody give me a gun! I'm going to kill this piece of vermin!" She never saw the blow that sent her flying backward into the snow.

Ransom grabbed Ivan to keep him from retaliating. The horses whinnied and pranced at the sound of her scream. In the chaos of the moment, Ivan glared at Ransom. "Pay him. I want her."

Ransom nodded almost imperceptibly.

"For all I know, she's part of your little ploy," Ransom said, drawing the tense situation into a less-threatening realm. He no longer cared about the gold. If Ivan wanted Cassandra, so be it. He wanted this over. Nothing mattered except finding Felicity.

"That's a chance you'll have to take. But then, you'll have her. Perhaps she'll be more accommodating to you." Malcolm eyed the saddlebags with a glint in his eye. "Do we have a deal, Mr. Hamilton?" He licked his colorless lips.

"Yes. Take the gold and go." Ransom put a restraining hand on Ivan and shook his head slightly. As Malcolm secured the first of the gold pouches, Ransom dropped onto his haunches beside Cassandra. He took her shoulders to help her to her feet. He winced and instantly let go when she cried out. Pain filled her teary violet eyes.

"What's he done to you, Cassie? Good God in heaven, what's he done to you?" he whispered. The rage he'd fought back moments earlier returned. God, but she was pitiful in her pain and the shame pinching fresh agony into her young face. Reflexively, he stood, battling with himself to keep from beating Malcolm to a pulp. Instead, he took a deep breath and extended his hand.

She accepted his help and slowly came to her feet. Tears spilled down her cheeks. "I want to die, Ransom. I just want to shoot him, then crawl away and die." As though intent upon shriveling into the frozen ground, her shaky voice was barely a whisper.

Malcolm hurriedly handed the gold up to two men behind him. He carried the third saddlebag over his shoulder and climbed into the troika.

"Come on, Cassie. We'll get you home so Cordelia can look after you." Tenderly, Ransom guided her to Ivan.

"Cassandra?" Ivan whispered, commanding her attention. His gaze vacillated between tenderness and brutality.

She shook her head.

Ivan mounted his horse and reached down for Cassandra. She shied away. "Please. Give me the stirrup and your hand. I'll swing up behind you." Then she sniffed and mounted behind Ivan.

Ivan steadied the horse while she adjusted. Slowly, tentatively, her hands gripped the sides of his thick coat. "Put your hands under my coat. You can hold on better and keep your hands warm," he told her.

Ivan touched the horse's flanks. "I'll meet you at the wharf, Ransom."

Although anxious, Ransom waited until they departed before mounting his horse. Then he said to Gerald, "I want that bastard. If I don't stop him now, he'll be back. You go to the wharf . . ." His words trailed away as he saw Raven Wing and Cloud Chaser approach with Felicity riding between them.

"Felicity?" Ransom breathed, barely able to believe the vision approaching him. "Thank God you're safe! Are you all right?" He spurred the horse forward.

"Yes," came her simple answer.

* * *

Holding back the tears demanded every ounce of Win's self-restraint. While she hadn't heard the entire exchange, she had seen that Ransom's choice was clear. Ransom had just purchased the wife he wanted. The conspicuous tenderness and concern Ransom accorded Cassandra made it obvious where his heart lay. She had her answer and for the moment, she didn't trust her voice.

"We need to talk."

"Whatever." She reined her horse away, knowing Raven Wing and Cloud Chaser would follow.

She kept riding, her misting eyes trained straight ahead. She didn't look back. If she saw Ransom, her flagging courage would unravel. For the moment, all she had left was the thin veneer of her dignity. Although dignity was cold comfort in a colder land, without it she'd dissolve into tearful misery.

He wanted to talk. What was there to say? Her worst nightmare had escaped the dream world and taken shape in reality. Cassandra was here and, if John Malcolm could be believed in this instance, she was free to marry. All Ransom had to do was get their marriage set aside. Divorced. Considering his far-reaching influence and the power of his money, such a task should be easy. He had promised forever, but who knew better than she how short forever could be?

She rode to the Tlingit village with Cloud Chaser and Raven Wing and lost herself helping restore tranquillity to the longhouse. When she had done what she could, she sought solitude at Spirit Dancer's meditation place.

She watched the gray sea lap at the cold, rocky shore with relentless fortitude. The water had no choice in battering the rocks, just as Ransom had no choice in his feelings for Cassandra, she decided. Just as she had no choice in loving him.

She didn't blame Cassandra. If Ransom wanted her, Cassandra would be his. The man was so overpowering and intense, Cassandra would never have a chance to want anyone else. And why should she? She had Ransom.

Win contemplated life in San Francisco. According to Adele, it offered an expanding culture with a theater and a number of intellectual societies. Perhaps there was a scientific guild. Maybe she'd find a colleague or two who didn't mind the fact that she was a woman. After all, money, of which Ransom said she had plenty, usually bought a certain amount of tolerance and acceptance in scientific circles. And she would have her child.

Their child.

Ransom's child.

She'd conceived the baby out of her love for Ransom and his passion for her. Their child wouldn't suffer being raised in an atmosphere of emotional denial and obligation. There would be love. Her love.

In the shadow of memory and the whisper of the wind, a familiar voice asked if she was quitting on what she wanted most in life. Startled, she glanced around for the speaker.

Only the mountain, the sea, the snow, and the wind kept her company.

You never quit on anything in your life. Are you starting now?

Head buried in her hands, Joey's image burned in her brain. "Tell me what to do, Joey."

Don't give up. Don't quit. Only losers quit. We aren't losers.

Lord, how many times had she spoken those same words to him?

"I'm not a quitter," came her defiant whisper in the face of the wind.

Then fight for what you want, Sis. That's why you're here. You love him. This is the chance you never had in L.A. Go after it with both hands and every weapon you can find. Fight dirty if you have to. But fight and don't quit. He's your destiny, Win. Believe in yourself and the power of love. For your own sake, don't quit.

Was that what she had been doing? Quitting? Rolling over without a struggle?

Perhaps.

But how did one fight for another person's love? Love had to be given freely. Ransom's affection wasn't something she could earn through hard work or snappy repartee.

Head rising a bit, she recalled his promises the night they consummated their marriage. In truth, he had promised her everything except love. He couldn't promise affection he didn't feel. While his sentiments for her seemed to grow, could they overcome his emotions for Cassandra, his first choice?

Staring out at the whitecapped gray sea, she stood, her resolve strengthening. "My destiny, huh? Well, we've lost enough in this deal. Let's find out if it's worth it."

The wind whispered encouragement with each step she took into the slanted sunlight.

The long shadows of the tall-masted ships dotting Sitka harbor pointed accusing fingers at two men on horseback leading an overworked packhorse down the wharf. The hustle and banter typical on the docks during the fleeting daylight hours were ominously absent. The sound of iron horseshoes against the weathered wharf clattered in an unmatched cadence out of tune with the waves lapping at the wooden pilings. The echo carried the portent of confrontation and alerted the wharf denizens.

One by one, faces appeared at the windows. Doors creaked as curiosity seekers exited onto the boards or stairs of buildings. Wordlessly, the duo exchanged concerned glances and urged the horses toward the dock where a dory and rowing crew awaited.

"Help me unload," John ordered the two men in the dory.

Neither sailor moved nor answered. Both watched the faces of the men filling the wharf around John and Vance as they dismounted. No sooner had their feet touched the wood than a contingent of twenty smartly uniformed Russian troops thundered in even cadence from between two buildings. The spectators parted, giving Prince Maksoutof's personal guard a wide berth.

"What's going on here?" John demanded of the man leading the troops surrounding him and Vance.

The officer responded in Russian, to which Vance shrugged. Although neither spoke Russian, the message became clear when the troops took possession of the horses and herded them and the two men down the wharf.

"I demand to know why I am being escorted." Malcolm jerked his left arm, testing his stoic jailer's hold. His actions resulted in a second soldier securing his right arm in a vise-like grip. "Where are you taking me?"

"What's going on?" Vance Gardener asked John as a pair of soldiers secured him.

"How the hell should I know?"

"You're the one who said we wouldn't have no trouble on the dock when it came time to leave."

"Shut up!" Half a head taller than Vance, John paled at the sight of the makeshift justice bench ahead. He swore under his breath. The euphoria of victory, which had been so sweet moments ago, soured.

Around them, men emerged from the shops, warehouses, and taverns as witnesses to what promised to be swift dockside justice.

Vance caught sight of the gallows erected behind the justice bench and tried bolting from his captors. A rifle butt in the gut doubled him over and a cold gun barrel at his back warned of the consequence of further resistance.

"Dammit, John . . ."

"Shut up, Vance. They can't do anything if you keep your mouth shut," Malcolm hissed. "I'll do the talking."

"Your talking got me into this." Vance groaned when the soldiers forced him to walk upright. "I shoulda never listened to you. I was getting back at Hamilton jest fine in my own way."

"You didn't think so when I came to Seattle. You were eager then, so keep your mouth closed now." John tossed his head to fling a stray lock of hair from his eyes. "Pretend you have some class, Vance, and we'll get through this and out of Sitka with our gold. All we've done is execute a business deal. We made a trade. Nothing more."

Looking far less confident than his partner, Vance surveyed the foul, pensive mood of the men lining the wharf and grumbled a pessimistic reply.

When the soldiers halted in front of the elevated bench, a voice called out from the crowd. "Ya crossed the line, Gardener. Ya know th' penalty!"

Vance shivered and visibly paled.

"What does he mean?" John hissed at Vance.

"We're dead men."

"We?" John straightened. "I didn't hear him mention my name."

Utter loathing crossed Vance's grizzled face and twisted it into a hate-filled scowl. He swore into his beard.

"This trial will come to order," commanded a voice with a Russian accent from the side of the crowd.

Dressed in intricately adorned formal courtroom attire over his heavy clothing, Baron Ivan Korinkov assumed the judge's seat. "By special authority of Prince Maksoutof, I call this trial of the Americans John Malcolm and Vance Gardener."

The soldiers parted and flanked the prisoners facing the justice bench.

"Vance Gardener, you are charged with murder on the high seas in the sinking of the *Margaret Elizabeth*. You are charged with conspiracy in the abduction of Felicity Forsythe Hamilton.

"John Malcolm, you are charged with conspiracy to commit murder on the high seas in the sinking of the *Margaret Elizabeth*. You are charged with conspiracy in the abduction of Felicity Forsythe Hamilton. And, sir, you are charged with woman beating."

Once Baron Korinkov read the charges, a flurry of whispers rippled the crowd.

"John Malcolm, what have you to say for yourself?"

"This is a farce! I don't . . ."

"Yes, you do." Hamilton emerged beside the Russian captain of the guard. "And it is hardly a farce. Unlike your marriage to my sister-in-law, this trial is legal. Furthermore, it is being conducted by a royal and legal representative of the czar and Prince Maksoutof."

For the first time in weeks, Ransom grinned. It was not a warm, comforting sight. "Checkmate." A cloud of steamy breath accompanied Ransom's deadly grin. The dangerous menace he radiated sent the men nearest him back a step.

John met Hamilton's hostile gaze for a full minute before nodding ever so slightly in defeat. The power play had ended in ruin and destruction. The gold had been his for a short time. The sweet taste of victory and the glory of confidence faded completely. He had played the game for the highest stakes possible and lost. He stared at the gallows, searching for the words that might save him.

Two soldiers parted. Patrick Feeny strode through their ranks. "So you be the gardener? Me mate on the only boat ta survive the *Meggie E.*'s sinking was a lad by the name o' Carl Owens. He was verra disappointed when ya dint show up."

Vance paled. "Carl? There weren't supposed ta be no . . ."

"Shut up!" John glared at Vance, who continued gaping at Patrick Feeny.

"He was so sure you'd come. But ya never meant fer him ta live, did ya? I betcha never expected no Russian ship ta pick us up neither, did ya?" Ransom's hand on Feeny's tension-bunched shoulders calmed him. "Ya ain't gonna get away with killin' me mates, Gardener."

"It wasn't my idea. It was John's!" Vance tried to turn away from Feeny. The unyielding vise on his arms held him in place. Around him, men murmured threateningly. "And it was his idea to snatch Mrs. Hamilton. He said she was a dimwit who wouldn't remember nothing that happened to her."

"Have you anything else to say?" Baron Korinkov asked from the judicial bench.

Vance's terror-filled gaze darted from Patrick Feeny to Ransom Hamilton to the sea of faces behind the wall of soldiers, then upward to the man seated in judgment. "All I did was give him the names of men who would help . . ."

"You spineless liar!" John twisted free of the soldiers and lunged at Vance. His hands curled into claws around Vance's neck and his eyes burned in a wild rage.

Chapter 29

Win's HOMECOMING GENERATED far more emotion than she expected or wanted. Cordelia and Adele sniffed softly into lace-edged handkerchiefs and touched her at every opportunity. Cassandra's open relief at seeing her alive and well heightened her discomfort. She preferred to dislike Cassandra, but the woman's tenderness and the memory of John Malcolm's brutal treatment in the clearing denied her even that. The terror of her own harsh treatment, although brief in comparison, afforded an unwanted compassion. Win endured her half-sister's affections in unflappable silence.

Cordelia's and Adele's genuine relief reminded Win of the extensive precautions Ransom had taken for her safety.

"Gracious, Felicity, those heavy furs must be uncomfortable. I'm sure a warm bath would do you good. If you like, I'll fix your hair and help you dress in your own clothing," Adele offered eagerly.

"I'd like to lie in the tub for a while, but first I need something to eat." She hoped her strained smile passed as genuine.

Waving her hands, Cordelia ducked into the kitchen and gave a few quick instructions. Charlet rushed out to see the house's mistress for herself, her round cheeks glowing in delight at her return. She promised a good fare in short order.

Win laid her coat, hat, muffler, and gloves at the foot of the stairs and cast a longing gaze toward her room. Regardless of what the future held, the lush furs were hers. The clothing represented her armor against the cold and a thoughtful protection provided by the man who owned her heart.

"I just can't believe you made it home from the totem pole village all alone," Cassandra marveled from behind Win. "Adele . . . Adele told me about your accident and the miracle that followed. It's . . . it's so difficult to believe after all these years."

"It's the Tlingit village. The totem poles are tributes and tell the history of the artisan who made them. Totems are carved with love and displayed with pride." Win gathered her poise and faced the woman Ransom chose to marry. For a long, silent moment, they regarded each other.

Anguish burned brightly in Cassandra's eyes. The source of her heartache was far more extreme than the bruises peeking over the edges of the modestly scooped neck of her dress. Win saw the patience and tenderness of a woman whose emotions ran as deep as her own.

"Have I lost you, too, Felicity?"

A sense of isolation emanated from Cassandra. A part of Win yearned to give the violet-eyed woman what she needed, but the Felicity that Cassandra knew had died months ago. She and Ransom would undoubtedly take that secret to their graves.

Win identified with her half-sister's loneliness and uncertainty. Sensing the goodness, the pain, and seeing Cassandra's remarkable physical beauty, Win felt inferior. How could she counter such a formidable opponent?

"I'm sorry, Cassandra. I have no recollection of you.

Other than what Adele and Ransom have told me, I don't know anything about you," Win whispered.

"Ransom?" Cassandra's face softened at the mention of his name and Win shuttered her reaction. "Papa loved him like a son."

"So I understand." Win ended the conversation by ducking into the washroom before joining the women in the dining room where an impromptu meal awaited.

Moments later, three sets of eyes watched her eat. She breathed a sigh of relief when they discussed Cassandra's ordeal and saved questions concerning her whereabouts until she finished eating.

"Please," Win said, her eyes roaming among them, "let me answer all your questions later. I'm dirty. I'm tired. And I need a little time to pull myself together. It's been a long, difficult day."

Cordelia tucked her arm around Win's and ushered her upstairs. "Your bath is ready. If you need anything, call."

At the bedroom door, Cordelia hugged her for a long moment, then rushed away, but not before Win saw the tears filling her green eyes. A wave of sadness washed over her as the older woman disappeared down the stairs.

So Cordelia knows he'll be sending me away, too, she thought.

The familiar bedroom sparked memories of nights spent in beautiful intimacy. A warm fire kept the encroaching winter chill outside the cozy, lamplit room. Undressing, she studied the room, steeping herself in the lingering remnants of tender emotions and shared passion. Not until she removed her chemise did she realize something was amiss. An analytical perusal sent her heart plunging in despair. The polished oak floor beside the secretary desk gleamed in the warm lamplight. Her journals were gone.

Sudden panic welled up. She wanted her journals. They preserved her fading past. They contained parts of her she might never reclaim any other way. Instinctively, she started for the door, but paused with her hand on the knob.

Ransom. Ransom must have taken the journals. Why? Why would he take her past at the same time he denied her a future with him? If she hadn't fallen in love with him, she might still own her past. She hastened to the nightstand and jerked the drawer out. The medical journal she kept rested securely on top of the other items. Thank heaven she'd stashed it in the drawer.

Her weary mind balked at handling yet another monumental problem. She added more hot water to the tub and climbed in, concentrating on nothing more complicated than washing her hair and body. Later, she'd ask questions. Later.

The soothing bath soaked a thin coat of agitation from her thoughts. For the moment, the fragrant soap and deliciously hot water satisfied her needs. She reveled in the steamy aroma, banishing all other thoughts and problems, until the door opened.

"Liss?" Ransom called from the other side of the bathing drapery.

Fully alert and drawn back into the eye of chaos, her heart skipped a beat before accelerating to trip-hammer rhythm. "What?" Her monosyllabic answer preceded the sound of the bolt being thrown on the bedroom door.

"Where were you? How did Raven Wing get you out of the village? Why did you ride away from me? What happened?" Ransom's boots hit the floor in series as he closed the distance to the heavily curtained bathing room.

Easy questions, she admitted with a sigh. "Spirit Dancer knew they were coming. He sent me away with Raven Wing. Cloud Chaser joined us later." The short answer covered everything.

Then he was kneeling beside her, cradling her face in his big palms, searching her pale features with fiery aquamarine eyes. "I was afraid they had you. It damn near made me crazy."

She wasn't sure which startled her most, his tender disclosure or the current running through her body when his lips closed on hers. The taste of his restrained passion whetted her appetite for what they had been denied for nearly two weeks. By the time he broke the kiss, both breathed heavily with ravenous need for fulfillment.

"I want to make love to you until neither one of us can walk." His warm breath teased her parted lips.

For an instant, she forgot he loved someone else. He wanted her. And there was nothing in the world she wanted more than him—now or ever.

"I accept the challenge." Water dripped from the hand she slipped behind his neck. She drew his mouth downward. She'd never get enough of his sweet kiss and she'd savor every touch and taste he permitted.

She claimed Ransom's mouth in a possessive promise of the molten heat coursing through her veins and aching for the euphoria that ultimately quenched the fire.

"Don't move," he warned when the kiss ended. In a flurry of movements, he shed his clothing and joined her in the tub.

Regardless of the conflicts raging outside the sanctuary of their room, all felt right for Win. She reached for him, desperately yearning for the fullness of him inside her body.

Neither spoke. The blatant need reflected in Ransom's gaze captured her trusting blue eyes. Ransom adjusted them in the water and held her over him, his manhood poised at the entrance of her silken heat. She was already breathless when his mouth closed on hers in fierce possession.

Win's arms glided around his neck and her fingers twined into his hair. Soapy water sloshed onto the tiled floor. The fire pulsing through her veins echoed the desperation of her love and need for response and satiation.

A small cry escaped from the back of her throat.

Ever so slowly, he lowered her onto himself, bringing her down farther and farther, sending himself deeper and deeper inside her, until he filled her completely. The agonizing slowness of his movements burned her. Already, tiny spasms racked her eager, moist depths.

Breathing hard, she broke the kiss. "Ransom," she pleaded. "I . . . I need!"

"God, Liss! You are so ready." His fingers closed around her hips just below her waist. "Take me with you."

She couldn't have stopped the tidal wave of desire surging through her if she had tried, which she didn't. She took all he gave in a frenzy, building the raging pyre searing her senses.

"Liss!"

She felt the head of his manhood swell and gave herself over to the climax she couldn't stall another second. Then she was flying with him in a blissful physical heaven where all her senses glowed with life and momentary satiation.

Breathless, they clung, each resting on the other's shoulder.

"Damn, how I've missed you," Ransom breathed, then kissed the hollow of her neck and shoulder.

She basked in his admission, until she remembered he loved Cassandra. Did he pretend she was Cassandra when they made love? A tiny shiver racked her body as she pulled away. Uncertain of her place in his life, words failed her. The fright of hearing him confirm her worst fears deepened the chasm festering between them.

She released him and sat up, her body reluctant to yield the wonderful part of him still deliciously filling her. "I'm glad to be home. I missed you, too."

A knowing grin erased the lines wrought by worry, weather, and age, and gave him a youthful, carefree appearance seldom visible on his chiseled features. "Speaking of missing someone, it will be nice having Cassandra with us. I believe we're in for some interesting developments where she's concerned. After what she's been through, she deserves someone who really cares for her."

A bucket of snow couldn't have frosted Win's afterglow more quickly than the sound of Cassandra's name on his lips, the lips fresh with her kiss. She wiggled free, not risking a glimpse of him, knowing he'd read her sudden anger.

Instead, she busied herself with rinsing so she could put more distance between them.

"What is it?" Ransom caught her hand. Water dripped from the sponge poking between her fingers.

"What happened to John Malcolm? Where is he?" Finally, cloaked in simmering anger, she met his patient gaze. "Was he really married when he wed Cassandra or was he running another con to make his offer sound even more enticing?"

A pregnant silence hung over them for a long moment and neither moved.

"John Malcolm and Vance Gardener will never bother any of us again. Consequently, it doesn't matter whether he was married when he wed her or not." A deadly cold hardened his narrowing eyes. "She is indisputably a widow now."

"Did you kill him?"

"No. Not exactly."

A charged silence filled the bathing room until she asked, "Is John Malcolm dead?"

"Yes."

"Is Vance Gardener dead?"

"Yes."

When he maintained the granite silence, she nodded. "You're not going to tell me they killed each other over the gold, are you?"

"No."

"Good. And you're not going to tell me they committed suicide in the throes of delirium over their success?"

"No."

She warmed to the challenge of his monosyllabic responses. "The nouveau riche seldom commit suicide when they've discovered so much to live for." His unwavering mask fed her growing ire. "How did they die, Ransom? How did Cassandra become a widow?"

"You don't need to know." His eyes narrowed in warning.

"Yes, I do. After all I've been subjected to, I need to know. I believe it's called closure."

The tic in his left cheek twitched twice, then stilled. Several long, tense minutes passed before he spoke. "We had a trial for them on the wharf. They were found guilty. Under Russian law, they were hanged."

"I see. On what charge?"

"The primary charge was the sinking of the *Margaret Elizabeth* and the death of her crew. Patrick Feeny finally had the opportunity to give his testimony."

"You're positive they were responsible for the *Margaret Elizabeth*'s sinking?"

"Yes. Vance Gardener had the backbone of a jellyfish. If he'd kept quiet, we might not have proven John Malcolm's involvement. But Gardener wanted to trade the sinking of the *Margaret Elizabeth* for the accusation of abducting you. Both knew I wouldn't allow anyone who hurt you to live. Gardener saw my reaction to Cassandra's treatment by John Malcolm and thought by giving me John, he'd save himself. But he guessed wrong. I wanted both of them to hang."

After another long moment, the implications of Ransom's terse words sank in. The gentle, passionate man she had just made love with had found a legal way of serving his own lethal brand of justice. Beyond the question of a doubt, he'd made his first choice in a wife a widow and cleared yet another obstacle in the way of his grand plan.

"I don't think Cassandra will grieve for him." Win slid her hand from his grip, then climbed out of the tub.

"No, I don't suppose she will. He was brutal with her." Ransom relaxed and stretched the full length of the tub. "Worse, he wasn't honest with her. He used her."

"That's one thing you've always been with me, Ransom. Honest. I appreciate it." Her soft voice masked the sorrow tightening her chest. She slipped on a warm wrapper and began toweling her hair dry.

He watched her sit beside the brazier and work the tangles from her long tresses. "What's wrong, Liss?"

She hesitated. There were so many things wrong. It was easier to count the things that were right. At the core of the wrongs lay her need for his love.

"Where are my journals?"

"In the bedroom. Aren't they?"

She shook her head. "They're gone." Another piece of her identity crumbled with the certainty she wouldn't see them until she no longer had the capacity to decipher the entries she had so painstakingly preserved.

In an obvious hurry to finish, he vigorously lathered his hair. "They have to be around here. Who would take them?"

"I don't know, Ransom. Who would take incriminating evidence that your current wife is crazy enough to think she's from the future and has filled volumes with nonsensical information no one can verify because it hasn't happened yet? Who would want such information?" Feeling herself stretch the bounds of control, she left the bathing room.

She settled in the big chair beside the fireplace and resumed brushing her hair dry.

"Look, I know you're upset about the journals being gone, but we'll find them." Then he swore and she heard water spilling and splattering in the tub.

A sad smile teased her lips. In spite of all the worries plaguing her, he could puncture her defenses without even knowing it. In that moment, she decided to accept whatever he gave her for as long as he'd have her.

Then he was standing in front of the fire, drying himself with a thick towel. Water dripped from the pointed clusters of raven hair framing his face. He paused, looking at her earnestly. "We'll find your journals, Liss. They were here when I finished reading them a couple of days ago."

"We'll find them." Even as she spoke the words, she didn't believe them. Like the shades of gray in the gaps of her memory, she felt their irrevocable loss.

"Liss?"

She flipped her hair back and looked up into his passion-darkened face. His blatant desire beckoned. Captivated, delighted he wanted her again so soon, she dropped her brush and unfastened the tie on her wrapper.

When she went into his waiting arms, the wrapper remained in the chair. Warm skin met naked desire. Everything felt so right. In his arms, she felt loved. Safe. Home.

"I do love you, Ransom." She pressed against his hard-muscled flesh.

In response, he swept her up and carried her to the bed. "I want to make love to you."

"You just did." She smiled, lost in the sparkling desire lighting his face.

"No. We satisfied a need." He brushed his lips over hers. "Now, we'll make love. I want you to feel it in every part of your delicious body. I never want you to forget it."

Later, she knew he had fulfilled his promise. Never would she forget his tender passion.

Chapter 30

SURROUNDED BY FAMILY and friends, Win took her place beside Ransom at the dining room table. Charlet outdid herself with the elaborate fare of brunch sausages, bacon, fruity pastries and pan-fried cakes, eggs, and porridge awaiting their pleasure in artistic array on the sideboard. But Win's normally hearty appetite fled with Cassandra's entrance.

Tall and regal, Cassandra's delicate chin remained high and her violet eyes intent on the chair Baron Korinkov held beside his. With a murmured thank you, she settled, then met Win's expressionless gaze.

Heart thundering, stomach roiling, Win held her half-sister's soulful look. Being cast out of her role as Ransom's wife meant a lifetime of emptiness. Still, a direct challenge might unleash an even more destructive result in the form of his enmity.

"Excuse me," Win whispered. The tears brimming her lower lids distorted her vision. She left the table, then the room without betraying the wild emotions roiling just below the surface. She didn't know why she couldn't keep the tears under control, only that she had to escape before she disintegrated into a weeping puddle in front of her adopted family and friends.

She fled up the stairs, stumbling when the shimmering tears spilling down her cheeks blurred her vision. She rushed to the sanctity of her bedroom, feeling the tumult blossoming uncontrollably.

The swelling emotions constricted her breathing and mushroomed until they escaped in a whimper as she closed the door. She scanned the room for a shred of serenity and found emptiness, loss, and incredible sorrow.

Curled up on the bed, she clutched Ransom's pillow against her breast as though she could hold him in her heart forever. The acceptance that the love she so desperately craved would never be broke the final floodgate. Breathtaking sobs gushed forth in body-wracking waves that released the jumbled mass of sorrow accumulated during her lifetime.

"I can't do it, Joey," she wailed into the pillow. "I don't know how to fight for him." She sniffed loudly. "She's here . . . it's real. And I can't pretend." A fresh wave of sorrow shook her body. The admission of defeat scorched her raw soul.

Caught up in her grief, the big hands scooping her up startled her into a scream muffled by the pillow.

"What is it, Liss? God, tell me. You're breaking my heart with these tears," Ransom implored. He rocked her like a child, stroking her disheveled hair. "Tell me." He kissed the top of her head, then pulled her onto his lap. "Tell me what has you so unhappy."

Telling him how she needed his love changed nothing. The lesson of wanting something that didn't exist came from her childhood. She had wanted her father's love. He had loved drugs and whiskey. She had wanted her mother's love. She had loved herself. Only Joey had loved her—and he had died.

"Look at me." Ransom curled a finger under her chin and lifted her face.

Still, she kept her eyes downcast. One glimpse of those warm, passionate aquamarine eyes and she'd be lost again. Sniffing, she abruptly shook her head. Tears continued streaming down her flushed cheeks.

"Did something happen you're not telling me about?"

The gentle stroke of his fingers along her damp temple quieted her sobs. Even as her tears ebbed, the sorrow of loss weighted her spirit. It hardly seemed right or fair for his touch to soothe her stormy soul. Suddenly angry with herself for succumbing to the narcotic of his nearness, she shoved him away.

"You're not going anywhere until you tell me why you're crying."

She sniffed, blinking hard. "I'm not crying anymore."

Another wave spilled over the dam of her lower lashes when she met his gaze.

"You're not crying any less, either." He thumbed a river of tears from her cheek. "For God's sake, Liss, tell me what's making you so unhappy."

"Life." She tried pulling her chin free, but he held her face turned to his.

"Life? As opposed to what? Death?" His expression softened as his eyebrows drew close together in uncertain amusement.

"Go ahead and laugh. In a macabre way, it's funny. Predictable, but funny." She freed her chin from his tender hold. "I shouldn't have deluded myself." Again, she pushed at him. He reacted by holding her tighter and stroking her hair.

Roughly, she brushed the tears from her cheeks with the back of her hand. "I should've known."

"You should've known what?"

"I'm still me. The packaging is different, but I'm still me."

When she remained silent, he prodded, "And?"

Her head shot up, grazing his lowered chin. "And? And the only person who loves me either hasn't been born yet or is dead!" Using both hands, she levered herself away from him and scrambled off the bed. "And . . . and I'll deal with that very well, thank you, after I get to San Francisco."

In a flash, Ransom shot from the bed. The pillow slammed against the headboard like a sharp slap. "What the hell do you mean, *after* you get to San Francisco?" he boomed loudly enough to rattle the walls. Rough hands grabbed her shoulders and spun her to confront the hardening angles and planes of his face glowing in fury.

"You don't have to shout at me! My shortcomings do not include deafness!"

"I didn't hunt you down in a blizzard because I had nothing else to do, Felicity. I haven't been sneaking through the cold, dark midnight to steal a few moments with you, then come home aching because I get some kind of sick enjoyment out of it.

"God damn it, Felicity! What the hell do you mean, go to San Francisco?" He drew a harsh breath. When he spoke again, anguish tinged his voice. "Why are you leaving me? Tell me what you want. I'll give it to you. Anything—except help you leave me. I'll stand in your way and carry you back every step of the way."

"Why? I—I th-thought you had what y-you wanted. Wh-why would you want me to stay? I couldn't bear watching you with her, Ransom." The fight left her with the words. The truth hung between resignation and rage. "It tears me apart."

"Watch me with who?"

The tightening flex of his fingers on her shoulders made her wince. Unwilling to reveal the depth of her anguish, she glanced away.

"What the hell are you talking about?" he demanded in a soft, dangerous tone.

"I'm talking about you, Ransom. You! And the woman you asked to marry you."

Ransom's jaw dropped. "Who?"

"Cassandra, you dolt! Who the hell did you think I

meant? She's the only one I know you asked to marry you."
She whirled away from him and stomped to the window,
wanting distance between them. "You make me so angry
sometimes. Did you expect me to hang around here after
you had our marriage dissolved?"

"What?" He stepped back, stunned.

Anger colored her cheeks as she faced him from across
the room.

After a moment of taut silence, a low rumble started deep
in Ransom's chest. It grew until it erupted and shook the
room.

Win's jaw set for a real fight. "Don't you dare laugh at
me." More heat colored her already pink cheeks. Humilia-
tion lanced her heart and launched her across the room. Her
small fists pummeled his chest. "Don't you dare laugh at
me!"

Big arms enfolded her, rendering her efforts puny against
his strength. "You thought Cassandra . . ." Laughter stole
the rest of his words.

She struggled against the velvet strength with which he
held her, lashing out at her helplessness to make him love
her or do anything except be at the mercy of the uncontrollable fate shaping her destiny. Tears of frustration burned
down her anger-bright cheeks. "Don't you laugh at me, Ransom Hamilton! Don't you dare laugh at me!"

"Sh-h-h-h-h, Liss. I'm sorry for laughing, but the idea of
me and Cassandra *is* laughable."

The bars of flesh restraining her eased. "You didn't think
so when you wanted to marry her."

He shrugged with indifference. "I didn't know Dr.
Winifred Beatrice McCanless when I asked her to marry
me." His arms tightened, bringing her so close she could
hear his heart beat through his clothing. "I didn't love Cassandra any more than she loved me. We liked one another.
And I'll admit we might have built a solid marriage—until
Ivan met her." A tender kiss on the top of her head started

the familiar heat capable of melting her coldest reserve. "It's Ivan who loves her, not I.

"Damn, when I thought I'd lost you, I knew real fear for the second time in my life. If you had died . . ." His voice trailed as his big hands moved over her small back.

"You would have been free."

"I would have been an empty shell. My heart would have died with you, Liss. I love you."

Questioning, her head rose. She pushed back and read the truth in his eyes. "You love me?"

"Yes, Liss. Of course I love you."

"How dare you love me!"

Incredulous, Ransom shrugged. "I didn't know I needed permission to love my wife."

"When . . . when did you decide you loved me?"

"I didn't decide anything." A disbelieving smile disappeared into his mustache with the formation of a generous grin. "Like your miracle at the dock, it happened. I woke up one day and knew I loved you. I had a lot of time to think about it while my leg was healing." The grin melted as his voice softened. "When I was afraid I had lost you forever, I knew I'd take whatever you gave me, Liss.

"The night you came into this room and took my hand and became my wife in all ways was one of the happiest nights of my life. Later, when you told me you loved me, I . . . "

"I don't believe this! You've known you loved me all this time and you didn't tell me? What was it? A state secret? You put me though hell by letting me think you wanted Cassandra! That you loved *her!*" With a mighty shove, she freed herself. The emotional tumult sent her across the room to the far side of the bed.

"I'm telling you now." His knit brows warned he was nearing the end of his patience.

"Thank you. I'm delighted you love me, Ransom. Damn delighted!"

"You don't look or sound it."

Tears continued flowing down her cheeks. "Well, how

would you feel if . . . Stay right there. Don't you dare come any closer. I'm mad at you, Ransom."

"Had I known telling you I love you would make you angry, I wouldn't have told you."

She scrambled onto the bed. "Stay away from me. I'm not done being mad at you."

"You can be mad at me all you want. Just tell me you aren't leaving me." The seriousness of his tone brooked no doubt that the game was over. "You're not going to San Francisco."

For a long moment, she studied his face. Vulnerability and apprehension sharpened his features. His predatory stance at the edge of the bed warned he'd accept only one answer.

"I'm not going to San Francisco without you," she whispered, realizing the future she dreamed was hers for the taking. He loved her. *Thank you, God!*

Her trembling hand reached out, inviting him to share the fullness of life together.

His big hand closed around hers. He pressed her fingers against his lips. "I promise, you won't regret the price you've paid for loving me . . . Winifred." Ransom's possessive embrace held her so close that his mustache tickled her forehead. "You have the most beautiful heart and generous spirit in any century. How could I not love you? You're the most precious treasure any man could hope for, and more than I deserve. God, I never want you sad or crying like your heart's broken. You've known too much of life's trials and not enough of its joys."

The soft brush of his lips against her hair tightened her arms around him.

"Did Spirit Dancer tell you that's why you're here?"

Astonished, she rocked back on her heels, wondering why she'd never asked that question. "No."

"Before you arrived, a powerful young spirit visited him while he was communicating with his own spirits. That new spirit was your brother."

"Joey . . ." Her heart did a flip-flop. *Dear God, Joey.*

"Yes, Joey. He couldn't rest until you had a chance to live for yourself and have someone love you with all his heart . . . without reservations, without conditions. That's how I love you, Winifred." A lopsided smile accompanied a slight nod. "A Tlingit test . . . I'm the luckiest man alive." His head tilted heavenward and he shouted, "Thank you, Joey! Thank you for Winifred!"

Win's heart swelled with a fierce love for Joey and her husband. Both bestowed her with the most precious gift possible and a future glittering with promise. Marveling at her good fortune, she touched Ransom's cheek. "I'm not Winifred anymore. Not really."

"Yes, you are."

"I am," she conceded, searching for the right words. "I'm more . . . and less. In this time and place, I've come to think of myself as Felicity Hamilton. And Liss."

He chuckled. "Felicity means pleasure, joy, bliss. Very appropriate."

"That's how I feel with you. I love you, Ransom, and I'll thank God and Joey and the Tlingit spirits every day of my life for this gift."

"So will I, Liss. I'm going to tell you I love you so often you'll be tired of hearing it."

"Never," she breathed, then brushed her lips against his. "Will you love our baby, too?" Feeling him tense, she bit back a tremulous smile. "The one we're going to have in May or early June?"

The storm returned with a frown. "You were going to San Francisco and not tell me?" Bewilderment and hurt hovered in his whispered question.

"Yes," she answered unabashed.

When he spoke again, pain etched his words. "Why? Why would you even think of taking our baby away from me?"

"Because I couldn't watch you with Cassandra when I thought you loved her." She cradled his face in her hands.

"The baby is the only part of you I thought might love me back. I couldn't risk losing him, too."

"I'd have followed you to the ends of the earth, Liss. Baby or no."

"I know that—now."

Suddenly, he grinned. "A baby? In the summer?"

"Our baby," she whispered, urging his lips toward hers. "Show me how much you love me before I get too big around to . . ." His reverent kiss silenced her.

The shadow of a memory flickered. Hadn't she read such a happy ending before? she wondered, before deciding no one could have imagined such a bizarre tale or so exciting a man.

Epilogue

"But why does she have to leave?" Felicity insisted on knowing. "What happened between you and your mother neither one of you will tell me?" She adjusted five-month-old Joseph Archibald to offer him a full breast. "If this concerns her giving my journals to Spirit Dancer . . ."

"No. It has nothing to do with your journals, though I'm sorry he destroyed them." Ransom's harsh expression mellowed as he watched his wife nurse their baby son. "I've delayed sending her away as long as I can. First there was winter. Then you wanted her with you for Joey's birth." He grazed his son's suckling cheek with the back of his finger. "You knew I wouldn't deny you anything. Then came Cassandra and Ivan's wedding, and finally the Russian-American signing for the purchase of Alaska. It's almost winter again, Felicity. She goes!"

"But I want her here for the birth of our next child, too." Try as she might, she didn't understand why Ransom was sending Cordelia away.

"Are you telling me you're carrying another child? A daughter?" Hope shone in his eyes.

She smiled and shook her head. "But since we're planning on a daughter . . ."

"No. Absolutely not. Besides, Cassandra will be here for you. The *Golden Sunset* is making a special docking this morning. When she leaves, Cordelia will be on her."

"But Ransom, with so many of our friends returning to Russia . . ."

He knelt beside her, still enthralled by the way her luscious body heated every chord of his being and yet inspired a serene contentment with his child.

As though knowing his father watched, raven-haired Joey flexed his fingers against the milky whiteness of his mother's breast, claiming the delicious orb for himself.

"But Joey should know his grandmother. Family is very important." She gave Ransom her best pleading look before admitting the futility of her efforts. For the last month she had enlisted Cassandra's aid in her efforts, all to no avail.

Ransom kissed Joey's head, then Felicity's breast. "I don't want to argue about this. I'll be downstairs. We don't have to leave for nearly an hour."

Saddened by the imminent departure of her mother-in-law and friend, Felicity watched her husband leave, wishing she knew the right words to change his mind.

The docks were alive with passengers, ships, cargo, whalers, and trappers.

All too soon Felicity bid Cordelia good-bye. Tears caught on her lower lids.

"I'm not sorry, son. Even if I could turn the clock back, I'd do it the same—especially knowing the happiness you two share." Cordelia returned Ransom's embrace with an extra hug. "I love you both."

"We love you, too." Ransom dropped a kiss on his

mother's forehead before releasing her. "You know, Ma, sometimes the clock does turn back."

Felicity watched without comprehending the unspoken messages in their exchange. When she would have questioned him, he turned Cordelia toward the *Golden Sunset.*

"Mother, may I present the owner of the ship you'll be sailing on. Captain Ulf Voss, my mother, Cordelia Hamilton." Ransom stepped back and captured Felicity's fingers in his.

Cordelia gazed in wonder at a fashionably tailored man who had once been her golden Viking, the warrior of the sea she sacrificed everything for except her life.

"I have waited and searched a long time for you, Cordelia." The Viking sea captain's sharp blue eyes softened in his weather-hardened face. A generous smile built new laugh lines around his eyes. The wind tugged at the graying blond hair falling around his ears.

"Ulf?" Gloved fingers covered her mouth in astonishment.

For a moment, Felicity feared Cordelia might faint. A glimpse of her husband's intent expression spoke the importance of the moment.

"Yes, Princess, it is I." Ulf caught her hand and lifted it to his lips. "Will you sail the *Golden Sunset* with me?"

"Oh, yes, Ulf. I'll sail with you anywhere." Cordelia hesitated. "How did you . . ." She turned to her son. "I thought . . ."

"I know what you thought. But you were right about a marriage without love. Thank you. Come back in the spring and perhaps we'll have a sister on the way for Joey." Ransom winked at Felicity. "But now you'll have the chance denied you so long ago." Ransom kissed his mother's cheek. "Now go."

A very happy Cordelia kissed Felicity again before shyly taking the arm offered by her aging sea captain.

Felicity waited until the couple boarded the *Golden Sunset* before caging her husband. "Who is he?"

"The owner of one of the most powerful shipping lines in the world, Ulf Voss." He put his arm around her shoulders as a shield against the cooling breeze. "He's the man my mother should have married, the one she loved."

Felicity looked a question at him.

"Let's go home and climb in bed, Liss. I want to make love to you."

"I want to know what's going on."

He lifted her into the carriage then sat down beside her. "I'm sure you can use your persuasive nature to coerce the story out of me."

Felicity laughed, already contemplating delightful ways of torturing the smallest detail from him. "You bet your bippy I can."

They laughed, neither having the faintest idea of what a bippy was, but sure that someday an entire nation would know what they did not. Today, they had each other and Joey and a golden future in a new piece of America.